KU-368-340

REVENGE
OF THE
STORMBRINGER

PETER
TREMAYNE

HEADLINE

Copyright © 2023 Peter Tremayne

The right of Peter Tremayne to be identified as the Author of
the Work has been asserted by him in accordance with the
Copyright, Designs and Patents Act 1988.

First published in Great Britain in 2023 by
HEADLINE PUBLISHING GROUP

1

Apart from any use permitted under UK copyright law, this publication may
only be reproduced, stored, or transmitted, in any form, or by any means,
with prior permission in writing of the publishers or, in the case of reprographic
production, in accordance with the terms of licences issued
by the Copyright Licensing Agency.

All characters in this publication are fictitious and any resemblance
to real persons, living or dead, is purely coincidental.

Cataloguing in Publication Data is available from the British Library

ISBN 978 1 4722 9605 4

Typeset in 12.54/15.4 pt Times New Roman PS Std by Jouve (UK), Milton Keynes

Printed and bound in Great Britain by Clays Ltd, Elcograf S.p.A.

Headline's policy is to use papers that are natural, renewable and recyclable
products and made from wood grown in well-managed forests and other
controlled sources. The logging and manufacturing processes are expected
to conform to the environmental regulations of the country of origin.

HEADLINE PUBLISHING GROUP
An Hachette UK Company
Carmelite House
50 Victoria Embankment
London EC4Y 0DZ

www.headline.co.uk
www.hachette.co.uk

For my 'Greek sister'
Maria V. Soteriades
Celebrating our fifty-five years of friendship

Si acuero ut fulgur gladium meum, et arripuerit judicium manus mea; reddam ultionem hostibus meis, et his qui oderunt me retribuam.

If I whet my glittering sword, and mine hand take hold on judgment; I will render vengeance to mine enemies, and will reward them that hate me.

Deuteronomy 32:41

Vulgate Latin translation of Jerome, fourth century

pRINCIpAL ChARACTERS

Sister Fidelma of Cashel, a *dálaigh* or advocate of the law courts of seventh-century Ireland
Brother Eadulf of Seaxmund's Ham, in the land of the South Folk of the kingdom of the East Angles, her companion

At Cashel
Colgú, King of Muman, Fidelma's brother
Gelgéis, Princess of Durlus Éile in Osraige, newly married to Colgú

Household of Fidelma and Eadulf
Alchú, their son
Muirgen, the nurse
Nessan, her husband

Household of the King
Finguine, Prince of Glendamnach, *tánaiste*, or heir apparent, to Colgú
Dar Luga, *banmhaor*, or stewardess, and formerly housekeeper, of the royal household at Cashel
Fíthel, Chief Brehon of Muman

Urard, scribe and secretary to Fíthel

Cuán, Abbot of Imleach Iubhair and Bishop of Cashel

Brother Dáire, the librarian

Rodaige, a master builder

Father Socra, the new chaplain at Cashel

Sister Sárait, an assistant in the chapel

Síonna, a female physician or *sui-liaig*

The Nasc Niadh, the Warriors of the Golden Collar, élite bodyguards to Colgú

Enda, commander of the *lucht-tighe*, or household guard

Luan, a warrior

Dego, a one-armed warrior

Aidan, a warrior

Cano, a young warrior

Luchar-súil, a sentinel

Female warriors of the Daughters of the Storm

Crédh, the champion and commander

Cera, the youngest warrior, who also serves as attendant to Gelgéis

Corbach, a warrior

From the township

Gormán, commander of a battalion of Colgú's warriors

Aibell, Gormán's wife

Della, mother of Gormán and close friend of Fidelma

Lassar, Dar Luga's sister from Ráth na Drinne

Rumann, a tavern owner

Gobán, a smith

At the fair
Corruine, a wandering apothecary

Characters frequently referred to
Fianamail, King of Laigin
Tuaim Snámha, ruler of Osraige
Brother Conchobhar, the late mentor of Fidelma

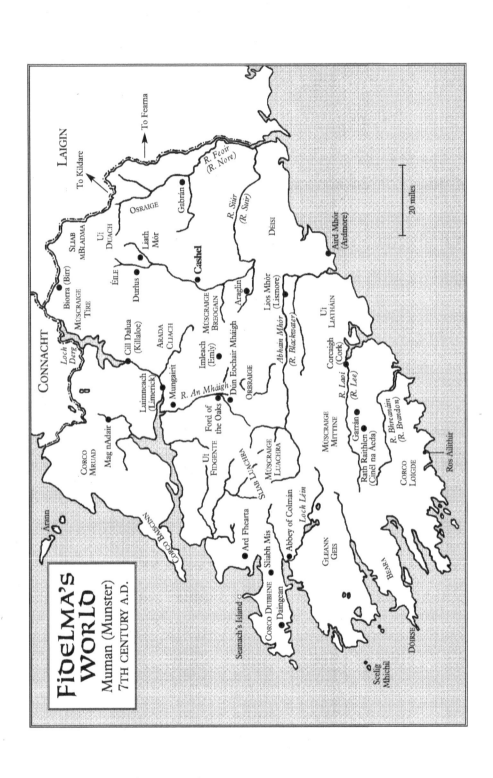

FIDELMA'S WORLD
Muman (Munster)
7TH CENTURY A.D.

LAIGIN

CONNACHT

To Kildare

To Fearna

R. Feoir
(R. Nore)

OSRAIGE

Gabrán

SLIAB
MBLADMA

Uí
DUACH

Liath
Mór

R. Siúr
(R. Suir)

DÉISI

Aird Mhór
(Ardmore)

20 miles

Biorra (Birr)

MUSCRAIGE
TIRE

ÉLLE

Durlus

Cashel

Loch
Derg

Cill Dalua
(Killaloe)

ARADA
CLIACH

MUSCRAIGE
BREOGAIN

Imleach
(Emly)

Araglin

Líos Mhór
(Lismore)

Luimneach
(Limerick)

Mungairit

Dún Eochair Mháigh

ORBRAIGE

Abhain Mhór
(R. Blackwater)

Uí
LATHAIN

Corcaigh
(Cork)

CORCO
MRUAD

Mag nAdair

R. An Mháigh

Ford of
the Oaks

Uí
FIDGENTE

SLIAB LUACHRA

MUSCRAIGE
LUACHRA

R. Laoi
(R. Lee)

MUSCRAIGE
MITTINE

Garrán

Rath Raithlen
(Cinél na Aeda)

R. Bhreanáin
(R. Brandon)

CORCO
LOIGDE

Ros Ailithir

Árainn

CORCO BAISCINN

Ard Fhearta

Sliabh Mis

CORCO DUIBHNE

Daingean

Abbey of Colmán

Loch Léin

GLEANN
GEIS

BEARA

DOIRSE

Seanach's Island

Sceilg
Mhichíl

AUThOR'S NOTE

This story takes place in the year AD 672. It is the Irish month of *Lúghnasadh*, which equates with modern August, sometimes referred to as *mí ag siúl léis an ghria*, or the month of walking with the sun. Fidelma and Eadulf have returned to Cashel following their adventure narrated in *Death of a Heretic*, which took place while they were visiting the Abbey of Imleach Iubhair. On their return, the marriage of Fidelma's brother, King Colgú, to Princess Gelgéis of Durlus Éile in Osraige, has taken place. It is a union many readers will have expected since they first met in the adventure of *The Seventh Trumpet*. Some time has passed since the ceremony and most of the prominent guests have departed. The last of the celebrations, a great fair (*Aenach Caiseal*), is now due to take place in the township, sheltering under the shadow of the fortress of the Eóganacht kings of Muman – *Caiseal Muman* (Cashel).

Regular readers will know that women of this period held parity of rights with men under the ancient Irish laws, and they could inherit, be lawyers, judges, physicians, scholars, ecclesiastical leaders and even warriors. Although their right to bear arms and be military leaders had become less prevalent than it had once been in Irish society and, indeed, among Celtic society generally, in Ireland at this time women could be warriors until changes in law at the end of the seventh century. It should be borne in mind that sporadic mention of female warriors, and their general exclusion from later historical documents is doubtless due to these changes in law as encouraged by Christianity. The relegation of the status of women in Ireland, it has been argued, commenced after the decisions at the Council at Birr (Biorra) in AD 697.

chapter one

The young warrior halted, immobilised as if he had suddenly become a stone statue. The sword point of his opponent was resting on his neck. He felt that if he swallowed, the movement of his larynx would cause the skin to be scratched by the tip of the blade. Enda, commander of the *lucht-tighe*, the household guard of Colgú, King of Muman, realised that the sword point was too close to be deflected. He had allowed his shield and sword to uncover his chest ready for what he had thought would be the position from which to deliver a decisive blow against his adversary. Too late, he realised that his challenger had invited the movement in order to be able to lunge forward, low and upwards, placing the tip of the weapon in its lethal position.

Several moments of silence passed and then Enda uttered, '*Air-maisid!*' indicating that he acknowledged the weapon had found its mark.

'*Logad?*' came the sharp question of his opponent.

'*Logad!*' Enda conceded.

The menacing sword point dropped immediately and his challenger took a step backwards, bringing up the weapon into a formal salute.

Around them, the audience of men and women burst into a brief applause before they began to disperse across the town square.

Their appearance proclaimed them to be idling spectators from various walks of life from the township: from merchants to artisans and various labourers; from women of substance to those who followed many occupations in the township that sheltered under the shadow of the great limestone rock on which King Colgú of Muman's great fortress rose and from which he ruled the most south-westerly and largest of the five kingdoms of Éireann.

Enda, with a stifled sigh of regret, sheathed his sword and surrendered his shield to his weapons carrier, who came readily to perform the service, as did the attendant serving his opponent. Enda now gazed at the female figure in front of him with grudging admiration. She was a full head shorter than he; less, now that she had removed her bronze war helmet, which was made higher by the image of a crouching, hissing goose. This was the symbol of the old pagan goddess of battle. His opponent was a young girl, not many years beyond the age of choice, with chestnut curling hair on which the sun caught red highlights. To say the girl was pretty might have been an exaggeration, but that she was attractive there was no doubt. Perhaps the line of her cheeks was too angular, the lips too thin, and the flashing hazel eyes set slightly too wide apart.

The skin was unusually tanned, although she was no worker in the fields. Her body was well formed, lithe but muscular. The calf muscles of her bare legs showed their strength, for she wore no metal guards on those shapely legs, just a short kilt, with a colourful linen shirt over which was a coat of protective chain mail, a form of armour that had been adopted by Celtic warriors long before their first encounters with the Romans. The girl now stood back with a broad grin of triumph at Enda.

'You will need to better your defence before we meet in the contest in four days' time, Enda,' the girl advised humorously as the young man removed his helmet and wiped his forehead with his hand.

'It is not often that I have the opportunity to try my ability with a champion of the Daughters of the Storm.' He returned her smile with a swift bow of his head. 'My compliments, Cera.'

'It is not often that our princess, Gelgéis, marries the King of Muman and we can come with her to demonstrate our capabilities,' the girl replied gravely. 'My companions and I are looking forward to the great fair, at which we will be able to stage these mock contests to show our skills.'

Leaving their attendants to collect their weapons, shields and armour, and take them back to the fortress, Enda and his young companion turned and began to walk side by side across the main square of the township towards Rumann's tavern. Here Enda knew that cool cider would be a welcome and fitting reward for their efforts in practising a mock combat.

Enda had been impressed when Princess Gelgéis had brought her troop of female warriors to her wedding. He had heard of the Daughters of the Storm, and had seen them at her fortress at Durlus Éile. However, he had never seen them in action. He knew that Gelgéis, as a princess of Durlus Éile, and of the ruling family of Osraige, was entitled to make her own choice of bodyguards. Although female warrior troops were no longer as popular as they had once been, Gelgéis apparently favoured the ancient tradition for her household to keep this company of female warriors. Enda had been attracted by the youngest of the troop, Cera, who also served as personal attendant to the princess. The attraction was mutual, and now the two of them found themselves practising with their weapons in order to be ready to perform a martial arts exhibition at the forthcoming fair.

Cera had explained to Enda that, centuries before, it was told that Óengus Osrithe had been the eponymous founder of the kingdom of Osraige, the 'deer people'. He had established a special troop of female warriors because his mother, Cindnit, had been a famous warrior herself. He had married Sadb the Thrice Powerful, who had also been a great warrior. Her fierce battalion of female warriors were called Na Scaileadha, the Protectors or Shields. But the tradition of female warrior companies was now disappearing. Now only Gelgéis maintained an élite troop: the Daughters of the Storm. They mostly gave exhibitions of their martial arts prowess at the many great fairs across all the five kingdoms.

The female warrior tradition was a strong one in society. According to the ancient storytellers, it was Scáthach who taught the martial arts to all the great heroes and champions at her academy. Did not Cúchullain learn his art under her? His famous warrior's leap, the *torann chless*, or thunder feat, was taught to him by her. Had he not learnt the mastery of his famous spear, the *Gae Bolga*, or 'belly ripper', at her hands? It had taken all the skills she had taught him that he had been able to overcome one of the most fearsome female warriors, Éis Énchenn. Aoife, Scáthach's twin, also had taught warriors of renown at her martial arts academy. Bec, of the Gamanrad, and the élite warriors of Connacht, acquired a fearsome reputation, as did Cathach Chatchenn, Ceidne, Erc, and other female champions of the Fianna, the High King's bodyguard. Even Fidelma's own namesake, Fidelma, the Nine Times Beautiful, had been hailed as one of the great female champions.

Now, however, smaller bands of female warriors still existed, and even ran martial arts academies, but only in conditions of extreme need did the provincial kings and their nobles call upon the services of female warriors in time of war. Enda knew that, under law, it was the right, and often the duty, of women to bear arms in defence of their people, but they were never forced to do so in the manner that some extreme proponents of the New Faith were now claiming, in order to make their case against the old laws and urge the removal of such rights from women.

Enda still found himself surprised when he encountered a female warrior like Cera, who not only could hold her own in single combat with him but was an able horsewoman, could cast a spear further than most male warriors he knew, and whose archery skills were so accurate that he would prefer her at his side in battle to many of the veterans he had served with.

The idea of a martial arts display at the fair had been the suggestion of Princess Gelgéis and King Colgú. It was thought that the contests between the visiting female warriors and the Colgú's body-guards, the Nasc Niadh, the Warriors of the Golden Collar, would inevitably arouse interest. Enda and Cera had spent time together practising, but it was not just Enda's admiration for Cera's martial ability that captivated him. She could hold her own on many topics of discussion. She was able to recite from memory the works of poets of the country and had even impressed Brother Dáire, the *scriptor* and librarian of Colgú's household, with such knowledge. Enda confessed that she was also physically attractive to him and was amazed that his feelings were reciprocated.

In the dark tavern, which Rumann ran in the centre of the township, Enda and Cera sat down with a jug of strong, cool cider and started to talk about the upcoming fair. Around them, however, the conversation had turned to the problems of rivalry between the princes and nobles who had not come to Cashel to pay their respects at the wedding of Colgú and Gelgéis. There were two notable absences. One was Gelgéis's own cousin, Tuaim Snámha, the petty king of Osraige, the buffer territory between the kingdoms of Laigin and Muman. Sometimes Osraige would side withLaigin and sometimes with Muman, whichever would give the greater benefit. At the moment, Tuaim Snámha was under treaty obligation to pay tribute to Cashel. In fact, it had been while facing down an uprising in Osraige that Colgú had first met Gelgéis.

The other absence, but one that was expected, was that of Fianamail, King of Laigin, who was always seeking ways to extend his kingdom into Muman.

'Do you think Tuaim Snámha will change his mind at the last minute and accept Colgú's invitation to attend the fair?' Enda asked, drawn into the subject being aired around him, while sipping his drink. He knew that it had been a considerable slight that Osraige's ruler had not attended the wedding itself. Some felt this could be ameliorated by his attendance at the fair.

Cera shook her head. 'Tuaim Snámha feels he is now in a strong position by ignoring this event. If Colgú shows displeasure against Osraige for this insult, it might not turn out well. Any move against Tuaim Snámha could involve intercession by Fianamail. He is a shrewd ruler, and the fact that he has survived so far is surely proof of it.'

Enda could not but agree. 'When Fianamail had to disband his army – an army he had brought to the borders of Osraige to support Tuaim Snámha – Tuaim survived even though he had surely been part of that conspiracy to rise against Cashel.'

The Chief Brehon of the five kingdoms, on behalf of the High King, had recognised Fianamail's territorial ambitions in using Osraige to occupy parts of Muman. The Chief Brehon had kept Fianamail in check by threatening to impose the *bórama* tribute if it was found that he had plotted further against Muman and, for two years, an uneasy peace had been maintained.

The *bórama* was the cattle tribute that had first been imposed on Eochaid, King of Laigin, when he had married the High King's daughter, Fithir, at the same time as he had raped her sister, Dáirine. This had led to the death of both girls. In revenge, the High King, Tuathal Techtmar, had defeated Eochaid's army, killing the Laigin King, and imposed the *bórama* as an annual fine on his successors.

'A pity there is no peace between Laigin and Osraige,' Cera sighed as she considered the situation. 'It has been a tense time for our people in Durlus Éile in case this marriage created an excuse for Laigin to form another alliance with Tuaim Snámha to attack Cashel.'

Enda grimaced. 'It is incredible to think that Fianamail of Laigin or Tuaim Snámha of Osraige would consider this an appropriate time to provoke Cashel. There is nothing for them to gain by defying the High King and his Chief Brehon over the *bórama*.'

'Perhaps Fianamail considers that the new High King, Cenn Fáelad, will have less resolve than his late brother, Sechnussach. Fianamail's ambition has always been to get the High King, and the Council of Brehons, to abolish the threat of the *bórama*.'

Enda took another sip of his cider and sighed. 'Princess Gelgéis's cousin is not to be trusted any more than Fianamail of Laigin. We have to keep a sharp watch on them both.' He hesitated. 'One matter I find confusing . . .'

'Only one?' The young girl smiled.

'Seriously. You are of the Daughters of the Storm, a warrior élite that is sworn to defend Osraige, so how could you refuse to raise your sword in defence of Osraige, if that was your choice?'

Cera pulled a disapproving face. 'We are sworn to defend the Princess of Durlus Éile,' she corrected. 'Our warrior band has its roots in Durlus Éile, which is part of Osraige, and our loyalty is to Durlus Éile first and foremost. Moreover, Tuaim Snámha currently pays tribute to Cashel and it would be madness for him to enter alliances with Laigin to attack our princess.'

Enda rubbed the back of his neck reflectively. 'Politics! I have little understanding of it. Well, if you could produce one battalion as formidable as the Daughters of the Storm, I do not think we should be concerned with any threats from Tuaim Snámha, or from Fianamail.'

Cera chuckled appreciatively. 'I wish you were right. But it is many a generation since we have fought in a large-scale battle. I suppose that you are old enough to have fought in Cnoc Áine six years ago?'

'A sad event,' Enda acknowledged. 'For a long time the Uí Fidgente had been stirring enmity against the Eóganacht of Cashel and it resulted in that battle. And now . . . well, now the Prince Donennach of the Uí Fidgente has become the best of friends to Colgú of Cashel.'

'I heard that the alliance was all to do with Colgú's sister, Fidelma?'

'Indeed. I was lucky to be at her side, as her bodyguard, during the time she performed her diplomacy . . . with, of course, her Saxon husband.' Enda grimaced. 'He doesn't call himself a Saxon but an Angle, as he comes from a kingdom called the East Angles. It sounds a strange place.'

'I wish I had been able to fight at Cnoc Áine.' There was a wistful tone in Cera's voice.

'Better not to have to fight anywhere,' Enda replied thoughtfully.

'And you say that as a warrior?' Cera responded, slightly surprised by the admonition.

'Even the great imperial Romans, with their mighty armies, wrote that war is the horror of mothers. I agree. There is much horror in war.'

'Then why are you a warrior?'

'I suppose that I have a simple attitude,' Enda admitted. 'As a warrior, I believe in the honour code expected of warriors: to defend the weak, the vulnerable, from those who want to impose their will by force and not in accordance with moral and legal codes.'

'So when a hosting is called, the warriors who go to serve should always do so only for moral and legal reasons?'

Enda smiled his agreement. 'This is why we must have warrior élites, trained not only in the use of arms but imbued with the code of their profession, which, as I say, is both moral and legal law. Morality must come first. If a hosting is necessary, such as that in the confrontation at Cnoc Áine, then it falls to the warrior élite to oversee the conduct of those volunteering to take arms and to make sure no accusation of immoral code can be made against the hosting. Thankfully, such conflicts are rare.'

Cera thought for a moment. 'But what if a king or the noble who commands the hosting has immoral purposes? How can the warrior élite, who take oath to the King, take a stand against him and prevent his entire army from descending into immorality when they follow his immoral purpose?'

'I presume you are again thinking of Fianamail of Laigin?'

'I was thinking in general terms,' Cera admitted. 'But Fianamail is a good example. He is supported in his ambitions by Bishop Molling Luach of Fearna. Fianamail even uses the bishop as his emissary to the High King.'

'Many churchmen, sadly, follow their own ambitious politics. Molling is one of them but there are many such in all five kingdoms.'

'I have met Bishop Molling, and Fianamail,' Cera observed, surprising Enda.

'You met the King of Laigin?' he asked, almost impressed.

'Our troop attended the triennial fair at Loch Garman. We had to demonstrate our prowess in martial arts at the fair. We also had to listen to Fianamail's denouncements, in which he claimed all the kingdoms were conspiring against him. I think he had an inflated sense of his own position. I felt he was demanding attention and admiration from everyone, and when that wasn't given he became unreasonable.'

'But you saw him in person? What sort of person was he?'

'When he came round presenting the awards for the best contestants in archery, riding and javelin casting,' Cera replied, 'I felt uncomfortable in his presence. There appeared no depth or warmth to him. His eyes were hard and he glanced at people without meeting their eyes, as if he was uncertain of himself. It was a remote look; that of someone not to be trusted.'

Enda gave a sniff of derision. 'Then he does not appear to have changed since I first encountered him.'

It was Cera's turn to be impressed.

'He had just succeeded Faelan, son of Colmán, as King of

Laigin. My impression of him was of a sulky youth. I and my comrades Dego and Aidan were chosen to accompany the lady Fidelma on a mission to Fearna itself. It was discovered that Eadulf, who was not Fidelma's husband then, had been taken captive by the fanatical Abbess Fainder. She was determined to put Eadulf to death according to some new Christian law introduced into her abbey from Rome. We had a meeting in the great hall of Fearna. Fianamail was made to sit in judgment about whether Fainder and her acolytes had broken the laws of the five kingdoms.'

'Who made sure Fianamail didn't misinterpret our laws?'

'Thankfully, the High King sent his Chief Brehon, Barren. At the end of the hearing, young Fianamail was summoned to Tara to be admonished by the High King. I must tell you the entire story when we have more time . . .'

He added this because he had seen a tall woman, clad in similar warrior's garb to Cera, enter the tavern. Her uncovered head showed a veritable mane of raven-black hair. Her eyes were dark and deep set, and her lips made a thin disapproving line in features whose bone structure was perhaps too angular to be called attractive. She seemed young but with a well-developed figure, which was obviously kept in a good muscular shape. She was approaching them with a scowl of disapproval. Enda recognised her as Crédh, the commander of the Daughters of the Storm.

'I was looking for you, Cera,' she announced as she halted before the table.

'I have just finished my sword practice with Enda for the fair,' returned the girl, immediately defensive. 'We were discussing some of the points of the engagement.'

The tall commander expelled her breath in a clear manner of disapproval.

'It is a contest that you are engaged in, not a joint enterprise.' Her tone was even more disapproving than her expression. 'Anyway, Princess Gelgéis is looking for you.'

'For me?' Cera appeared confused.

'I think that I have made myself clear,' Crédh sniffed. 'Remember, as the youngest among us, you also have the role of *inaillt* to the princess.'

The term did not exactly mean a handmaiden, but an attendant, one who waited upon a lady of rank when required.

'I shall attend this instant,' the girl flushed. Standing up, she offered a brief embarrassed glance of apology to Enda before she hurried from the tavern.

'You should not distract those serving me from their duties,' Crédh said, scowling at him as they were left alone.

Enda, as commander of the household guard, considered Crédh ranked as his equal and had made that clear to her on previous occasions, for he had already noticed that she seemed to carry herself with an air of superiority.

'I did not consider it a distraction,' he replied gravely. 'We were two warriors discussing the finer points of our profession. It is helpful in the days before the martial arts demonstration.'

'We consider it a contest,' snapped the tall woman. 'In a challenge there is a winner and loser. The two adversaries do not discuss their options before the tournament. This is supposed to be a contest that imitates a battle of life and death.'

Enda regarded her gravely.

'Let us hope the warriors on both sides realise the contest is only a simulation and not reality,' he said softly.

CHAPTER TWO

Why would anyone be attempting to beat a tattoo on a goat-skin drum in the middle of the night? That was the first question that occurred to Fidelma as she reluctantly came awake in the warmth of her bed and tried to separate her dream thoughts into reality.

She lay for a few seconds listening to the tapping sounds before the realisation slowly came that it was an urgent knocking on the door of the bedchamber. She blinked, trying to focus in the darkness. Then, throwing off the warm woollen blanket, she swung out of the bed. Beside her, Eadulf groaned slightly in his disturbed sleep. She glanced anxiously for a moment in the direction of his tossing figure. He had not been sleeping well recently and once or twice his words were almost distinguishable, but, they being in his native language, she could not make them out. The urgent tapping continued and she felt her way towards the door.

A figure stood outside holding a flickering candle in an unsteady hand.

It was Muirgen, who acted as nurse to Fidelma and Eadulf's son, Alchú, as well as helping with the domestic affairs of their household. Fidelma came properly awake rapidly.

'Is it Alchú? Is something wrong with my son?' she demanded before the woman could speak.

'No, lady,' the old nurse reassured her in a calm tone. 'The boy is still asleep and there is no harm to him. It is Enda who says that he must see you urgently.'

Fidelma knew that Enda, as commander of the household guard, was not one to disturb her in the middle of the night without good reason. She turned to look for her robe and found Eadulf was still groaning as he struggled to awaken.

'What is it?' he grunted, forcing himself to sit up.

'I am not sure. But Enda wants to see me,' she replied, tightening the robe around her. 'It must be something important.'

She had barely finished the observation before Eadulf was out of bed, hauling on his robe.

'It's not yet dawn,' he observed with a note of complaint, glancing towards the window.

Muirgen led the way with her candle to an adjoining chamber, where Fidelma and Eadulf usually received their guests.

'Call me, if you need me, lady,' she said, as she stepped aside to allow them to enter.

By the fireplace, the tall, youthful figure of Enda was waiting with ill-concealed tension. A lantern had already been lit and the log fire, left as smouldering grey ashes a short time before, had been encouraged into a blaze.

As they entered the room, Enda turned and offered a perfunctory salute, encompassing both Fidelma and Eadulf. Afterwards, they both agreed that they thought he appeared rather pale and disturbed. It was unusual to see such agitation on the face of the usually stoic warrior.

'My apologies for disturbing you, lady, but your brother, the King, requests your presence immediately.' His voice seemed edged with some emotion she could not interpret.

'Is my brother well?' Fidelma demanded.

'He is well, lady.' There was some hesitation in Enda's assurance before he added, 'A body has been found in the royal apartments.'

Fidelma stared at him for a moment in bewildered silence.

'Is Princess Gelgéis well?' she pressed quickly. It had been only a month before that her brother and Gelgéis had finally married.

Even as Enda was about to nod his head, Eadulf asked the more pertinent question: 'Whose body has been found?'

There was a pause while Fidelma tried not to show her irritation at how slowly she was able to extract information from the young man.

'Your brother and his lady are well, but they are in distress and need your assistance.' The young warrior's reply was curiously staccato and he was clearly not revealing what he knew.

'Do you know the identity of the body that was found?' Fidelma demanded.

Enda's facial muscles seemed to tense. 'Cera,' he responded tightly.

Eadulf exchanged glances with Fidelma. They had both seen the young warrior several times in the company of the girl Cera over the days since the wedding celebrations, and not always at the practice sessions for the forthcoming fair.

After a moment or so, it was Fidelma who pressed forward with the inevitable question.

'You say that her body was found in the royal apartments? In what manner did she die?'

Again, the reply was slow in coming. It was clear Enda was trying hard to keep his emotions in check. His voice had dropped almost to a mumble.

'Come, Enda, speak clearly,' Eadulf admonished, sympathising but considering the best way of getting information from an emotional person was to be detached. 'You have been our companion in many situations and are used to the presence of death.'

Enda attempted to make a gesture with his shoulder but it did not convey any meaning. It was almost as if he were about to sob.

'We understand you knew this girl, Enda.' Fidelma tried to be sympathetic. 'Tell my brother that Eadulf and I will join him as soon as we have attired ourselves in more presentable fashion.'

Enda inclined his head a fraction in acknowledgement and left the chamber. It was unusual to see him move with his head bent forward as if bearing a heavy burden on his shoulders. It took Fidelma and Eadulf a short time to splash their hands and faces in water brought to them by Muirgen, and then complete their dressing. Fidelma took a moment or two to look in on their son, Alchú. The young boy was sleeping peacefully. Fidelma received an assurance from Muirgen that she would watch him carefully in case there was any likelihood of danger to him. Then Fidelma and Eadulf made their way across the shadowy courtyard to the royal residence, where the entrance was lit by brand torches, which were beginning to flicker in that curious pre-dawn breeze that always heralded the coming of the light.

There was a guard on duty at the main doors of the residence. It was the one-armed warrior, Dego. The warrior's life had been saved by Eadulf, but at the cost of his right arm. Dego had displayed a great resilience and, after months of practice, could now use his sword in his left hand with the same dexterity that he had previously shown with his right. His determination at overcoming his disadvantage had so impressed King Colgú that he had kept Dego in the *lucht-tighe,* the household guard of the royal residence.

Dego took a step forward, recognised them and saluted with his good hand.

'The King and his lady are awaiting you in his private reception chamber. Enda has just returned there.'

'Where is the body?' Fidelma asked.

'It is untouched and lies where it was discovered, lady. It was found in one of the rooms of the King's new sanctuary.'

Fidelma was surprised. The *tech-termonn*, the 'sanctuary', was the name her brother had given to a special set of four sleeping chambers that he had designed with his master builder, Rodaige. It had been built while Fidelma and Eadulf had been on their recent travels, and inspired by her brother's obsession with security and Rodaige's descriptions of some of the new constructions that many of the northern nobles were commissioning after hearing reports of such buildings from missionaries returning from Rome and the Holy Land.

Colgú had wanted to extend the royal quarters so that, after his marriage, he and his bride would not have to share the main palace accommodation with distinguished guests and visiting relatives. The idea that he had put forward had been to have a special isolated apartment built on top of an especially constructed artificial base of rocks rising four metres against the south-west side of the main building. It was accessible only by one narrow flight of steps from within the main building. This led to a single corridor with four doors, two on each side. Through these four doors were the individual rooms. Three were bedrooms, and one was a *fothrucadh*, or bathing room, with a door connecting it to the main bedroom, which was for Colgú and Gelgéis.

The other two rooms, on the right-hand side of the passage, were for the use of Colgú's *banmhaor*, or stewardess, Dar Luga, and Gelgéis's attendant.

'Do you say that the body was found in one of the bedchambers?' Fidelma wanted to be more precise.

'The body was found in the *fothrucadh* next to the main bedroom,' Dego replied. 'That has caused a shock as the sanctuary was built for security. Someone must have gained access despite that, although no one should have been able to get in without encountering the guard at the single entrance.'

'But someone did?' Fidelma queried.

'No one has been apprehended,' admitted Dego. 'I hear the killer has simply vanished.'

Fidelma's eyes widened a little.

'Is the body in the sanctuary now?' Eadulf asked.

'Indeed. Dar Luga, the stewardess, is watching over it. Colgú felt he should take the princess out of the sanctuary to the small reception chamber down here. As I said, he is there now with Enda.'

'Was Dar Luga in the sanctuary during the time of the attack?' Eadulf frowned.

'She was, but I should let others attest to that,' Dego replied, emphasising his words with a shrug. 'I was on duty here at the main doors so not privy to what actually happened. I should say that, apart from the household guards that were on duty, your brother has alerted no one else about the events. He felt it unwise to make a general alarm until he had consulted you.'

Fidelma moved with Eadulf towards the main door. Then she hesitated and turned back to Dego.

'Who was the guard at the entrance to the sanctuary when the event happened?'

'Luan was on duty, lady.'

Fidelma thanked Dego as he reached forward to release the latch and push open the main door into the royal residence.

As they entered, the figure of another warrior emerged from the shadows of the corridor's lamp light. It was Aidan, also a member of the household guard, whom they knew well. He had been standing at the foot of the main stairway opposite to the great doors of the feasting hall. He saluted them and stood back silently. Further down the corridor they saw Luan, a companion in previous adventures. He stood sentinel outside the door to Colgú's private reception chamber on the lower floor, which was opposite the entrance to a small flight of wooden stairs, which ascended as the only entrance to the sanctuary.

Observing Fidelma and Eadulf's approach, Luan turned, rapped on the door behind him and, hardly pausing for an answer, thrust it open to allow them to enter without pausing. Enda was there, standing uneasily inside. The pale face of the young Princess Gelgéis turned to them, her expression one of relief. She was sitting on a couch to one side of the fireplace. She had a thick woollen shawl clutched tightly about her in spite of the warm summer weather, and her hair was unloosed. It was obvious she had left her bed in a hurry and there had been no opportunity to comb or dress her hair.

Standing before the fire, looking dishevelled and wearing a loose robe, was Fidelma's brother, Colgú, his hands clasped behind his back and his face creased in a worried frown. His red hair was askew and it was clear that he had made no attempt to attend to himself since waking.

'Has anyone examined the body?' Eadulf demanded immediately on entering, quite forgetting the protocol of not speaking first in the presence of the King.

No one seemed to think it worthwhile to remind him of conventions.

'It was easy to ascertain that the poor girl was dead.' Colgú's tone was almost querulous as he shifted his weight slightly. 'That was obvious to me by her wound. Her throat was cut. There was much blood over her chest.'

'Before we go further,' Fidelma interrupted as Eadulf seemed about to put another question, 'explain what happened, brother. I presume that you discovered the body? How was that?'

'I was awoken in the dark of the night by an unusual noise,' Colgú said after a moment or two for thought. 'Something had fallen in the adjacent room, which we use for washing. I rose from the bed, took a candle, and lit it from an ember in the fireplace. Then I went to check from where I thought I heard the noise.'

He saw his sister's frown and smiled without humour. 'I did have the acumen to take my sword for protection.' He paused a moment. 'Gelgéis was still asleep. I went to the door adjoining our room to the *fothrucadh* and, lifting the latch, opened the door quickly. In the shallow light of the candle, I saw a female body lying over a bench, but there was no one else in the room. The killer could have only just escaped through the far door, which leads into the passage. I went to open it and found it locked. There was no key on the inside of the door and no sign of it on the floor. It had been locked from the outside. I hurried back into the bed-chamber. Gelgéis was awakening and so I unlocked my door into the passage and peered out. As there was no one about, I shouted to raise the alarm. I turned to ensure Gelgéis was awake and told her to put on a robe.'

'Who answered the alarm?'

'Luan was on guard at the foot of the stairs and came hurrying up. Moments later, Dar Luga, whose room is opposite ours, opened her door and emerged. She was still half asleep.'

'So neither of them had been roused by the killer?'

'This was the worrying thing. Neither of them had seen or heard anything before I had called. Certainly no one had passed down the stairs by Luan. And that is the only exit.'

'Did anyone go back into the room where the body was?'

'I asked Luan to come and search the rooms of the sanctuary. There are only four. Then I told him to alert the warriors below the stairs. I wanted to bring Gelgéis down to this chamber, so I asked Dar Luga if she would sit with the body until I sent for you. Dar Luga needed to go back to her room for something; for her robe, I suppose. I ensured Gelgéis was safe here with Aidan on guard. Then I returned to join Dar Luga and Luan. We went back into the room where I had seen the body. That is when I was able to get a large lamp lit and we realised the dead girl was Gelgéis's attendant, Cera.'

He paused, glanced at Enda, who was standing stoically, hands clasped behind him, staring into the middle distance as if not part of the gathering.

'And you identified the body?' prompted Fidelma.

'We all knew her,' confirmed her brother. 'Cera was personal attendant to Gelgéis; she had her room opposite to the *fothrucadh*. Enda, alerted by the alarm, came into the sanctuary and joined us. However, I sent him to awaken you.'

19

'Where was the body in the room . . . you say it is a washing room?'

'The room we use for our toilet and dressing,' confirmed her brother. 'Cera was lying half on a bench, as if she had fallen backwards. The wound and the blood that came from it were clearly visible.'

'You said the door from that room into the corridor was usually locked?' Fidelma asked.

'It is my practice to have the doors of my bedchamber and the bathroom locked before we retire. The keys are always left on the inside of the doors. But, as I have said, the bathroom key was not there.'

'Are you are saying that this girl was in your bathroom at the dead of night but had no key to enter? Did she have a spare key?'

'She had no key.' The word came as a frustrated sigh.

'You said that you saw the girl's throat was cut?' Eadulf asked.

'It was,' Colgú replied heavily.

This brought forth a suppressed sob from Gelgéis. Colgú reached forward, picked up a cup from a table and handed it to her. She sipped at it slowly and then looked at Fidelma.

'I am sorry. Cera had been in my service only a short time, but she had finished her martial arts training and joined my bodyguard. She was so young.'

'I need to be sure of something,' Fidelma said after a moment or two of thought. She looked at Enda. 'The girl was young but also a member of the troop of female warriors – the Daughters of the Storm. Being one of them, she was fully trained. Yet, from the sound of it, she was overpowered and dispatched before she could raise any alarm. Her death was done quietly and quickly. Only the fall of her body awoke Colgú. So her ability at self-defence was not perfected?'

Enda finally stirred, as if emerging from some sleep. There was anger in his tone.

'On the contrary, lady. I have been practising martial arts

training with Cera these last weeks. I can say she was one of the best opponents I have ever met.'

'Enda, are you saying that the assassin was just lucky or more finely trained than she was?' Fidelma asked.

'I am saying that whoever killed her was no mere assassin. It was either someone with remarkable skill or, at least, someone she knew well so that her defences were down and she was caught unaware.'

There was a silence while they considered this. Then Fidelma spoke again.

'So we have no idea why Cera had left her own chamber to cross the passage in the middle of the night and was able to enter the bathing room, which was locked, where she was found?'

No one answered her. It took her some time to frame the next question.

'One point of clarification, Enda. I presume that you came in answer to Luan's alarm?'

'The relayed alarm, to be precise. Dego was outside the residence when he told me.'

'So, now I need to get a picture of the first moments of discovery.'

Fidelma went to the door, opened it and beckoned Luan, who was still on guard outside, to come into the room.

'Just a few questions at this time. You were on duty, guarding this stairway into the sanctuary during this night?'

'I was. My duty started at the first *cadar*.'

Eadulf knew the day was divided into four sections, the first *cadar* starting at midnight.

'When my brother raised the alarm, where was he standing?'

'He was in the passageway, outside the door of his own bedchamber, which was open.'

'And no one had passed you to go up or down the stairs to the sanctuary during this time?'

'No one passed me, lady. When I was called, I was asked if I had seen any intruder and then I was told to call the alarm. Dar Luga was just emerging from her room opposite the King's bedroom. After I had called the alarm, I made a hurried examination and can confirm that the door to the bathing room, where the body lay, was locked and the key missing. That is, the door to the passage. The King had brought his lady down to this room and Aidan was told to look after her while we went back upstairs to join Dar Luga. I had already had a quick examination beforehand to make sure no one was hiding in the rooms there. I went through the King's bedchamber and confirmed the door to the bathing room was locked. There was no key on the inside or the outside. Then Enda arrived and was asked to fetch you immediately, and I was sent for a spare key.'

'A spare key? Where was that kept?'

'In this very chamber. Where we are now. The King asked Dar Luga to remain with the corpse and I asked her to see that nothing was disturbed in the room while we made a further search in all four rooms. But we found no sign of any intruder.'

'During this early time, apart from yourself, was anyone else on guard above the stairs?' Fidelma asked.

'Once those who had their rooms in the sanctuary had retired for the night no one else was allowed to pass.'

'So who were the last to retire?'

'The *banmhaor,* Dar Luga, retired last. She came late from the kitchens with a jug of water. I think that was not long after I had heard the bell sounding the start of the first *cadar.*'

'You saw no one access the sanctuary after that?'

'Everyone who had a right to be in the sanctuary was already inside. I never left my position until I heard the King shouting.'

'So no one could have entered or left by way of the interior stairs after you came on duty?'

'No one, lady,' Luan confirmed confidently. 'And the stairway is the only entrance or exit.'

'Only Colgú, Gelgéis, Dar Luga and the girl Cera were in the sanctuary during this time?'

'Except for the killer, of course,' Luan confirmed with a grimace. 'As I said, I took a passing scrutiny of the four rooms to make sure no one was concealing themselves. I was certain that they were not, but I admit it was only a brief examination. Perhaps someone could have been hiding somewhere. But they would have had to be hiding there before I came on duty. There are a few small store cupboards but I felt I needed help to search them properly.'

'Had a proper search been made before everyone retired for the night?' Fidelma pressed.

'It is the duty of the commander of the household guard to make certain the rooms are secure before the King and his lady retire for the night,' Luan replied, glancing at Enda. 'I am sure Enda would have ensured no one was hiding in these rooms.'

Fidelma turned to the young warrior.

'I made the search, lady,' he volunteered in a dry voice. 'There was no sign of any intruder when everyone in the sanctuary retired.'

'Eadulf and I will make another inspection shortly,' Fidelma said. 'We need to check for ourselves, having learnt some methods of evading searches, no matter how well conducted.'

Eadulf was a little impatient as he asked: 'I should make an examination of the body unless there is a physician that you wish . . .?'

Colgú was distracted. 'The new physician is not due to arrive for a few days. You know we have been without a physician in the fortress for some weeks.' He glanced to Fidelma. 'I know Eadulf is not considered a fully qualified physician, and the law—'

'Eadulf has served us countless times in the capacity of an adviser on medical matters,' Fidelma replied quickly, seeing a dark shadow cross Eadulf's face. 'We should use him.'

'Then I will go immediately and make some observations,' Eadulf cut in, in irritation. 'I presume that there is no other objection?'

'It is widely known that you have studied the healing arts at the northern medical school of Tuaim Drecain. But you did not complete the training before you decided to journey to Rome to study more about the latest Roman interpretations of the New Faith,' Colgú pointed out. 'But, if Fidelma has no objections . . .'

Fidelma looked at her brother in surprise.

'Eadulf's knowledge has proved essential to my success in resolving many a frustrating case. You know that. He often carries the traditional *lés* or medical bag on his journeys, and that has been of great service.'

'As you say,' Colgú said slowly, 'Eadulf's opinion, in these matters, is always highly valued. It was just that it occurs to me that our laws say no unqualified physician is allowed to practise.'

'In this case, I doubt any objection can be raised if Eadulf examines the body,' Fidelma returned pointedly.

'Then Enda can accompany you and Eadulf to view the body. I and Gelgéis will wait here.'

Eadulf and Enda left the room, but Fidelma held back when she caught sight of a perplexed look on Luan's face.

'You have something on your mind, Luan?'

'Will you step outside a moment, lady?' he asked.

Fidelma glanced quickly across to see that her brother was deep in conversation with Gelgéis. She stepped out and closed the door behind her.

'What is it?'

'Well, a thought did occur to me,' Luan admitted, lowering his voice to almost a whisper. 'It is a thought I don't like, but . . .' He ended with a shrug.

'All thoughts are useful, Luan.'

'Cera served as an attendant to Princess Gelgéis. She was also the youngest of the female warrior troop and she told me that it was a tradition for the youngest to act as attendant to the princess as patroness.'

'I heard this when the duties of the Daughters of the Storm were explained to me,' Fidelma replied patiently. 'What point are you making, Luan?'

'Two things. Firstly, how was she able to be out of her own room in the middle of the night? Secondly, what was she doing in the *fothrucadh*, which had been locked and secured?'

'Do you have any conclusion?' Fidelma asked quietly.

The warrior looked nervously around: 'I said that I did not like the thought.'

'Like it or not, explain it, and why you came to it.'

'We are all thinking that this was some attempted assassination of Colgú or the Princess Gelgéis or both.'

'It is logical and the first thought that occurs,' Fidelma agreed. 'But why don't you agree?'

'My thought was, what if it was not Colgú and Gelgéis who were the intended victims of the attack? What if it was Cera, who *was* the victim?'

'I don't follow you.'

'What if Cera had been passed the keys to the *fothrucadh*, next to the royal bedroom?'

'You speak in riddles,' Fidelma said impatiently. 'Are you saying that she was attempting to assassinate my brother and his wife? Then who killed *her*?'

Luan hesitated a moment before responding. 'The last person securing the sanctuary was the commander of the household guard.'

Chapter Three

'What are you implying, Luan?' Fidelma asked quietly.

'What I am saying is that the last person to go up into the sanctuary, to make his check when everyone had retired, was the commander. We know he had some sort of relationship with the girl Cera. He also had access to the keys of the rooms. Maybe something went wrong between them.'

'Something went wrong?' she repeated.

'They were always practising martial arts with naked blades. But I think there was more going on than just practice.'

Fidelma hesitated. 'We will talk of this later, Luan,' she said quietly but firmly. 'Not a word to anyone else about your thoughts. Now, I shall see what Eadulf can tell me about his examination of the body.'

They came to the top of the stairs into the sanctuary and paused by the first door. Fidelma called out to Dar Luga, and to Eadulf, who had preceded her, to announce her arrival. It was but a moment or so before the plump, matronly, but now anxious-looking, woman opened the door. For Fidelma it was disconcerting to see the usually smiling, plump former cook and now *banmhaor* of the fortress, standing with pale, drawn and almost distraught features. Fidelma noticed that there seemed to be a misty hue of sweat on her pale face. For a moment or so it seemed Dar Luga was hesitant in recognising her.

'I am glad you have come, lady,' Dar Luga whispered. 'Who would have done this to such a young girl?'

She backed into the room so that Fidelma could enter. Fidelma saw Eadulf was on his knees behind a figure lying across a wooden bench. Enda was standing at a door on the other side of the room, which Fidelma presumed was the entry to the main bedchamber. Luan had followed her in and now stood by the door that opened to halfway down the passage behind. A quick glance confirmed that the room was a typical bathroom. The far wall contained a window comprised of several panes, which she guessed, once dawn came, would prove to be of coloured glass. An unusual stone construction in the corner showed a means of heating water, and nearby was a large wooden tub in which to immerse oneself. Fidelma realised that she would have time to examine the room later. Now she turned to Dar Luga.

'You don't look well. Sit yourself.' Fidelma turned and pointed to a wooden chair facing away from the corpse.

'It was a shock to be awakened with this news,' the elderly woman agreed, sitting. 'It seems an age since Colgú said he would send for you, and all the time I have been sitting with . . . with . . .' She indicated the corpse on the bench.

'We'll try not to keep you long.' Fidelma glanced across to Eadulf with a silent question. He looked up with an eloquent shrug. There was, in fact, little he could say other than to confirm that the girl's throat had been cut by some sharp blade. Fidelma thought that Cera had undoubtedly been an attractive girl in life. In fact, she recalled that Dar Luga had once referred to Cera as being of 'the age of long tresses', a colloquial expression that implied the girl had barely reached the age of choice, although it was obvious to Fidelma that she was more the age of twenty.

'A very bloody and brutal attack,' Eadulf announced. 'The incisive drawing of a blade across the throat was done by no amateur but someone who knew precisely what they were doing.' Then he frowned. 'One thing bothers me.'

'One thing only?' Fidelma was in dry, black humour. But she noticed that he had thrown an almost furtive look at Enda and Luan, so she turned to them.

'Perhaps it will save time if you two start a more detailed examination of the rooms in this sanctuary to see if there is anywhere an intruder could hide?'

'But we have already . . .' began Luan, before catching Enda's eye. Then he shrugged. He and Enda left on their task. Fidelma turned back and motioned Eadulf to continue.

'I was going to say something about the method of the killing,' he explained. 'The wound demonstrates that the killer knew what they were about. Death would have been produced, if not immediately, then within moments.'

'Are you saying that she was killed by . . . a professional? Like a martial arts expert?'

'There is another thing that occurred to me. Don't forget this girl was not just a personal attendant to Princess Gelgéis but a member of the Daughters of the Storm, the professional guards to the princess. That means she was well trained both in the martial arts and unarmed combat. Yet, from the way the blade was used, it is clear she was attacked from behind and died without a struggle.'

Fidelma realised that Eadulf was spelling out exactly what Luan had been suggesting to her. Cera's assailant was also proficient in martial arts and had managed to overcome her defences in this way.

'There are plenty of people with well-trained skills in martial arts in the fortress,' she murmured, not even realising it was some automatic defence for the thought that Luan had put into her head.

Eadulf glanced up at her as though reading her mind. He tried not to show a reaction but turned quickly back to his task, becoming absorbed in his examination.

The embarrassment of the moment was interrupted by a low moan from Dar Luga. Fidelma had entirely forgotten that the stewardess appeared ill and was sitting in a corner of the room. Fidelma turned to regard the matronly stewardess with concern.

'Let us find somewhere more comfortable for you to be seated before I ask you the few questions that are necessary. Then you must do something about this ague that has afflicted you.'

'I am sorry, lady,' the woman said. 'I have been feeling something coming upon me since I first woke up. We can go to my chamber.'

Fidelma helped the elderly woman to her feet and towards the door. Outside the bathroom, Fidelma led Dar Luga to the room she occupied opposite the main bedroom.

Once in her small chamber, the stewardess lowered herself on to the bed and helped herself to a glass of water, which stood nearby, next to a small jug. She took a sip and screwed her face in an expression of distaste.

'Water does not taste well after it has been left standing in a warm room overnight,' she explained, putting it back on the table. She seemed to misjudge placing it, because it immediately tipped over and smashed on the floor.

At once Dar Luga tried to rise and was apologising, but Fidelma calmed her.

'Leave it for the time being. I just want to ask a question or two and then you should go down to the kitchen and see if you have something for this ague.'

Dar Luga seated herself again, while Fidelma was peering round the small room.

'Surely it is unusual for you to spend the night here? I thought you had an apartment on the far side of the fortress.'

'Last night I stayed here. Colgú allows me use of this room in the sanctuary if I am working late.'

'And so you were working late last night?'

'I was cooking for your brother. I had to finish off some preparation in the kitchen and the first *cadar* had started when I retired.'

'So you came to bed after midnight?' Fidelma queried unnecessarily. 'And you slept?'

'I think that I slept immediately. I was only awoken when Colgú raised the alarm.'

'Did you hear anything before Colgú raised the alarm?' Fidelma pressed.

Dar Luga shook her head. 'I am afraid I tend to sleep soundly, lady,' she replied quietly. 'As I said, I retired late; I felt exhausted and brought water with me from the kitchen. I passed Luan at the bottom of the stairs and we exchanged a few words, but perhaps this ague had started, for I felt exhausted and I came up and slept at once. The cry for assistance awoke me, but it took me a few moments to realise it was the King shouting. I recall that I took a drink of water to wake myself. The King's door, being directly opposite, was open. He was helping Gelgéis from the room. She was barely awake. Luan had already come up to the top of the stairs and was trying to open the passage door into the bathroom where the girl was found.'

'Did Colgú explain what the alarm was about?'

'It took a while to penetrate my mind. Colgú was shouting that his wife's attendant had been killed. He shouted to Luan to look for the culprit, and was asking whether anyone had passed Luan on the stairs. No one had. I think Colgú added that the door to the passage from the bathroom been locked and I should have a spare key. That is, as stewardess. I looked, but I could not find it.'

Dar Luga groaned a little. She raised a hand to wipe away the perspiration from her face.

'You are definitely not feeling well,' Fidelma observed. 'You must get Eadulf to get you a potion.'

'It is just an ague,' Dar Luga protested. 'It is probably made worse by the fact that I was late to bed. Too much talk about the new chaplain to the fortress. Then, being awoken suddenly and shocked by these events has not improved things.'

'You should get Eadulf to examine you,' Fidelma advised. 'You should not ignore these things, for you are perspiring.'

The plump women shook her head. 'It will pass. I will go to the kitchens; that is, if I have your permission, lady. I have some medications there.'

Fidelma reluctantly nodded agreement. 'Very well. I know we are awaiting a new physician to arrive at the fortress, but remember, Eadulf can help.' She hesitated. 'Just one final question. Can you be certain that there was no sign of the attacker fleeing after you awoke and Colgú was creating the alarm?'

'I remember Luan came and made a search. He later came back with Enda, who had access to a spare key to the bathroom. That was after the King escorted his lady down to the chamber and asked me to stay with the poor girl's body to make sure nothing was disturbed. I was hard pressed to do so until assured no one could be hiding in the sanctuary.'

'Why didn't Luan stay with the corpse? Why were you asked?'

'Luan had duties and, of course, Enda was sent to get you and Eadulf. Also . . . also . . .' Something was puzzling her. 'Also . . . there was something else. Something about a locked door? What was it? I can't remember.'

Dar Luga passed her hand over her forehead to wipe away the perspiration.

'Very well,' Fidelma said soothingly. 'You go down to the kitchen and make sure you mix yourself something for this chill. Enda and Luan seem to have disappeared. If you see them when you go down, ask them to come back up.'

Dar Luga rose slowly and began to move along the corridor. It was clear from her movements, and the difficulty with her breathing, that the plump stewardess was feeling the worst for her cold.

Fidelma made a mental note to get Eadulf look in on her when he could.

When she returned to Eadulf, she found him placing a linen sheet over the body of the girl. The early-morning light was now strong through the window, and the lamps and candles were no longer necessary. Fidelma had not previously spent any time examining her brother's pet project, the sanctuary. Personally, she thought it a curious and unnecessary thing to build a sanctuary within a fortress like Cashel. Now she realised that the large window in the bathroom had, as she had guessed, various coloured panes of glass.

Fidelma stood and gazed at the windows thoughtfully. She recognised that the glass was quite purified – what was called *glóine*. It was far superior to the standard glass that was more commonly used. Glass, with its variations of colours and density, had been well known in the five kingdoms from the time beyond time. But it seemed that her brother had chosen the purest form, which was opaque rather than totally pellucid. She remembered that Colgú had told her that Rodaige, his master builder, had been on a journey to Ailech, the new fortress of Ferg mac Crundmail of the northern Uí Néill. It was called 'the sun palace', for the window features allowed light to bathe the entire building.

From behind her, Eadulf observed her examination. 'They are nice windows,' he said. 'Whoever made them must be gifted. Apart from a small air panel, which a man's head could hardly fit through, the panes do not open. I checked. Even if they could open, they are eight or more metres from the ground outside, and also within sight of the sentinels walking the battlements opposite.'

'So, you are saying that no one can get in through the windows?'

'Not unless they could climb up unobserved, and their shoulder width is the size of a small person's head. And, of course, the other possible entry route, from the roof, can be dismissed.'

Eadulf was gazing up at the sloping roof. Fidelma followed his eyes and saw, to her surprise, that there was a *forlés*, a round skylight, set high in the roof.

'Each of these rooms has one,' Eadulf informed her. 'I took the chance to have a quick look in the main bedroom. It has the same window in the wall and the same skylight.'

Fidelma was not surprised. *Forlés* had become popular in the palaces of many nobles.

'Unless one is an acrobat,' she said, gauging the distance from floor to the skylight, which was about four metres, 'there is no entrance or exit by that means.'

She knew that, had anyone possessed the agility to descend on to the sloping tiled roof of the extension from the outside, they would have had to have exceptional acrobatic powers to enter through one of the round skylights and drop down into the room without making a tremendous noise, even if they had landed on the bed to cushion their fall.

'What about that hatchway?' she suddenly asked. She had noticed it near the stone-built area, in which a fire could be made to heat water for the bath. There was a hatch, secured with bolts, in the wooden wall surround.

'I don't know,' Eadulf admitted. 'I've just seen it. But from the pile of logs and wood, I would say it is where wood and water must be drawn up from the ground to this level.'

'Hauled up eight metres from the ground level?' Fidelma snorted. 'Very impractical. Why not a bathroom on the ground floor? And a spark from the fire could easily catch the building alight.'

At that moment, Luan re-entered the room.

'Do you know how this operates?' demanded Fidelma before he could say anything.

'It is for the wood and the bathwater,' confirmed the warrior. 'However, as you see, it is always secured from inside this room.

The arrangement is that at certain times the hatch is opened and, by means of a rope and pulley, a basket of wood, logs, is hauled up ready for the fire. The same system pulls up water for the evening bath. Of course, this is only used by the King and his lady. It is not accessible from the outside. Someone in this room has to open the bolts.'

'And the wooden screens there?'

'That is for their . . . er . . . the *fúalatech* and er . . .' Luan flushed and it was clear he was pointing out this was a toilet.

'Very impractical,' repeated Fidelma in disapproval. 'A bathing room and such should be on the ground and not up in the air! I'll look more into that as it is a weakness.' Then she turned her frown on him. 'Where is Enda?'

'You asked us to leave while you questioned Dar Luga,' the warrior replied.

This produced a scowl.

'I suggested you both make a more careful search of the rooms and cupboards. Have you done that?'

Luan looked lost. 'I beg your pardon, lady. I thought you used that as an excuse to do your questioning in private.'

Fidelma's mouth tightened. 'So now it seems that people can read my thoughts when I ask them to perform a task for me?'

'Enda did say that he was going to the roof of the main building in order to look down at the sloping roof here to see if there was any way it could be reached from the main roof.'

Fidelma grimaced and she glanced up at the *forlés*. So Enda was thinking about the skylights as well.

'If there is, I doubt if anyone could get through those skylights,' she said. 'Anyway, we would have heard him if he had managed to get into the room above us.'

'I have not seen Enda since then,' Luan admitted. Then he added quietly, 'Did you think any more about what I said, lady?'

'I understand what you suggest, Luan,' she replied sharply. 'All movements, and the movements of all, will be investigated. You may be assured of that. One thing I do think that you should think about. You realise that Enda was more than a friend to the girl? That much is obvious.'

'I was trying to be observant,' Luan protested. 'I was speculating.'

'No speculation without information,' muttered Eadulf.

Fidelma grimaced irritably at his ironic use of one of her frequent sayings. She turned back to Luan.

'Don't misunderstand me. I accept what you are saying. You have observed well. Behaviour that is not the usual is always worth observing.'

She was aware of Eadulf beginning to move around the chamber, peering at various items. He saw that she turned in curiosity to him.

'I am just wondering if we have overlooked anything,' he said. 'Our mystery is how the killer entered and left the chamber.'

'The easy way is this ridiculous arrangement for hauling up wood and water,' Fidelma said. 'I did not realise it existed.'

'But the hatch there is locked, and the rope to the basket is kept secured by the pulley, which means the pulley can not be used unless someone inside the sanctuary is controlling it. And even if it was being used in the night, the sound of it would have disturbed people.'

Fidelma turned back to the door. 'If the key to that door was missing, how was it opened?'

'A spare key had to be sent for, lady,' Luan reminded her. 'Enda knew where it was and came and opened the door.'

'So where did the assassin go when he locked the door almost in Colgú's face?'

'No one came down the stairway. I can swear to that. He had to leave by one of the other rooms.'

Fidelma went across to the window in the wall. Looking through this, she saw, a short distance away, the tall limestone south-western wall of the fortress. It rose higher than Colgú's *tech-termonn*. On top of this wall, she could see a sentinel on his patrol.

Fidelma sighed deeply. 'Well, we can say with certainty that the intruder could not get in by these windows. And there are no windows in the other chambers?'

'Those rooms have no windows because they are built against the major walls of the rest of the residence building,' Luan confirmed. 'These rooms have the only windows in this residence. However, all four rooms have the skylights.'

Fidelma ignored his determination to bring the skylights up again.

'It looks as if the assailant must have come up the stairway or had been hidden in one of the rooms before the night guard started,' she countered. 'He killed Cera here after he emerged from hiding.'

Eadulf was trying to visualise what Fidelma described.

'When your brother entered here from his bedroom, the killer was leaving by that door,' he reflected. 'Or had left moments before when he heard Colgú coming to the room. The killer had time to take the key, close the door behind him and lock it. Now, the question: had he already been in this room when the girl arrived? Or had he entered with the girl?'

'Even more puzzling is that, once in the small passage, where did he go? Even if he was able to get in through the wood hatch, how did he get out and leave the hatch locked after him from this side?' Fidelma stood looking round thoughtfully for a moment into the passage. 'It seems to pose more questions than the ideas answer,' she said.

Eadulf glanced around the bathroom, this time more slowly than before.

'So, if we exclude the *forlés*, there are only three possible ways the killer could have entered this room. The first is the door from the passage. The killer could not have passed Luan on the stairs, so they had to have been hiding in the chamber of either Dar Luga or Cera herself all the time. But then they would have been there when you and Enda searched earlier. Finally, we are back to the hatch for wood and water.'

Luan was shaking his head indignantly. 'No one passed me on the stairs after Dar Luga went to her chamber. Neither could an assassin have hidden in the other rooms without some collusion by either Dar Luga or Cera. I find that impossible to imagine.'

'Then are you saying that the killer was some spectre able to render themselves invisible?' Fidelma asked caustically.

'A trained warrior might be able to enter via the *forlés*.' Luan was defiant. 'That is why Enda went up on the roof of the main buildings to see if there is a way down to them.'

'Even if there was a way down to this roof, one can see just by the height of the rooms that even a warrior with catlike abilities could not enter through the skylight without disturbing whoever was in the room below,' Fidelma replied firmly.

'Probably we should search for a rope,' Eadulf pointed out in a soft tone.

Fidelma smiled wanly. 'A worthy thought, and yet we seem to be ascribing great acrobatic powers to the attacker.'

'No need to point out that we have many acrobats in Cashel,' Luan replied with sarcasm. It gave Fidelma pause.

'That is true,' she reflected. 'We have performers arriving for the fair. But I am sure, Luan, you will tell us that it is not beyond the capabilities of our own élite household guards to achieve this feat. However, even the best of them would make a noise.'

The warrior gestured with a half-shrug. 'It would not be something I would like to do unless my life was in jeopardy.'

Eadulf gave a small dismissive gesture with his hand. 'If the killer could swing down a rope into this chamber then it is also possible they could do so directly into Colgú's chamber, and kill him and Gelgéis before they raised any alarm.'

'If they were the intended victims,' Luan muttered.

Eadulf looked perplexed but it was Fidelma who answered. 'So you still think that Cera was the intended victim? Why kill the young girl? I would presume that she was roused when she heard the assassin and was trying to raise the alarm.'

Luan shook his head. 'I have learnt from you both that motive is important, so I am wondering about the peculiarities of this killing.'

'Peculiarities?' Eadulf frowned.

'It was nearly halfway through the first *cadar* of the day. All was in blackness and silence in the sanctuary. Whether the assassin had been hiding somewhere, awaiting an opportunity, or whether they had just entered, is another matter. However, they make their move. Now, remember, Cera's bedchamber is immediately at the top of the stairs opposite to the bathroom, now locked. I am standing on guard only a whisper's distance away. If the assassin had disturbed Cera and she awoke to investigate, then why not call me? To gain access to the bathroom – although Colgú says he always locked it – she would have crossed the passage. Did she find the door open? If so, Cera entered to be attacked and killed. She would have seen the killer. But then she was killed with her back to the killer. Why did I hear nothing? Why didn't Cera call down to me when she left her room if she was alarmed?'

'Do you have an alternative explanation?' Eadulf asked patiently.

'If the girl was neither the intended victim nor was trying to raise the alarm, but was colluding with the killer, the assassin could have been in her room. Thus they made sure no alarm was raised. Cera and her companion crossed to kill Colgú or Gelgéis. Something went wrong, resulting in the assassin turning on Cera.'

'That seems unlikely,' Eadulf replied curtly. 'And the killer would need a key to this room. It's nonsense. Two assassins and one turning on the other outside the bedchamber of the victims?'

'I have already pointed out that it was known where the spare keys were kept and who had access,' Luan replied quietly.

'We are discussing theories,' Fidelma said with a worried expression, but trying to mollify Luan, who had flushed in annoyance at Eadulf's responses. 'And it seems that we have not really decided who the victim was meant to be.'

'We won't know the motivation until we find the killer,' Eadulf sighed. 'So let us resume considering the idea that the killer . . . he or she . . . had entered the sanctuary and managed to hide themselves until the moment they felt appropriate. But where? Colgú's room has its own door leading on to the passage directly opposite Dar Luga's room. There is a connecting door between Colgú's chamber and this bathroom. This room has a door that is more or less at the top of the stairs directly opposite the girl's room. Colgú's custom was to lock both the doors that lead into the passageway. Both doors can be seen from the stairway, which was where Luan was stationed. I think we can rule out the assassin coming into this bathroom from Colgú's room. I think he could not have been hiding in this room, even behind the screen for the toilet.'

'Where, then, is there a hiding place?' Luan demanded, with a wave of his hand to encompass the area.

Eadulf compressed his lips for a moment. 'If the assassin was not hiding in Dar Luga or Cera's rooms, then we are back to the wood entrance, and Luan's idea of Cera being an accomplice who opened that hatch at night.'

'But she would have had to let down the rope, which, if the pulley was used, would have made a noise loud enough to wake the dead,' Fidelma pointed out.

'I stick to the fact that I did not hear Cera crossing the passageway from her room to here,' Luan said. 'She did not call out and give an alarm. Consider the facts and motive.'

'Motive?' Eadulf was irritable. 'You keep intimating that you know something more of the motive?'

Luan looked nervously at Fidelma. 'I understand what you say about Enda being in love,' he said. 'It's just that we should not concentrate on the idea that the intended victims were Colgú and the Princess Gelgéis. Isn't love considered a motive? Or rather, as Brother Dáire was trying to teach us the other evening, love is often a motive for death. But I have nothing to add that is conclusive.'

'It is not love that is a motive, but *amore peribat*,' Eadulf corrected in rebuke. 'Unrequited love. Love to hatred turned.'

'At the moment, we are gathering information,' Fidelma firmly interrupted. 'Let us continue for the moment. If we take one of Luan's theories as plausible, then Cera was the victim, so why didn't the assassin kill her in her own room? Why come here?'

Eadulf was lightly dismissive. 'Luan is suggesting that the assassin was Enda. I cannot accept that. How could it be? His love was turned to hatred. He killed Cera out of some newfound hate. He did this during his final inspection of the sanctuary. Then he transported her into this room, making a noise so Colgú raised the alarm. He managed to escape. Where did he hide? In a cupboard? Or climb to a skylight? He certainly couldn't escape through the wood hatch. I think the idea that Enda was her lover who had suddenly turned killer because of one rejection is nonsensical.'

Luan breathed in sharply in anger.

'I don't think Luan is suggesting that,' Fidelma cut in. She was worried because she had never seen Eadulf so belligerent. Even the anger she had seen a short time before, when Colgú had questioned his right to officially examine the body, had surprised her. She wondered why he was being so quick tempered and almost petulant.

'Then that leaves only the use of gymnastic power to get down and back through one of the skylights.' Eadulf was again sarcastic.

'The skylights in Dar Luga and Cera's bedrooms are higher than on this side of the sanctuary. It is a longer drop or climb. Or maybe the assassin is someone else, and Luan and Enda were not so thorough when they conducted the search after the body was found.'

Luan took an angry step forward. 'Brother Eadulf,' he said dropping the usual epithet 'friend Eadulf', 'in my culture there is a law that protects one against the snarling, barking and biting of those who use sarcasm. We often call it *aer*, or *groma* in its less vindictive form. I am prepared to accept your snarling at me because you are merely a *cú glas*, a grey dog, a mere foreigner . . .'

'Luan!' Fidelma almost shouted, moving quickly as if to step between them.

Eadulf's face remained taut. He had difficult in articulating. Then, gaining some control, he said slowly: 'All I point out is that these rooms should have been thoroughly searched before the household retired and doubly so after the body was discovered and it was clear that there had been an intruder. It is no help to claim that the search did not find the intruder . . . unless it was no search at all.'

Luan's posture was definitely aggressive.

'Lady,' he said coldly, 'please inform Brother Eadulf of the law book, and the section in it on satire and sarcasm.'

'I do not think we need that, Luan,' Fidelma replied coldly. 'We are here to resolve a murder and a mystery, not to start fighting with one another. Perhaps we should reflect on the maxims of Brehon Morann. When a lawyer starts to exchange impartiality for emotion and bias, then all hope of judgment and solution is lost. Whatever offensive thoughts have displaced the dispassionate ones, let us leave them and return to the main problem.'

There was a moment of silence.

It was Eadulf who shrugged and abruptly stepped forward with his outstretched hand to Luan.

'I apologise. I have been too absorbed with some problems recently. Not being able to resolve them, I am not in the best of tempers. Please forgive me.'

Luan was not one to hold a grudge. He immediately responded with a smile and stretched out his own hand to meet Eadulf's.

'Good,' Fidelma said hurriedly, although she was somewhat disturbed by Eadulf's apology. 'Now let us review the situation. Luan is posted at the foot of the stairs and the chambers are sealed from entry below.'

'If we dismiss the possibility of the assassin hiding in Cera's chamber,' Eadulf offered hesitantly, 'then there is only one solution. The killer was hiding in Dar Luga's chamber.'

'We have yet to consider whether the killer was hiding in Dar Luga's chamber,' Fidelma agreed.

'When Colgú raised the alarm, the door to this chamber was locked. The killer had almost slammed it in Colgú's face to avoid identification or even capture. The assassin then locked the door from the passage. They could not go down the stairs or they would have encountered Luan. It did not take long for Colgú to go back to his bedroom door and emerge into the passage that way, but in those few moments the killer had vanished. When you heard the alarm, Luan, and came to the top of the stairs, what did you see?'

'I saw the King at his door, shouting. I gathered that Cera had been attacked and the bathroom door was locked from the passage side. So I went to the King's door, brushed by him and went into the bathroom. I was carrying my lantern. I saw the girl was beyond help and there was no one else in the room. I confirmed there was no key in the lock. I turned back. The King was helping Princess Gelgéis along the passage by which time Dar Luga had been roused and was trying to help. He instructed me to check for an intruder in Cera's room, which I did. The King instructed Dar Luga to stay with the body.'

'Did you hear anything before Colgú raised the alarm?' pressed Eadulf.

Luan thought for a moment. 'Things happened quickly. I believe I heard a door being shut sharply. That was probably the bathroom door.'

'The door that was found to be locked from the outside,' Eadulf stated.

'I am told my brother's practice was to ensure his bedchamber and the *fothrucadh* doors were locked when he retired,' Fidelma remarked.

'Did Cera retire to her room at the same time as Colgú and his lady retired and locked their rooms?' Eadulf asked.

'Cera did so after her duties as attendant to the princess.'

'But Dar Luga came late to the sanctuary. That was admitted by her and seen by you. She was the last into the sanctuary.'

Luan agreed. 'It was after midnight that Dar Luga went to her room. Last night, as I mentioned, we spent a brief few moments exchanging words while she ascended the stairway to her room.'

'By that time the doors to Colgú and Gelgéis's rooms were locked?'

'I heard the King turning the keys not long before Dar Luga came.'

'Before you went to get the spare key and found Enda, where did you look for the missing key?' Fidelma asked.

'There was little time to search because of the nature of the incident. I had tried the door and found it locked. As I said, I had my lantern. There was no key fallen to the floor outside nor on the floor inside. The intruder must have taken the key.'

Fidelma looked thoughtful. 'Surely, Dar Luga, as stewardess, would have access to keys to all the rooms?'

'I believe she might,' Luan admitted.

'But you went to Enda rather than ask her?'

'I did not think. I knew the master keys were also kept by the household guards, under Enda's authority. As I said, they were in the King's private chamber at the bottom of the stairs.'

'I have thought of another complication,' Eadulf said slowly. 'As personal attendant to Gelgéis, surely Cera had a key to the bathroom so that she could enter when needed?'

Fidelma shrugged. 'We shall have to see if Gelgéis knows the answer to that question. We must now look at the evidence and see what our options are. Whatever the motive, it is obvious that the victim was the subject of a knife attack. No one has mentioned that the knife used in the attack has been found.'

Luan shook his head. 'I did not see a knife near the body.'

'I saw no knife,' Eadulf confirmed.

'So the attacker took it with them. There is enough blood on the body and robes that some traces might show us the way the attacker went. Have you looked for bloodstains along the passage?'

'Along the passage?' questioned Luan.

'The killer must have left this room to go into the passage and then into another room. There was no other way. So if they were carrying the knife and covered in blood, there should be traces.'

'We should check in this room first for the discarded weapon,' Luan pointed out.

It did not take long for them to search the obvious places in the room for the weapon. There was none. The attacker must have had no time to conceal the weapon before he had to escape to avoid Colgú. As Fidelma had pointed out, there were enough splashes of blood around the bench on to which the girl had fallen. There were drops on the floor and smears, which had been trodden about by those who had found the girl.

Fidelma sighed. 'I want all the rooms searched again.'

'Again? All the rooms?' Luan was puzzled. 'The King's bedchamber as well?'

'That is what I meant by all the rooms,' she replied sharply.

'Also any cupboards or chests where a dagger could be hidden. The key also. Any traces of blood should be recorded.'

'We did search several large cupboards used for keeping of clothing and personal items. Should I search those of . . .?' Luan was protesting.

'Search those most carefully again in case the culprit believes that we would not bother to look in such places. Look for blood traces. The killer must have had blood on their clothing. But the dagger that made this wound should tell us more about the killer.'

Luan was heading for the door to the passage when he paused and glanced back at the body.

'What about the arrangements . . . the preparation of the poor girl's body? The obsequies? Isn't that a task that Dar Luga should be in charge of?'

'We will make sure the matter is taken care of,' Fidelma assured him.

Luan briefly raised his hand in acknowledgment and left.

Eadulf had gone once again to the window, poking at the frame as if testing the width of the opening. He stood back with a shake of his head and then peered yet again to the high sloping ceiling to the *forlés*. He stood with his hands on his hips looking around the room in a slightly perplexed fashion.

'This is a mystery,' he sighed. 'The mystery of a locked room . . . So it is only through that passage door that the killer came and left. A locked room with a key that was on the inside.'

'And, if so,' Fidelma replied in a tired voice, 'it adds even more mystery to what we know already. I've just realised it.'

'More mystery?'

'You were the one that brought it up,' she replied.

He frowned. 'How so?'

'You pointed out about the knife and the bloodstains and the key. When the killer fled, taking the key and locking the door behind them, there should have been a great deal of blood being spread in his trail. This blood would have saturated the clothes of the killer. It would have been on the weapon.'

'What makes that more mysterious than it already is?'

Fidelma pointed to the door around the handle. 'There are no bloodstains on the handle and lock, or around that area of the door. No one has said that they have spent time cleaning the door. Neither has anyone noticed any bloodstains on the outside of the door in the passage.'

Eadulf pursed his lips together and let forth a quiet whistling breath.

CHAPTER FOUR

When Fidelma and Eadulf came down the stairs from the sanctuary, they found Aidan had taken Luan's position outside the door of Colgú's reception chamber. He silently acknowledged them, then knocked on the door before opening it to let them pass inside. Colgú and his wife were seated before the small table where they were finishing the brief first meal of the day. They had apparently sent for clothes better fitted for day wear. That they had been up since before dawn, and had awoken in circumstances of stress, still showed on their drawn and pale features.

What surprised Fidelma and Eadulf was that Enda was also there, kneeling by the fire, having apparently rekindled it into a crackling blaze. To them, the fire seemed unnecessary because dawn would shortly bring the midsummer sun and the clear sky already gave an indication of the warmth to come. Enda appeared uncomfortable as he rose to face them.

'I thought that you were doing some investigation regarding the roof?' Fidelma queried dryly. 'Did you complete the task that I gave you and Luan to do before that?'

'I did complete it,' the warrior muttered. 'No one was concealed in the sanctuary and I could find no way of gaining easy access to the sanctuary roof. So I thought it best to come here to ensure the King and his lady were safe.'

'What news?' Colgú interrupted, asking Fidelma and ignoring the tension of her exchange with Enda.

'Death was caused by one cut.' Eadulf felt he should contribute his finding. 'It was immediately fatal. It was professionally done. The person who delivered the stroke knew exactly where to thrust their blade.'

Colgú was practised enough in warfare to understand Eadulf's logic.

'Would you say that it was a deed done in panic?'

'The way the girl was held from the back and the way the blade was used would indicate no panic.'

Colgú cast an anxious glance at his wife, but his curiosity overrode the worry that this news was upsetting to her.

'You imply that the killer was no stranger to the art of killing,' Enda interceded unexpectedly.

'I think we could go beyond implication. The wound was made by someone who knew how to inflict death immediately; someone who practised the martial arts or was, perhaps, a physician; someone who has studied the body. Even a mortician would have the same knowledge.'

There was silence for a few moments.

'There is little else to tell you at the moment,' Fidelma went on hurriedly with a quick look at Enda. 'Until we begin our questioning of everyone involved—'

'But you have been up in the sanctuary with the corpse for some time,' interrupted her brother in a snappish tone. 'Who else do you have to question before you can tell me something more positive?'

Fidelma returned his irritation in a cold voice. 'You should trust me as a professional in my job, brother. You should know I will not make hurried decisions . . . not even for you.'

It needed no expert to see the red-haired King and the red-haired *dálaigh* were brother and sister. Their fiery eyes, chins thrust out belligerently, challenging one another, even their manner of speaking, with tones of defiance, suggested their close relationship.

'The major concern is why this girl was attacked,' Gelgéis said, speaking for the first time. 'Can you tell us anything about that, Fidelma?'

'Anything said now will simply be speculation,' Fidelma replied.

'I have already heard speculation that it could have been a deliberate attack on the girl and not on me or Colgú.'

Fidelma's mouth tightened. Luan had obviously been making free with his theories.

'I don't think it is speculation to accept the obvious,' Gelgéis added.

'Not so obvious. At this time the obvious is that it might be another attempt to eliminate my brother from the kingship. It might even be an attempt by the dissidents of Osraige, angry at you, Gelgéis, being married to the King of Muman. But it is right that the theories should be raised. I will not condemn Luan for postulating it, even though I do not accept it as yet.'

Colgú was angry but it was an anger born of fear for his wife.

'Someone broke in to the specially built *tech-termonn*, a place that my master builder told me was totally secure. Until we can identify the killer, it is impossible to say what the motive was.'

'When the day is lighter, I shall want to examine the way that wood and water are hauled up to the *fothrucadh*. That seems to be the first weakness in the security of the sanctuary to me.'

Colgú hesitated a moment as if he was going to protest, but then shrugged as if surrendering to logic.

'It is done by pulley and rope. The hatch through which the rope is hauled is bolted from the inside after the wood and water are taken in. The water, when used, and the waste ... well, that is flushed through a special lead piping.'

'I would still like to see the operation,' Fidelma insisted, before turning her gaze to Enda. 'So, when I told you and Luan to search the apartments more thoroughly, I was told that you had decided to extend the search to the roof of the royal complex, in order to see if there was a way down on to the roof of the sanctuary. You say that you found no one could use that means of entrance?'

Enda shifted nervously. 'I found no easy way down from the roof of the main building to the roof of the sanctuary. If anyone could manage it, it would be almost impossible to enter quietly through one of those *forlés*,' he answered. His voice had become somewhat listless. It was as if his mind were no longer a functioning part of his body. Fidelma began to suspect that the trauma of Cera's death had now registered with him.

'You do not look too well, Enda,' she said thoughtfully. 'I know you have been on duty since before the first *cadar* of the day. Perhaps you would like to retire for a short while to rest?'

'I could do with a short time of rest, lady,' Enda conceded, turning to Colgú, apparently embarrassed. 'I am afraid I do need to absent myself for a short period.'

'Of course.' Colgú motioned with his hand in a gesture of dismissal.

'I shall need to have a talk further with you, when you are up to it,' Fidelma added as he made for the door.

Fidelma waited until Enda had left the chamber and then turned towards her perplexed brother.

'You should know that Enda had a personal involvement with girl, Cera. This will account for his awkward behaviour.'

Princess Gelgéis raised her head with a sad smile. 'Personal involvement? I thought as much, even though Cera never confessed it to me. She and Enda were paired for part of an exhibition of the martial arts during the fair in the township.'

'This I know, lady,' Fidelma replied in a gentle tone.

Colgú grimaced, expressing his frustration. 'Carry on as you see fit, Fidelma. All I ask is to be told what you know when you know it.'

'That request is superfluous.' Fidelma was immediately irritable again. 'You shall be informed at once. But it will take as long as it takes.'

She turned back with a smile of reassurance to Gelgéis, who was still trying to conceal the anxiety on her features. She had obviously been fond of her young attendant.

'Do not worry, Gelgéis. I shall do my best to resolve things quickly.'

'Until we are certain of the motive for this killing, I suggest some intervening action must be made to protect ourselves,' Colgú said firmly.

'Intervening action?'

'For the next few nights Gelgéis and I will double the household guard. We will remain in the sanctuary unless you tell me there is some vulnerability to the construction. I thought that I, with Rodaige, my master builder, had covered all entries that were at risk.'

'I am not leaping to any conclusion until I have assured myself that it is the right one,' Fidelma replied.

Princess Gelgéis intervened, looking apologetic. 'It is no affront to your own household guard. It is not that I mistrust or doubt the capabilities of the Nasc Niadh, the famed warriors of Cashel. But my personal guards, the Daughters of the Storm, have served my family well. So I shall need to make some arrangements to ensure they can carry out their duties to me.'

'I understand,' Fidelma reassured her.

'I have already sent for Crédh, the commander of my guard,' Gelgéis added.

Fidelma caught Eadulf looking at her with a questioning expression. She knew what he was thinking and hoped that he would keep his thoughts to himself. Cera had also been a trained warrior of Gelgéis's personal guard. That had not prevented her from meeting her death.

'I will have a word with Enda when he is rested,' Colgú said. 'We will see how best the security arrangements can be made.'

There was a knock on the door at that moment and Aidan's head appeared around the opening.

'Crédh is here,' he announced.

'Then let her come in,' Colgú ordered as if the warrior should have done so without being asked.

The tall figure of Crédh entered and stood glancing quickly round the room. She carried herself upright and her dark eyes moved quickly, assessing the company. There was something challenging to her thrusting jaw, thin lips and the narrow hook of her nose. Then she took a step forward before lowering her head in acknowledgement to Gelgéis, and then, more briefly, Colgú.

'I received your summons here, lady.' She addressed Gelgéis in a voice that seemed mechanical, as if devoid of emotion. 'I heard on my way here that young Cera has been killed. In what manner was she—'

'I will explain later,' the princess cut her off abruptly. 'Meanwhile, my husband and I will be increasing the guard duties. My husband's sister, the lady Fidelma, who is a *dálaigh,* will be in charge of the investigation into Cera's death, and it is my intention you should work with her as and when she needs your help.'

'I understand, lady,' the warrior answered at once. 'It shall be as you say. Are there any special instructions at the moment?'

'I want you to work out a schedule so that a member of your company is always within call of me from now on. Fidelma, is there anything else?'

Crédh turned almost reluctantly to Fidelma. It was obvious from her expression that she resented being placed under the authority of others.

'There is little to be done at the moment. But perhaps some questions might arise later.'

Gelgéis suddenly rose determinedly. 'I am exhausted already, but I will take this opportunity to go with Crédh and discuss what duties I would like my warriors to undertake. That is, unless you have objection, husband?'

After Gelgéis and Crédh had left and instructions were relayed to Aidan, Fidelma stretched out in the chair Gelgéis had just quit. Brother and sister were now less formal with one another and Eadulf once they were alone.

Colgú helped himself to *corma*, a strong liquor, and made a motion of his hand to indicate Eadulf should help himself also.

'Of all things, this had to happen at this particular time and with Finguine and Fíthel absent from Cashel,' Colgú groaned aloud. 'The two people I needed here more than anyone.'

At once an expression of annoyance crossed Fidelma's features. Finguine was her brother's *tánaiste*, or heir apparent, to the kingdom, while Fíthel was the Chief Brehon of the kingdom, an office she had once aspired to.

'Why should the absence of Prince Finguine and Fíthel make a difference?' she asked testily. 'Fíthel may be your Chief Brehon, but am I not qualified enough to investigate this case?'

For a moment or so it appeared that her brother did not understand her point. Then he shrugged.

'Of course, the matter is within your competence,' he replied in a waspish tone. 'I am referring to other important matters that you might have forgotten.'

'Other important matters?' She was puzzled. 'Matters more important than murder in your own sanctuary?'

'The resolution of the crime and the punishment of the perpetrator are important to you, Fidelma, and I accept that. Don't forget that I have this kingdom to govern, the largest of the five kingdoms on this island. Muman is a diverse kingdom with seven squabbling relatives all claiming succession to the kingship, all of them disputing my being confirmed as King although it was done in accordance with the law. After them, we have the Osraige, the

Déisi and the Uí Fidgente all wanting to dispute having to pay tribute to Cashel.'

'You sound hard done by, brother. You can always abdicate and enter a religious house, as some nobles have done. I suppose we each have chosen our role in life but, once chosen, we should pursue it as best we can.'

'Do not forget your role is as my personal legal adviser,' Colgú replied sharply. 'That also places you on my council, which is not due to meet until *Cét Gaimrid*, the first of winter. Now this happens, with me hosting the great fair in the township in three days from now. That is an event that our prestige rests upon.'

'If nothing else, Cera's death has reminded me of that,' Fidelma acknowledged in a tight voice.

Colgú agreed with a frown. 'Well, I had not forgotten about the martial arts contests. I hope this matter can be resolved before that.'

'Before the fair or before the next council? I have already said that an investigation and resolution will take as long as it takes, brother. I know you want the fair to go ahead as a symbol of uniting Cashel and Durlus Éile, and by association, Osraige, but what do you mean about the council? You seem to have something on your mind by which you are distracted and worried about a council meeting and the absence of Finguine and the Chief Brehon Fíthel? Is there anything you wish to share with me?'

Colgú spread his hands in an expression of vulnerability.

'It is only that I have been told to expect an emissary from the High King soon. Apparently, there are important matters that he wishes to lay before me and the council of the kingdom. That is why I regret the absence of my heir apparent and leading legal counsel.'

'What's that about?'

'I have no idea. However, my council should know their presence at the fair would be an important political matter. Not everyone in the kingdom is happy about my union with a princess from Osraige. Do you think the absence of Finguine and Fíthel at this time could be interpreted as signs of dissension?'

'During the two years since you first met Gelgéis, and in spite of the number of times the wedding ceremony had to be cancelled for various unrelated matters, you have been strongly supported by Finguine and also by the Council of Brehons of this kingdom,' Fidelma pointed out.

Eadulf had been sitting quietly to the point where Fidelma had almost thought he was dozing. Now he spoke. 'Fidelma is right, Colgú. You worry too much about these tasks and what people think. You have other people to plan the fair.'

'And there is much to plan. Dar Luga, although I appointed her my stewardess of the household, cannot fulfil all the roles of the advisers that are missing at this time. Those are essential for the good governance of the fair. She has experience of the catering, but not enough experience in other matters – the entertainments, the contests, the horse racing and other events.'

'Enda should stand in as adviser,' Eadulf pointed out. 'He needs something that can distract him at the moment. He has attended enough fairs to know what is expected and I am sure that, given support, he is capable of performing whatever duties are needed.'

Colgú was thoughtful. 'Fidelma has drawn attention to the fact that he seems to be affected by the death of this girl. I presume that is why you wanted to speak to him later?'

'It is. It seems he had become very close to her. I am not sure Eadulf is right that distraction is the answer,' Fidelma said. 'I feel he should be given some time to sort out his thoughts.'

'Very well,' Colgú replied. 'I have no objections. But then it is a question of who will replace him.'

'Luan has been acting second in command for long enough – I am sure we can continue without making drastic changes. But another thought: Gormán, your former commander, and his wife are still staying with his mother in the township.'

Gormán was not only the former commander of the household guard but had commanded a full *catha*, or battalion, of Colgú's warriors when the King called a 'hosting' in defence of the territory.

Colgú thought for a moment. 'Very well, but we can decide on security for the fair later. I am worried that we are not only awaiting our senior officials, but we have many newcomers that we have to learn to work with.'

'Such as?'

'We have only recently appointed a new physician and an apothecary for the household and are awaiting their arrival.'

'I thought that you were happy to accept that Eadulf could fulfil part of those roles this morning?' Fidelma pointed out, realising the comment might be taken as an insult.

'You do not have to tell me that Eadulf is adept at that sort of examination. He has helped you in such cases many times. I merely point out that we need a general physician and apothecary who will not be questioned under the laws that have already been raised.'

'It was my understanding that these offices would be already filled before the fair started. I thought a physician had already been recommended and approved by Abbot Cuán. Are they not due to arrive soon?'

'They are expected any day. But, at the moment, the fact is that there is no fully qualified physician in the fortress. In spite of his acknowledged talent, Eadulf is not one.'

Fidelma glanced uneasily towards her husband. 'But he has been good at what he has done, otherwise he would not have garnered the reputation that he has.'

'Eadulf did not even complete his qualifications and is not regarded under our law as a qualified physician,' repeated Colgú. 'Anyway, I hope the physician arrives soon with her staff.'

Fidelma noticed that Eadulf's features were moulding into an expression that ranged from irritation to annoyance, then to anger.

As a distraction, Fidelma picked up on her brother's words. '*Her* staff? The physician is a woman?'

'Her name is Síonna; she was the professor of medicine at Mungairit. I know that you and Eadulf visited the abbey not so long ago and saw its vast teaching complex. Perhaps you know her? Abbot Cuán, representing me in his position as Bishop of Cashel, chose her as having the best reputation for the master physician here.'

'We know the abbey at Mungairit,' Fidelma agreed, looking to Eadulf as if for confirmation. 'I don't remember her name spoken of.'

'Is the matter relevant?' Eadulf suddenly cut in, in a belligerent tone. He was unable to suppress the anger that was building up in him any longer. 'I agree that I am not fully qualified and you have laws about people practising medicine without qualifications, but I have not been challenged before. My examinations have been accepted in evidence for the record when submitted to any brehon.'

Colgú, after a moment's surprise, seemed to miss the point that his comment had provoked.

'If you are worried that your position needs to be supported by a qualified physician, then I am sure Síonna can do that when she arrives. You have been asked to do only what it is known that you can do, Eadulf. For that we are grateful.'

'I am well aware that my status is on sufferance here,' Eadulf snapped in anger.

There was a sudden silence and Colgú looked bewildered.

'On sufferance? I do not understand.'

'Your laws are specific, not just on medical practices but on the status of who is allowed to practise medicine . . . especially foreigners, even if one is married to someone of noble birth. This is the third time my situation has been challenged.'

Colgú glanced in surprise at Fidelma and back to Eadulf as he had used the common term for a foreigner – *cú glas* or grey dog. The polite form would have been *deorad,* for an exile. The expression clearly showed Eadulf had some problem.

'You have always had our complete support, Eadulf,' Colgú assured him quietly. 'Has it seemed otherwise? Do you feel that you are only tolerated here? Then I must protest that you are anything but tolerated. You are part of the family.'

Eadulf felt an almost uncontrollable resentment suddenly rising up within him. His mind seemed to have gone back to the day when his great desire was to leave Cashel and make his way to some more peaceful spot, away from the nobles of Muman and their King and the interminable constrictions of learning new laws; away from the advice of the various well-meaning dignitaries; away from the hustle and bustle that came with the politics of being in close proximity of Fidelma's family and the oppressive feeling that he was only accepted for her sake.

His mouth tightened and his brows came together as he realised the path of his thoughts and the inevitable end. He was questioning his relationship with Fidelma. Yet, he realised, his life had become inseparably linked with her and also with their son, Alchú, 'the gentle hound'. Why had Colgú's remarks raised such old resentments, which Eadulf had thought he had long since dealt with? He had not felt such emotions since those earlier days when he was being advised what he should know before marrying an Eóganacht princess.

Fate had led Eadulf to meet Fidelma at the Council at Streoneshalh in the abbey of the Northumbrian princess, Abbess Hilda. They were on opposite sides of the great debate on the merits of the insular churches, the philosophies of the Irish missionaries and the revised philosophies of Rome. It was a fateful meeting, which eventually made them embark on a trial marriage for a year and a day under Irish law in which he had become *fer comtha,* with rights as her husband for the period. Afterwards he had accepted full marriage and merger into the royal Eóganacht family of Cashel.

The reality of full marriage was not as simple and unremarkable as the exchanging of vows of the trial marriage, for was not Fidelma's brother, Colgú, claimed as fifty-ninth generation from Eibhear Fionn, son of Golamh, called Milidh, who brought the children of the Gael to Éireann? And what was Eadulf? In this land he was called a *cú glas* – a grey dog – the term for an alien. More polite folk called him a *deorad* or *deorad deo* – an exile or exile of God. He had been an hereditary magistrate in his own village of the South Folk in the kingdom of the East Angles. Now he had to rely on Fidelma's brother for his status, for he was now deemed a *fine thacair* – 'a kinsman by summoning'. In law, that meant legal protection and adoption. Colgú had formally adopted him into his family. But he had no bard to recite his *forsundud*, the praise poems of the generations of his ancestors. Even when he and Fidelma married, with the blessing of Colgú and many of the nobles and churchmen, the law on marriage made clear that it was not a union of equal rank and property.

Indeed, the law classed him as a man supported by a woman's position and property. In spite of his marriage and connections, he was still looked upon as a foreigner.

Eadulf suddenly realised how quiet the room had become and that Fidelma and her brother were staring at him curiously. Fidelma's expression seemed mingled with sadness and hurt.

'I am sure no one is questioning your abilities, Eadulf,' she told him quietly. 'We will talk of private matters at the appropriate time.'

Eadulf realised he had relapsed into a sulky silence as he considered his problems. He mentally rebuked himself as to why such thoughts had suddenly overwhelmed him and caused him to make the outburst. He would have a hard task in explaining his thoughts, even to his own understanding.

'The case is in my sister's hands,' Colgú began, breaking the uncomfortable silence. 'If you are dissatisfied with your role in this investigation . . .?' He was still clearly puzzled by Eadulf's unexpected eruption.

'I am satisfied with Eadulf's examination and judgement of the current case,' Fidelma interposed quickly before Eadulf could respond. 'The girl was murdered. It does not need someone of high qualifications to observe that Cera had had her throat cut. It falls to me to identify the culprit and determine why this heinous crime was committed.'

'Very well,' her brother sighed. 'So there is nothing to hinder the preparation of the body for the obsequies and burial at the appropriate hour tonight or tomorrow night? We had best send for the new chaplain, Father Socra, and give him instruction.'

'I have met this Socra only once when he arrived here with his few followers some days ago.' Eadulf could not help but seize the opportunity to reassert a normal tone in the discussion. 'When I asked him why he took the title "Father" when we usually use the term "Brother", he told me he was your personal priest. I pointed out that the scripture of Matthew claims that Jesus taught: "Do not call anyone on earth your father, for only one is your father, He who is in heaven." This Socra did not like that and he claimed that Rome now accepted that priests should be addressed as "Father" as they were spiritual fathers. He sounds as if he is an advocate of Rome's religious interpretations, but how it is perceived here? The insular churches have rejected Rome's rulings many times. Yet he has become the priest here. So what do you call his office?'

'Father Socra officially replaces Brother Fidach. He now becomes my *sucart meisi* – my table priest – with the full approval of Abbot Cuán, acting as the Bishop of Cashel. I am told Father Socra is well able to take charge of all the duties expected of him.'

The term 'table priest' was the one that Eadulf had realised was sometimes rendered in Latin as 'chaplain', the name coming from the early Christian religieux who were keepers of the sacred relic, the *cappa*, or little cape of the Blessed Martin of Tours.

'In that case, we should inform Socra that he should collect the body of Cera and take it to the chapel to begin the obsequies,' Eadulf said.

'A new chaplain, a new physician and apothecary . . .' Fidelma was reflective. 'It seems sad how people are changing here. Those that I thought would be here for ever have died or vanished. I know little of this Father Socra except he comes from near Durlus Éile. I heard Abbot Cuán had appointed him as an acknowledgement to Princess Gelgéis. He looked rather young when I met him briefly on his arrival. Do you think that he will be comfortable being here?' She asked the question of her brother.

'Why would he not be comfortable?' Colgú was puzzled.

'My understanding is that he was trained at an abbey on the banks of the River Bhearú, the river that separates Osraige from Laigin.'

'I remember it,' Eadulf suddenly said. 'The abbey of Sléibhte stands on the border of the Laigin kingdom. Once across the river and you are in Fianamail's kingdom.'

'Sléibhte is still in the territory of Osraige,' Colgú replied with a hint of disapproval. 'What better person to have been appointed to the chapel here, now that I am joined in marriage to a princess of Osraige?'

'Only the River Bhearú separates Osraige from Laigin,' Eadulf repeated as if speaking to himself. 'We must take into account that Osraige has been a centre of turbulence on your eastern border and has been used several times to engender discord and rebellion here. We must not forget that you had to force Gelgéis's cousin, Tuaim Snámha, the petty king of Osraige, to pay tribute to Cashel. It was clear that some members of his family, with exceptions, were plotting with Laigin against this kingdom. They are not all like the lady Gelgéis.'

Colgú was quiet for a moment, but his features showed his displeasure.

'I hope you recall that the appointment of Father Socra was made out of respect to my wife,' he said dryly. 'Even so, before coming here to take up his role, Father Socra was examined by Abbot Cuán. His loyalties are to Gelgéis and to supporting the settlement made by Tuaim Snámha of Osraige.'

'One should also hope that his loyalties are to the New Faith,' Eadulf muttered.

'Well, whatever title he calls himself I am happy to accept Socra is of the Osraige and his loyalty is to Gelgéis,' Fidelma replied, assuaging her brother's defensive tone but wondering why Eadulf was continuing to be in such an uncharacteristically peevish and petulant mood.

'Possibly it is correct never to take things at face value,' Eadulf commented dryly. 'I, more than most, should remember the line from Phaedrus, when he observed that things and people are not always what they appear to be. I would have thought the experience of investigating murders and other high crimes would have caused this to be an essential lesson.'

Colgú's irritation increased. 'Whether the abbey that Father Socra comes from is in Osraige or across the river in Laigin seems irrelevant. Socra was given the role of priest here as a tribute to my marriage to Princess Gelgéis,' he repeated. 'He was recommended by Abbot Cuán, as Chief Bishop of this kingdom.'

Eadulf smiled feigned benevolence. 'I was making my point in a clumsy fashion due to not having fluent command of your language. I am, as is made clear to me, a foreigner. I was merely saying that if it transpires that the murder of Gelgéis's attendant was made in an attack that is a protest at your marriage, we must start considering who would be behind it. Such an attack would help sever any trust between Cashel and its border territories, leading to other dissensions. It is simple wisdom to remember that Sléibhte is so close to the Laigin border that it straddles it.'

Fidelma cleared her throat noisily as she watched the emotions on her brother's face. She had never seen Eadulf in such a mood before.

'Whether Socra comes from Osraige or even Laigin, his obligation is to fulfil his duties to his religion, not to the geographic area he comes from,' she said.

Eadulf's jaw thrust out defiantly. Although he knew he should let the subject drop, he still felt the burning resentment that had prompted his comments in the first place.

'You, especially, are aware of the many attempts to overthrow your brother. Only a few months ago we had the Council of the seven princes of the kingdom here in Cashel, and uncovered a conspiracy that was astounding. I do not think I should apologise by maintaining that we should not be diligent in uncovering possible enemies plotting and planning your brother's downfall.'

Colgú exhaled a deep breath. 'Your point is taken, Eadulf.' His voice still bore a tone of testiness. 'Of course, I have not dismissed the possibility, nor will it be dismissed until the evidence is clear. But we must not let geography dominate our suspicions.'

'True,' Eadulf agreed softly. 'But sometimes it helps.'

Colgú ignored him and it was Fidelma who decided to change the topic.

'We have seen how it is almost impossible to enter your sanctuary apartment. Unless this hatch within the bathroom shows a weakness, it seems the only way in is if the intruder was an acrobat.'

Her brother tried to soften his scowl. 'I told you, I designed the plans with my master builder. If there was a secret way in, which is the only alternative, do you think it would have been hidden from me by him?'

'You did not build that apartment with your own hands.' Eadulf was still quarrelsome. 'As you acknowledge, you had a master builder and all his workmen.'

'All were sworn to secrecy.'

'Oaths are often violated and secrets revealed,' Eadulf muttered.

'Then we should send for Brother Dáire.'

Fidelma and Eadulf stared at Colgú in bewilderment for a moment.

'Brother Dáire?' Fidelma echoed in surprise.

'Our young librarian,' Colgú replied heavily.

'I know very well who Brother Dáire is,' Fidelma replied in a tone of heavy sarcasm. 'Why is he needed?'

'Because he can bring us the plans for the buildings. My master builder lodged them with him in the library when the building was finished.'

chapter five

For a moment Fidelma looked at her brother speechlessly.

'I do not believe it,' she finally said, as softly as if saying a prayer.

Colgú was uncertain at this dramatic reaction.

'What do you mean?' he asked defensively.

'You have designed and built a sanctuary; a special and secure place. The purpose, you say, is security, which was necessary because of the experiences that you have suffered, mostly from our distant relatives who have cast envious eyes at the kingship. You had plans for a special chamber drawn up by your master builder, by which plans you felt you could rest safely. Your concern was the fact of your marriage to a princess of Osraige – for her safety as well as your own – because twice Osraige and Laigin have tried to manipulate her in order to inflict harm on you. And yet, after all that . . . I discover that I have a fool for a brother.'

Colgú coloured hotly. 'And I am a king who has a sister who often oversteps the boundaries of expected etiquette. Explain to me what you find so foolish.'

'You make efforts to create a special sanctuary. It is supposed to be impregnable. Now you tell me that plans of it have been lodged in the library of this fortress. A library that is open to all who desire to use its facilities. Where is your sense of security?'

'The security is in the way it was built, not in the plans!' Colgú snapped. 'Even with plans, there is no way anyone can get into the sanctuary unless they are an adept, or one of the Children of Danu, who could change into a bird and take flight. I do not believe in such creatures any more than you do, Fidelma.'

Fidelma smiled cynically at his outburst.

'It seems that you have spent time in the library reading ancient stories as well as offering your security plans to the librarian. I tell you what I believe in, brother,' she said. 'I believe in human dexterity and endeavour. I believe in the ingenuity of the determined. You would have done well to come across the words of the Roman Stoic Seneca, who put them in the mouth of Hannibal the Carthaginian.'

Colgú frowned angrily. 'I do not have time to indulge in quizzes about Latin literature.'

'*Aut inveniam viam aut faciam.* It means: I will either find a way or make one.'

Colgú flushed angrily, knowing that his sister could always come back with a good riposte.

'The librarian, Brother Dáire, would have kept the plans securely,' he replied stubbornly.

'The plans are in the library for anyone to see,' Fidelma pointed out again. 'What the human mind can conceive, the human mind can deconstruct.'

Colgú resorted to scorn. 'A few months ago you proposed Brother Dáire to the council when Brother Conchobhar was killed. Now you suggest he will allow anyone to see what is secret.'

'I would still propose him. I do not blame *his* integrity, but the person who put plans in the library where anyone can access them.'

'Well, I am sure that Brother Dáire would not allow anyone to examine them without a good reason and my permission,' her brother retorted hotly.

Eadulf almost felt like holding up his hands to call for peace. When brother and sister argued, there was no quarter.

'The point is not worth arguing now,' he declared. 'If the plans are in the library, they have been there for some time. The damage, if there has been damage, will already have been done. Certainly, they were available before last night. We cannot make them disappear retrospectively. Let us see them and perhaps find out if there are any weaknesses in them that could have been used. From what I have observed of the building, I would agree that only an acrobat could scale the walls to reach the windows or skylights, or that place in the *fothrucadh* where the wood and water is hauled up. Either that, or there is some secret place where the assassin could have hidden and so avoid entering the single stairway when it was guarded.'

'The sanctuary should be totally secure,' Colgú muttered, as if seeking some approval for his building.

'It's past dawn now,' Fidelma said decisively, 'so send word to get Brother Dáire to bring the plans to the south-west corner where the pulley and rope are placed. We can observe that position at the same time.'

When they sent the request for Brother Dáire to join them, it was Aidan who reminded them of the time. The second *cadar* of the day had already started and Enda had apparently neglected to give the order for the change of the guards. The summer sun was high and bright above the eastern mountains and spreading its warmth over the fortress as it travelled across the sky. Colgú immediately ordered the sentinels of the second *cadar* to take the places of the first watch, who were stood down. Aidan went off to find Brother Dáire while Fidelma, Eadulf and Colgú walked around the wall of the residence to the side with the artificial stone construction on which the sanctuary was built.

It took no time to realise that the stone foundation could not be climbed, nor could the rope and pulley be used unless someone in the building above had unlocked the hatch, unloosed the rope and helped to raise the nearby baskets for wood or the barrel containers of water. Fidelma's perplexity was obvious. Even if the intruder was able to fly, they would still have to have someone open the locked door from the inside.

It seemed that Brother Dáire had already been working in his library. He later confessed that he found the early mornings a time of peace and quiet for working. He surprised them as they were returning to the main residence and, once inside Colgú's private reception chamber, he placed a locked metal box on the small table. The plans for the sanctuary had been locked inside at the request of Rodaige, the master builder. Brother Dáire was not one to engage in long preambles and so, after he greeted them, he took a key, unlocked the box, and spread the plans on the table.

'So what are you looking for?' he demanded.

'Before we go into the details of the King's sanctuary,' Fidelma began, 'can you confirm that these plans were placed by Rodaige, the master builder, in your safekeeping in this box in the library? Do any other copies exist?'

'I am assured by the King and Rodaige that no other copies exist,' replied the young librarian.

'I observed that you had a key to the box. Who else has a key?'

The librarian was surprised. 'The only key now rests with me in the library.'

'I presume the King and his master builder had free access? Were they the only ones to have access?'

'Even when the master builder was here, no one other than he and the King kept the plans. Each day, the master builder locked the plans back in the box and handed the key to me. Since the work was finished, and the building was completed, no one has disturbed them.'

'You say *when* the master builder was here? He is no longer here?'

'Rodaige, the master builder, is now working at the abbey of Cluain Eidhneach.'

'No one would have been able to see the plans without you knowing about it?'

Brother Dáire's face was grave. 'You may rest assured that I maintain the strictest security and, even if it was known that the plans are kept locked in this box, there is still no way anyone could access it without a key, nor would they be able to do so without my noticing the box had been moved for inspection. Not that the plans would lead you to any secret ways in the apartment.'

'Why would they not?' Eadulf queried immediately.

'The only way into the sanctuary is the one you see.'

'Very well,' Fidelma sighed, as she began to look over the plans to check. 'The purpose of this is just to make doubly sure that this apartment was designed to be isolated from the rest of the royal apartments and there is no other way into them.'

'You could see that with your own eyes,' Colgú snapped. 'What you see is on the plans.'

'It is what one cannot see that interests me,' returned Fidelma. 'I am looking for any secret connections. I am looking for hiding places that might have been overlooked. The base on which the rooms are set is an artificial mount of stone. Might there be a way of climbing up unseen and entering through the wooden floors?'

Brother Dáire shrugged. 'What you see is what there is marked on the plans. Rodaige was particular that the stone mount was a solid construction.'

'Sometimes things are not marked. The main building, which we have used since the ancient times of Nad Fróich, has been rebuilt several times and who knows what secrets it holds?'

'The old royal apartments were well built and the walls solid,' Colgú replied. 'There is no way through those walls and certainly no way through the artificial base of stones to the sanctuary. I watched the construction each day.'

'The old residence rises a few metres above the roof of the sanctuary. Why is that? Why is your new building so small and placed in such a confined area, which is entirely overlooked by the old building?'

'It was Abbot Cuán who persuaded me to consider the idea. He had picked it up from stories that pilgrims brought back to his abbey from Rome. My master builder, Rodaige, adapted those ideas with others that he had seen elsewhere in these kingdoms. It is known that the emperors and the bishops of Rome, who are often subject to attack – especially from the invading idolaters from Africa – started the custom of building places of refuge or retreat where they might seek sanctuary.'

'So you picked up the idea from Rodaige's stories? Who actually designed it?'

Colgú smiled. 'I have little idea of the design.'

'Are you saying the design was that of your master builder, Rodaige?'

'He is responsible.'

Fidelma sniffed in disapproval. 'It says much of our world if we have to build special sanctuaries, fortifications within fortifications, to be able to feel that we are safe.'

'Well, there is much talk of the wars that the Greeks are fighting against the Sarkini, as Hippolytus called them,' Colgú protested, surprising them. 'I heard stories from Rodaige, who heard it from returning missionaries.'

'Sarkini? I have not heard of them,' Fidelma frowned.

'I was told by Rodaige that it means those who dwell in the eastern lands.'

Eadulf shifted his weight. 'I have heard about them also, Fidelma. When I was in Rome, I heard that Constantinople was besieged by these Sarkini some years before, but, thankfully, the Greeks were victorious. I have heard pilgrims say that these Sarkini are now returning and have recently conquered an important

Greek island called the Island of Roses. Because of this, the concept of building sanctuaries has become popular in order to maintain the security of the rulers.'

'And this is why it was designed,' Colgú agreed. 'The idea was to have the bedroom for myself and Gelgéis, a room for an attendant and a room where we could wash privately. When it was designed, it was found it needed a square-shaped construction so a spare room was added. The design was made on a single floor and with only one entrance by a single flight of stairs, which could be guarded.'

'But you had to raise the floor to one above this and on an artificially constructed stone mound. Therefore the elevation provided a weakness.' It was Eadulf who pointed this out. 'I am thinking of this *fothrucadh* – the wash room where you have a fireplace for heating the bathwater. The wooden floor, even on a stone base, will eventually be untenable. It will catch light.'

'Not so,' replied Colgú. 'The base of this new floor has been simply filled with blocks and stones. If you remember, that flooring for the fireplace and surrounding is of stone. The wooden floors are in the bedchambers. So the only way in and out is the stairway entrance from the floor.'

'No secret tunnels were made?' Eadulf was disappointed. 'I suppose it is a clever plan.'

'It is a bizarre idea, but one the master builder developed directly from stories told by returning missionaries. It seems that ten years ago raiders from a city called Alexandria were attacking places around the Sicilian coast and the islands. Bishop Peregrinus, of an island called Lipari, was so concerned about such attacks that he had a special shelter built for him – a sanctuary just like the *tech-termonn*.'

Fidelma looked over the plans again, then shrugged. 'This sanctuary is the equivalent of this shelter of Peregrinus? And there really are no secret tunnels or hiding places?'

'The building is observed most of the time, so no one could try to excavate under it, which is impossible anyway. The sentinels patrol the outer wall of the fortress or are to be found in the watch-towers,' Colgú confirmed.

'And, as we saw, the floors of the chambers are of strong oak and yew,' sighed Eadulf. 'The walls and pillars are of the same woods. In other words, it is like a rectangular wooden castle.'

'We are left with the conclusion that only an acrobat could attempt to enter through the *forlés*. An acrobat . . . or an athlete.' Fidelma paused. 'It seems we have abandoned any idea of a secret hiding place.'

'But Enda has said there was no easy access from the roof of the taller building to the roof of the new apartment,' Colgú rejoined.

'Show me the plans again,' Fidelma sighed.

Brother Dáire sat down at the table and smoothed them out once more. Fidelma peered over his shoulder.

'You are right,' she finally said. 'Unless one is able to leap from roof to roof, it is impossible to enter that way.'

'It is impossible to enter at all,' her brother confirmed.

'But there is always some way of dealing with the impossible,' Fidelma said softly.

Colgú was cynical. 'There is no way in, unless this unknown killer simply walked up the stairway, passing Luan, who was guarding it.'

'Unless, of course, the killer was known and had a right to be in the apartment,' Fidelma remarked as the thought came to her.

The others stared at her, wondering if she was joking.

Brother Dáire broke the silence by beginning to roll up the plans to return to the box.

Colgú rose with him. 'I shall join Gelgéis. We need to catch up on our interrupted rest.'

After he and Brother Dáire left, Fidelma uttered a long, trou-bled sigh. 'I suppose there is little else to do for the moment. But do not think that we shall be catching up with our sleep any time soon. I suppose we should speak with Father Socra about the obsequies.'

There was a tap on the door and Eadulf went to open it. He was met by the excited figure of Luan.

'Lady!' he gasped, looking over Eadulf's shoulder to Fidelma. 'We have found something that you must see.'

In spite of his excitement, his features were clearly troubled. Fidelma felt a decided chill of expectation.

'What is it?' she asked quietly. 'Did you find something in the search I asked you to undertake?'

Luan made no direct reply to the question except: 'You and "friend" Eadulf had best come and see for yourselves. I think we have found that which you sought, but you will not like the conclusions.'

'Have you found the murder weapon?' Fidelma asked immediately.

'We have, but—' began Luan.

'We will come,' Fidelma interrupted him.

Luan led the way up the stairway to the sanctuary. To their surprise, he took them straight to the chamber opposite the master bedchamber of Colgú and Gelgéis. It was Dar Luga's room.

Dego was waiting for them at the entrance. He stood back and motioned them inside. Luan followed them. It was a small, dark room, because, on this side of the sanctuary, only the *forlés,* high in the sloping roof, provided light. Fidelma was reminded that the rooms on this side were built against what had been the main wall of the residence. There were neither windows nor, indeed, any access between the two buildings. Although it was now well after dawn, Luan and Dego had lit lamps to explore the shadowy corners of the room. Luan crossed to one corner where there was a wooden trunk. He bent to this and pulled up the lid, pointing down with a slightly dramatic air.

On top of the contents of the trunk, mainly a pile of folded woollen and linen garments, were some bloodstained pieces of cloth wrapped around some objects. Luan lifted back the cloth. The bigger object was a short-bladed, brass-handled dagger.

Fidelma stared silently down for some time. It was Eadulf who broke the silence.

'It does seem Luan has found what we were looking for.'

Fidelma bent forward and, using her fingertips, extracted the bloody cloth that wrapped the dagger, laying it on a nearby small table. She was also aware of the pieces of shattered glass from the accident that Dar Luga had had earlier, therefore she was careful as she unwrapped the cloth. She placed the dagger to one side. There was another bloody metal object with it. It was revealed as an iron key ring with two keys attached. They were curiously cut and Fidelma recognised the types and patterns that the fortress smithy often made. Each was a simple straight-shafted key, although the end was decorated. The blood was not entirely dry on either object. Fidelma had no doubt that the keys were those to the bathroom door.

She put down the objects on the bloodstained cloth and stared at them for a while. Then she turned to Eadulf, while quickly glancing around the chamber.

'Where is Dar Luga now? She was going to the kitchen as she did not feel well. Has she returned?'

Luan looked ill at ease as he responded. Like most who worked in Colgú's household, he was fond of the matronly housekeeper and looked on her as a maternal figure, often going to her with problems that he felt she could help with.

'I think the *banmhaor* is still in the kitchens, lady. I know she was not feeling well and was resting. Shall I go and fetch her?'

'Not yet,' Fidelma replied shortly. She turned to Eadulf, whose face was still registering shock. 'What do you make of it?' she asked. 'Does the weapon tell you anything?'

'Only that it is a good choice of weapon to carry out this sort of butchery,' he said bitterly. 'It is small enough, and sharp.'

'But they tell you nothing else?' she pressed.

'Well, it is certainly a warrior's dagger,' Eadulf observed, peering closer at the object. 'Such daggers are not even regarded as battle weapons. They are mainly ceremonial ornaments, or used at feasting to cut an individual's portion of the meat and . . .' He halted and peered more closely and then spoke with reluctance. 'But it is consistent with the wound on the girl's corpse.'

'You were also about to say that women of status carry them in small sheaths at their waists?' Fidelma added.

'I was.'

Fidelma placed the dagger and keys to one side while she began to unroll the bloodstained cloth that had been wrapped around them. It was made of coarse linen. She held it up, turning it this way and that to the light.

'It is rather like a skirt,' Eadulf said. 'Isn't it rather short? Is it some sort of short covering that warriors sometimes wear when they are practising single combat?'

Fidelma could not restrain her smile at the idea, but it was a sad smile.

'I somehow doubt that any of our warriors would agree to be seen in such a kirtle.'

Luan affected a cough. 'Begging your indulgence, lady, I recognise it as a *fútheróc.*'

Fidelma's reply was almost sad. 'You recognise it correctly, Luan. It is an apron . . . an apron as worn by a cook or someone preparing dishes.'

The silence was palpable. Dar Luga had never given up her original role of overseeing the cooking for the royal household, even though she had been elevated first to the position of housekeeper, and then to *banmhaor*, stewardess, of the royal house. A cook's apron was therefore evidence that pointed to her as much as the knife and keys it was wrapped around.

'Neither of you have spoken with her about your search here?' Fidelma asked Luan and Dego.

Luan shook his head on behalf of both. 'Not since you spoke with her and she went to the kitchens. Didn't she say that she was going there to prepare something for an ague she had developed? When we made the discovery, I felt it better that you should be the first to be informed, lady. She must have known we would be making a thorough search. Therefore, she would surely not have left such things lying about if they implicated her in this crime.'

Fidelma recognised the logic in his comment. She knew from past occasions that Dar Luga was quite fastidious when she was preparing the various dishes for Colgú's special feastings. It was illogical for her to remove herself to the kitchens if she knew of the presence of these exposing items, and that a search would take place.

'Luan has a good point,' Eadulf said.

'Lady, you know Dar Luga well. She has served many years in the royal household. Even though we found this bloodstained apron, dagger and keys in her room, I would maintain that they must have been hidden without her knowledge.'

'At the moment, that is an assumption,' Fidelma admonished. She had picked up the dagger by the blade, using the bloodstained apron, and was examining the small but ornate silver decoration with some red enamel on the handle. 'The pattern doesn't spring immediately to memory although I feel that I have seen such a symbol before,' she said softly.

Eadulf peered over her shoulder. 'It's small, but if you look closely it looks like lightning flashes, a leaf shape, and there is the small head and body of a bear to one side. I've seen it before. I can't be sure but I think it was at the Council at Streoneshalh. It was borne by one of the delegates . . . I think. But it is certainly not a symbol used by the Angles.'

'It looks like a symbol of war.'

Fidelma looked down at the dagger for a moment and then placed the object back on the cloth.

'There is much blood on these items. Yet when the killer fled, there was neither blood on the door handle of the bathroom nor on anything else. When you searched, did you find this room was clean, with no signs of blood?'

'A few spots, but that is basically correct, lady,' Luan admitted. 'If the killer was wearing the apron, then maybe it prevented the wide dispersion of blood?'

'If we follow one theory of the event,' Eadulf said, 'the killer wiped the door handle of the bathroom as they left. Then they took off the bloodstained apron, wrapped the dagger and keys in it, and all in the space of moments. The killer brought the bundle here to Dar Luga's room to hide.'

'Have you checked that the keys are of the *fothrucadh* where Cera's body was?' Fidelma asked.

'I thought that it was obvious,' Luan replied nervously.

Fidelma picked up the keys and handed them to Luan.

'Do so now,' she instructed. 'In law nothing is obvious until proven.'

Luan was looking slightly offended as he took the keys and went off to perform the test.

Fidelma was about to move to the far side of the bed with the intention of using the lighted lamp that was on the side table, when Dego told her to be cautious.

'There is some broken glass around there, lady. Have a care of where you tread.'

'I remember. Dar Luga broke it while I was questioning her,' she said, her lamp causing pinpricks of light to dance on the broken fragments.

Fidelma held the dagger under the light. In her mind came images of the legendary female warriors and of the many female battle-goddesses. She wished it all made sense to her. At least they could agree that the image on the cast brass handle was a symbol used by female warriors.

Luan returned with the obvious answer.

'As I assumed, lady,' he said in dry rebuke, 'the keys were from the *fothrucadh* where the body was. I think they were Dar Luga's own set of keys, which she was allowed to have as stewardess.'

Eadulf wore an uneasy expression. 'I am afraid the evidence does make sense. I believe you thought so when you reflected that the killer could have been someone who entered the apartment without being questioned or raising alarm.'

'Dar Luga is a suspect,' Fidelma replied stonily. 'We must be diplomatic in our questioning, but we cannot dismiss her as a suspect just because we have known her for so long.'

'But there is no reason why she would attempt to kill your brother and his wife,' Eadulf said. 'What if Cera was the intended victim? She might have reason there.'

Luan was shaking his head. 'I refuse to believe Dar Luga is capable of murder. What reason would she have to kill the girl? Dar Luga was a friend to everyone.'

Fidelma shook her head in sad contradiction. 'That statement has several weaknesses. Reasons for murder are all unknown until they are discovered. A murderer can have friends, families, before they commit an act that makes them into a killer. That does not make them less a friend or part of a family. It does not turn them into an alien. Even in the right circumstances, a matronly grandmother can conceal emotions that can explode into a murderous intent.'

Luan looked at her with scepticism. 'But Dar Luga . . .? I believe that these items were hidden in her room without her knowledge. I do not believe Dar Luga would turn into a murderess.'

'Belief is not fact. Anyway, it is not your task to make a judgement.'

Luan handed the items to Fidelma with a sullen attitude. 'So the keys fit the lock, lady. They must be the ones the killer used to enter and relock the door when they escaped after the killing. Now what?'

'Find me a bag to carry these items in,' Fidelma instructed, ignoring his surly manner.

When a bag had been found and the bloodstained items put into it, Fidelma stood for a moment or two looking round the room, giving it a final examination.

'Let us assume that the account Dar Luga gave me and Eadulf was correct,' she said, almost speaking to herself. 'Somehow Cera enters the bathroom of my brother and his wife. She is attacked by the killer. A noise, perhaps a dying scream, awakens my brother, who rushes into the bathroom room to find Cera slain, the killer has fled into the corridor and even locked the door behind them. The killer has an apron, which perhaps is used to absorb the blood splatters. They also have the dagger and the keys.

'By this time Colgú is shouting an alarm. Luan is standing guard on the stairway, the only entrance and exit to these bed-chambers. He comes running up the stairs in answer. Colgú stands at his bedchamber door, the only exit he has on to the corridor as the bathroom door is locked. When Luan arrives at the top of the stairs he sees Colgú at his door and Dar Luga has by now emerged from her room opposite. She seems tired. Do you follow thus far?'

'Of course.' Eadulf frowned in annoyance.

'So we have questions.' Fidelma smiled thinly. She turned to Luan. 'How long was it from when Colgú raised the alarm, to when you got up the stairs to a level to see the passage outside the murder room and for Dar Luga to come out of her room? She was in her night attire – was there blood upon it?'

'It was a short time, lady. I did not see any blood on Dar Luga's clothing, but it all happened so quickly that I could not swear to that on oath.'

'The killer, in those moments, has fled from the bathroom and locked the door behind them, at which point Colgú has raised the alarm. But where is the killer? They must have run straight to Dar Luga's bedchamber to take off the apron and then hidden it with the keys and then . . .'

'Vanished,' Luan responded.

'We now know they had to go into Dar Luga's room to place the bloodied items. So, if they vanished . . .?' Fidelma left the question in the air.

'They escaped,' Luan amended.

'Then escaped how? As we know, there are no outside windows, only the *forlés* high above. It would take more than an acrobat to achieve that as an exit after hiding the items and before Dar Luga was roused from her sleep in answer to Colgú's call.'

'Or did the killer hide and wait until everyone had left, then simply come down the stairway and leave as well?' Luan suggested.

'But the stairway has been constantly under surveillance since the alarm. And someone has always been inside. So how could anyone have left without being seen or heard?'

'So we are back to saying that they could only have come into Dar Luga's room, or else Dar Luga is the culprit.'

'She told us that she was awoken when Colgú raised the alarm,' Fidelma reflected. 'It was dark and she awoke with the onset of the ague. Her first reaction was to reach out and take some water. When I was questioning her, she took some more water, and that's when she broke this glass.'

Luan smiled grimly, glancing to the shattered fragments. 'It fits that she was asleep and so it was possible and dark enough for the killer to slip into her room and hide the things before Colgú raised the alarm.'

'But the same query follows,' Fidelma pointed out. 'The killer came to this room and then what? Dar Luga found Colgú at the door, raising the alarm. She answered him and even returned into her room to get a robe. If we accept this, how had the killer time to hide the items and disappear?'

Something made Fidelma and Eadulf look up at the skylight together. The room had been searched by Luan and Enda before Dar Luga was left to keep watch over the corpse while Fidelma was summoned. So where was the bloodstained killer at that time, unless . . .? When all the possible answers had been found wanting, only the improbable was left. They were quiet as they looked at each other with reluctant expressions. There seemed only one logical conclusion, which no one wanted to admit.

CHAPTER SIX

'It is difficult to accept the logical conclusion,' Fidelma began slowly. 'Yet what is the alternative? The logic seems without question. Dar Luga killed the girl and, hearing that she had disturbed Colgú, she then exited the bathroom, remembering to lock the door behind her, which gave her time to run back to her own room, taking the apron, the dagger and keys, put them in a careful bundle and place them in her trunk. She drew attention to the ague as an effective means of hiding her lack of breath in hurrying to hide the items and her emotional state.'

'The killer still could have hidden here before Dar Luga was awakened,' Luan protested, but there was little conviction in his voice.

'Still wearing the bloody apron and holding the weapon and keys?' Fidelma smiled with scepticism. 'There were only moments between the killer fleeing the bathroom and Colgú raising the alarm.'

'He could have hidden until Dar Luga left the room to join Colgú, emerged and then hid the items in that chest and then . . .'

'And then . . . suddenly vanished? Perhaps floating up like some mystical bird to the skylight? Or, perhaps, being of athletic propensity, the killer was able to perform Cúchulainn's famous salmon leap and reach it?'

Luan flushed at Fidelma's irony. His lips compressed in a hard line. 'There must be a way,' he said stubbornly.

'When faced with impossible explanations one should admit defeat and accept the least unlikely,' Fidelma advised with a weary grimace.

'Perhaps we are not furnished with a possible explanation at the moment,' Luan replied somewhat bitterly.

'We will question Dar Luga first,' Fidelma said.

'Should we not look for alternatives?' Luan's question was more of a demand.

'What alternatives? I certainly have no alternatives. Do not think that I am not appreciative of any suggestions and ideas. But I am afraid the only path I can see is that we put the facts before Dar Luga and ask her version.'

'We will treat Dar Luga gently,' Eadulf added. 'And with the respect that she deserves.'

'In fact, Luan, go and find Dar Luga. Tell her to join Eadulf and me in our own apartment. That will put her at ease. We will be there shortly. Do not tell her anything of what we have discovered here.'

Luan hesitated a moment before turning and leaving them. He was clearly unhappy with the task.

Eadulf waited until he had vanished before saying: 'I am afraid, like Luan, I think there must be another explanation. I just don't believe Dar Luga is capable of murder.'

'We must follow where logic dictates,' Fidelma replied.

'How long has Dar Luga served your house?' Eadulf pressed. 'As I recall, she is the sister to Lassar, the wife of Ferloga, who keeps the tavern at Ráth na Drinne. Both sisters were well respected, and aren't they both known to your friend Della?'

'Even murderers have relatives and friends. Judge only by the facts.'

With Dego leading the way, they returned down the stairway to the main entrance hall.

'My brother does not seem to have luck with his stewards,' Fidelma observed dryly, turning to Eadulf as they reached the lower floor. 'There was Madagan, who was then replaced by Beccan. Beccan was murdered to keep him silent when he was involved in a conspiracy. Colgú never sought to replace his office, allowing Dar Luga to control the affairs of the household. As you will recall, she was doing the work of the steward of the household, albeit officially as just cook and housekeeper.'

'I remember,' Eadulf confirmed. 'At the Council of seven princes, when we were threatened by insurrection and by the pestilence, no one objected to her being confirmed in the role of stewardess by your brother. She has been loyal to your family. That's why I believe she could not have done this killing.'

'Belief is one thing; judgement of the facts is another. To judge something, you must have patience until you have all the information to do so,' Fidelma replied in a stony manner. In her own mind, she was inclined to agree with Eadulf, but she was also aware that, as a *dálaigh*, she must not allow personal feelings to interfere, especially in a case of murder.

A young warrior named Cano had replaced Dego on guard at the main doors. That reminded Fidelma that the day had progressed into the second *cadar*. It had been a long night. She realised that Dego was looking exhausted and was about to suggest he go for his rest when she remembered Enda.

'We were to see Enda when he was rested. Have you seen him?'

'That I have not, lady. Certainly he was behaving very curiously this morning. I overheard some of what Luan was saying to you.'

'Well, forget it. Imagine waking up and finding your loved one murdered. Would that not make you behave in a manner that seemed unnatural to those who knew you?'

'How swiftly attitudes change,' Dego admitted with a sigh. 'Last night there seemed an air of merriment, as if we were still celebrating the wedding of the King. Everyone was overjoyed at this marriage of the King. Now this event casts a dark shadow over everything.'

'As you say, now things have changed. So, among our warriors here in Cashel, do you know of anyone who is a malcontent about the King's marriage?'

Eadulf always admired how Fidelma could manipulate a conversation to gain information and then drop in an unexpected question that provoked a thought-revealing response. With Dego, however, he was disappointed.

'You know us too well, lady,' the one-armed warrior replied. 'We of the Nasc Niadh take an oath as warriors to give our lives in defence of the legitimate King and his family.'

'Are the Nasc Niadh affronted by the fact that the Princess Gelgéis brought her own female bodyguards to her marriage?'

Dego chuckled. 'You refer to the Daughters of the Storm? A group of young girls ready to put on a ceremonial show of martial arts at the forthcoming fair in the township? They are not real warriors.'

'But they have reputations as real warriors.'

'Reputations? That was in the ancient stories. That was in the old times when, saving your presence, lady, women could command entire armies. Indeed, when we gave up the old goddesses of war, who were always women. But after what Luan has said, may I ask if Enda is still in command of the household troop?'

'Enda remains in command until otherwise announced.' Fidelma was annoyed. It seemed everyone was listening to Luan's theory. 'If you see Enda, remind him that I have need to question him.'

'If he is not to be found? Who commands, lady?'

'There is no reason to think Enda will not be found,' she said shortly.

Dego saluted with his one good arm.

'Where will you be, lady?' he called after Fidelma as she and Eadulf left him to begin to cross the courtyard.

'We are returning to our own apartments to await Luan and Dar Luga. Then we will wash and rest.' She hesitated a moment. 'Doubtless if any changes are to be made, my brother will give the orders.'

It was now almost mid-morning, with the summer sun spreading its light over the limestone buildings of the fortress. In crossing the courtyard to their own apartments, they passed old Brother Conchobhar's apothecary opposite to the chapel door. They used this route so often that it was automatic, although Fidelma could not help the feeling of sadness as she viewed the deserted, empty building where her old mentor and tutor, Conchobhar, had been cruelly slain.

He had been a close mentor since the death of her father, Failbe Flann. What was more, and the reason why he had been slain, was that he had been Keeper of the Sacred Sword of Nuada, Gatekeeper to the House of Death, the symbolic keeper of the knowledge of her family to the time beyond time. In him reposed knowledge of the generations of the Eóganacht who claimed their descent from Eibhear Fionn, son of Golamh, who brought the Children of the Gael to the island. The sword *Frecraid*, 'The Answerer', was the symbol of the power of the Eóganacht dynasty to rule Muman. It now hung in the Great Feasting Hall of the palace. With an ironical twist of fate, Fidelma now found herself Keeper of the Sword, with a suspicion that she could not even share with her brother.

She was suddenly aware of Eadulf nudging her.

'The door of the apothecary is open,' he pointed out.

She looked across to see the door was moving slightly in the morning breeze.

'We'd better secure it,' she said, going in the direction of the building. 'The place should be empty.'

As she pushed open the door with the intention of making a check, she paused on the threshold, Eadulf close behind her. The nostalgic pungent smells that she expected to catch her breath were no longer heavy on the air. Usually the claustrophobic and almost choking odours of herbs and musty spices forced her and Eadulf to stand at the threshold and adjust their senses. This first room was where the old apothecary used to mix his potions, and at the back was where many a corpse had been examined and prepared for burial in the adjacent chapel.

Fidelma was one of the few who knew that a trap door at the back led to a souterrain, an underground chamber, which in turn led into an ancient and surprisingly large cavern in which the ancient Sword of Nuada had been stored.

Fidelma was about to turn and swing the door shut to secure it when Eadulf, peering over her shoulder, laid a hand on her arm.

'That's odd,' he said softly, and pointed.

In the morning sunlight, little as it was that entered the shadowy apothecary, she followed his gaze to the bench where Brother Conchobhar used to mix his herbs. A few jars and a pestle and mortar stood there, and nearby the remains of some fresh plant. Someone had obviously been mixing some concoction.

'I didn't think anyone was allowed in here after Brother Conchobhar died,' Fidelma commented.

Eadulf moved forward and looked down at the remains of the plant. The leaves that were left were large and deep green. There were some roots that were black, conical and tapering. There were traces of violet-blue flowers. But a good portion had been mixed in the mortar, especially the roots and leaves.

'What is it?' Fidelma asked, peering over his shoulder.

'I am not sure what you would call it in your language,' Eadulf admitted. 'It is a highly poisonous plant. We call it wolfsbane because, when I was a child, the farming folk in my village would poison wolves with scraps of meat soaked with it. Aconitum . . . that's what the educated religieux called wolfsbane.'

'You mean *ciarsú*?' Fidelma provided the name in her language.

'Whatever it is called here, it is very poisonous,' Eadulf replied. 'It looks as though someone had made a recent attempt to distil it.'

'I've seen this flower in summer months in the mountain fields. Why should anyone be mixing this plant and its roots?'

'When I was studying, we were told that it should not be used, but some apothecaries did so. They claimed it was good for all feverish conditions and palpitations of the heart. However, I think more deaths followed its use than cures.'

'Well, we had better shut and secure the door, and ask who is responsible later. Whoever was making this should not have left the remains just lying there.'

They checked around before they exited, then closed the door and secured it. Eadulf was standing outside while Fidelma made sure the lock was fast, and he happened to glance at the door of the chapel, which was opposite.

'Here is a reminder that we were supposed to alert the new chaplain to arrange to take the body of the poor girl for preparation and the traditional watching,' he whispered, indicating with his head.

Fidelma saw that a youthful figure in religious robes was emerging from the side door to the chapel. The figure was accompanied by a female figure, who seemed to tower over him. She was dressed in black, but not religious robes. Both Fidelma and Eadulf recognised Father Socra, the new chaplain, for they had both met him briefly on his arrival. He was young but already had some silver flecking his curly, sand-coloured hair, which he wore in long fashion, and so unkempt that it fluttered as the wind took it.

In fact, there was no colour to his dirty undyed robes other than the sparkle reflected from a silver chain from which hung the glinting silver emblem of the Chi-Rho, the 'XP' being the first Greek letters of 'Christ'. It was one of the several emblems by which Christians had recognised each other in the early days. Fidelma had to admit she had not taken a liking to the young priest. There was something brooding in his brown eyes, an early ageing that did not go with his youthful fair skin, and those eyes seemed too close together. His brows arched over the bridge of his nose, which had a prominent hook form. His thin lips were dark red as if he had used some red berry juice to brighten them. Fidelma knew that it was wrong to have taken an immediate dislike. *Cucullus non facit monachum,* she had once been fond of declaring – do not judge people at face value. Yet now she was doing just that and trying to justify it as a simple human failing.

'*Bonum mane,*' Father Socra greeted them. They had already noticed that he preferred to use Latin at every opportunity. Perhaps this was because, from what she had seen, the religieux preferred to identify his interpretation of the New Faith as being from Rome. Most of the insular clerics tended to use Greek, as the language from which the early Christians had formed most of their philosophies and beliefs.

Eadulf responded on behalf of both of them, '*Salve tibi.*'

Almost at the same time, they turned their gaze towards Father Socra's tall companion. She was younger than Fidelma and her hair was raven black. Her skin would have been pale had not the sun added colour, indicating a life that had been spent mostly in open-air pursuits. Curiously, her eyes were bright and pale. She was clad in black and wore no jewellery, but she carried a traditional *lés,* a bag that proclaimed her to be a physician. This was confirmed a moment later when Father Socra introduced her.

'May I present Síonna from Mungairit, who will be taking up the position as physician in the fortress?'

The woman made no attempt to hold out her hand in greeting but gave a swift, almost jerky nod of her head to encompass them both.

'It is easy to recognise Fidelma of Cashel, and I presume her companion is Brother Eadulf,' she said, without any accompanying smile. She spoke in a curious throaty tenor as though she had a sore throat.

'It is pleasing to welcome you to Cashel, Síonna. I understand from my brother, Colgú, that he has been impatiently awaiting your arrival from Mungairit. Your face is familiar, though. Have we encountered one another before? Eadulf and I have both been visitors to your abbey.'

Síonna made a quick negative gesture with her hand.

'I think not,' she replied. 'But then Mungairit is, as you will know, one of the largest of the teaching abbeys.'

'I am told that you were the professor of medicine there?' Eadulf tried to assume a friendly tone in order to encourage a smile from the stony-faced woman.

'You were told correctly,' she replied without any corresponding emotion.

'We had not thought you had already arrived in the fortress,' Fidelma said, changing the subject slightly. 'We were not informed.'

Síonna frowned, hesitating a moment before she answered. 'I arrived late last night, too late for me to formally announce my presence.'

Father Socra now intervened, his face wreathed in an eager smile.

'I happened to be at the main gate when Síonna arrived. The gatekeeper did not seem to have any instruction. I took it upon myself to vouch for her in the absence of Dar Luga, the stewardess, and provided a bed for the night in the accommodation for the religieuse.'

'Dar Luga was unavailable?' Fidelma asked in surprise. 'I thought she kept a late night, last night. When did you arrive?'

Again it was Father Socra who answered. 'I think the bell for the first *cadar* of the day had already sounded. So Síonna probably arrived sometime just after midnight.'

'That is right,' the physician confirmed. 'I missed my way earlier and hoped to make the fortress by dusk. But dusk closed in rapidly. Having reached the township, I hesitated, thinking to find an inn, to stay. But as there were still lights in the fortress and at the main gates, I continued up here directly. It was lucky that Father Socra was able to pass me through the main gate.'

'And your assistants are with you?' Fidelma put the question.

'My assistants?'

'We heard that you were being accompanied by an apothecary and some other helpers.'

'I expect the arrival of an apothecary and his assistant. I have not been informed that they have arrived yet,' Síonna replied.

'So no one has been using old Brother Conchobhar's apothecary?' Eadulf asked softly.

'What apothecary is that?' queried the physician, clearly puzzled.

It was Father Socra who indicated the building opposite, asking, 'Why should they use it anyway? I have been told it was locked up after the death of Brother Conchobhar.'

'It's just that someone seems to have been using it.' Fidelma was dismissive. 'We simply supposed the new apothecary might take over the use of the building and its store.'

Father Socra seemed puzzled. Then it was as if he realised time was pressing.

'I was just taking Síonna to make introductions to the King's steward and also to the King. Our new physician is anxious to see what work needs to be done.'

'In that respect, you are a little late,' Fidelma said.

'Late?' Both their faces showed their bewilderment, but it was Father Socra who responded with the question, 'What is meant by that?'

'There has been a death in the royal chambers,' Fidelma said, addressing Father Socra. 'An attendant has been killed. We were coming to inform you. It is the King's request that you take the body under your care and prepare it for the obsequies.'

Síonna was the first to recover from the surprise of this news.

'An attendant in the royal chambers? I trust your brother and his lady are well? This death was not connected with them?'

'My brother and his lady are physically unharmed. The attendant, a young girl called Cera, in the service of Princess Gelgéis, has been killed.'

'Cera? Killed?' Father Socra seemed surprised. 'Wasn't she one of those Daughters of the Storm? They are female warriors that Princess Gelgéis insisted should accompany her,' he explained shortly to his companion.

'She was,' Fidelma confirmed. 'Then you knew her?'

'As chaplain I should know all,' Father Socra replied. 'Cera? No woman should lend herself to a man's role,' he added in disapproval. 'I supposed she was killed trying to be what a woman should not be.'

Fidelma frowned, attempting to follow what he meant.

'Are you asking whether she was killed while practising with her weapons?' Eadulf asked, before deciding to make a clarification. 'It was a secret killing.' He decided to use the legal term that meant 'murder'.

The man's eyes showed a momentary flash of understanding. His thin lips actually seemed to harden for a moment.

'Who did it?' asked Síonna.

'That is a matter not yet known,' Fidelma replied solemnly.

'Am I to examine the corpse? I presume you need a statement from a physician?'

'Eadulf has already examined her corpse,' Fidelma assured Síonna. 'There is now no impediment, Father Socra, to your removing the corpse to the chapel for preparation and burial following the traditional *aire* or watching period. I presume, for the obsequies you may need to consult the lady Gelgéis or the commander of the Daughters of the Storm.'

The sandy features of Father Socra turned quizzically to Eadulf. 'While I have heard of your reputation, Eadulf, I did not think that you held the appropriate medical qualification. If that is so, surely it will lead to complications under the law?'

Fidelma immediately offered the defence. 'In the various crimes and matters that we have been engaged in solving, Eadulf's opinion relating to medical knowledge has been accepted by all authorities. No one has challenged his official reports so you need have no concerns in carrying out what is deemed necessary as to the obsequies in this case. I can, with the authority of my brother, the King, give you, Father Socra, permission to take the corpse and prepare it for the watching ritual and burial, and perform all the due ceremonies needed.'

She turned to Síonna. 'Not realising that you were already in the fortress, my brother gave permission, as did I as a qualified *dálaigh* and legal adviser to my brother.'

Síonna showed no interest.

'I hear what you say, lady. I think I had better make my presence known to the steward of the King's household. Where might I find him?'

'The stewardess is Dar Luga. At the moment, I am conducting the investigation with her, and she will be busy for a while,' Fidelma replied disarmingly. 'I think any advice as to how things are done would be best coming from my brother. At the moment my brother's heir apparent, his Chief Brehon and even Abbot Cuán, the Bishop of Cashel, are all absent from the fortress. I remain as legal adviser to my brother so will see to it that the legalities will be followed until the Chief Brehon arrives – that arrival being shortly expected.'

'Then you are legally authorised to instruct me?' Father Socra asked almost in a complaining tone. 'The body has to be washed, dressed and prepared for burial. I have only been once to the cemetery since I came here so I may need local advice as to how the body is usually taken down the hill to the burial ground after the official period of watching.'

'Then all you need is to ask.'

The chaplain was still frowning in thought. 'You said that this attendant was Cera, one of the Daughters of the Storm? Then I must tell you that I had reason to remonstrate with this girl, Cera, when she attended service in the chapel last night. She is . . . was . . . barely of the age of choice. I told her that she was committing a grave sin before God by her pretence to attain a man's role.'

Fidelma and Eadulf exchanged glances of surprise.

'She was in the chapel last night?'

'She was a shame to Osraige.'

'Then you knew her prior to your arrival at the fortress?' Eadulf asked abruptly. 'So you knew her before and recognised her in the chapel?'

There seemed some hesitation in Socra's reply. 'I knew that she served Princess Gelgéis in Durlus Éile and was one of those who mock the name of warrior.'

'You have made clear that you disapprove of women taking up the martial arts. You knew Cera in Durlus Éile. Is that where you are from?'

Father Socra shrugged. 'I only saw her in Durlus Éile one time. I am from Sléibhte in Osraige. I was born in the countryside there and went into the abbey when I was young.'

'We know you came from that abbey. Wasn't it founded by Fiacc, a prince of Laigin, who declared himself abbot? It stands only a river's width from Laigin territory.'

Fidelma realised that Eadulf was making the same point that he had made in conversation her brother earlier.

'Did you know where Cera came from?' Fidelma asked hurriedly.

'I know neither of her nor of her family. I am sure such questions about the background of the girl are best addressed to Princess Gelgéis, as Cera was accepted as her attendant. Anything else about her would be addressed to Crédh, who calls herself commander of those monstrous women.'

'Of course,' Fidelma acknowledged. 'I think you have made yourself clear that you disapprove of the tradition of women in martial arts or in any military role. I presume that this is a religious scruple? I trust it does not include women in any professions and that you are happy, as you have demonstrated, to welcome Síonna as a physician? Indeed, that you do not have problems accepting me as *dálaigh*. That would present difficulties in my role as personal legal adviser to the King.'

For a moment or two it seemed Father Socra was having trouble swallowing. Finally he turned Fidelma. 'You say that you are legal adviser to your brother; that it is your brother's instructions that I arrange to pick up the body? I have a few people in the chapel that can help me. My main assistant is Sister Sárait.'

'Our practice here is that the body is usually interred at the appropriate time,' Fidelma pointed out. 'In this case, that would be at midnight tonight. But, as I have said, Princess Gelgéis may desire a longer period for the body to lie in the chapel for the period of the *aire* or watching. It is natural that you, as chaplain, will see to these ceremonies.'

Usually the body of a person of respect was watched for a minimum night and a day before being taken to the burial ground.

Father Socra inclined his head in acknowledgement, but he did not seem content.

'This is not good,' he sighed.

Fidelma stared at him, trying to fathom his attitude. 'No death is good, especially when the victim has been murdered.'

'I'd better get Sister Sárait to commence that tolling of the *clog-estechtae* – the death bell – and organise the transportation of the body to the chapel.'

'Sister Sárait? She is your assistant?' The name was unfamiliar to Fidelma.

'She is one of the servers who came with me to help me in my new office,' Father Socra replied.

'Did she also come from the Abbey of Sléibhte?' Eadulf asked.

'She joined our party at Sléibhte,' Father Socra acknowledged stiffly. 'I have no recollection her being in the abbey before she joined us. You seem unduly interested in who has come from Sleibhte?'

'I am interested in all places,' Eadulf assured him.

'I shall find Princess Gelgéis and take note of her wishes, then. Unless the stewardess is available to give instruction, I can take Síonna to our librarian, who can give her information about the fortress and her new position.'

Fidelma and Eadulf watched for a moment as the two made their way across the courtyard.

'Well,' murmured Eadulf, 'we now have a priest, a chaplain, who is going to be the last word in misogynists. So he does not like women engaged in martial arts and, I don't doubt, engaged in any of the professions. Did you notice the way he seems to take control of this physician, Síonna? He seems to be telling her what to do.'

'It's probably just his manner but I think he will soon be disabused of such attitudes. I don't think she liked him. If he espouses his religious ideas here, he will soon find those ideas are not popular.'

Eadulf snorted. 'He wanted to challenge my position immediately while even Síonna accepted it.'

'Taking of challenges, we must talk about your . . . your outburst to my brother,' Fidelma observed quietly.

Eadulf flushed and his mouth clenched shut for a moment.

They had turned and continued towards the doors of the building in which their apartment was located. They had just reached them when there came a shout. It was Luan, who was almost running across the courtyard from the royal residence.

He came to a breathless halt before them. His panting breath was more one of emotion, for warriors prided themselves on their fitness and the short run should not have caused him any discomfort. His entire demeanour was odd.

'Lady, I am sorry . . .' he began, then stopped as if gasping for breath.

'Steady, Luan,' Fidelma advised calmly. 'Catch your breath and tell us what is upsetting you.'

Luan took a few deep breaths.

'Lady, I regret to have to report that Dar Luga has been found dead.'

CHAPTER SEVEN

Eadulf arose from the kneeling position by the side of the prone, plump figure of Dar Luga. The body was lying by one of the tables in the large kitchen at which food was usually prepared for the King and his guests. There was a half-filled glass on the table and a jug of water from which the woman had apparently been drinking. Luan had ordered the kitchen to be cleared of early morning workers. He had placed some members of the household guard at various points to secure the area before allowing Eadulf to perform a thorough examination without interference. Fidelma stood behind Eadulf, waiting for him to finish.

When he finally rose, Fidelma asked quietly: 'She was complaining of an ague earlier. Has that something to do with her death?'

Eadulf glanced upward with a serious expression. 'Undoubtedly so, but it was no ordinary ague. If only we had been able to spot the symptoms.'

'What do you mean – spot what symptoms?' Fidelma asked in concern. 'Are you saying this was a pestilence that we should have noticed?'

'Not a pestilence.' Eadulf shook his head. 'She has been poisoned.'

Fidelma gave a sharp intake of breath and stepped forward to stare down.

'How can you tell?' she asked.

'See the paleness of the skin has changed; see the blue around the mouth and the discoloration around the eyes? There is a rigidness that has appeared as distortion of the muscles since we last saw her and will soon lock in a rigor.'

Fidelma looked at the half-empty glass on the table and pitcher of water.

'You mean she came down here, realised we would find the evidence against her and decided to take poison as a way of escaping justice?' Her tone reflected her disbelief.

Eadulf bent forward, placed the tip of his finger in the glass and held it against his lips.

'Clear water,' he said. 'But she was being poisoned and I think she was dying of that poison even when we were speaking with her earlier in the sanctuary. I am afraid that we know what it was: the wolfsbane that we found in old Brother Conchobhar's apothecary. It does not work immediately. It is why I said that she must have already been poisoned even when we saw her earlier. So she must have taken it in her room before she saw us. I want to see her room again now. I need to confirm an idea.'

Luan had been waiting nearby and Fidelma told him to instruct a guard to remain and let no one near the body. Then she asked whether he had sent word of the stewardess's death to anyone.

'I waited for you and Eadulf, lady,' he replied. 'It will be best if you informed The King.'

'Then send word by one of your men to my brother. He might even be with the new physician, a woman called Síonna, who arrived in the fortress last night. She can be asked to examine the body for cause of death. We should not go beyond the bounds of protocol now that we know she is in the fortress. I have no objections now that Eadulf has had a chance to examine the body.'

Eadulf was about to raise a question when Fidelma forestalled him.

'We can pre-empt her complaint by making the invitation,' she explained. 'You have made your examination and we know what path we must take. Now Síonna has arrived we have to defer to her as the physician in this fortress. But she will not interfere with our investigation.'

They returned, with Luan, to the sanctuary and into the room Dar Luga had occupied. Eadulf went straight to the bedside table and crouched down by the side of the bed, looking intently at the floor.

'What are you looking at?' Fidelma asked.

'Remember the broken glass? You said that Dar Luga had spilt some water she was drinking early this morning.'

'You mean the liquid in that glass was what contained the poison? You think she attempted to destroy it on purpose?'

'The reason why she might have done so, we can discuss later. But for the moment . . .'

Eadulf gave an exclamation and reached forward. He picked up a piece of the broken glass and raised it to eye level. He could see that there was a small trace of liquid in the angle of the broken piece. He dipped his finger into its contents, placed it against his lips and gave a soft exhalation.

'Wolfsbane,' he confirmed. 'It is usually lethal a couple of hours after it has been ingested. It stops the heart from beating.'

'And has done so,' Fidelma observed quietly. 'Dar Luga drank the poison to escape the inevitable conclusion. Was she the guilty one?'

'Not necessarily. It also supports my argument,' Eadulf contradicted. 'The poison was placed there even before she answered Colgú's alarm. She awoke confused and took a drink from the poison. I think the water was placed there deliberately by someone else.'

'An opinion?' Fidelma asked.

'An opinion equally as valid as your own,' replied Eadulf mildly.

'At least we can agree that the poison was already working when we saw her, but we did not identify her condition.'

'From what I know of this poison, even if I had recognised the condition, then it might have been too late anyway,' Eadulf admitted.

Fidelma was quiet for a moment, deep in thought. Then she said: 'There seems another way of interpreting this matter. Dar Luga was the culprit and took poison to avoid justice.'

'There is a more important way for us to consider this matter,' Eadulf replied in a tight voice. 'That is: Dar Luga was a friend and confidante to many of us in the fortress. She was like a mother to many of the young attendants, and even warriors found need to recourse to her care. She is now dead and someone poisoned her. I still refuse to believe she murdered anyone, and these events do not prove anything else.'

Fidelma flushed. 'As a *dálaigh* I have to put friendship aside. It is secondary. My first task is to discover the truth, whether I like the truth or not. She was the only one in the sanctuary, the only one with access, when Cera was attacked.'

'Discover the truth? I know what my truth is,' Eadulf muttered cynically.

'I would prefer that you to listen to the points of evidence and advise me strictly on those. Your task is only to tell me the medical evidence as you know it. If I am wrong on fact then I should be advised as to where I am wrong,' she replied testily.

For a moment or two, Eadulf swayed angrily as if a trembling fit had seized him. It seemed to Fidelma that the same shortness of temper he had experienced earlier that morning against Colgú was about to erupt. However, he exhaled a few long breaths with tightened jaws. Fidelma realised that there seemed to be a summoning of a great effort of will to control himself. Watching his expression, she immediately regretted her own shortness of temper. She knew this was not the first time that Eadulf had displayed this curious momentary lack of control.

'I realise I am not qualified to do anything other but answer your questions,' he replied shortly. 'I have never ceased to hide facts.' He bent down to pick up the larger pieces of glass by the bed and put them in his *lés*, his small leather bag.

Fidelma watched him with regret.

'Sometimes I express myself too sharply, Eadulf,' she said, trying to imply an apology in her tone without stating it clearly.

There was an uncomfortable silence when he did not respond. Then she spoke again.

'I was going to admit that there were two ways of interpreting this matter. I would have mentioned your path had I proceeded. However, I will try to put the points in the order that I would present them. We have discussed that the *forlés* were inaccessible unless the killer could miraculously float up to them. So the conclusion is that there was no way in or out of the room. Therefore, the killer must have remained in that room. So who remained in that room? We must consider the facts.'

Eadulf retreated into a sulky silence. Fidelma waited for a short while and then continued.

'Putting these things together, we could speculate this: for some reason Dar Luga wanted to kill the attendant Cera. She did so but roused your brother, who discovered the crime. Dar Luga managed to escape back to her own room. She then hid the dagger, the apron and keys, but, realising there was no way of escaping herself and the inevitability of her guilt, she had an amount of wolfsbane, which she had prepared in old Brother Conchobhar's apothecary, and swallowed it. The poison, as you say, worked after a period of time.'

'We are going over the same ground.' It was Luan who interrupted, voicing his opinion for the first time since they had returned after discovering Dar Luga's body. They had almost forgotten he was there. 'And you will also remind us that this room, her room, was probably the only escape route for the killer. Therefore, you claim, she was the killer.'

Fidelma did not rise to his hectoring tone.

'Sometimes it is wise to go over the same ground and apply second thoughts to the evidence rather than hearing it once. Making up one's mind by first impressions is also a way of missing things,' she replied stoically.

'And that is your theory, lady?' Luan asked dryly. 'I don't think you need me to point out its weaknesses.'

'Tell me them, anyway,' Fidelma invited. Several times that morning she had been surprised at Luan stepping out of the character she knew of him, to advance theories in a contrary manner.

'To follow your interpretation, you have to assume Dar Luga must have been a woman in such turmoil of hatred that she set out to kill Cera. Yet Cera was a young girl, whom she had apparently previously liked and admired since she first came to Cashel only a few weeks ago. I had been told that Cera was friendly with Dar Luga. There was no animosity between them. So why would Dar Luga act in such a brutal and bloody fashion against the young girl? What had stirred her thus? And, more important, why had she already decided to imbibe poison? Remember, she had already prepared it. Why does she take it and then meekly wait to die, sitting with the body of her victim and then, calmly gives her version when she is questioned by you, before going down to the kitchens to continue to await death? I do not believe that is the truth.'

Fidelma stared at the young warrior with some amazement mixed with growing approval. In the several years she had known Luan, she had never considered him in any way other than as a warrior in her brother's service and as a member of his household guard. It was from Enda and Gormán that she would have expected such discussion. Warriors of rank were expected to have studied and obtained knowledge on many subjects and be analytical in their approach. She had not expected it of Luan. However, he displayed good reasoning and, she had to admit, there was logic in it.

'So, in rejecting that interpretation, Luan, what is your idea?' she invited with a tight smile.

'Dar Luga says she was woken by the shouting of the King. She said that she was in a state of bewilderment and so had to take a drink of water before she rose and answered the King's alarm call. We now know that drink was of the poison. The door of the room where Cera's body was found was locked from the passageway. I had to send for the spare key. That meant I had to fetch Enda to get the key. The King ordered Dar Luga to come through his bedchamber into the bathroom to keep watch on the body while he took Gelgéis to his downstairs reception room.'

'And so?' Fidelma prompted.

'So that left a period that meant anyone could come and go without witness. As I understand from friend Eadulf, the poison was in that first mouthful of what she had when roused by the King. It would be illogical to poison herself at that stage.' He hesitated. 'I think she probably drank the water even before she went to bed. The murderer had somehow hid, and during the period while Dar Luga was watching the body and while I had gone to get the key was when they escaped.'

There were several moments of silence after Luan finished speaking. Finally, Fidelma nodded slowly and her mouth formed into a tired smile.

'Your speculation also has many weaknesses, Luan, but I appreciate it for an alternative idea of the events,' she acknowledged.

'Where is the weakness?' the young warrior demanded belligerently.

Eadulf broke his silence with a long sigh. 'The main weakness is the question of why the killer poisoned Dar Luga. The killer must have anticipated the need to poison Dar Luga before they even broke into the apartment. Did they reason that when Cera was killed Dar Luga was going to be regarded as a suspect? The killer must have already prepared the poison and placed it by Dar Luga's bedside, having estimated the time it would react . . .'

'You've argued yourself out of the theory,' Fidelma smiled sadly. 'Only one person could have prepared the poison and imbibed it, and that was Dar Luga herself.'

'It is the central mystery,' Eadulf agreed. 'If Dar Luga were poisoned by the killer by drinking the water by her bedside, why would that be? As Luan has unemotionally argued, the poison must have been placed beside her bed before Cera was killed, whether Cera was the intended victim or not. The attempt on Dar Luga's life was contemplated long before the event. If so – why?'

'I think there is still a weakness in claiming Dar Luga is the murderer,' Luan replied stubbornly. 'I think it comes down to the fact that there was no motive for her to kill Cera.'

'On the contrary, the facts reinforce the argument that she was the killer,' replied Fidelma. 'The main mystery of this extraordinary killing is the total impossibility of the killer gaining entrance to the sanctuary. We are left with the conclusion that the killer was already here . . .'

'. . . So we have to accept that Dar Luga was responsible?' Eadulf ended. 'But I agree with Luan. I cannot accept that Dar Luga was the killer.'

Fidelma took a deep breath to quell her frustration. 'The only other explanation we are presented with is an impossible mystery; a series of events that are unfeasible, irresolvable. In other words, there is no explanation at all.'

'That is about the sum of the matter,' Eadulf agreed after a moment. 'I say that knowledge of the character of Dar Luga precludes the very idea that she is the killer. Knowledge of character and lack of clear motive should be taken into reasoning.'

'Nevertheless, the ball of twine must be untangled, and that cannot be done just by emotion.'

'Then you have to untangle the twine before you decide where it leads,' Eadulf replied dryly.

A flash of irritation crossed Fidelma's features. However, with a grimace she reluctantly agreed. She was unhappy with her deductions.

'Then we must find the end of the twine. The only means to proceed is to discover if there is an alternative way the killer could have entered the secure chamber, and, indeed, managed to exit from it once the alarm had been raised,' she said.

'When one path is blocked, we should turn to another,' Eadulf replied ruthlessly. 'Too much time has been spent on the "how" and none on the "why".'

'The King believes that he was the intended victim,' pointed out Luan. 'If so, we don't have to ask the motive. There are plenty of conspirators who would like to take his place.'

'If he were the intended victim, it does not change things,' Fidelma said.

'It would if one maintained Dar Luga was the assassin. Her loyalty to the King was well known, just as she was loyal to Cathal, your cousin, when he was king.'

'But what if this was a case of mistaken identity?' Fidelma rejoined, suspecting that she was beginning to argue for the sake of not giving up her theory.

'How so?'

'What if Cera was part of an attempt to kill Colgú by those from Osraige and was herself killed to protect . . .' Fidelma let her voice trail off as she realised how weak the argument sounded.

'That does not lead us anywhere,' Eadulf said stubbornly.

'Only if we insist the killer was one of those in the sanctuary,' Fidelma pointed out in another train of thought. 'If the killer was from outside then we could accept that they intended to kill Colgú or Gelgéis. As Gelgéis is a princess of the Uí Barraiche, which is the royal house of Osraige, then the suspects are just as many as if we believe the intended victim was Colgú. Don't forget the Uí Barraiche have close connections with the family of Fianamail of Laigin.'

Eadulf was reflective.

'As Gelgéis is of the Uí Barraiche, her death would give excuses to Osraige and Laigin to intervene in the affairs of Muman, claiming retribution.'

'And if Colgú and Gelgéis *were* the intended victims, that makes the case against Dar Luga even weaker,' Eadulf pointed out with a thin smile.

'Not necessarily,' Fidelma snapped. 'I know you have suspicions about Laigin and Osraige. But, really, just because Father Socra comes from the border between the two territories, do you think it is sufficient grounds for suspicion?'

'Perhaps I am oversuspicious,' Eadulf acknowledged. 'You must admit that we have found that the petty king of Osraige is not entirely enthusiastic in acknowledging Cashel and paying tribute to it. Moreover, his non-appearance at the wedding of his own cousin to the King of Cashel was surely a sign of his antagonism.'

'Perhaps it is too obvious a sign,' Fidelma suggested. 'But what if the victim really was meant to be Cera? What do we know of her? I mean, do we have any personal details? Other than she was one of the Daughters of the Storm and also served the Princess Gelgéis as a personal attendant, and that she was from Durlus Éile, we know little about her.'

'Perhaps that is why you should question Enda,' Luan intervened. 'I don't think you completed your questioning with him.'

Fidelma turned to him with annoyance, paused and realised she had momentarily overlooked Enda.

'Has Enda been seen since he said he was going to rest?' she asked thoughtfully.

Eadulf turned to Fidelma, his argument forgotten for the moment. 'Remember how upset he was when he brought us the news this morning? Perhaps he was too upset to speak.'

'Remember, lady, that you told me that his emotions explained his odd behaviour to me?' Luan said.

'I had not forgotten,' Fidelma admitted. 'That was why he was given absence from his duties to recover . . . although we agreed to talk further.'

'He might not know much about Cera's background, but Gelgéis would doubtless know more,' Eadulf said. 'But until some facts about her are made clear, there is another theory. It has just occurred to me that we should be judging things from a different perspective. I mean about Cera being a victim and Dar Luga being a killer.'

For a moment or two Fidelma and Luan both stared at Eadulf in surprise and then realisation came to Fidelma.

'You mean that we are looking at this matter in the opposite way? That Dar Luga was the victim, not Cera? But that is—'

'Illogical?' Eadulf smiled grimly. 'Perhaps not. There are many who have resented the fact that your brother raised Dar Luga from being his housekeeper to the level of *banmhaor*, steward of the household, and thereby an adviser to the King.'

'But he did that at the Council of the seven Eóganacht princes, when the kingdom was being menaced. They all consented.'

'The princes might have accepted it, but they doubtless resented it.'

'Would that be motive enough to assassinate her . . . just the fact that Dar Luga suddenly became a person of influence in this kingdom?' Fidelma queried.

'That depends on whoever felt affronted by the appointment. There were certainly enough who would aspire to be in your brother's place.'

'But to the point of making an attempt on her life?'

Abruptly there came to their ears the slow deep-toned ring of the chapel bell – the *clog-estechtae*, the death bell.

'That means I have an unpleasant task to fulfil,' Fidelma said grimly.

'Unpleasant?' Eadulf queried.

'I have to inform my brother personally about Dar Luga, and I should tell him about our speculations. We also have to ask Father Socra to prepare the death rituals for Dar Luga as well as for Cera.'

Telling Colgú was, Fidelma realised, not going to be an easy matter. Dar Luga had looked after Colgú almost like the mother he had lost when she had died in giving birth to Fidelma. She stood quietly for a few moments.

'I will inform my brother,' she reluctantly. 'But I will I keep my speculations to myself. I would ask you not to repeat such speculations nor express any opinion until I say so.'

'What if we are asked?' Eadulf frowned. 'There is a lot of speculation in the fortress already, and once Dar Luga's death is known there will be stories spreading like a wildfire in a dry summer month. How can we then keep quiet and allow rumour to gather? It is not like you to exhort silence on the matter.'

'There is a saying that when words may cause disquiet and apprehension, then a silent mouth is melodious and soothing.'

'I cannot agree, lady,' Luan argued. 'It will be hard for the entire inhabitants of Cashel to accept this news. Everyone knew Dar Luga well. If there is any speculation that she might be a murderer and that she then took her own life to escape retribution, the fear and anger will be widespread. Believe me, lady, such gossip and speculations on these deaths and their connections will spread, whatever you say.'

'I expect you to say nothing, as I shall until I have something positive to say,' Fidelma retorted in annoyance. 'You have both said just how respected Dar Luga was and that from being his housekeeper, my brother raised her to the role of stewardess. This fact alone is going to be a hard blow for him to take.'

'It is a hard blow for us all and if we do not—' Luan was cut short.

'If you feel unable to accept saying nothing,' Fidelma's voice was suddenly icy, 'if you cannot accept a simple order, then I have to resort to the ultimate sanction and place a *géis* on you to do so.'

Luan was shocked. Even Eadulf, who had encountered the *géis* before, was amazed that Fidelma felt committed enough to go thus far. The *géis* was a sacred and absolute prohibition and injunction to a certain action. The breach of the action resulted in dire consequences to the one who broke it. It had its origins in the time beyond time and was greatly feared by the people who, even with the adoption of the New Faith, continued to implicitly believe in the *géis*'s supernatural powers. While Fidelma often made little of such things, the fact that she felt compelled to mention that she, as sister to the King, might use it to enforce her authority now was to Eadulf, at least, surprising.

'There is no need for that, lady,' Luan said nervously, glancing conspiratorially over his shoulders as if he expected to see some wraith rise up behind him. 'I will respect your wishes and say nothing.'

Fidelma and Eadulf followed Luan down the stairs into the main hall of the residence. At the bottom of the stairs stood one of the guards, Aidan.

'Your brother and Enda have returned to the residence, lady,' he said in greeting to Fidelma. 'They are in the small reception room now.'

'Enda as well?' Fidelma was surprised.

'Yes, lady.'

Fidelma turned to Luan. 'Go and find Father Socra, the chaplain. Take a diplomatic moment to advise him that he needs to come alone to me or to my brother, the King. You understand? Not a word of why he is wanted until I have spoken with Colgú.'

Luan raised his hand in acknowledgement and went off on his mission.

Fidelma and Eadulf left Aidan and entered Colgú's small reception chamber. Fidelma's brother was seated in his usual chair before the fire while Enda stood at the table to one side, helping himself to a glass of cider. It was Colgú who looked up with anticipation on his features. He glanced from Fidelma to Eadulf.

'What news?' Colgú demanded. She realised he was pale and nervous.

'I have bad news,' she began.

He made a dismissive emotion with his left hand. 'This is too small a world to maintain secrets.' His voice was harsh with emotion. 'I heard whispers from a member of the kitchen staff whose brother works in the guards' barracks and mentioned it to me. Dar Luga has been poisoned. I sent the new physician to investigate. Was that supposed to remain a rumour until you told me?'

'It was to remain no rumour,' Fidelma replied grimly. 'I had sent a message to you and asked the physician to attend to examine the body.'

'And the details? I suppose Eadulf examined the body before you sent for the physician?'

'I am the *dálaigh* in charge and Eadulf acted with my authority,' she snapped.

'She was poisoned, but whether she took it, or was given it and forced to imbibe it, we have yet to determine,' Eadulf admitted immediately, deciding the idea of the *géis* no longer mattered. 'There is a conflict of opinion about the subject and we have yet to make a determination.'

Colgú let out a long sighing breath. 'So Dar Luga is gone? She was working in the fortress when my cousin Cathal of the Eóganacht of Glendamnach became King, before I was confirmed his *tanaiste* – the heir apparent – by the seven princes. When Cathal died of the pestilence, I relied on her in so many ways. She might have remained as my housekeeper and cook and we probably would have been content. It was you, Fidelma, who advised me that she was correctly the *banmhaor,* and I appointed her in name as well as position. There will be much lamentation for her.'

'Do you censure my suggestion?' Fidelma asked quickly, listening for the tone of criticism.

'Not I,' Colgú replied with a sad shake of his head. 'We will have to give new instructions to Father Socra.'

'Of course,' Fidelma confirmed. 'I sent Luan to inform him. And don't forget that Dar Luga was sister to Lassar, wife to Ferloga. They both run the tavern at Ráth na Drinne. Someone will have to ride to the tavern to inform her, as she will doubtless want to take part in, and inform others of, the obsequies. My friend Della was also a good friend to both sisters, so she should be informed.'

'It shall be done. In fact, I have sent for Della's son, Gormán, to come to the fortress. Gormán and his wife are staying with Della for a few days. Gormán, as one of my best commanders, could be useful at this time.'

Fidelma frowned and could not help casting a glance to where Enda was standing statuelike with no expression on his face. It seemed that he had not moved since she and Eadulf had entered.

She was about to ask what her brother had in mind for Gormán when he said: 'What do you think Dar Luga's death has to do with that of Cera? One death from stabbing but the other from poison.'

'As of this moment, we have nothing further to add while our investigation continues,' Fidelma replied. 'However, there are practical matters to be decided.'

'Practical?'

'Until we are sure about motives, we should rearrange the security in this place,' pointed out Fidelma.

Enda, who had been standing in self-conscious silence, suddenly flushed and felt obliged to speak. His words came out as a protest.

'I am commander of the household guard. Breaches in security are my responsibility. Gormán resigned his command long ago.'

Fidelma met his affronted gaze evenly. 'For the moment you are also a witness, Enda. I was under the impression that you felt that you needed to absent yourself from this investigation, being affected by the death of this girl Cera.'

'You think that I . . .?' began the warrior.

'I have yet to examine whether you bear any responsibility, directly or indirectly. So we must deal with that. What I propose is to follow the method we adopted during the Council of the seven princes; and I think what my brother may have had in mind is to invite Gormán to take charge of security in the township, especially during the time of the fair.'

She glanced at Colgú and received a nod.

'If Gormán is still staying in the township with Aibell, his wife, then this is ideal,' she went on. 'If there is some hidden plan to this matter affecting the kingship, it might be linked to the fair, which would be a good opportunity to infiltrate strangers into Cashel. I suggest that Gormán be temporarily reappointed in command of a battalion of the Nasc Niadh, to be deployed in case of any threat to the township that might take place during the time of the great fair.'

Enda was red in the face with mortification. He turned to appeal to Colgú.

'In that case I must ask to be released from your service, as this demonstrates there is no confidence in my abilities.'

Fidelma regarded him with disapproval. 'Enda, lack of trust in your ability is not what is being said here. No one has dismissed your rank and privileges as commander of the household guard. But the law of witnesses must be followed. We know well that you are qualified as a *fiadu* – one who sees – and therefore you are legally a witness in the law: a witness to the events of this morning, for it was you who commanded the guard. There are various caveats in the text of the *Barrad Airechta* where you could be challenged on points of evidence, especially when it seems that you might be constrained by your relationship with Cera.'

There was a momentary expression of anguish on Enda's face and his shoulders suddenly slumped in resignation as if he could no longer suppress the grief in him.

'I am legally in your hands, lady,' he finally accepted in a small voice.

'You are not being accused of anything,' Fidelma replied gently. 'Once all is clear to me, then you can immediately resume your role as commander of the household guard. Meanwhile, I think it best if you wait in the next room while I have a brief word with my brother.'

After the door closed behind him, Colgú asked: 'You do suspect him of something. What do you want me to do with him?'

Chapter Eight

'Do you want me to put Gormán in command in Enda's stead?' demanded Colgú.

'Not at all,' Fidelma replied calmly. 'I am just being guided by the law as one must be, relating to the matter on giving evidence about an illegal death. Enda had developed a romantic attachment with Cera, the victim in this murder. I must examine him on that point, which might subsequently raise all manner of questions about his actions. It is not so much about uncovering the culprit as ensuring that actions in the aftermath of the event are correctly taken.'

'I am in your hands in the interpretation of the law,' Colgú agreed. 'But I wish all my personal council were here.'

'In that I agree. We must try to fulfil important offices here in the household in case this matter does concern some attempt to threaten the stability of the kingdom. With Dar Luga's death we have no one in charge of the running of the household. Finguine, your *tanaiste*, is away and so is Fíthel, your Chief Brehon. And when does Abbot Cuán arrive?'

'Very shortly.'

'At least the new physician arrived last night.'

'Her position is only advisory to the council. She had barely introduced herself when she was summoned to the kitchens to examine the body of Dar Luga. I presume Síonna will officially confirm what Eadulf has already discovered about her death.'

'I don't think there will be any disagreement,' Fidelma confirmed. 'We actually found the place where the poisonous plants had been distilled. That was in poor Conchobhar's abandoned apothecary. I presume Síonna and her helpers will be taking that building over?'

Colgú's surprise only reflected momentarily before he shrugged. 'I had not thought about it, but I suppose it is logical that she should take over that building as it probably still contains many of the things she will require.'

'That is good, but remember you will need someone to replace Dar Luga, to fulfil or assist the duties of steward. Dar Luga had a principal role in organising the fair in the township.'

It was Eadulf who made the suggestion. 'If I am allowed to propose a name, would not Brother Dáire be able to fulfil the role of steward, if only for the time being? I know a full council would have to confirm the proposal, but now no steward exists and a steward is needed.'

'Brother Dáire?' Colgú was surprised. 'From an advisory seat on the council to becoming steward . . . he is gaining quickly in status in my household. Yet he is very young.'

'Young as he is, since he arrived here he has served us well,' Fidelma pointed out. 'We might not have survived during the Council of the seven princes without his advice during times of danger. We needed his practical aid.'

'He not only gave us proper advice when we were confronted with the possibility of a major pestilence, but his research into some of the ancient manuscripts also led to the identification of the conspiracy that nearly overturned the kingdom,' Eadulf reminded her.

Colgú was rubbing his jaw thoughtfully.

'You are right that his age should not be held against him,' he finally conceded. 'Very well. So shall it be, but *pro tempore*. We will temporarily appoint him as *rechtaire*. But the council will have to confirm anything permanent.'

'The only person I feel uncomfortable with is your chaplain,' Eadulf announced.

'Father Socra will have to be consulted,' Colgú said immediately. 'As chaplain, he has the right to advise the council, especially now that he has two funerals to organise.'

'I am not sure he was given any special instruction by Gelgéis about the interment of Cera,' Fidelma mused. 'With Dar Luga, he should consult with Lassar, her sister, when she arrives from Ráth na Drinne. I have officially accepted Eadulf's report and presume that Síonna will make a report about Dar Luga's death to Fíthel when he arrives. That should not conflict with what we already know.'

'You say that there is a matter of concern about the administration of poison.' Colgú suddenly frowned. 'I believe that Father Socra is one of those very much in favour of the new Roman interpretations of matters. If there is any possibility that Dar Luga took her own life through poison then he might refuse to bury her in the normal place. Last time he was here, Abbot Cuán was telling me that Augustine of Hippo condemned suicide as an action against the New Faith. He interprets the Commandment "You shall not kill" as also applying to killing oneself.'

'New Roman law should not overturn our own laws on such a matter,' Fidelma replied. 'When Brehon Fíthel arrives here, he will give the interpretation of the law. I will support his judgment because I am sure we will be in agreement.'

'Well, let us be sure a wise decision is made,' Colgú advised her. 'I am told that a hundred years ago the Romans passed a secular law against the act of suicide and after that the New Faith, through this Augustine, also called it sinful.'

Eadulf was trying to remember something. He suddenly grinned cynically. 'I can recall that it was discussed at the Council of Arles. But they were thinking only of protecting nobles. They declared that if a slave committed suicide and, accepting the slave belonged body and soul to its master, then the cardinal sin of suicide was not the responsibility of the master. So that contradicted the idea that the soul belonged to the master.'

'If you prefer,' Fidelma told her brother, 'I will check our own laws of *fingal* to ensure that we are covered.'

Eadulf knew that the word *fingal* was also used for suicide because to kill oneself was the same, in philosophical terms, as to kill a relative or kin. In such a closely related tribal society as this, suicide was a heinous crime. It was considered even more abhorrent than in the new laws of Rome. But if the law also declared that every dead person was absolved of their own liabilities, that did not stop their entitlement to the legal ritual of burial.

'I will leave the legalities to you. If Father Socra makes an issue of it, that may antagonise the many people here who held Dar Luga in high esteem. I shall inform Brother Dáire that he will be taking over, in a temporary capacity, as my steward.' Colgú left to do so, looking tired.

After her brother had gone, Fidelma stretched out in a chair and closed her eyes.

'We still have not caught up on our sleep,' Eadulf murmured.

She was about to respond when there was a knock on the door. A moment later Enda entered the room.

'I saw that the King had left, lady. I believe you wanted to speak with me?'

It was Fidelma who motioned him to be seated in front of the fire.

'I am sorry to have to make this examination.' Fidelma's regret was genuine. 'However, if this matter has to come before the Chief Brehon there is no need to tell you how pedantic he can be on all matters of law, however obscure. Sometimes one comes to believe that, with Fíthel, it is the law that is more important than justice.'

Enda sat quietly. He seemed to have lost some of his youthful animation.

'What is it that you want of me, lady?'

'You do understand why I have to follow the procedures of the law in dealing with this matter, Enda?'

The young warrior raised his head and the face he turned to her still wore that curious mixture of uncertainty and pain.

'I know that what you are doing is to find the killer of Cera and now of Dar Luga, lady. I know the law must be followed. Both women were dear to me. Dar Luga almost raised me as my own mother while Cera . . . Cera . . .' He hesitated.

'I appreciate your feelings, Enda,' Fidelma said in a soothing tone. 'I know from how you reported the sad news this morning that Cera's death was devastating for you.'

'It was our intention to marry, lady.'

'Was there any protest at this plan?'

'Protest?' Enda was bewildered.

'Did those you told of your plan to marry support you?'

Enda gave a half-shrug. 'We were not going to announce it until after the fair in case anyone thought our martial arts contest was faked and not worth attending. You may know, lady, there is much wagering at fairs and I know that many have already placed bets as to the outcome of the contest.'

Eadulf was puzzled. 'But if this was an exhibition, a friendly contest, how could there be wagers on winners and losers?'

'The contest is adjudicated and points given. In that way a winner declared.'

'I still can't see how such a combat can be judged.'

'The contest is in three parts. Points are given for riding a war horse over a course and striking at three apples raised on pointed stakes along the course – the best mark is awarded for slicing the apple in two with a sharp sword. Then, dismounted, the contestants aim three arrows at a target, and then there is casting three javelins at a target. Points are given here, too. Finally, there is the sword and shield contest at which you aim to touch the opponent with a sword tip three times – the word *airmaisid* is uttered, declaring that the strike has hit. The points are added up and the winner declared by the adjudicator.'

'It sounds dangerous,' Eadulf observed.

'The skill of the warrior is to make the touch without breaking the skin.'

'And who adjudicates this?'

'This year it will be Gormán. You must know, friend Eadulf, that he is our greatest warrior and leader of the Warriors of the Golden Collar.'

'So,' Fidelma went on hurriedly, 'everyone knew that you and Cera were practising for the contest. But, you are saying, no one knew you were planning a wedding afterwards?'

'We had told no one.'

'Not even Crédh, Cera's commander?'

Enda was hesitant. 'She might have suspected our relationship, but not our intention.'

'Did the fact that you were paired together, representing Muman and Osraige, concern either of you?'

Enda looked puzzled. 'It was decided that Cera and I would be matched together because she was chosen from among the women warriors, but they were representing Durlus Éile and Princess Gelgéis rather than Osraige. We had been practising frequently so that we would not dishonour the celebrations of the King's nuptials. Why would that make anyone suspect anything more?'

'Well, it should not in itself. But Durlus Éile, like it or not, is part of the territory of Osraige,' Eadulf pointed out. 'Even that in itself might have upset someone.'

'Let us return to last night . . . or, rather, early this morning,' said Fidelma. 'You were charge of the household guard last night?'

'As well you know, lady.'

'And when were you alerted by Luan?'

'Sometime in the middle of the first *cadar*.'

'What then? What did you do?'

'I was almost at the bottom of the stairway, about to make my inspection of the guard posts, when Luan came down in a state of great excitement, demanding the key to the bathroom. He told me the door had been locked and the key was missing, and that the King was raising the alarm about someone injured and an intruder in the apartments. I gave him the spare key but followed him up. The King and his lady were up and standing at the end of the small passage. Dar Luga was standing in her doorway but looking ill. The King bade Luan unlocked the door and . . . and . . .'

'You saw the body of Cera?' prompted Fidelma.

Enda regained his control of his features before saying, 'Yes.'

'What did you do?'

'I checked to ensure she was dead. Realising she was past help, I held her close for a moment.'

'Getting blood on your tunic?'

'Yes. Then the King, who was taking his lady down the stairway to this chamber, asked Dar Luga to remain with the . . . with Cera until you were sent for. Dar Luga, however, asked Luan and me to take a quick look of the rooms first, to assure her that no intruder was hiding there. After we did so and assured her, I came to fetch you, as the King had instructed.'

'And Luan?'

'He went to assist the King. We had no idea that Dar Luga was an intended victim as well.'

'You say Dar Luga was looking unwell. I can confirm that. You did not suspect that she had been poisoned?'

'If only I had realised that she had been. I thought she had a cold. I confess, there is a great anger on me, lady.'

'The anger for revenge?' queried Fidelma, examining him carefully.

'It would not be true to say that such feelings are beyond my thoughts. But I have been trained in the code of the Warriors of the Golden Collar. Such thoughts must be resisted, for the law is paramount.'

Enda seemed to be having difficulty keeping his mouth in a firm line. He blinked several times and Fidelma and Eadulf noticed the tears forming in his eyes. When he spoke, his voice trembled with emotion. His words were like suppressed sobs.

'I have to try to forget that Cera and I had hoped to exchange marriage vows. I will discard vengeance for the sake of justice.'

Fidelma examined the tearful young man.

'Thank you for confirming these matters, Enda. You have our condolences. But it makes my next questions even more imperative. Will you be able to answer them for me?'

'I will do whatever I can to provide you with the information that you require.' Enda glanced up at her. 'What information do you need?'

'Let us go back to what you know about Cera. For example, when and where did you meet?'

'How does that help?' Suspicion flitted across his face for a moment.

'It might facilitate in eliminating whether Cera was the intended victim or just in the wrong place at the wrong time. Let us start with when and where you met her. Presumably it was when she came in the company of Princess Gelgéis to attend the marriage?'

Enda shook his head. 'I met her before that. It was during the period of *fogamor*, the harvest season, two years or more ago.'

'That was when . . .' began Eadulf.

'When Osraige rebels, led by Cronán of Gleann an Ghuail, were attempting to lead an uprising against Cashel. Had it been success-ful, it would have allowed Fianamail of Laigin to find an excuse to march his army into Osraige, uniting it with his kingdom.'

Fidelma was thoughtful for a moment, recalling the memories of how she, Eadulf and Gormán had first met Gelgéis of Durlus Éile. Gelgéis had been against Cronán's plan and had declared for Cashel. Fidelma and her companions had uncovered the Laigin conspiracy. She was trying to think of Enda's possible role in it. The young warrior seemed to read her thoughts.

'In putting down Cronán's uprising, your brother, the King, led a hundred mounted warriors of the Nasc Niadh to Durlus Éile. It was where he first met Gelgéis. I was then commanding a nine-man troop. I first met Cera in Durlus. She was the daughter of a blacksmith in the town. She was already one of the troop called the Daughters of the Storm, and also an attendant to Gelgéis, which was some sort of tradition. When Princess Gelgéis began to visit Cashel regularly, she was often accompanied by Cera, and our friendship grew.'

'And apart from being one of those Daughters of the Storm and attendant to the princess, is there anything else you know about her background?'

'As I said, she was daughter of the smith in Durlus Éile and, as such, she was of high status.'

Eadulf, who had been listening, recalled how he and Fidelma had been helped by a smith in Durlus Éile. He knew that a smith in this society was regarded as nobility and even the lowest rank of smith was on the same level as a brehon of lower rank, with an honour price to the value of three to four milch cows.

'But she had no other powerful family connections – only from the nobility of her father's profession?'

Enda smiled faintly. 'Also from her own profession. She was not related to any princely family. That suited me. I am a warrior and I have trained as such. That is my code of life. It is true that I have been honoured by the King to command the household guard. That is enough responsibility for me. So I was comfortable with my position in life and she was as comfortable with her position.'

'If you had married, did you see a change in your respective roles?'

Clearly, from his expression, Fidelma saw that the idea had not occurred to him.

'There should be no reason why our domestic roles should alter,' he replied.

'So what you are saying is that during your friendship with Cera you found nothing in her status, her honour price or her life that would indicate that she either made enemies or would be placed in such a position that someone would want to kill her.'

'Absolutely none,' Enda replied firmly. 'The idea that her murder was planned is nonsensical. I can only think that she was killed to prevent her from identifying the infiltrator of the sanctuary.'

'It is a reasonable conclusion,' Fidelma admitted reluctantly. 'So let us return to Dar Luga as a suspect.'

Enda did not hesitate. 'I refuse to believe that she was the attacker. I have known Dar Luga since I came to Cashel as a youth. I accept that she was poisoned, but will not believe that it was self-administered. She was killed by the same person who killed Cera. I cannot say who it was yet, but I swear I will find out.'

'It is my duty to find out,' Fidelma reminded him. 'I trust you will remember your warrior's oath as you have just described to me.'

'An honourable reputation is more lasting than life,' he returned the old saying.

'What it comes down to,' Fidelma summed up, 'is your explanation that Cera disturbed the intruder, but why was Dar Luga poisoned? Cera could have been in the wrong place at the wrong time, but Dar Luga . . . well, she was asleep in her bed. It doesn't make sense. So let us return to the idea that Cera was the victim of an attack; that she was the target.'

'Even that idea is not sound.' Enda was not to be budged from his belief.

'Why do you say that?' Fidelma pressed.

'Consider. Let us say that Cera was alerted by a noise. She left her bed – left her bedroom without alerting Luan, who was just feet away on the staircase. She went into the *fothrucadh*. Surely finding the door unlocked, when the King unfailingly locked it each night before retiring, could have warned her that something was wrong. But she was able to enter and was killed with her back to the assailant, who then fled because the King had been disturbed. It sounds absurd.'

'That is the interpretation, Enda,' Fidelma agreed.

'If she was the intended victim, why was she not killed in her own chamber?'

'A good point,' Fidelma conceded.

'You were told by Luan that he had heard nothing – not Cera coming out of her room and crossing to the bathroom – before responding Colgú's alarm,' Eadulf said.

'Luan did say he heard a door shut, which we presume was when the intruder ran out of the bathroom, locking the door behind them,' Fidelma corrected.

'The intruder argument leaves us another problem. Cera's room was directly opposite the bathroom room,' Enda pointed out. 'I think this proves that she was not the intended victim.'

'Why so?' Fidelma asked.

'As I said, Cera was not killed in her own chamber. But if we say that the killer's intended victims were the King and his lady, why did the killer not attempt to enter into their bedchamber directly, if he was able to enter their bathroom? Why did the killer not attack the King when he entered the bathroom, alerted by the falling of Cera's body during her attack? Why go into the bathroom, which created noise enough to alert Cera from her sleep so that she went into that room and met her death? And how did the killer get into that bathroom?' Enda asked. 'It was the King's custom to lock the door from the inside before going into his bedchamber where he had also ensured the door was locked on the inside. How did the intruder find a key? I had to give Luan the spare set to open the door.'

'It is a good point,' Fidelma answered. 'Just as good as the question of why Luan heard nothing before – except, possibly, the closing of the door as the intruder fled. Why no sound? Not the movement of Cera from her room, not the attack . . . no sound until Colgú raised the alarm.'

'Questions, the same questions,' Eadulf muttered.

'And no answers forthcoming,' Fidelma snapped.

'And if Dar Luga was the killer,' Eadulf said, 'why did she not use a more subtle means to murder the King and his wife? As a cook she could have used poison without suspicion. Anyway, if Dar Luga was the attacker and Cera the victim, why not kill Cera in her own chamber? Again, she could have done so easily and without drawing attention.'

Eadulf was thoughtful, as he considered these arguments. 'Following on from what Enda was saying, there is another point that has been worrying me.'

'The mystery of why Dar Luga was given, or took, poison before the murder of Cera?' Fidelma asked. She had reluctantly kept Eadulf's previous question to the front of her mind. 'Another question without an answer.'

'It is a question that is obscured for the moment. We are close to accepting that Cera was simply attacked for being in the wrong place at the wrong time: that she was silenced so that she could not raise the alarm or identify the intruder. That would be what our friend Enda thinks is the answer.'

Enda looked annoyed. 'And you do not?'

'It leads to more questions,' Eadulf pointed out.

'What questions?' Enda demanded.

'If Cera was eliminated just because she was a witness, then the intruder would have probably acted in panic. They would have lashed out in an attempt to silence the witness. Cera was a warrior, trained in martial arts. She would have known how to defend herself. Even Fidelma knows the art of self-defence. I have seen her in action. No, this was no frenzied attack, nor that of someone surprised in the midst of an activity.'

'I agree,' Enda sighed, 'Cera had her back turned unprotected to her assailant when her throat was cut. The dagger was used in such a way that it caused death almost instantaneously.'

'That has been worrying me all along,' Fidelma uttered with a long sigh. 'It was not a frenzied attack. It was one swift thrust of a weapon held in the hand of someone who clearly knew the most lethal place to aim. And Cera stood there – perhaps in shock – and did not defend herself. But that rules out the idea that the killer was an intruder who just wanted to silence her on the spur of the moment.'

Enda was looking mystified. 'What are you saying?'

'I think the conclusion is obvious. Cera knew her killer and was too shocked to employ the defences that should have been second nature to her. Perhaps that confirms what we have already learnt.'

'Confirms what?' Enda was still bewildered.

'One thing we do know now,' Fidelma said grimly. 'Cera was killed by someone she recognised. That someone must have been a warrior.'

Enda stared at her, his face pale. He turned to Eadulf, and then back to Fidelma again.

'A warrior?' His voice was hoarse. 'What proof do you have of that?'

'We can go further,' she replied. 'I think Cera was killed by a female warrior.'

It took Enda some time before he shook his head in confusion.

'Are you serious?' Eadulf whispered to Fidelma. 'A short time ago you were certain it was Dar Luga who was the killer. Surely this speculation goes too far?'

'Not far enough,' Fidelma replied complacently. 'The dagger that cut her throat was one of the small ceremonial ones carried at a warrior's belt. Moreover, this style of dagger was the type used only by members of the Daughters of the Storm.'

CHAPTER NINE

There were a few moments of silence while Eadulf and Enda took in what Fidelma said.

'Then you can identify this dagger, lady?' Enda asked.

Fidelma took the dagger from her marsupium and held it gently by the blade in order that the image on the handle could be observed.

Enda stared at it as if mesmerised.

'This is not the symbol of the Daughters of the Storm,' he asserted immediately.

'But it is similar to the ones worn by the Daughters of the Storm?' Fidelma pressed.

'Only in that it is a small dagger,' Enda replied. 'It is not even of the craftsmanship of this island.'

Eadulf was looking embarrassed. 'I am afraid that I knew it was not the symbol of those carried by the Daughters of the Storm. It reminded me of a similar style that I had seen during the debate at Streoneshalh.'

Ignoring Eadulf, Fidelma frowned in annoyance. 'Tell me about this, Enda. Where did this come from?'

'All I can do is confirm what friend Eadulf says. It is not the symbol used by the Daughters of the Storm. They use the symbol of an attacking goose.'

Eadulf nodded. 'I have seen their symbol,' he agreed. 'So what does that symbol mean? Why is it different from this one?'

'The crouching goose is called the *giraing*, the wild goose. It is just a depiction of the goddess of battle. The goose is usually shown in the position that it would assume to defend against an attacker and . . . I would imagine this dagger belongs to another female warrior band.' He turned Eadulf. 'Where did you say you saw this?'

'I saw something similar at the great Council at Streoneshalh, where Fidelma and I first met.'

'This was found with blood on it in Dar Luga's bedchamber, together with the missing key to the bathroom door and an apron.' Fidelma was now hesitant as her theory was confronted. 'All covered in blood. It matches the wound inflicted on Cera.'

'Well, you can see the symbol was on the handle when it came out of the mould,' Enda pointed out. 'A symbol using a special mould would mean that several of these small daggers were produced. Therefore the smith who did this was making several of these dagger handles with the symbol. Different groups share symbols in common on their daggers.'

'You mean, if we identify this symbol, we will know what company of warriors uses that symbol?'

'That is so,' replied Enda, thoughtfully. 'You are right that it was not a weapon carried by male warriors.'

'So who uses this symbol?'

'This emblem is called a *saignén* – a lightning flash,' Enda replied. 'It is a symbol of one of our ancient goddesses, a goddess of battle, Macha. The lightning flash implies storms – thunder and lightning – which were often connected with battle. Most female warrior bands have similar emblems.'

'If this is not one that Cera would have carried,' Eadulf mused with firm emphasis, 'it is that carried by her assailant. But if this lightning symbol is not the emblem of the Daughters of the Storm, then whose is it?'

'If it is similar to one you saw at Streoneshalh,' Fidelma concluded, 'then is it Saxon?'

Eadulf shrugged as if trying to draw on his memories. 'The Saxons, Angles and Jutes have troops of female warriors. But I am sure that I have seen the symbol before and I keep thinking of Streoneshalh.'

Fidelma sighed in frustration. 'So all that can be said is that it is definitely not used by the Daughters of the Storm? It is neither Cera's own dagger nor that of any of her companions?'

Enda shrugged and she accepted it as confirmation.

'I am afraid that the dagger does not provide the proof of identity that we were hoping it would,' Fidelma added, trying to disguise her disappointment. 'Well, we will have a word with Crédh. She might be able to identify its origins.' She put the dagger back in her marsupium.

There was a short silence before Enda prompted: 'Is there anything else that you wish of me, lady?'

'I have cleared up the questions I wanted to raise with you for the moment,' she confirmed.

'Am I free to go about my own affairs now? Can I return to my duties as commander of the household guard?'

'You can continue. These are dangerous times. I have advised my brother that Gormán should be in charge of the security in the township during the fair. But you will remain with your responsibilities here in the fortress.'

'I understand, lady.'

'Before you go back to duty, you should take some rest. I also want you to be assured of our sympathy. We will find whoever killed Cera.'

'My thanks and appreciation, lady.' There was a slight jerky motion at the corner of his mouth. 'I cannot rest now, lady. I must go to the chapel to take part in the watching of the body, as it begins now.'

Enda was at the door when he paused and turned back to her, still with a worried expression.

'Would you advise me on a matter that causes me some bother me, lady?'

'If I can, Enda,' she answered.

'Cera's body will be watched in the Christian chapel with a Christian ritual. It will follow the usual custom and she will finally be taken to the burial ground and interred with symbols of the New Faith. Is this so?'

'That is the usual procedure.' Fidelma was bewildered. 'Why do you ask?'

'Cera was not a Christian.'

Fidelma glanced at Eadulf, thought for a moment and then shrugged. 'There are still many in the five kingdoms who continue to believe in the Old Faith; many who follow the old ways and philosophies. You cannot completely change a people from their beliefs that have existed from the dawn of time to new philosophies in scarcely two centuries. What worries you about this?'

Enda hesitated a moment and then said: 'You were once a religieuse, lady. Can you advise me what I should do in ensuring that the girl's beliefs are not disregarded?'

'I was not exactly a religieuse. I was a religieuse in name only. My cousin Abbot Laisran persuaded me to enter Cill Dara as legal adviser to the Abbey simply because, at that time, I had no other means of job security. That was before Colgú became heir apparent to King Cathal. So I could not say that I had complete knowledge of religious rules, either of one faith or the other. I am sure all will be well.'

Eadulf nodded agreement. 'I have observed that most who have embraced the New Faith in this land have done so by belief and logic. Unfortunately, in other lands, especially those lands that inherited the old Roman Empire, they had no choice. They were ordered to accept the New Faith. The empire still exists, but now it is ruled by the Pope and his Curia. They inherited the empire of the Romans. This land is different, and here people get buried according to ancient customs, whether they are believers or not.'

Enda seemed reluctant to accept this assurance.

'Cera believed in Danu, the Mother Goddess,' he sighed. 'She believed in all the old deities and their influences.'

'I still fail to see what it is you want, Enda. What can we do?'

'If Cera's body is to be taken, prayed over and watched by those believing in the New Faith, which I still understand so little about, what if she is buried deep underground with the ceremonial of the New Faith? Will this not impede her journey to the Otherworld? My knowledge of the differences is not a deep one, lady. Are we only allowed one journey after death? The New Faith says if we obey their rules, we go directly to a sunny afterlife, but if we do not obey their rules then we go to some eternal fiery furnace.'

Fidelma felt a sudden sympathy for the young man. 'I consider it not a good thing to accept the concepts of the New Faith about obtaining eternal happiness in another life by following strict man-made rules or, by refusing them, having to endure eternal suffering, pain and punishment. Such ideas are not good to base your life on.'

'Cera used to say, better is the afterlife that Donn, the collector of souls, promises. When people die in this world, he comes to gather their souls and assembles them on his island in the west. When they are all congregated, he sails with them across the western ocean until they reach Hy Brasil – Tír na nÓg, the Land of the Ever Young; the ancient Land of Promise. There is no discrimination among the dead. One does not have to be approved by priests before you are given permission to sail westward with Donn. No judgement is needed as to whether you deserve to go to a place of reward or a place of punishment.'

'The Otherworld was a good prospect at the end of a life here,' Fidelma admitted, still unsure what Enda was implying.

'But what if Donn misses Cera's soul because she has been taken by the Christian god and has alien rituals performed over her body before it is buried in some dark secret place? I have come across this same argument among the people in the western mountains, who remain practising the Old Faith.'

Fidelma did not answer at once. She, too, had heard these ideas among several when she had been sent by her brother to the remote valley of Gleann Geis, whose inhabitants still adhered to the old ways, when she had to persuade their chieftain, Laisre, to allow a Christian church to be built in his territory. She often wondered whether she had done the right thing. Yet her family had accepted the New Faith two centuries before when her ancestor Conall Corc was welcomed into it by the Blessed Ailbhe of Imleach.

'Were these thoughts brought about by some confusion in your own mind?' she asked Enda. 'I do not remember you being so concerned before.'

Enda's expression was sad. 'I admit that Cera and I did discuss the matter of our beliefs several times.'

'Was Cera trying to convert you to the old ways?' Eadulf asked. He had been brought up in the Old Faith and deities of his own Anglian people. He was aware how his life had changed once he had been converted to the New Faith.

'Perhaps.' Enda shrugged. 'I don't know. I think she disapproved of those who, once taking oath to the old deities, of actually fighting in their name, had then converted to the New Faith and become more fanatical in the name of the new deity. Fanaticism was never sanctioned by the Old Faith.'

'Fanaticism in all matters is to be condemned,' Fidelma agreed. 'Was she talking of any ruler or a person in particular?'

'I had the impression she had recently seen someone who had caused the thought to come to her. Someone she once knew, who had become a fanatic. But she accepted my belief as I began to accept her beliefs. It was toleration, not conversion.'

Fidelma leant forward and patted Enda's arm. 'Enda, you have to believe in what you believe. Cera believed in the Old Faith. From her viewpoint, surely the Mother Goddess, Danu, will have understood this, as would Donn, the gatherer of souls. Anyway, Donn is said to gather the souls at the moment of death. I can see why you are concerned. According to those testaments that were agreed by Council, it is said that those who die in the faith of the Christian God are assured of eternal salvation, but they still have to go through a lengthy purification before they are allowed to enter an eternal life of happiness. They have to endure what they call purgatory. They take it from the Latin term *purgare,* an act of cleansing. But with Cera and her belief, even now the perishable body you will see being waked in the chapel is no more than a shadow. If you accept her belief, her soul is even now in Tech Duin, the House of Donn, on the island to the west, being made ready for the journey across the western ocean to the land of promise.'

Enda made a suspicious sniff that was almost a sob, and stood with his head bowed a moment. Then he raised it and tried to smile.

'Thank you, lady. I'd better have a word with Father Socra. Then I shall try to rest later.'

After he left, Fidelma turned to Eadulf.

'We have more important tasks on our hands, Eadulf. Let's find Crédh and see if she can enlighten us any more about this dagger.'

Fidelma and Eadulf were told that the Daughters of the Storm were meeting in the guards' barracks, and were surprised to find Gelgéis was also there. Fidelma had thought she would be resting, as Colgú had told them. She was seated before a table on which there were the remains of a largely uneaten meal. Crédh, the commander of the female warriors, had been seated with her, but at their entry she rose and stood to one side. They were aware of the other female warriors standing in an interested group.

Fidelma glanced at the abandoned meal, which had apparently been intended for the princess's breakfast. The only item that had been touched was the flagon of cider. Seeing it, Fidelma felt guilty because she realised that she and Eadulf had not eaten since they had been summoned by her brother in the middle of the first *cadar* of the day. They both had to eat and get some rest before the day was much older.

'What news?' Gelgéis demanded abruptly, as they entered.

Fidelma took a seat before her, as was her right, not only as the King's sister but as a *dálaigh* bearing the second highest degree, *anruth,* that the secular or ecclesiastical colleges could bestow.

'No positive news so far,' she admitted. 'I presume that you have heard about Dar Luga?'

'Colgú has told me,' the princess confirmed sadly. 'He said that she had taken poison. I conclude that she was the attacker.'

'We do not think so.'

'Then why did she take poison?'

'Whether she took it of her own accord or whether it was administered by some other agent is a matter yet to be decided.' Fidelma paused, then asked: 'What are you doing here? I thought my brother said that he would remain with you until this matter is resolved?'

'Colgú has business to attend to. He has left the fortress and so I came here to be with my own bodyguard.'

'Where has he gone?' Fidelma was surprised.

'He took two of his warriors with him and rode down into the township. He said he had business to contract about the upcoming fair. And to make sure a rider is sent to a place called Ráth na Drinne.'

'That's a short distance south of here, where Dar Luga's sister resides,' Fidelma explained. 'He has sent to inform her of Dar Luga's death.' She hesitated. 'Since I am here, I do need to ask you a few questions, as well as Crédh . . . just for clarification, you understand.'

136

Princess Gelgéis raised her right shoulder slightly and let it fall. 'I doubt I know anything that will be of help that you do not know already. I sleep soundly and the first I knew this morning was that Colgú was out of bed and shouting at the door of the bedchamber. Then he was urging me to wake. I know he was giving orders to Luan, the bodyguard, and then instructing Dar Luga. It was not until he hurried me down the stairway to his reception chamber that I realised Cera had been slain and that Dar Luga was supposed to look after her corpse while preparations were made.'

'I understand. But I just wanted to confirm how long Cera had been with you?'

'Do you ask about her time specifically in my service or in the service of the Daughters of the Storm?'

'As your bodyguard and as your attendant.'

'It is two years since she qualified from the school of martial arts. The custom is that the youngest member of the Daughters also serves as attendant in my immediate household.'

'And Cera was a girl from Durlus Éile?'

'She was the daughter of the local blacksmith, Gobán. Because of her father, she became familiar with the creation of swords and weapons and therefore she joined the academy of martial arts run by Bé Chuille . . .'

'Bé Chuille?' Fidelma was surprised. 'But she was a female warrior goddess of legend. I did not know of this academy.'

Gelgéis forced a tired smile. 'The one I speak of was no deity. She remains a female warrior of Osraige, but she took the name Bé Chuille in honour of the goddess who led the defence of this island when the evil witch warrior, Carmun, with her three foul sons, named Dubh, Dotha and Dian, tried to seize the five kingdoms.'

Fidelma nodded slowly as memory of some of the stories of her old mentor, Brother Conchobhar, came back to her.

'This academy still exists?'

'It does, but academies for female warriors are few in these times, due to the influences of the New Faith.'

'So Cera trained at this martial arts academy and graduated and joined your household?'

'Joining first the Daughters of the Storm, as Crédh will tell you.' She indicated the female warrior, who still stood silently. She was obviously uneasy at Fidelma's presence.

'This tradition of your house,' Fidelma went on, 'is it that the youngest of your company of guards also serves as a personal attendant to you, or is it an older tradition and it is in service to the ruling princess?'

'It is a tradition held for many generations. After my steward, Speláin, was killed when we went to visit my cousin, Abbot Dair-cell, of the Abbey of the Blessed Cáemgen, when I was made prisoner, I came to rely on Cera as my personal aide. I remain much in debt to you and Eadulf for tracking down my captors and releasing me.'

'As I recall,' Fidelma commented, ignoring her appreciation, 'Cera was not travelling with you on that occasion?'

'I did not need her services on that trip. After you rescued me, when eventually I returned to Durlus Éile, Cera continued in my service. I think you must have met her on your first visit to Durlus? That was during the harvest season of two years ago.'

'I remember our meeting well but I do not recall Cera,' Fidelma replied.

'It was certainly at that time that Enda met Cera,' Eadulf interposed unnecessarily. He had been standing silently while Fidelma and Gelgéis had their conversation.

At that moment Crédh seemed to give a snort of disgust and Fidelma turned to her with interest.

'You wish to add something?' Fidelma asked pointedly.

'Forgive me, I did not mean to interrupt,' the female warrior replied without sounding apologetic.

'Were you going to comment on the relationship between Cera and Enda?' Fidelma pressed.

Because Crédh was still standing where shadows obscured part of her features, Fidelma could not see the expression on the girl's face.

'It is not my place . . .' Crédh began.

'Step forward into the light,' Fidelma ordered as if she were giving a military command.

Crédh took a stiff step forward and halted. Then she frowned and looked at Princess Gelgéis as if seeking her intervention.

The princess merely waved her hand towards Fidelma.

'In this matter, Fidelma, as *dálaigh* and legal adviser to my husband, the King of Cashel, will ask questions and expect answers.'

'Although we have met before,' went on Fidelma, 'we have not spoken to any extent. As commander of the Daughters of the Storm, you would be Cera's senior?'

'Except where her duties as attendant to the princess were a priority.'

'Did the dual roles conflict?'

'Not at all.'

'The ceremonial duties of your warriors attending Gelgéis's wedding were impressive. I also understand that your company will be giving displays of your martial arts talents during the fair that is scheduled in a few days.'

'That is so,' affirmed Crédh.

'I have noticed the emblem of your troop of warriors is that of a crouching goose. It is crouching and hissing as if in defence or in attack. I believe it is called a *giraing*. Is that so?'

Crédh gave a slight affirmative motion with her head. 'It is an old emblem of the goddess of battles.'

Fidelma reached into her marsupium. She pulled out the small dagger and handed it to Crédh, hilt towards her.

'What can you tell me about this?'

Crédh turned it over in her hands with a thin smile.

'It is a personal dagger,' she replied. 'Most warriors carry one.'

'And most female warriors?'

'Of course. This is a small one, such as carried by female warriors.'

'It bears an emblem.'

Crédh looked at the brass handle carefully. 'It is the *saignén*, the lightning flash. It was the symbol of Macha, one of the triune war goddesses. You will know them . . . Macha, Badb and Mórrigna. It is the emblem.'

'The symbol, I am told, identifies the female troop.'

'I cannot recall what female warrior troop uses this emblem, but it is familiar.'

'A member of your troop would not carry such a dagger?' Fidelma pressed.

'Why would they? Our troop is proud of our symbol and would not carry the symbol of another troop. On admittance to the Daughters of the Storm, each warrior is presented with a dagger with the *giraing* emblem on it. When they leave or die, it is supposed to be returned to their commander so that it may be passed on.'

'Does that happen? Or do some women keep their daggers?'

Crédh smiled with cynicism. 'After a conflict not everyone is in a position to pass back their daggers.'

'I presume that you found Cera's dagger with her?' Gelgéis asked abruptly.

Fidelma looked at Eadulf, who shook his head.

'It should be returned,' Crédh added.

'We will ensure it is done,' Fidelma replied.

Eadulf, who had stood quietly for some time, decided to sum up in a resigned voice: 'Are you saying that we must find a group of female warriors who used this lighting flash symbol as their emblem and, even further, find a member who cannot account for a lost dagger? Even worse, a dagger bearing the symbol could have been passed on or inherited and lost. It short, you are saying that such identification is just about impossible.'

'As I said, I have a vague memory of having seen the emblem before, so that troop might still exist, or existed recently but no longer does so. However, I would say that this was not carried by a warrior of the five kingdoms.'

'Why not, if it carried the emblem of war goddesses of the five kingdoms before the coming of the New Faith?' Fidelma demanded.

'You will know that there are people in other lands that share the ancient goddesses with us. Like the Dál Riata beyond the sea.'

'That will be a long search,' Fidelma sighed.

'Perhaps your librarian could help,' Crédh said, suddenly surprising them.

'Brother Dáire?' Fidelma asked unnecessarily.

'He might know as he was talking about something similar a few days ago. He was talking about Ernmas, the mother of the war goddesses, the mother of Macha.'

At this point Princess Gelgéis was growing visibly tired and impatient.

'I have to say, Fidelma, that I am tired from lack of sleep. Are these questions to the commander of my bodyguard really necessary?'

Fidelma inclined her head. 'I, too, am tired, Gelgésis, as is Eadulf and others, including my brother. Tired minds do not function well the longer we are deprived of sleep, I agree. Yet I think you will know the role and authority of a *dálaigh*. In the case of unlawful killings it behoves no one who is called upon as a witness to pretend that they are not entitled to respond when asked to do so. Do you understand?'

Gelgéis's cheeks had brightened in embarrassment at Fidelma's sharp riposte. She was silent a moment but her shrug was enough to give consent for the questions to continue.

Fidelma turned back to Crédh. 'So let us return to your

intervention when we were speaking of Cera and her relationship with Enda. You seemed to wish to comment on that, but you said it was not your place?'

'There is nothing to add,' the girl replied, her expression wooden.

'I believe that I do not have to remind you about the powers of a *dálaigh*,' Fidelma emphasised again. 'We were speaking of the relationship between Cera and Enda.'

'I have nothing to say . . .'

'Except that you did not approve of such a relationship?'

'It is not my place . . .' she began again.

'Then I will take it that you did not approve?' Fidelma repeated sharply.

The girl blinked; her jaw tightened and she stared back with sullen belligerency.

Princess Gelgéis was frowning at her bodyguard.

'If you answer the questions then we may all get some rest,' she said. 'It has been a long night. Anyway, this is not the first occasion that I have heard that you disapproved of Cera's relationship with the commander of my husband's bodyguard. Was this a personal matter or was it one concerning your duties as commander of the Daughters of the Storm? If it was the latter, why have you not come forward to me to speak of it? You made no objection when it was initially planned that Cera and Enda would be matched together for the mock combats during the fair.'

The girl still hesitated.

'You do not do yourself any favours by prevarication,' Gelgéis intervened irritably.

After a moment more of hesitation the girl said softly: 'It was a personal matter.'

'Personal?' Gelgéis echoed in annoyance. 'Did you disapprove of the idea of Cera having a relationship with Enda or vice versa?'

'I did not want Cera to have a relationship with Enda.'

Gelgéis looked speculatively at the girl. 'Do you mean that you were in love with Enda? Were you jealous of her?'

There was a pause before Crédh said: 'It was Cera whom I wanted to be my friend and companion.'

There was a soft 'oh' from Gelgéis, as everyone knew what the girl meant.

Such relationships between people of the same sex were not forbidden by law but it was recognised as a cause for divorce in married couples by which it was used as a no-fault judgment. However, in those areas controlled by abbeys who were adopting the new rulings from Rome – devising 'Penitentials', as they were called – such relations were deemed forbidden and made a subject for punishment. The term *bhanacht*, for female sex, was declared a prescribed act. The only surprised reaction that registered was that the relationship seemed to have been hidden from Princess Gelgéis.

'So, Crédh, do we presume that the feelings that you felt for Cera were not reciprocated?' Fidelma prompted.

'They were not,' agreed the girl quietly.

'Did you accept that?' Fidelma asked, hearing the resentment in her tone.

'I am not sure that I understand.'

'I am presuming that you made your feelings clear to Cera at some point and that she rejected you. Did you accept that?'

The girl's jaw tightened. 'I had to accept her rejection. What else am I supposed to do when such emotions overwhelm you?'

'A Roman, Maccius Plautus, declared that love is rich with both honey and venom. When love is gone, the venom remains. Rejection of love has been known to be a reason for murder.' Fidelma was serious. 'Did you kill Cera?'

chapter ten

'Did I kill Cera?' Crédh's eyes widened in shock at the question. 'How can you kill the one you love? That is impossible. It is not logical.'

Fidelma smiled sadly. 'It is the oldest reason for murder. Love is a disease that blankets us with such emotions that one can feel that one is drowning. Such suffocation can come upon one that the rejected lover feels they must strike out to breathe freely. But doing so will suddenly alter the world around them. Their world will turn into a vision of madness. Spectres of fear and hate are conjured to add to the darkness that will surround them.'

Eadulf was regarding Fidelma with astonishment. He knew that Fidelma had been betrayed and rejected by her first love, a young warrior named Cian. She was then a young student attending Brehon Morann's law school. Cian was a self-centred personality, firmly believing that it was his right to be admired, praised and served by those he befriended. When he had abandoned her for another, Fidelma found the experience devastating. That had made her refuse further close relationships, being sceptical of even developing a closer relationship with Eadulf, although not denying the attraction she felt towards him. Then there came her meeting with her former lover, Cian, on the pilgrimage voyage. In that meeting she had recognised Cian for the narcissist he was and finally felt able to accept Eadulf's love as genuine.

'Do you think that I would kill her?' Crédh almost shouted. 'Kill the very person I was in love with?'

'It has been known,' Fidelma replied quietly, without emotion. 'Where there is love, there is always grief. When did you make your feelings known to her?'

The girl's changing expressions showed her emotions as she stood trying to calm them.

'Weeks ago,' Crédh finally admitted in a slow, considered tone. 'A few days before our party set out to come here for the marriage of Princess Gelgéis. She told me then that it was impossible for her to reciprocate my feelings. Then, some weeks after we arrived here, I noticed her much in the company of Enda.'

'Did you question her about her intentions?'

'I did.'

'And what was Cera's response?'

'She told me that she was in love with Enda and they hoped to be married. She went further and said she could only share pity for me and could never indulge in *féin-truailliú*.'

Eadulf understood the term as literally 'self-pollution', but realised it meant love for the same sex.

'So Cera rejected your love and, you say, you accepted the rejection? It did not make you incensed? There was no sense of rage; no seeking revenge on the person who rejected your love?'

The girl was standing stiffly as if at attention. 'All I can say is that it was not so. Such a production of feeling would mean the opposite to loving someone.'

'That is a good philosophy. But it is said that there is only a fine border between love and hatred. The two concepts are often confused.'

'I have also heard it said,' Crédh agreed indifferently.

'I return to the question,' pressed Fidelma. 'Did you accept Cera's rejection of your declaration totally?'

'My answer would depend on what you mean by acceptance,' countered the girl. 'I did not kill her.'

Fidelma's eyes widened a little as she realised Crédh had a use of language that was well developed.

'You must have had some emotion, some anger, and some resentment?'

'If you imply that I accepted it in a way that I should have turned off all my emotions at that stage, that would have been impossible. I think you would admit that. Such emotions, once emerging, cannot be blown out like a puff of breath blows out a candle. But I did not enter into madness and kill her. I accepted there was nothing further I could do at that time.'

'I bear in mind what Catullus said.' Fidelma examined the girl thoughtfully. 'He loved and hated, and did not understand why he was tormented at accepting that both were valid at the same time. Were you tormented, Crédh?'

'I loved but did not hate,' replied the girl firmly. 'I accept that I am also tormented in that someone has killed the object of my love.'

Princess Gelgéis was shaking her head in bewilderment. 'I do not understand why you are dwelling on Crédh's private emotions, Fidelma. Surely you should be investigating who is responsible for this attack?'

'That is precisely what I am doing,' Fidelma replied coldly. 'With respect, Gelgéis, in trying to find a motive for the attack on Cera I must ask questions such as these.'

Gelgéis raised her shoulders in resignation. 'I suppose you have to do what your training tells you to.'

'Then I have to ask you, over the years that Cera served you, have you never been disappointed in her service? Never had any criticism? Never any suspicion that she was involved in any matters that were not in your interests?'

'Easy enough to answer that. I never was dissatisfied or critical of her at any time.'

'So you can offer no ideas as to why Cera was killed or, for that matter, why Dar Luga was poisoned?'

'Your brother believes that he and I were the targets of the break-in to his sanctuary,' Gelgéis declared. 'So far I have seen no reason to doubt him.'

'If the intention was to attack my brother and you, how were you both not roused while Cera, in her bedroom on the other side of the passage, was? If Cera was roused and came from her room into the bathroom room next to you and was attacked there, then why did she not raise an alarm? The only sound that woke Colgú must have been when Cera's body fell. How had the killer been so fleet that when Colgú went into that room, the killer had already exited, locking the door behind him and vanished? It is difficult to understand.'

'I understand your problems, Fidelma. There is little I can do to help.'

Fidelma turned back to Crédh. 'I just want to confirm a few other points. Your company, the Daughters of the Storm, came to Cashel specifically as a ceremonial bodyguard to Princess Gelgéis?'

The girl raised her head a little and made a noise like a snort of disgust. 'There is nothing ceremonial about our warriors. We train hard and can fight even harder. We have seen male warriors flee from our blood-dripping weapons. I am surprised that you do not know our history. The son of the founder of the royal family, Oengus Osrithie of Osraige – the son called Birn Buadach, the victorious – became known for the victory of his battalion of women warriors. Through their victories he was placed as ruler of Osraige. Even Tuaim Snámha has to admit that his ancestors descend directly from him.'

'Are you saying that the Daughters of the Storm have to take their oath of allegiances to Tuaim Snámha of Osraige?' Fidelma asked thoughtfully. 'Your oath of loyalty would be taken to him?'

'Tuaim Snámha gave up the tradition of female warriors in his retinue just as many other kings and rulers have done throughout the five kingdoms,' Crédh replied. 'There are so few female warrior groups now. Thankfully, the Princess of Durlus Éile maintains the tradition of a small female warrior group – the Daughters of the Storm – who have often appeared at the annual games and exhibit their dexterity in arms to show they are the equal to their male comrades. We also enter the archery contests and javelin throwing, and are better horse riders than most males who demonstrate against us.'

'Of course,' Fidelma acknowledged. 'And that is what you were going to be engaged in at the forthcoming celebration fair here. I remember your group taking part in the competitions of the Aenach Life, the great fair presided over by the High King, years ago. That was the last time I recall the female warriors from the Royal Branch taking part. But those times are dying. I used to watch the chariot races when I was young, and now chariots are no longer used as machines of war, and even the few used for exhibitions seem to have disappeared as well.'

'Since I became commander of this troop, these girls accompany me not just for ceremonial duties and exhibitions of martial powers. They have proved their worth in several conflicts, by which I mean as mercenary warriors, hired out for military service, usually in the petty conflicts in the north-west kingdoms. Now it seems as if their martial powers are needed.'

She added the latter sentence with an emphasis that Fidelma was not sure was irony or concern.

'I can assure you that if it were just a matter of martial powers that are needed, then the Nasc Niadh – our own Warriors of the Golden Collar – are not lacking. However, I have to point out that no military power in the five kingdoms is a protection against a single, motivated assassin. If Colgú and Gelgéis were the intended victims, then we must all be vigilant. If you will forgive us, we will continue with our investigations.'

Fidelma and Eadulf left the warriors' quarters and were crossing the courtyards towards their own apartments when Eadulf paused. He saw the doors of the royal residence were open. There was no one on guard, but from the door a woman was struggling to exit with her arms around a bundle wrapped in a linen cloth. She was tall and dressed in black, even to her headdress of the type often affected by devout religieuse. Eadulf called Fidelma's attention to her.

'I don't recognise her,' he muttered.

Fidelma glanced across and then, without responding, turned and walked towards the woman. Eadulf followed.

The woman seemed taller from a distance than she appeared when they came close to her. Only her pale face gave relief from the blackness of her covering. This blackness of dress strangely accented her not unattractive features. They were enhanced by bright, pale eyes. Her tallness and erect posture gave the impression that she was young and fit. Her features seemed somewhat familiar to Fidelma and she realised that she had seen her once or twice around the chapel. She recognised that this must be one of the religieuse helpers to Father Socra.

'Are you Sister Sárait?' Fidelma asked, recalling the name that the new chaplain had given them.

The woman had halted on the steps of the residence when she saw them approaching.

'I am assisting Father Socra,' answered the woman, perhaps a little too defensively. Now, close up, Fidelma realised the religieuse had the face of an older woman; perhaps a year or two younger than Fidelma was herself. The religieuse continued: 'I was sent to collect some personal belongings, some clothing, from the room of the girl, Cera; some clothing suitable for the dressing of the corpse.'

'Do you need assistance?' Eadulf volunteered.

Sister Sárait turned her head to indicate a young warrior, Cano, who had emerged behind her.

'This warrior helped me choose the items from her room.'

'Sister Sárait wanted clothes to dress the corpse,' the youthful warrior explained in a defensive tone. 'She is new to the fortress and I saw her coming from the *scriptorium* looking lost. She had been asked by Father Socra to pick up the clothes. It would not be seemly to bury the poor girl in the bloodstained clothes she was wearing when . . . when . . . Anyway, I had assumed that it would be all right.'

As Fidelma recalled, Cano was actually the youngest recruit to the *lucht-tighe*, the household guard. It seemed an apt name for the youth, as it meant 'the wolf cub'. It also suited his personality: eager to please, gazing up at his superiors and almost tensely waiting for his orders. Fidelma felt that she was nearly obliged to throw him a bone to scamper after. She smiled at the youth before turning back to the religieuse.

'That's all right, Sister Sárait,' Fidelma assured her. She examined the woman with a smile of reassurance. 'We have not met you officially.'

'I realise who you are, lady, now,' Sister Sárait replied. 'Also, I know of Eadulf, the Saxon, your husband.'

Eadulf made a tired grimace.

'Eadulf the Angle,' he corrected softly. 'I come from the kingdom of the East Angles, where I was a *gerefa,* an hereditary magistrate, before I joined the religious.'

The woman let a perplexed expression cross her features, not recognising the terms.

'Do not worry,' Eadulf assured her before she asked the inevitable question. 'I know your language has no separate word for an Angle and so it is my fate to be a Sasanaigh, a Saxon, in this country.'

'Let us formally welcome you to Cashel,' Fidelma intervened with a smile. 'We must meet later so that you may be welcomed properly to the fortress. In my brother's fortress, we all regard ourselves as kin.'

'Thank you, lady.'

It was Eadulf who delayed them as Fidelma was about to leave. 'We were told by Father Socra that you came with him from Sléibhte?'

'That is so.' There was some hesitancy in her reply.

'It must have been a tiring journey. I have been that way myself. I know it fairly well.'

'Not exactly. Anyway, Father Socra's party came by way of the river, the Bhearú, from the place of the quadruple lochs, and then south to the abbey of Cainneach,' Sister Sárait replied. 'It was only from Cainneach that we had to take to the roads. But the journey was not so exhausting.'

'Sometimes the River Bhearú can be dangerous,' Eadulf observed. 'I do not mean the flow of the waters and occasional rapids but the fact that the east bank is in Laigin.'

The woman's expression seemed to tighten.

'No harm should come to members of the Faith going about God's business,' she replied piously.

'I suppose living on the border between Osraige and Laigin, one becomes used to many problems. Raids and such like.'

Sister Sárait sniffed in a dismissive gesture. 'My home is in Iar-muma, West Muman. Borders are usually in people's minds, or in their ambitions. Those who live on a border are the same people whichever side they are on.'

'But they can be manipulated by kings who want to extend their powers,' Eadulf observed with a smile.

The woman was standing nervously, clutching the bundle almost defensively across the front of her body.

'You must forgive Eadulf,' Fidelma interrupted with a disapproving look at him. 'It is too early to discuss politics and philosophy. Do you have all you need, Sister?'

'Oh, yes, this young warrior was most helpful,' the woman replied. 'So was the other one.'

'The other one?' Fidelma was perplexed.

The youthful Cano came to her aid. 'Enda is still inside, lady. He was most helpful in choosing the clothing that the poor girl, Cera, should be clothed in for the watching ceremony.'

Fidelma looked in puzzlement at him. 'I thought he would be in the chapel or, at least, resting. He has been up all night. Are you saying he returned here and went up to the sanctuary to sort clothes?'

The question was superfluous as it had already been answered.

'He is inside, lady,' repeated Cano.

Fidelma turned to the religieuse. 'Then you should be on your way to the chapel. We will doubtless speak later to welcome you properly. As I said, we consider this fortress peopled with family and we like to know all who serve here, especially those who serve in the chapel.'

For a moment she stood watching Sister Sárait carrying her bundle towards the chapel. Then she turned back to the nervous young warrior, Cano. 'Enda is inside, you say?'

'He is, lady. He looks quite exhausted, though.'

At other times the comment would have drawn forth a rebuke. Opinions volunteered about their superiors by youthful guards were considered a breach of convention. Instead, Fidelma smiled at the boy and repeated: 'Your commander has been up all night. So have we.'

Cano blushed as he realised there was a gentle rebuke there. He hesitated and then took his station by the main door of the royal house.

Fidelma turned to Eadulf. 'I think it time we had some food and a rest as the day moves quickly on.'

They turned and walked to the entrance of their own apartments. As they entered, old Muirgen came forward with a worried look on her features. They could hear their young son, Alchú, playing in an adjacent room.

'My man brought me the news, lady. I am distressed to hear of Dar Luga. She was a great support for me when you brought me here as nurse to your son.'

'She was a support to many,' Fidelma agreed in a low tone.

'Alchú loved her. He has not been told the tragic news, lady.'

'He will also have missed his morning ride,' Eadulf pointed out.

'Nessan could lead him around on his pony for a bit,' the old nurse offered. Nessan was Muirgen's husband and now chief swineherd at the fortress.

'Yes; better than nothing,' Fidelma agreed. 'We are both exhausted after this night's tragedies. Meanwhile, we want something to break our fast and then we must rest for a while. Some fruit and barley cakes will do, and warm goat's milk.'

'Cider for me, otherwise the same,' Eadulf added, stifling a yawn, before turning into their main room.

Fidelma hesitated and seemed about to call after him but then shrugged and turned into the other room in which she could hear the sound of her son playing. She played with the boy while Muirgen went to fetch her husband to arrange for him to take the boy for some exercise. When Fidelma returned to join Eadulf, she found he had dozed off in his chair. She did not disturb him until Muirgen returned with a tray of food and their drinks. Eadulf came awake reluctantly, coughed and then reached out for his cider, taking a deep swallow or two.

As they ate, there was an unusual silence between them. It was Eadulf who became aware that Fidelma was frowning as she nibbled at an oatcake. Then she put it aside, took a sip of her goat's milk, before setting it down. Her deliberate movements alerted him to the quizzical expression on her face.

'Well?' he found himself saying defensively. 'You have that critical expression on your face.'

'I am worried, Eadulf,' she said quietly. 'You seemed to be in conflict with my brother earlier this morning. You have been displaying a shortness of temper that is unlike you. You will recall that I said we would talk about it later. I think the time is now. What upset you when my brother was speaking?'

Eadulf was quiet for a few months and then he heaved an almost languid sigh.

'Memories,' he said shortly. 'Perhaps they are a way of realising one is becoming older and wiser, but also they bring clouds of blackness.'

'I believe that you will need to explain that.'

Eadulf shifted uncomfortably in his seat.

'When one is young, life is full of excitement. One is keen to travel to other places and meet other people than those one grew up with. One has a hunger to explore; to see other places; to ask questions and to gather knowledge. Born and raised in one place, one does not know enough about life or the realities of what it means to turn one's back on the place where one grew up, where one was educated; to turn one's back on one's culture; to find oneself embracing new philosophies and entering into a society where the language is not one's own. One can adapt to all that when one is young. As a youth, one can accept and judge the new world.'

Fidelma had not heard Eadulf talking in this manner before, nor the formal use of the pronoun and proform to refer to people in general.

'You are starting to question these matters now?' she asked, puzzled.

'I have begun to feel at times . . . what is the term you sometimes say for a foreigner? A *murchoirthe* – one who is thrown on a strange shore by the sea?'

'Something has brought this thought into your mind. What was it? Was it when my brother spoke of your ability to conduct the medical examinations and the restrictions set by law?'

Eadulf hesitated and then nodded briefly. 'I suppose that was part of it. It reawakened memories and the realisation that I am, indeed, a "grey wolf", as Luan put it; an alien here without honour price and rights, contributing little or nothing.'

Fidelma made an angry sound, almost like a sharp bark. 'Contributing little or nothing to society? Who has said this thing? Luan?'

'He spoke in anger. It doesn't matter. Few would say it to my face although it is in their thoughts. It is what I believe others see me as.'

'Do you feel it is what I think?' she demanded.

'It is not what you express,' he replied firmly. 'It is what is stated in your *Lánamnas*, the laws of marriage. Those laws are clear. I am considered to have married in the third degree, being a man who cannot even provide for my wife.'

'That is from the *Bregta Crólige*.' She could not help correcting him. 'It is only stated as a generality.'

Eadulf realised that once he had started, he had to finish.

'Fidelma, one of the happiest periods was when we lived as man and wife under the simple proposition recognised by your law. We lived together for a year and a day without sacrament to see how life treated us. I was your *fer comtha* and you were my *ben chorrthach*. Perhaps it was a bad day when we married in more formal terms – as I was without an estate in a foreign land.'

'Did not old Brother Conchobhar tell you that if you marry a woman from the glens then you marry the whole glen?' Fidelma reflected. 'I am a *ban chomarbae* – a female heir with a life tied up in an interest in my father's land and able to pass that on with a minimum amount of wealth to my son – to our son. Would that be so in your country among the Angles?'

Eadulf shook his head and muttered: 'But your law says that I live on sufferance.'

'You do not,' Fidelma was growing ill tempered. 'My brother took you into our family as a *fine thacair*, that is, one adopted under the law. In adopting you, my brother extended to you the rights of the protection of this kingdom and his family. So not just by marriage have you become my kin, but with Colgú standing in lieu of my father, he has extended to you half of what would be my dowry. That very sum makes you rich and a landed noble of this kingdom. You are under the protection of my brother, the King, and his family. And, over the years you have worked with me, you have earned fees due to one who assists a *dálaigh*. So I remind you that you have built up an investment in the land that you share with me. Now, Eadulf, by your adoption, you stand as a man of full status, and no one has the right to consider you a non-person, without rights. You are no foreigner, or an outsider.'

Eadulf found he could not answer her incisive legal knowledge as she spelt out his legal position.

'Sometimes I do not feel that I am as you describe me. I have no scribe to recite a praise poem before me . . . no tradition of having my lineage declared or family praised for their pedigree.'

Fidelma shook her head sadly. 'Would you want it to be so? It is a tradition here that I often think is overrated. Sometimes I think that the only difference between people of status and no status is that those of status are better thieves and killers than those of no status. That was how status was achieved among the tribes in ancient times.'

'You do not have to appease me, Fidelma.'

'Nor would I. You are an hereditary *gerefa* of your people, which I am informed is one of rank, not a high rank but one who equates with our "cow lord" or yeoman farmer. Such a man can also be a magistrate; a law giver. If you are so concerned with the lack of your family status, as opposed to the family in which you have been adopted here, then we must send ambassadors to your people in the kingdom of the East Angles, who will compile your ancestry, for no people are without ancestors, whether they be memorable dynasties or not. More importantly, it is not who they were that matters but who you are.'

'It is not what I see here,' contradicted Eadulf. 'Your people always keep your genealogies listed so carefully and they go back almost to the time beyond time. Our king lists have only been orally recited until recently. With the coming of literacy, it is the Angles who have been the first to set down their king lists. Not that it is of use to me.'

Fidelma sat patiently, a troubled look on her face.

'You are prevaricating, Eadulf,' she said softly. 'You are saying that you feel a foreigner here. How else am I to interpret that except that, in spite of the years you have been with me, that you are the father to our son, and that I love you, that has obviously not been enough to make you content to be with us . . . or to be with me?'

'That is not what I am saying,' Eadulf said thoughtfully, as if he were puzzled at the very conclusion.

'Then how else can I judge it?'

There was a continuing silence between them as Eadulf sat frowning, wrestling with her words and his feelings. He finally gave an exasperated sigh.

'I am often clumsy at expressing concepts in words, especially when they are not in my own language. Often the nuances are lost to me; the images and distinctions, even the tones of the emphasis make me realise I am floundering in a flow of ill-chosen expression that drowns the real meaning.'

'Explain, then, as best you can,' she invited.

'Very well. First of all, I must impress that I care so much for you that without you I am but a ghost walking. Does this word "love" imply the depth of feeling? There are words in your language that I am not sure would be better expressive of my emotions. If I am not using the right one to say that I feel the right level of love and friendship, I am sorry. I feel friendship, the affection, the devotion, the ardour of passion, the continuing sense of happiness and delight and pleasure at being in your company. Does any of it signify that one likes another to such a depth that they see them as one person? I do not know. I am just the prisoner of words. Every word I list can be misinterpreted. It is the feeling that passes between one another that is important. Not the words.'

Fidelma was sitting with a faint smile at the corner of her mouth. There was something remote and yet sad about the expression.

'For someone who does not know how best to express themselves, you have a strong vocabulary, Eadulf. So if there are no problems with the emotions that bind us together, no weakening of our commitment to one another, what makes you feel so alienated from me?'

Eadulf shrugged as if in a state of helplessness. 'Not from you,' he protested. 'I find it difficult to analyse it. Now and then a word, an expression, sets off a question in my mind. I find myself asking what I am doing here. Why do I feel so alien? When I examine myself logically, I find that it has not been anything that you say or do. I love you as much as I ever did. It is nothing your brother and many others here have said, or in how they have behaved towards me, that have prompted these black thoughts.'

'Black thoughts? Such as?'

'I have recently had bad dreams,' Eadulf confessed.

'It is true that you have woken me several times in the night with your restlessness. Can you remember what these dreams were about or what feeling they left you with?'

'In the dreams I was back in my youth. We were talking about the king lists of my own people. I was born when Anna was King of the East Angles. He was killed when I was fifteen. That was during the invasion of Penda's Mercian hordes. It was a time of vicious conflict. When, two years afterwards, our next king, Athelhere, led our people to defend us against Penda and his Mercians, who continually tried to annex us, I witnessed others being slaughtered. My own father was one of them. That was when I became the hereditary *gerefa* of Seaxmund's Ham.'

'That is something I could never understand – how one could inherit a title or position from one's father.'

'That is the way of my people. The eldest male always inherits. By the time I became *gerefa*, as you know, our kingdom was changing from the worship of Woden to the teachings about Christ,' went on Eadulf. 'I, myself, was caught up in this, being a convert of three scholars from this land – Fursa, Foillin and Ultan. They were from Connacht and they started to convert us Angles to the New Faith. Our king gave them an old deserted fortress at Cnobheresburg as an abbey. I was taught by these missionaries about the New Faith, and it opened such knowledge for me. That is why I first came to this land: to study at the abbey of Tuaim Drecain and started to learn about the healing arts. Before I graduated from there I decided to travel to Rome where I heard about the changes to the Faith that the scholars there were making. That was how I returned to my homeland and went to Streoneshalh to attend the great debate at the great white abbey of the Blessed Hilda.'

'I remember well, Eadulf,' Fidelma assured him. 'The scholars of the new Roman ways arguing against those from this kingdom and their students; arguing the basics of the original teachings against the amendments Rome was now adopting. And, of course, that is where we met. But you mention bad dreams? What dreams now?'

'I dreamt of my father being slaughtered during the great battle in Winwaed. I dreamt of my mother giving up all ambition for life after my father was killed. My dream seemed to show that these things in my life were confused and that I would see my father and mother combined in some strange way, grieving and lamenting over a grave, and it was my grave. I stood beyond the grave, trying to comfort them, but they did not hear me. Nothing I could do would prevent them lamenting. I felt they were grieving that I had turned from the gods – from Woden, from Thunor, from Freja and, above all, from my own people. I had pride. Was I not a descendent of Uffa? Yet instead of helping my people with my new-found knowledge, I had left them and gone in search of more knowledge.'

He paused in thought. Fidelma said nothing, waiting until he was ready to continue.

'I dreamt of the countryside around Seaxmund's Ham. Seax-mund was the chieftain that drove out the Britons so that the Anglians of the east could settle there. Seaxmund built the town and named it after himself. It was where I was born and raised; raised among the sun-baked fields with our sheep and pigs. It was where I was raised in the low flat country and where I used to swim and also fish in the gushing river. I remember my father once tell-ing me that when Seaxmund took the land from the Britons he could not think what to rename the river, so they retained the name the Britons gave it and hence it was known as Fram. My father was told by a Briton whom he owned as a slave that it meant the brisk river. It was well named as I once had a little boat and sailed it all the way down that river to where it finally could empty into the great sea.'

Fidelma listened patiently as Eadulf poured out his account almost without taking breath. He had never been so loquacious in all the years they had been together. She chose a moment when he paused.

'What you are telling me, Eadulf, is that you are experiencing a grief for your homeland, specifically for the village where you were born and raised. The memories that you have of where you grew up have emerged to cause grief. You grieve not from bad memories but from good memories; from lack of hearing your lan-guage regularly and being among your people. It weighs on you. Indeed, it vexes you.'

Eadulf thought for a moment before his shoulders slumped in resignation.

'I wish old Brother Conchobhar were still with us,' Fidelma

sighed. 'He had an uncanny knowledge of how to interpret such dream visions, understanding what they meant because often the meaning was something other than was obvious.'

'Although I did not know him as well as you, Fidelma, I also miss him and his wisdom,' Eadulf agreed.

'Well, I have a little knowledge of things that he said. I think we would agree that something is stirring your memories of your home and people. When was the last time you were among them?'

'It was the time that you were with me,' Eadulf replied. 'You remember, after we were shipwrecked on the coast of Dyfed? That was when we decided that we would join as soul mates for a year and a day under the terms allowed in your wedding traditions before we might formally marry.'

'That was about six years ago,' Fidelma reminded him. 'I remember it well.'

'We travelled to Aldred's Abbey in answer to a message asking for help from my friend Brother Botulf.' Eadulf felt excited at the memory. 'The abbey was not far south from my village.'

'I remember,' Fidelma smiled tightly. 'Aldred's Abbey stood on the shore of a great sea. Such a sea I never saw: a bleak, cold, restless ocean.'

Both fell silent for a while, remembering being in that place together.

Suddenly Fidelma stood up and took a small hand bell from a table and rang it. She stood, head to one side, listening to the echoing notes. They had barely faded when the door opened and Muirgen appeared.

'*Corma.*' Fidelma ordered the strong, distilled liquor. '*Corma* for both of us, and more oatcakes.'

Muirgen looked surprised.

'But, lady, you have not rested yet.'

'The *corma* will help us rest,' Fidelma replied confidently.

When Muirgen had gone to conduct her mission, Fidelma went

back to her seat, slumped down and glanced at the still-troubled Eadulf.

'I have been selfish, I think,' she suddenly announced.

Eadulf stirred and turned a puzzled face to her. 'Why you? What have my dreams and irritableness to do with your being selfish?'

'Sometimes I fail to remember that you are in an alien land, existing in a culture and in a language that is not yours, and that it is perhaps unnatural to cut yourself off entirely from the place where one had one's birth and education, and from family, however distant that family now is.'

'Well, it was the choice I made,' Eadulf said. 'I admit that I should not have shown my irritation earlier.'

'I have a suggestion,' Fidelma went on. 'I should have thought of it sooner.'

'Which is?'

'Once we have identified the perpetrator of these deaths and brought whomever it is to justice, then we should talk again. You will be honest with me about your thoughts, and if you still feel the same then as you do now, there is a solution.'

'A solution?' Eadulf's perplexity increased.

'What we did six years ago, we can do now.'

'Six years . . . you mean the time when we visited my home? Visited Seaxmund's Ham?'

Fidelma smiled. 'Seaxmund's Ham in the land of the South Folk in the kingdom of the East Angles,' she said, mimicking the way Eadulf would introduce himself.

Eadulf was shaking his head. 'But under what pretext? You have obligations to your brother, the King.'

'The Archbishop of Canterbury in the kingdom of Kent, what used to be the land of the Cantii, is Theodore of Tarsus, a Greek whom I met in Rome . . .'

'I remember him also, not only from our days in Rome but

when we passed through the town of the Cantii on our way to the kingdom of the East Angles. What has he to do with what we speak of?'

'Theodore, being a Greek, is not as insular as some of your countrymen,' Fidelma pointed out. 'Since replacing Wighard, whose murder we solved in Rome, he has been consecrated in Canterbury and now encourages instruction in Greek and Latin. He also encourages astronomy, music, literature . . . This he does in spite of the narrow views of many of your countrymen. You remember the fanatic Wilfrid at Streoneshalh, who demanded everyone pay obedience to Rome? He argued not just obedience in Oswy's kingdom but, because Rome has appointed Canterbury as its principal church among the Anglo-Saxon, he now insists that all the churches in these islands must make obeisance to it.'

Eadulf shrugged. 'I know. That idea has been rejected by the Britons, and even those in Dál Riata and other kingdoms. Sadly, some Romans of the New Faith continue the idea of the old empire in another form. Wilfrid is happy with that concept.'

'Exactly so. Wilfrid is now persuading Theodore to find out which of our religious centres, our abbeys, would support a primacy in the five kingdoms, which would then recognise Canterbury as the principal church. As you know, there are several abbeys claiming they should be the primacy. The leading ones are Cill Dara, Ard Macha and Imleach. We could use this as an excuse for our trip by volunteering to take letters from Abbot Cuán, setting forth Imleach's case that the abbey is older than Canterbury or any other centre, and present it to Theodore. That gives us the excuse to make the voyage and continue on to Seaxmund's place, or Ham, as you call it; to go to your home town.'

'It is a journey that will take some thinking about.'

They were interrupted by Muirgen returning with the *corma* and glasses.

'A toast to that journey,' Fidelma raised her glass.

Eadulf seemed suddenly overcome with a strange reluctance to contemplate the journey.

'Well, it might take some time to get over the first hurdle,' he said.

'The first hurdle?' Fidelma queried.

'Resolving the murders of Cera and Dar Luga.'

Fidelma flushed. For a moment or so she had almost forgotten them while thinking of how best to resolve Eadulf's problem and contemplating the possibility of returning to his homeland.

CHAPTER ELEVEN

The summer sun was still bright but there were a few clusters of white cloud when Fidelma rose from her brief rest. During what was called the middle month, she had been used to rising in the daylight. Now she estimated that they had slept for a quarter of a *cadar* and thus it was well into the third *cadar* of the day. She decided to let Eadulf continue to lie abed while she went for her wash. Muirgen had already anticipated her needs. The toiletries had been prepared and, when she had washed and dressed, she went to confirm with Muirgen that all was well. Apparently, Nessan, Muirgen's husband, had taken young Alchú with him earlier while he attended the sheep in the northern pastures below the fortress.

Eadulf was only beginning to stir when she left their apartment to make her way into the courtyard. As she did so, a noise at the main gate caused her to turn to see who was entering. She recognised Gormán, the son of her old friend Della, and with whom she and Eadulf had shared so many adventures.

She went across to the gates and waited until he had dismounted and the stable boy had taken care of his horse.

They greeted one another with troubled expressions.

'Dar Luga's death has caused great sorrow for my mother,' Gormán opened. 'She cannot believe that anyone would wish Dar

Luga harm. But to poison her is beyond comprehension. Is there further news?'

'None as yet,' Fidelma replied. 'I am hoping to see your mother, Della, later today but, as you can imagine, this might be difficult. I presume she will be at the rituals this evening or tomorrow.'

'My mother sent for Lassar, Dar Luga's sister. They will come to the fortress as soon as she arrives. Lassar will stay with us until the rituals are over. My wife, Aibell, will join them.'

They began walking slowly across the courtyard to the royal residence together.

'Resolving this problem might be a slow process, Gormán. There are no surviving eyewitnesses,' she told him. 'We are not even sure how the killer could have entered the sanctuary where it happened.'

'We have been in tougher situations,' replied Gormán confidently. 'Is friend Eadulf well? I presume he is working with you?'

'He is resting as we were both up half the night. He will doubtless join us shortly. Has my brother spoken to you of what he now expects?'

'He rode down to my mother's farmstead earlier this morning to give us the news. He has said that he would like me to take command of the local *catha* and deploy the battalion in case of trouble during the days of the fair.' He hesitated. 'He whispered to me that even Dar Luga was a suspect. Thankfully, my mother did not hear that for she would have left the King in no doubt of her opinion. Colgú also felt you had some reservations about Enda's involvement. Enda was my trusted second in command for a long time when I was in command of the Golden Collar.'

Fidelma grimaced. 'Colgú left the fortress before I had finished my questioning of Enda. He was going to marry Cera, the girl who was killed. His behaviour prompted me to clarify that he was involved emotionally. However, there is no slight on Enda that I questioned him, and I have confirmed he remains in command of the household guard.'

Gormán whistled softly. 'That is good, but tough for him, being in love with the victim.'

Gormán had no suspicion of Enda, for he had known the young warrior well and over many years.

'I am in charge of the investigation and will remain so even when my brother's Chief Brehon returns. The situation demands it be so,' Fidelma said.

'Brehon Fíthel is still absent?' Gormán asked.

'He is expected to arrive soon, as are Abbot Cuán and Prince Finguine.'

'My mother has been doing some baking as if a great famine is about to descend on us. Aibell has been helping her. They will have some sort of stall at the fair. I wonder if we are to have more unrest stirred up by Fianamail of Laigin or the dissidents in Osraige?'

'At the moment, your guess is as good as any,' Fidelma replied. 'But what better time and place to try to stir up trouble than during the celebrations of the marriage of Princess Gelgéis to my brother? You and your warriors will safeguard the township in case the event inspires unruly conduct among those coming to the township and there needs to be intervention to calm the situation. To be honest, I thought it might be better to advise Colgú to cancel the fair if it presents a security risk.'

Gormán gave her an almost sympathetic smile but shook his head.

'Believe me, lady, that would cause even greater problems. Apart from the ambitions of Laigin and dissidents in Osraige, there is also Prince Cummasach of the Déisi, who has never been happy paying tribute to Cashel. As we know, he just waits for the right opportunity. No, I agree with the King that the fair must go ahead. People have already started to arrive for it: various artisans and entertainers, and the farmers bringing livestock. The horse traders are already finding encampments. Don't worry, I am sure that I can deploy the battalion in such a way that, if there is trouble brewing, it can be dealt with before it becomes too serious.'

They halted outside the main doors of the residence. Fidelma regarded him with serious resignation.

'I hope that it won't be an idle boast, Gormán. You have been with Eadulf and me enough times to know that my brother faces danger from ambitious members of his family as much as from those gathered on the borders. Why, even within days of his succession as King, following the death of Cathal from the pestilence, he had to lead his warriors and allies into battle to assert his position.'

'I served him at Cnoc Áine,' Gormán reminded her softly. 'The Uí Fidgente and their allies tried to overthrow him. Now they are the best of friends with us.'

'Thanks to our negotiations with Prince Donennach, the Uí Fidgente are no longer a threat.'

'Perhaps so. But there are others, and threats from outside continue. Fianamail, the King of Laigin, will do anything to assert control over Osraige and weaken us.'

'Perhaps you are right,' Fidelma said reluctantly, 'the fair must go ahead. It would increase Fianamail's inflated sense of self-esteem if he thought that we, in Cashel, are so concerned about him as to even think of cancelling . . .'

'Nothing should get back to him about our concerns,' Gormán agreed. 'The plans for the security at the fair must remain secret.'

They had conducted the conversation in the courtyard outside the main doors of the royal resident. The young warrior, Cano, had been replaced, and Fidelma and Gormán were just turning to enter when the tall, dark figure of Síonna, the physician, appeared from the door of the library. She paused when she saw them, then turned abruptly and hurried across to the deserted apothecary of the late Brother Conchobhar. Gormán had hesitated as if he would greet the physician but she did not slacken her pace nor glance back. Fidelma had noticed with interest the recognition that seemed to light in Gormán's eyes before it quickly died.

'You know her?' she asked.

Gormán grimaced a little in bewilderment. 'I thought I did. Who is she?'

'That is Síonna, our new physician. She was apparently a *suiliaig*, a professor of the healing arts, at Mungairit.'

'Is Síonna the new physician in the fortress?' Gormán still sounded puzzled.

'Have you met her before? I know you have visited Mungairit.'

Gormán shook his head. 'I met no physician there named Síonna.'

Fidelma sighed. 'The strange thing is that I also had a distinct feeling that I had seen her somewhere before. I thought it must have been at Mungairit, whenEadulf and I visited the abbey. Anyway, she comes highly recommended as a physician.'

Gormán was still standing with a hand absently massaging his forehead, as if it helped his concentration.

Then Eadulf came trotting across the courtyard to greet Gormán.

'It is good that you are still here, Gormán. Good that you and Aibell had not started back to your farmstead in Muscraige Luachra. Your mother, Della, will be glad of your company at this time. Dar Luga was her close friend.'

Gormán was about to reply when he abruptly clapped his hand to his forehead.

'It was not at the Abbey of Mungairit but the fortress at Dún Eochair Mháigh, the fortress of the prince of the Uí Fidgente.'

Eadulf was totally bewildered by the outburst, but Fidelma realised where he had picked up the conversation.

'At the fortress of Prince Donennach?' Fidelma was surprised. 'Síonna was a physician there?'

Dún Eochair Mháigh, the principal fortress of the Uí Fidgente, at the crossing of the River An Mháigh, was the nearest major fortress to the farmstead that Aibell had inherited and where she and Gormán had decided to set up their home.

Eadulf was looking from one to the other, puzzled.

'Unless my memories have become distorted and taken on images or other realities, she was not there as a physician,' Gormán replied.

'What else would she be?' Fidelma asked impatiently.

Gormán had to think for a few moments more and then his expression lightened. 'Of course; she was there demonstrating her prowess as an exponent of martial arts.'

'What?' Fidelma reacted sharply.

'As you know,' responded Gormán, 'I was imprisoned in the fortress during the time when all was not good between the Uí Fidgente and Cashel.'

'I remember that time very well. I visited the fortress twice. But I have no remembrance of Síonna in either role – physician or demonstrating martial arts. Her face has a curious familiarity but nothing more. Are you telling me that the woman that you saw just now was a female warrior from the territory of the Uí Fidgente?'

'I know little else about her. Is it important?' Gormán asked, wondering at Fidelma's reaction. 'After all, it is well known that some people will adopt many roles during their lives.'

'But if she was a warrior, exhibiting martial arts – indeed, as are the Daughters of the Storm now visiting with us – then the change from that to being a professor of the healing arts is a curious leap rather than being a simple step.'

'Leaps in life are not unknown, lady. I am sure, if you cast your mind to considering the idea, you will conjure the memory of many who have changed their lives in even more drastic form.'

Eadulf, feeling excluded, felt he should contribute. 'There are warriors who have become priests, and priests who have become warriors.'

'Certainly there are some kings who have abdicated of their own volition and entered into the religious life, even going into the seclusion of hermitages,' Fidelma admitted.

'Therefore, it is not beyond understanding that a female warrior could renounce the martial arts for the healing arts,' Gormán pointed out.

'But don't forget that, if she was a warrior, then she would have had to study extensively to become a professor of the healing arts: a minimum of eight years, and perhaps ten or more. Do you think that she looks as if she has been studying for that long? Not to mention that, before that, it would have taken time to become proficient enough in the martial arts to be given permission to travel freely through the territories, performing such exhibitions.'

Gormán shrugged. 'It was some time ago when I saw the person who looks like this physician practising martial arts. I am sure it was before the battle of Cnoc Áine.'

'That was so long ago,' Eadulf pointed out.

Fidelma inclined her head. 'We will return to the matter later. We had better find my brother and discuss the situation.'

To her surprise she found that Dego had come back on duty at the door of her brother's private reception chamber. He acknowledged them with a friendly nod and smile, and a special glance of affection at Gormán, whom he had served under for many years.

'Do you mind if I ask a question of Gormán?' he asked, before opening the door for them.

The three of them halted inquisitively.

'I know one should not ask for information relating to wagers from anyone with inside knowledge,' the warrior began. 'I am not really seeking specifics but . . .'

Fidelma glanced disapprovingly at the warrior. 'Relating to a wager? You know the law and you also know better, Dego. This is best not said in my hearing.'

'Nor in mine,' echoed Gormán, also disapprovingly. 'You know the rules on wagering that govern the Warriors of the Golden Collar.'

Dego looked unhappy. 'It was not for personal benefit. It was only to ask, in view of what has happened here. Will there still be a contest between a warrior representing the Nasc Niadh and one of the Daughters of the Storm during the fair? You see, many have already started to make wagers. I do not know whether to encourage them or to confirm that the contest will no longer be going ahead. Certainly, the contest between Cera and Enda is cancelled.'

Gormán glanced at Fidelma, wondering whether he should answer. 'I do not have that knowledge,' he admitted. 'Certainly, no other contest has been scheduled.'

'If there are alternative plans,' Fidelma relented a little, 'the details will be read out on the *faithche* – the fairground – so everyone is informed. Why are you asking?'

Dego was hesitant. 'There has been some talk.'

'You should wait for the decision of my brother, who will confer about it with Gormán,' Fidelma said short-temperedly.

'Well . . . I just wanted to know if Father Socra is entered in the archery contest. You see, I know that almost as soon as he arrived here he began practising daily with Enda's household guard.'

'Practising daily?' Fidelma was surprised. 'You are definitely talking of Father Socra, the chaplain?'

'For a member of the religious, he has many accomplishments that put most of our martial arts trainees to shame. I thought you knew.' Dego glanced from Fidelma to Gormán.

'I would not know this unless I am told by . . .' the senior warrior began. 'I no longer join the household guard in their practices. You should ask Enda.'

'Father Socra does not practise with the guards but does so in the isolated grounds beyond the chapel.'

Fidelma had turned to Dego with interest. 'How have you watched

Father Socra? How does this relate to what is due to take place during the fair?'

'I have glimpsed him from the battlements. I was interested as, with my one hand, I can no longer shoot a bow but at least I can train others to do so.'

'So you are training our bowmen to meet challengers in the archery contests scheduled at the fair?'

'Exactly so, lady. The other day I was on guard along the northern wall, which overlooks the grounds behind the chapel. The priest was there practising against a target. He showed outstanding ability as a marksman with the longbow. He did not see me at first, but eventually I went down to join him and asked him how he came by such ability.'

'And did he answer?'

'He told me that growing up along the banks of the Bhearú, as a youth, he had to ensure that his family were fed – thus he learnt his skills chasing hares, otters, beavers . . . even badgers. He gained competence with his bow by hunting for food.'

'Not unusual,' Gormán commented.

'Did he show any other competence with weapons?' Fidelma queried.

Dego raised his shoulder in an eloquent shrug. 'I only saw his use of the longbow. I would say with that he was the better of many of our warriors. Aidan is our best bowman and he is, as you know, my friend, and therefore I thought to see if this Father Socra was participating in the fair so that I could compare their prowess.'

'I know Aidan is a good bowman. Are you saying that you believe that Father Socra might be his match?' Gormán asked thoughtfully. 'Well, I know nothing of who will enter the contests. But, as the lady Fidelma says, you will have to wait and learn on the day of the fair.'

They left Dego unhappy as he opened the door of Colgú's reception chamber. Inside they found him, having returned to the fortress while Fidelma and Eadulf had been asleep. He was by himself, finishing a mug of cider. After Fidelma had assured her brother that she had no further developments to report, Colgú turned to Gormán.

'Are you satisfied that one battalion is adequate to safeguard the fair?'

'I am. Anything more would alert enemies or cause anxiety among the people. However, a question comes to mind. Who is going to take charge of planning the domestic part of the fair?'

It seemed the idea had not occurred to Colgú. Gormán helped him.

'There was some discussion about plans when Dar Luga visited my mother the other day. I presume they talked about the stalls for buying and selling foodstuffs. My mother will be helping, but it is being suggested that the wife of Rumann will be in charge.'

Rumann ran the main tavern in the centre square of the township.

'What else comes under this role?' queried Colgú. 'I had forgotten all this was previously arranged by Dar Luga.'

'As well as foodstuffs, there are stalls of clothing and such like. Most of these will be in the square outside the tavern. However, what of the musicians, jugglers, fools and clowns, and all the other entertainments?'

Colgú seized the lifeline that Gormán was really suggesting.

'I believe that we can carry on as Dar Luga intended. Rumann, his wife and Della, your mother, will be able to give you all the information and contacts about organising in that area.'

'What about the contests – horse racing, games of skill, especially the martial arts contests?' Gormán pressed almost remorselessly. 'Enda was arranging those, but he spoke to me yesterday about the actual contests supposed to take place between the Warriors of the Golden Collar and the Daughters of the Storm. He asked me if I would take over the coordination of the event.'

Colgú was surprised. 'Did you point out that you had the dual role of being in charge of security was well as being adjudicator in the military contests?'

'I did.'

Colgú rubbed his chin thoughtfully. 'I know you have mediated over contests in previous fairs, Gormán. I want you to continue in those roles, especially as you have been an adjudicator in many of the events.' He paused, looking embarrassed, and spoke slowly. 'You know Enda was due to face the girl Cera, who was appointed champion of the company of female warriors from Osraige – those that Gelgéis uses as her traditional bodyguards?'

Gormán shifted his weight, obviously uneasy. 'I did know that.'

Fidelma decided to intervene.

'It might be a wise choice to dispense with the contribution from the Daughters of the Storm altogether,' she said.

'Obviously the main mock combat between Enda and Cera is cancelled,' Colgú said, looking unhappy. 'The point is I know that event had created some excitement among the people – my personal bodyguard being in a contest with my wife's personal bodyguard. A short time ago I had a discussion with my wife on the matter. She had talked with Crédh, the commander of her bodyguard. She now feels that it is essential that the contest continues for the sake of appearances. She believes we should show that we are neither intimidated nor fearful.'

'Princess Gelgéis wants the martial arts exhibitions to go ahead?' Fidelma tried to conceal her amazement.

'The entire fair was to culminate in a contest between a chosen warrior of the Golden Collar and one from the Daughters of the Storm,' confirmed Colgú. 'I have had the opportunity to question Enda about it. He is still willing to represent the Golden Collar against any champion of the Daughters of the Storm.'

'In spite of what has happened?' Eadulf demanded. He was astonished.

'Enda said he would agree *because* of what had happened,' Colgú replied curtly. 'I have given my sanction to it. It remains only for Gormán to accept the role of adjudicator of the contest. If he agrees, that is the end of the matter.'

Gormán considered for a moment. To the astonishment of both Fidelma and Eadulf he finally said: 'It might be wise to maintain the event. I mentioned to the lady Fidelma earlier, a lot of people are expecting great things at this fair, celebrating this union.'

'Wise?' Fidelma queried sceptically.

'Uppermost in everyone's minds is this: if this attempted assassination was some sort of Laigin-inspired plot using Osraige and the claims about how the people of Osraige are treated, then this cancellation might be playing into their hands. How many were expected to witness this contest?'

Colgú rubbed his chin reflectively. 'The last I heard, it seemed everyone was interested. These girls who are challenging the Nasc Niadh would have been something to talk about. There are so few female warrior companies these days.'

'If you have spoken to Gelgéis as well as Crédh, have they suggested who would replace Cera? And has Enda really agreed to face a substitute?'

'Crédh herself has volunteered to represent them. Enda has agreed to it.'

'I don't like it,' Fidelma declared. She glanced with warning at Eadulf in case he felt he should say something about Crédh's confession about how she had felt about Cera and the idea that there might be another reason as to why she wanted to face Enda in combat, even though a mock one.

'I have seen Crédh at one or two exhibitions in other parts of the kingdom,' Gormán said. 'I am surprised that she was not put forward as the challenging champion in the first place. She is certainly one who is admired in the profession she has chosen. I think we should definitely go ahead with her appearance in the martial arts contests.'

'Excellent. Are you agreed, Fidelma?' Colgú asked.

'I have grave reservations,' she admitted. 'But I cannot say I have alternatives to offer. The more I consider the matter, the more I realise that the fair has to go ahead in all its prospects, otherwise greater problems will be created.'

Colgú took this as an endorsement and looked round with satisfaction. 'So what is next?'

Gormán seemed hesitant but finally asked: 'Have you appointed an official replacement for Dar Luga? I mean someone who is now steward of your household with whom we can liaise, not only on matters arising about the fair?'

'Fidelma proposed Brother Dáire and I have made the temporary appointment. It is, of course, up to my council, when they convene, to confirm that appointment.'

Gormán's expression was one of disapproval. 'A librarian, one versed in booklore . . .? I am sorry, lady,' he turned to Fidelma. 'I am afraid I do not regard that as a good choice. The steward must be an efficient organiser, control the staff in order to run the entire fortress. With Dar Luga it seemed you were keen on a housekeeper running the affairs of the household. And now it seems you are keen on a scholar more used to organising his books than the politics of kingship to assist Colgú maintain this unruly kingdom.'

Fidelma did not hide her irritation at his questioning her choice. 'What do you expect? That my brother should appoint a warrior to run his household? A steward must have more talents.'

Gormán made a dismissive motion with his hand, ignoring the slight against his profession.

'I would accept that poor Dar Luga was needed in stocking provisions, controlling the keeping of the royal apartments . . . indeed, someone keeping everything well ordered and spotless for visiting guests and relatives. The organising of this fair is a case in point. I would accept that Brother Dáire has book learning that few other people have. But remember the times that to maintain security a combination of all these talents was needed?'

Fidelma sniffed sardonically. 'It sounds as if *you* would be applying to be steward here, Gormán.'

The warrior looked offended and was about to retort but then suddenly grinned wryly instead. He quickly shook his head.

'I have enough on my hands trying to run my own life. Aibell and I spend more time in Cashel than we ever planned to when we married. We have the farmstead to look after at Rath Menma. As you know, we have barely had any time to be there.'

'I can assure you, Gormán,' Colgú's voice was heavy, 'as soon as the fair is over, and hopefully by that time, Fidelma will have resolved this death riddle, then you can go to Sliabh Luachra, or wherever your farmstead is . . .'

'South of Sliabh Luachra,' Gormán corrected pedantically. He spoke with justification because Sliabh Luachra, the Mountains of Rushes, had an unenvious reputation. It was a series of peaks rising to a height of five hundred metres, whose glens were rush-filled marshland containing dangerous bogs and impenetrable woodland. This consisted of seven glens, which attracted ruthless robber chieftains, who took refuge in this impregnable fortress. The farmstead, which Aibell had inherited from her mother, was the place where Fidelma and Eadulf had rescued Gormán and Aibell not so long ago. It was much further south than the dangerous territory of the brigands of Luachra.

Colgú sniffed as if it were of no importance.

'Anyway, we must give an indication to Gormán of how we want this fair to be arranged,' Fidelma pointed out hastily.

'I remember some of the old fairs, lady,' Gormán joined in hurriedly, 'so if I followed those general lines . . .? I am sure I can manage with the advice of Rumann and even my mother, Della.'

'Don't forget that this is one of the occasions we are using to introduce Gelgéis, as my queen, to the people,' Colgú reminded him. 'After this, during the month of the Dog Star, Mí Madramhail, we have to go on the traditional *accmaing,* a circuit, in which we must visit the principal fortresses of the seven Eóganacht princes. Each has its own fair, so that all the principal areas in Muman are able to acknowledge Gelgéis.'

'So does that mean there will be some ceremony at the start of this fair?' Gormán asked.

'It does. The nine days of the fair are to express support, through the assembly of people of every grade without distinction, for the King's rule. We need to open with a raised platform on which Gelgéis and I will be seated alongside my advisers and counsellors.'

'Presumably Finguine, as heir apparent, will be there?' Gormán asked. 'Abbot Cuán of Imleach Iubhair, as Bishop of Cashel; Fíthel, the Chief Brehon; and Brother Dáire as steward? They will all have their roles at the opening ceremony? All on the same platform?'

'Of course. Why do you ask this?'

'They will all be on the same platform?' Gormán queried cynically.

'Of course,' Colgú replied, annoyed. 'You sound disapproving? Seeing the King and his council is the purpose of having this gathering.'

'I understand what Gormán means,' Fidelma said.

'This is a weak spot,' Gormán agreed. 'If there are any about who would do Cashel harm, that moment and position is now the weak point – the spot where you all will be most vulnerable.'

'That is true,' Fidelma said. 'I do understand that it is a tradition that the King and his new wife and his advisers are there to be acknowledged by the people. We must ensure that the traditions are kept to because, if ignored, people will take it as a show of weakness. Eadulf and I will not be on that platform but will mingle among the crowd, keeping a watch. I am sure Enda will be on the platform?' She glanced at Gormán with the question.

'My warriors will be concentrating in the main square during that part of the ceremony,' he replied.

Having discussed and divided some tasks between them, the meeting ended. Fidelma and Eadulf accompanied Gormán back to the main doors of the residence, then watched as he retrieved his horse, rode back through the main gates and started down the path to the township. Then Fidelma heaved a deep sigh and was about to turn back into the building when there was short blast from the trumpeter at the gate. The notes announced an arrival of one of rank at the fortress. It was Prince Finguine, the *tanaiste*, Colgú's heir apparent.

chapter twelve

Finguine was the elder of the two sons of Fidelma's cousin King Cathal Cú-cen-Mathair, whose approaching death from the pestilence had brought her back to Cashel to undertake a mission as his last request. Days later, Cathal was dead and Fidelma's brother, Colgú, endorsed by the Eóganacht *derbhfine,* the family council, had been chosen as King. Finguine had then been selected as heir apparent.

Fidelma smiled to herself, thinking how this successional system of kingship confused Eadulf, imbued as he was with his culture's law of primogeniture. In Fidelma's culture, there was no such concept of inheritance by the eldest. The generations of the family – usually three – met in council and nominated the one who would take over, based on whomever was considered the most worthy and best able to fulfil the office.

Finguine, with his warrior guard, had ridden into the courtyard and was dismounting. They seemed in an unusually silent and sombre mood as Finguine left his horse for his companions to attend to while he came striding directly towards Fidelma and Eadulf. He was not smiling as he greeted them.

'I was told the bad news in the township. Poor Dar Luga will be a great loss to our household. I did not know the girl, Cera.

From what is being said, no one has been formally accused of the killings.'

'Not yet,' Fidelma confessed.

'But of all people – Dar Luga? We all loved her. No one could believe there was cause to kill her.'

Only Eadulf saw the flush that came to Fidelma's cheek and saw her slight uncomfortable movement, knowing that only a short time ago she had been almost convinced that it had been Dar Luga who had killed Cera. Finguine was too involved with his own perplexed thoughts to notice.

'I suppose the targets were Colgú and his wife? There is a lot of gossip about Tuaim Snámha being involved; especially when he refused to attend his own cousin's wedding feast.'

'It is good that you have returned,' Fidelma acknowledged. 'This is now a period of intense unease. We have just been talking about it with my brother and Gormán.'

'I see a lot of strangers in the township below,' Finguine pointed out. 'They are early comers to the fair. Is that still scheduled to start in three days' time?'

'It is. Gormán commands an entire *catha* of warriors to ensure the fair goes ahead without disturbance. The event will be an opportunity for those who disapprove of Colgú's wedding to make some demonstration. Gormán should be able to deal with that. But if the intrusion in the sanctuary apartments and the murders were an attempt to create some sort of coup, then it is essential to get the matter clarified as soon as possible.'

'I was told that the girl, Cera, was due to represent Gelgéis's female bodyguards in one of the martial arts bouts at the fair. Someone told me that a replacement will be chosen and it will still take place but with other contestants. Is that wise?'

'Colgú and Gelgéis seem to think so, and Gormán agrees with them. Enda has been asked to fight the leader of Gelgéis's bodyguard.'

'It would not have been my choice of proceeding,' Finguine said doubtfully. 'Surely any suspects might well be within the ranks of the Daughters of the Storm.'

'It is a first thought, but the female warriors are all sworn to Princess Gelgéis's service, not to that of Tuaim Snámha. I questioned their leader very carefully.'

Finguine did not seem convinced but did not pursue the matter.

'Well, I must wash the dust of travel off me and then I had better talk with your brother about convening a council so that decisions may be taken.'

'Fíthel, the Chief Brehon, and Abbot Cuán are not yet arrived,' Fidelma pointed out. 'So the council is lacking two essential members.'

'And with the death of Dar Luga, we are missing the steward of the fortress who sits upon the council,' Finguine said.

'Brother Dáire has been temporarily appointed as steward,' interposed Eadulf.

Finguine's eyes widened slightly and he shrugged. 'We were also waiting on the arrival of a physician and a chaplain. They would sit in advisory positions.'

'They have both arrived,' Fidelma confirmed.

Finguine gave her a sharp look. 'You do not sound enthused about them.'

'I have yet to make up my mind.'

Finguine hesitated for a moment as if to ask for an explanation. Then he smiled grimly. 'I shall see you both later. I want to refresh myself and then speak with the King.' With a hand half raised in salutation, he turned towards his apartment.

It was as they were crossing back across the courtyard that Fidelma and Eadulf became aware of raised voices.

'What on earth is that?' Eadulf demanded, halting.

'It sounds like a lot of shouting in the warriors' barracks.' Fidelma tightened her features in condemnation. 'They should not be making a disturbance at this time. This is a time of watching the corpses and reflection.'

'Luan should be in charge of discipline if Enda is still resting. I could go over there and tell them to keep the noise down. That is, if they will take any notice of me.'

Once again Fidelma thought she heard a tone of bitterness in his voice. She hesitated uncertainly before agreeing: 'Very well.'

Eadulf walked slowly towards the guardhouse by the main gate. He had never heard such undisciplined boisterousness from the Warriors of the Golden Collar. At least he could see one warrior respectful of his duty, being on guard at the main gate. Eadulf knew him but had trouble trying to remember his name. The man acknowledged him with a grin, jerking his head towards the barrack building.

'You would think they'd have enough of conflicts without creating one among themselves.'

'What is going on?' Eadulf asked.

The warrior was smiling cynically. 'I think it is some dispute that has broken out with sides being taken.'

'I don't understand. Something is dividing the household guards?'

'There is a rumour that Enda has been dismissed by the King and Gormán is now back in command. The men are unhappy.'

'What nonsense is this? Where is Luan? Isn't he in charge?' Eadulf asked.

'Luan left them to their arguments. He's doing the regular round of the guards on the walls. However, Enda is inside and, by the sound of it, not having much luck in quelling the argument.'

'Enda is inside? You don't feel that you should help him or alert anyone?'

'Not I. I am on duty at the main gates of the fortress. What sort of guard would I be to abandon my post to attend to some internal argument, leaving the gates without a sentinel? Anyway, there are two companies of the household guard in there. Should I stand up and tell eighteen warriors to behave when the commander of the household guard cannot do so?'

'Are you sure that Enda is inside?' Eadulf demanded.

'I would not say so, otherwise,' returned the sentry, his good nature now withdrawn at hearing the rebuke in Eadulf's tone.

Eadulf simply exhaled in disgust, turned and made his way to the barracks door.

When he opened it, he saw pandemonium. The warriors seemed to be forming a circle in the centre around two others who were clearly shaping up to one another. The shouting ranged from encouragements to warnings. Eadulf's eyes narrowed as he took in the spectacle. The fight was already under way. The only thoughts that flooded into his mind were what authority he had to call a halt to it. He knew he had no legal authority, but when the warriors gave him space to see the two who were confronting each other, he gasped.

Aidan was one of them, and blood was dripping from his nose and mouth as he crouched in a defensive attitude, arms held up in protection. Before him, his face distorted in an anger that Eadulf had never seen before, stood Enda. The eyes of the young warrior were glazed with hatred; the lips seemed twisted back, showing his teeth as if they were fangs. He was about to launch himself on his opponent, hands held forward as if he would reach out and seize the throat to twist the life out of the man.

Eadulf tried to swallow, but his mouth had gone dry at the unexpected sight.

'Stop this!' he suddenly found himself shouting, finding his unwilling muscles pushing between the combatants. 'This must stop!'

The surrounding warriors now began to calm down and two of them turned to Aidan and began to drag him away. But Enda was still attempting to launch himself across the space to his opponent.

Sounds were coming from the warrior's mouth that Eadulf had never heard during the years he had known him. It was like the snarling of a beast. Eadulf's instinct was to quit the scene as quickly as possible. However, stubbornness took over and he pushed himself firmly in the path of the advancing warrior. He knew that if Enda's flaying hands made contact with him, he would be the worst for it.

Standing his ground firmly, wishing he could close his eyes and hope the oncoming warrior would vanish, Eadulf saw a muscular arm and fist raised. Some instinct made him reach out as if to encircle the fist in the cup of his right hand.

'Enda! Stop! Enda! It is I, Eadulf!' he shouted.

It was as if cold water had been poured over the warrior. A shudder went through his frame and suddenly he halted. Eadulf could feel Enda's breath on his face. But the warrior halted, his right arm still raised, the fist ready to descend to connect with Eadulf's face. Enda's distorted face seemed to be frozen in a mask for a few seconds. Then the eyes blinked and the tightened muscles began to slacken and resume a normal pattern. He blinked again and then stared first at his fist and then at Eadulf's protective hand. Slowly his eyes locked on to Eadulf's own.

'Friend Eadulf?' His voice was puzzled as he voiced the familiar friendly form of address.

'Enda,' Eadulf forced a smile, 'are you feeling well?'

Enda was still looking puzzled as he glanced around as if becoming aware of his surroundings. He unclenched his fist and allowed his arm to drop to his side. He turned back to Eadulf.

'Was I in some sort of fight, friend Eadulf?'

'You were. Why?'

Enda was thoughtful. 'Someone said something,' he muttered. 'Hurtful. Cera . . . she is dead.'

'You were supposed to be resting.'

Enda was frowning as if trying to remember something.

'Aidan made some remark and I hit him,' he explained. 'That was wrong. It was as if the battle mist had descended. It should not have happened.'

'That is true. Perhaps I should call someone to take you back to your quarters so that you can get some rest. We all thought you had gone to rest.'

Enda hesitated, about to say something, and then seemingly changed his mind.

'I am all right. I will make my own way back to my quarters.'

He turned for the door and the other warriors began to disperse. Eadulf waited until the door closed behind the young warrior, then turned with a disgusted look at the now quiet and sheepish-looking warriors.

'I have no authority here, even though I am married to the King's sister,' he announced. 'Had I authority I would say that your behaviour would make me ashamed that you are all members of the élite household guard. Now, where is Aidan?'

Aidan was sitting on a bunk on the far side of the barracks while another member of the guard was bathing his face. A bruise was going to develop around his right eye.

He looked up as Eadulf came across.

'I think it was my fault,' he pre-empted Eadulf's question.

'I presume Enda did that?' Eadulf nodded to the discolouring eye.

'He did.'

'And why?'

'I was stupid. I didn't know the depth of the feelings he has for the murdered girl.'

Eadulf exhaled deeply. 'You made some remark about Cera? That was insensitive.'

'It was not about the girl particularly,' protested the warrior, 'but I'll grant I was pretty stupid. I merely said something about there being other pretty members of the Daughters of the Storm for him to fight during the Fair. He is supposed to uphold the honour of the Nasc Niadh against the female warriors from Durlus Éile. I was told that a new opponent was to be chosen. I know it was a stupid thing to say, especially as it was whispered that he was having an affair with Cera. I did not know how serious his feelings were.'

Eadulf gazed at the warrior sadly. 'As you stay, it was stupid. In fact, it was incredibly stupid and no wonder he lost his temper.'

'Should I go and apologise to him? I really did not mean to insult him.'

'I would wait awhile, and take some sort of intermediary with you. I will try to have a word with him when he has calmed down a little.'

'I suppose we are all on edge since the events in the King's apartments,' Aidan sighed. 'Is there any further word as to who was responsible?'

Before he could reply, another member of the guard added: 'Many of us felt very close to Dar Luga, for she was almost a surrogate mother to us. We were more distressed by her death rather than that of the girl.'

He was a broad man with a barrel chest and thick black beard. Eadulf remembered his nickname was Temnan, the dark one, because of the luxuriant growth of his black beard.

Eadulf regarded him for a moment or two, hearing his defensive tone.

'All deaths should be distressing,' he said.

'But many of us fought in the encounters with Osraige during their plotting with Laigin against us.'

'And that means?'

'Let there be no misunderstanding. We like Princess Gelgéis and like our King's choice of her as a wife. But we do not lose sight of the fact that Durlus Éile is in the north of Osraige and Osraige have plotted with Laigin.'

Eadulf had these exact same thoughts, but it was not well that the élite warriors of Colgú used them to create dissension among themselves.

'I would urge you to consider a little more carefully before a further public expression of your words,' he advised sharply. 'I shall forget that I heard them. They will not be passed on from my lips. And while you think on Dar Luga's death, remember that Cera was from Durlus Éile and served Princess Gelgéis.'

Aidan was still massaging the side of his face by his reddened eye.

'This we do not forget, friend Eadulf. Nor do we forget that many from Osraige have accompanied Princess Gelgéis to witness her marriage to Colgú. Who knows but that some may come with evil intention?'

'It is also good you remember that many do not,' Eadulf replied sharply. 'Remember them and do not act on prejudice of place, lumping everyone with the same identity.'

'Is there any more news in your investigation?' Aidan tried to turn the conversation.

'You will know soon enough when there is such news. In the meantime, be watchful but take no action until you have discussed it with Fidelma or myself.'

'It will be as you say,' Aidan agreed, becoming spokesman for the rest. There was a pause and then he added: 'Is it true, though, that Colgú and Gormán are trying to persuade Enda to continue to fulfil his agreement to fight one of the Daughters of the Storm?'

'You sound as if you disapprove.'

'That is because many of us do. It is not because they will represent Durlus Éile or Osraige,' he went on hurriedly, 'it is because Enda's mind now seems unbalanced.'

'Unbalanced? Because he struck out at you when you mentioned the single combat demonstration?' Eadulf asked. He did not wait for the answer. 'Consider this: Enda was in love with the girl. After this contest, it was the intention of Enda and Cera to be married. I think that should explain his actions when you made your remark.'

'But Luan said . . .' began Aidan.

Eadulf's eyes narrowed. 'Luan said . . . what?'

The younger warrior shrugged. '*Is* Enda going to fight another of the female warriors?'

Eadulf hesitated but decided not to justify the matter. He simply said sharply: 'Yes, he is.' He did not wait for any reaction but turned and left the barracks.

Outside he found Fidelma with their son, little Alchú, walking towards the stables.

'It's a nice summer evening,' Fidelma greeted him. 'I thought it would do us good to take a short ride through the eastern woodland.'

She was expecting Eadulf to make an excuse but he agreed, quickly explaining what he had just witnessed.

'I find it hard to speak with Enda with reason,' Fidelma sighed.

'I do not understand how your brother has persuaded him to remain in the martial arts contest after the death of Cera,' Eadulf said.

'It is Colgú's decision, supported by Gelgéis,' Fidelma shrugged. 'It would not have been mine. Well, let us hope Enda now takes some rest, as an active brooding mind does no good to anyone.' She suddenly exhaled loudly. 'I need fresh air. Let's go for that ride.'

It was a warm sunny evening when Fidelma led the way on her favourite Gaulish pony, Aonbharr, the supreme one, through the main gates of the fortress, followed by little Alchú on his pony. Eadulf brought up the rear with a sheepish-looking Aidan at his side. It was pure chance that the duty fell to Aidan that day. While Eadulf was becoming more proficient at his horsemanship, Fidelma had once stipulated that, whenever he rode with their young son, he should be accompanied by one of the household with a fine knowledge of horsemanship.

They turned down the path towards the township below, but then Fidelma turned eastward at the foot of the limestone outcrop on which the fortress was built. There was a lively atmosphere coming from the township, indicating the preparations for the coming fair. Fidelma rode across the main highway, the Slige Dála, 'the way of the blind', which, she knew led via Osraige all the way to the High King's residence at Tara. Eadulf also had come to know the better riding tracks, away from the noise and bustle that people coming to set up their stalls and pitches for the fair would be making. He realised that Fidelma had chosen a roadway that still had to be maintained and fenced by law as the 'great road' although it was only a fourth-class road that connected one fortress with another. It could, however, take single-horse-pulled wagons passing in opposite ways without problems. The road led to the small fortress of Cumascach, an old retired warrior who had once served Fidelma's father.

Eadulf knew that Alchú liked the ease of this ride through stands of perpendicular oaks, with their broad trucks and crooked branches, before the landscape became green fields, mossy glens and heather-covered hills, with patches of poisonous buttercups and, beyond, red clover being pollinated by bees in the warm sunlight. These stretches were alive with butterflies, their different colourings too numerous to count, and even day-flying moths added to the colours.

Now and then one or two kestrels circled above, some hovering over the roadside looking for small mammals. They were easy to identify by their russet-coloured wings and dove-grey crowns and tails. Eadulf knew these birds of prey nested in holes in the trees that grew along the roadway. The kestrels would emerge now and then in search of their quarry.

In front of him, Fidelma was silent. He knew her mind was probably oblivious to the passing countryside and so he concentrated on answering his young son's questions. He knew that Fidelma was struggling with the facts of the day's events and trying to find answers to the questions.

Eadulf breathed in deeply, turning his face towards the warmth of the setting sun as it caught him between the branches of the trees, and was actually enjoying relaxing into the ride, although he probably would not admit it. He still maintained that travelling on horseback was not his favourite method of journeying. Eadulf was happy to allow his horse to amble along. Alchú, already a seasoned rider, wanted a more rapid canter and Eadulf allowed him to pass, signalling to Aidan to keep close to the boy, even though Fidelma was in front.

However, they had not gone far before they had to close through a coppice of willow trees taking advantage of the lime-rich soil watered by a shallow-running stream. As they were emerging from the coppice, a figure was approaching them on horseback at a quick trot. Eadulf recognised a female figure. She noticed them and slowed down to a walking pace so they could pass on the path. Her hair was loose and as the wind blew it back from her face, Eadulf had no difficulty in recognising Síonna. She was also carrying her *lés,* or medical bag.

She acknowledged the company, slowing her horse but not apparently intending to halt.

Alchú, riding ahead of Eadulf, halted his pony and greeted her so that she was obliged to stop and return his greeting with a forced smile.

'What's your name?' she asked in a friendly manner.

'My name is Alchú, which means "the gentle hound",' declared the little boy proudly. 'And what does your name mean?'

'Oh, I was named after a big river. My name is Síonna,' the physician replied in a good-humoured, confidential tone.

'That is not the name of the big river that flows around Cashel,' declared the boy with a frown. 'That is called the Suir, the "sister river".'

'My, but you are well informed,' Síonna smiled at him.

Fidelma glanced proudly at her son. 'If you travel to the

north-west of our kingdom, Gentle Hound,' she said, 'you will find the river of this name. It rises among the chalky peaks far to the north and flows through the kingdom of Connacht before it enters the kingdom of Muman.'

'So why are you called after that river and not the one here?' the boy demanded of the physician.

The woman chuckled indulgently. 'Síonna was the granddaughter of the sea-god Lir in the time beyond time and it was said that there was a pool over which was a tree on which grew nine hazelnuts. These nuts carried wisdom, knowledge and inspiration. The nuts dropped into the pool, and there was a salmon swimming in it that swallowed one of the nuts. But the old gods forbade anyone to go to this pool and fish for that salmon because they would inherit the knowledge—'

'But Síonna did?' the boy interrupted excitedly.

She inclined her head. 'Síonna did,' she affirmed. 'She was not worthy enough to eat of the nuts of knowledge and so the water of the pool rose in anger and washed her down the length of the river to the sea. It is said that her body was found at the mouth of the great river, which was then named after her.'

'So the river was named after the goddess and you were named after her?' smiled Alchú, happy with the story.

The physician gave a little laugh. 'But I am no goddess,' she told the boy.

Fidelma was examining her with curiosity. 'I am surprised to see you on this track, Síonna. You only arrived at Cashel at midnight last night, and before you had time to settle in my brother sent you to examine the body of Dar Luga.'

'From a medical viewpoint, a simple case of poison.' She paused and grimaced humorously. 'I understand Brother Eadulf had diagnosed that before me. The rest is up to you.'

'You opined it might be self-administered, and that had an effect on Father Socra.'

'My opinion was that it was impossible to tell whether it was self-administered or someone else administered it. I am not responsible for Father Socra's interpretation of what I said,' dismissed the physician.

'That is true,' admitted Fidelma. 'Anyway, at least you have been able to relax for the rest of the day.'

'I have an old friend who grows herbs in a valley not far southeast of here,' she replied slightly defensively.

Eadulf had edged his cob up to them and greeted her with good humour.

'I have heard the story of your name used for the original of rivers in different locations. Isn't it the same tale associated with the goddess Boand, who gave her name to a river where the great warrior Fionn Mac Cumhail touched the cooked flesh of the salmon of knowledge. He licked his finger and, thereafter, when he needed knowledge, he sucked his finger and it came to him.'

'I am sure your son will choose the story he likes best,' the female physician replied. 'You have a smart boy, lady,' she said to Fidelma. There was no guile in her tone, just a straightforward statement of fact.

'But you, of course, would choose the story that justifies your own name?' Eadulf smiled.

'That is natural.'

'I have heard that the well from which the river gushes is called Connla's Well, and wasn't Connla the son of the great female warrior Aoife, the daughter of Ardgeimm, whose roar was like the bellow of a bull?'

'You obviously know the versions of the story,' conceded the physician, a wary note coming into her tone.

'But speaking of female warriors—' Eadulf continued.

'I thought we were speaking of rivers,' interrupted the woman sharply.

'There is a point where the subjects cross. I was thinking of

Aoife the twin sister of Scáthach, who taught Cúchullain the martial arts while her sister was having an affair with him?'

The physician frowned. 'The stories that are told by old men are many and varied, Brother Eadulf. You could tie yourself in knots trying to make a single and comprehensible tale of the myths, and eventually you would find that there is no logic in it at all. Most of the stories of the legends and ancient origins are so varied that one should never look for logic in them.'

Little Alchú had become bored by the conversation, allowing his horse to wander further along the road. Fidelma gave a quick word to Aidan to follow the boy.

She smiled apologetically to Síonna. 'I agree. One looks to myths for being more than just exaggerated stories from history. Do I take it that you are not interested in the ancient stories of history?'

'History is nothing more than the myths that people accept.'

'That is an interesting way of looking at it. However, it seems to imply that you have had bad experiences from history.'

Even Eadulf was puzzled at Fidelma's words but he saw the physician's mouth had tightened. She glanced at Eadulf rather than Fidelma.

'As you are known as one who has studied in a medical college here, you are doubtless interested in the rational approach and demand a lucidity of logic? Life is not always a straightforward mathematical series of equations but leaps across unknown confusion.'

Eadulf had to admit that his and Fidelma's attempts to draw the physician into commenting on her reported life as a female warrior before becoming qualified in the healing arts was not going well. He decided on another tack.

'I suppose our logic is being tested at the moment with the deaths that have occurred. But, as a physician, do you not wonder why you will probably be called upon to treat wounds and even save the lives of the young women who will be displaying their prowess as warriors during the fair? Even the most careful, when using sharp weapons, will have accidents.'

Síonna's expression had hardened and she stared at him for a moment.

'I am a physician. When I look at those willows, I do not see it as making excellent wood for a bow. I see it as a tree that produces *salicin,* a substance from its bark that we can use to treat painful headaches and fever. My task is to treat those who need my skills.'

'I just wondered how you felt having rejected the aptitude of a warrior for the skills of a physician.'

There was no mistaking the reaction on the physician's face now that Eadulf had decided to abandon all subterfuge.

'I have never tried to disguise my past,' she replied coldly. 'But with due respect, Brother Eadulf, I will not supply you with further subject for gossip. It is none of your business.'

She dug her heals into the flanks of her horse and sent it at a swift canter back along the path, leaving Fidelma and Eadulf gazing thoughtfully after her. Then they both became aware of little Alchú calling for their attention further along the path. They reset their features and went to join their son with broad smiles.

chapter thirteen

Dego was one of the guards on duty at the gates when they arrived back at the fortress. As they entered they saw a strange warrior, accompanied by Brother Dáire, crossing the courtyard from the residence building and moving towards the entrance to the guests' quarters. The stranger was clad in colours that were familiar to Fidelma. As Fidelma and her party dismounted, she beckoned to Dego.

'Who is that strange warrior?' she asked. 'If I am not mistaken, those are the colours of the High King.'

'He arrived not long after you left, lady,' Dego replied. 'He says he is an emissary of the High King.'

'An envoy from Cenn Fáelad?' Eadulf sounded impressed.

'That much is evident from the colours he wears,' Fidelma was impatient. 'What does he want?'

'He would speak only with Colgú and none other. He was conducted directly to the King and they spoke alone. Thus you know as much as I do.'

Fidelma and Eadulf handed the charge of Alchú back to Muirgen and hurried across to see Fidelma's brother. She was not only curious to hear about the business of the new arrival, but anxious to learn if there were any new developments since the arrival of Finguine. They found Colgú in his private reception room, sitting in his favourite chair and looking morose. He held a mug of cider in his hand. On the table there was a half-unrolled parchment with an official seal. Fidelma guessed it was some message from the High King.

Colgú looked up as they entered, but showed no surprise. He looked exhausted. Without a word, he gestured to a table on which there was a jug and mugs. Then, surprisingly to her, he carefully rerolled the parchment and put it aside. Fidelma hesitated and then, realising she was thirsty, she walked across and poured herself a liberal measure of the cider before taking a seat opposite Colgú. Eadulf followed her example.

'We saw the envoy as we arrived,' she ventured.

'An envoy from Cenn Fáelad has arrived here to add to my troubles.' Her brother's tone was bitter.

They settled themselves.

'Is it trouble?' asked Eadulf. 'Are we allowed to know?'

Colgú replied with a thin smile: 'The High King is seeking approval to convene a special council of the five kingdoms concerning amending our laws.'

'Can you tell me what that is about?' Fidelma prompted again. 'I am your legal adviser. I suppose that I am entitled to know.'

'It has nothing to do with this case.' Colgú appeared quite exhausted. He took a sip of his cider and seemed to think a moment before replying. 'The High King is minded to call a special council of the kings of the five kingdoms, their Chief Brehons and their advisers. It will be called to discuss possible changes in law.'

'But the Council of Brehons, the judges of the five kingdoms, meets every five years to discuss the laws and whether there is any need to update and amend them. Holding a special council is unusual,' Fidelma pointed out.

'You will have to wait until my advisory council convene. This has to be done with the sanction of my Chief Brehon, Fíthel. Thankfully, Finguine has arrived, as you know. But I must wait until Fíthel and Abbot Cuán arrive. That was why I asked the envoy from Cenn Fáelad to wait. Then I can send a response to the High King's request.'

Even Fidelma was surprised at her brother's unwillingness to let her have some indication of what the High King wanted.

'The last time a special council was called to amend our law system was back in the days of the High King Laoghaire mac Néill, two centuries ago,' she commented. 'That was when the laws had to be amended so that they did not clash with the teachings of the New Faith, which was spreading through the five kingdoms.'

'It was said that amending the laws then took three years,' Colgú added. 'That was when Muman was represented by Conall Corc and his Chief Brehon, Rossa.'

'Anything new is a matter that has to be discussed by a full council of judges and lawyers of this kingdom before any brehon council representing all the five kingdoms can hold a grand council to discuss it,' Fidelma said thoughtfully. Her eyes widened when she contemplated the idea.

'Is the proposed change so important?' Eadulf asked.

'It seems a curious proposition,' Fidelma said. 'A change to our laws, you say? What type of changes and in what area? Does it affect Urradhus Law?'

This was a reference to customary law.

Colgú gave a shake of his head. 'It is so far reaching that this proposal, if it is accepted, would mean amending several of the Cain Laws affecting all the five kingdoms. That means it will affect customary law,' he admitted. 'Also it could affect Cairde Law, the international law agreements with people beyond the seas.'

'So the Urradhus Law, which is the common laws of our people developed over time immemorial, would be amended,' Fidelma observed thoughtfully. 'Look at the introduction of what they called "The Penitentials". They were not considered anything to do with our law system and those rules and punishments were thankfully confined in certain abbeys and imposed by the autocratic abbot princes there. They are nothing to do with our culture.'

'However, law conferences should not concern us immediately,' snapped Colgú, when he realised how subtle Fidelma was in extracting information. 'We will not discuss this until all the members of the council are here. Before that we have another important legal problem to resolve.'

'We are still investigating,' Eadulf replied, presuming Colgú meant the identification of the killer.

'I was visited by Father Socra,' Colgú said.

Fidelma raised an eyebrow slightly. 'He has some objection about the obsequies?'

'He has received the medical statement about Dar Luga from the new physician, Síonna—'

'She could only conclude Dar Luga was poisoned,' Eadulf interrupted in a defensive manner. 'I did the examination and I know the finding.'

Colgú sounded almost apologetic. 'She added her opinion,' he said. 'She felt that the poison could only have been self-administered. As the official physician here, she presented that report, which is now an official record.'

Eadulf drew in his breath. 'But that is only an opinion,' he protested.

'She was allowed to give it. This permits her to put any blame, or explanation of the death, where she thinks,' Fidelma reminded him in a heavy tone.

'But she did not know Dar Luga. She only arrived hours before the deaths in the sanctuary. She does not know our investigation.'

'If it is the wrong conclusion then I have to prove it is so,' Fidelma said sadly. 'It is my fault because I did not think she would make opinions as she had only just arrived here.'

'But at this moment, I am told I have made the wrong conclusion,' Eadulf protested.

'Father Socra is taking the physician's viewpoint,' Colgú told him. 'As we have previously discussed, his reaction is predictable. Father Socra has been quick to point out that Dar Luga, as a suicide, should be interred separately and prohibited from receiving the blessing of the New Faith. That is what the law says, as well as the rules of the New Faith.'

'It *is* what the law says,' Fidelma sighed. 'But the law also says this must be proven. As I said that I would, I have reflected much on this and, even though I was inclined to consider that the poison was self-administered at first, I am now of the opinion that Dar Luga was as much a victim as was Cera. I intend to prove it.'

'So why did you believe the poison was self-administered at first?'

'The fact that only she could have been in the sanctuary, except for you and Gelgéis, at the time when Cera met her death. So it seemed logical that, when we found Dar Luga poisoned, it must have been self-administered, which could be interpreted as a means of escaping justice.'

'Now you think it is not logical to accept the facts?' her brother asked, picking upon the words.

'We have to consider what are facts and what are opinions.'

'The evidence against Dar Luga is the fact that my sanctuary was secure enough by the very efficiency of the design that I made. Anyway, that building is nothing. What has been erected can be pulled down. I think Gelgéis would approve of the building being destroyed.'

'Would you really pull down your newly constructed sanctuary to appease Gelgéis's apprehensions?' Eadulf asked in surprise.

'If that is what causes her trepidation.'

'I would argue that there is no place that is safe in the fortress. If we supposed Colgú and Gelgéis were to be the victims then the assassin failed. The assassin would not try a second time,' Fidelma said.

Her brother was sarcastic. 'I hope that you are not going to throw in one of your favourite pieces of Latin from Publilius Syrus about *fulgar non ferit in eodem loco bis . . .*'

'True, lightning doesn't usually strike in the same place, but I don't think Syrus said it,' she countered. 'I didn't intend do anything of the sort. What I would have said was that I can understand Gelgéis's reasons for not wishing to spend future nights in a place where such tragedy has happened.'

'Yet the sanctuary was designed and built with security in mind. Unless you are an acrobat and swing from the walls to the skylight, you can only enter by means of the stairs outside the door here,' Eadulf acknowledged.

'That was the intention of the plan when I asked my master builder to design it. A totally isolated set of chambers with only one way in and out,' Colgú confirmed.

'I never liked the idea when I heard of it,' Fidelma admitted. 'It left no way of escape if the building caught fire. When I was investigating the fire at Imleach I learnt that whether you build in wood or stone, both can be consumed by fire. One of the things I must do is to explore every inch of the building tomorrow morning because the only way of proving that Dar Luga was not the guilty one is to show that the rooms must have been accessible by means other than the stairs outside.'

Colgú tiredly shook his head. 'Then it will be a long search.'

'Maybe Rodaige, your master builder, neglected to point out a weakness and insert it on those plans he left in the library?'

'You have seen the plans, and Rodaige, as I told you, has left Cashel.'

'Remind us,' Fidelma said. 'Where has he gone?'

'He went to work on the abbey at Cluain Eidhneach.'

'The ivy-covered field that Fintán established a century ago?' mused Fidelma.

'The abbey is being rebuilt, as Imleach is. Anyway, the master builder is not here, but you and I will make another examination of the sanctuary if you want. I shall show you there is no other way into the chambers.'

'I thought that Cluain Eidhneach was in Laigin?' Eadulf sudden intervened suspiciously.

Fidelma continued hurriedly, 'Anyway, we were speaking of your chaplain raising objections as to the method of burial of Dar Luga. Has he refused to proceed with the traditional watching of the body before the burial tomorrow night?'

Colgú spread his hands helplessly. 'He raised the point that the new physician says she believes that the poison was self-administered and this is *fingal*. He claims he must refuse services and burial on this basis. If only Abbot Cuán were here, or even Brehon Fíthel, to face down Father Socra as to religious law.'

'So he will not accept my ruling on questions of our law?' Fidelma felt her temperature rising at the idea that her knowledge of the law could be arbitrarily dismissed.

'Here's the problem.' Eadulf spoke to avert her anger. 'Temperament. He is the type who would probably resort to law if you argue religion and to religion if you argue law. He is biased, anyway.'

'Have you seen Finguine yet?' Fidelma asked. Only Eadulf heard the irony in her voice. 'As your *tánaiste*, your heir apparent, he should take some of the burden to help you face Father Socra.'

'I need both legal and religious opinion . . . I need your opinion, Fidelma,' Colgú replied.

Fidelma shrugged as if his previous words had not impacted on her. 'You have always had it when asked and, often, whether you wanted it or not. But I am not sure what to do if Father Socra just refuses and accepts Síonna's opinion. He has the right not to perform the funeral of Dar Luga.'

'And you know what that will lead to,' replied her brother. 'Dar Luga was a mother figure of all my warriors, not to mention the friends and relatives she had in the township. We can do without provoking widespread antagonism. But what else can we do? I even asked the opinion of Brother Dáire . . .'

'Which is right and proper as he is now your temporary steward and member of your council,' Fidelma replied, though with some hesitation. 'What did the librarian say when you told him about Síonna's decision?'

'Brother Dáire says that if Dar Luga's death is officially *fingal*, suicide, then Father Socra would appear to be in the right if he believes in the laws passed by the Roman councils of the New Faith. But he points out that despite the legal verdict of suicide, that does not prevent a religious burial either under the Old Faith or the New Faith. Those councils of Rome often give contradictory opinions. Brother Dáire also appears to offer support to what I am advised so far.'

'Contradictory opinions about what?' Fidelma frowned.

'He believes that it would not be wise for us to cancel the arrangements for the township fair. He believes it would be ill luck.'

Fidelma smiled cynically. 'Ill luck? Ill luck in what way? And is he saying that it would be increasing whatever ill fate there is already, when we already have two murders on our hands?'

Her brother winced. 'I was hoping we could come up with some resolution on the identity of the murderer before the start of the fair.'

'The start of the fair is in three days,' Fidelma reminded him. 'I see no prospect of any resolution before that.'

'Most importantly,' Eadulf said, 'tomorrow night, Father Socra is expected to hold the services and accompany the remains of Cera and Dar Luga to the burial site.'

'If the remains are not buried then it will create great unrest, just as Brother Dáire says,' Fidelma agreed.

'Abbot Cuán is expected to arrive in time to bless the festivities,' confirmed her brother. 'So his support cannot be counted on to force Father Socra not to fulfil his priestly functions.'

'With all due respect,' Eadulf agreed, 'is there no way this chaplain can be persuaded to fulfil his duty? If not, there might be a way of avoiding the problems.'

'I am open to suggestions.'

'Appoint someone else to do so.'

'But that would bring us into conflict with Abbot Cuán.'

'If that must be. However, I think the abbot will support us.'

'Brother Dáire has told me that it is written in the chronicles that certain auspicious signs are needed to ensure the fair is blessed, and that these should always be taken note of. He believes that we should not continue with the fair as if nothing has happened, for we are doomed unless the auspices are observed.'

'I never took him as one who believes in such signs,' muttered Fidelma.

'He made one suggestion to avoid these matters.'

'Which is?'

'He says that he has learnt from history that people will always believe what they are told. If you don't tell anyone that there have been deaths, then people will accept there have been no deaths. So the suggestion is that no word of the deaths should be mentioned until after the fair is over. Thus the three days of celebration will take place, people will enjoy themselves, the auspicious signs will be counted as soon as the people disperse. Then the deaths will be announced.'

Fidelma stared in amazement. 'But people know already,' she gasped. 'There are two bodies being waked in traditional form in the chapel; they will be buried tomorrow night. How can you say that no one will notice?'

'If things are managed appropriately—'

'I do not believe I am hearing this. There is no way on earth that information on these deaths can be withheld. It is immoral. Even thinking of the idea is dangerous. One word, and the *derbhfine* of the family, let alone the council of the seven Eóganacht princes, will have you removed from the kingship.'

'I know it.' Colgú's voice was broken with emotion. 'I said I needed your counsel, Fidelma. I only raised these points as we speak as family.'

'It is a thought that should be stillborn in the mind. I will see Brother Dáire and demand an explanation for such bad advice. At least I am your legal adviser, even if I am not the Chief Brehon of your kingdom.'

'I would not have followed that advice anyway. I can assure you of it. At least Finguine favours the holding of the fair, as does Gormán. Anyway, that leaves the problem of Father Socra. He was even reticent about Cera because she was a female warrior, but I think Gelgéis stood up to him over that. I have advised Enda to keep a silent tongue about her religious beliefs otherwise it is obvious how Father Socra will react. But as for Dar Luga, unless Abbot Cuán arrives tomorrow and persuades Socra to change his attitude, we will be in trouble.'

'Dar Luga's sister and other relatives and friends will be here by then. I hope I can make it clear to Father Socra that if he refuses to officiate at her funeral then he will be answerable to many here. If only Síonna had not been so free with her opinions and stuck only to the facts.'

'Dego tells me that Enda helped one of the religieuse choose some clothes from Cera's room to dress the body for the *aire*, the watching ceremony.' Colgú was reflective. 'Perhaps Gelgéis might find a way to delay the burial of Cera until midnight the day after tomorrow. It would allow more time for Abbot Cuán and Fíthel to get here and support the burial of Dar Luga.'

'Well, it might give more time for Lassar from Ráth na Drinne to travel here with friends of her sister to attend the obsequies,' Fidelma agreed.

'Speaking of Enda helping to choose grave clothes, I hope word of Father Socra's attitudes will not cause more problems. Have you seen Enda again since you discussed that idea of continuing the martial arts contest?'

Fidelma nodded. 'I have told him to take time off until he can bring his mind back to his duties. He had become rather sensitive.' She hoped word of the confrontation in the warriors' barracks had not reached the King.

'Maybe we are a little unkind on him since he was in love with the girl and this has hit him hard,' Eadulf ventured.

'I told both Brother Dáire and Enda what I have been advised,' Colgú said firmly. 'The main event that people are coming to see are the exhibitions of martial arts by the female warriors of Gelgéis. Gelgéis believes that it is attracting people because it is so rare to see female warriors demonstrating their capabilities these days. Since the influences of Rome, through the New Faith, such exhibitions are no longer numerous and neither are female warriors in the battle hostings of the kings.'

'Therefore it is accepted that the exhibition by the Daughters of the Storm will not be cancelled?'

'Nor the single combat. The important thing is that most of the people in the surrounding townships are coming to see the Nasc Niadh perform. Everyone in Muman knows and admires the Warriors of the Golden Collar. So Gormán is insisting the exhibitions between those chosen warriors of the Nasc Niadh and the Daughters of the Storm go ahead.'

'You have spoken carefully about this with Enda?'

'Enda had to accept my decision,' Colgú told them with a frown.

'Why so?' Fidelma immediately said.

Colgú's brows drew together and his cheeks coloured.

'Why? I am King of Cashel, fifteenth in line from Conall Corc, who made Cashel his fortress capital, and I do not have to justify my decision.'

Fidelma grinned mischievously. 'Who is greater, the King or his people?' she whispered softly, reminding him of the ancient law that states that the people are the greater, for they ordain the King; the King does not ordain the people. 'A king has to justify all his decisions if they are questioned.'

Her brother flushed. 'Anyway, I put the proposition to Enda. At the moment, he has a reputation as one of the most respected warriors of Cashel, being commander of my household guards. Even Gormán accepts that.'

'I hope Enda's spirit is in it,' Fidelma suggested. 'The murder of the girl affected him greatly. Indeed, I think the matter should not be forgotten. Someone else should have been chosen.'

'You are in favour of cancelling the contest?'

'I did not say that. But it could be rearranged. What made you come to the conclusion that the martial arts exhibitions were essential?'

Colgú looked uncomfortable. 'Gelgéis is patron of the Daughters of the Storm, and they came with her not only as her personal bodyguard but to demonstrate their skills in our kingdom. This was agreed when you and Eadulf were away in Imleach.'

'And you came to these conclusions by consulting with Gelgéis?'

'As I said, it was proposed at the council and agreed. Now that it has been announced and people are talking about it with anticipation, it would be seen as insulting if the entire contest were cancelled.'

'I am only referring to the contest between champions of the Golden Collar and the Daughters of the Storm.'

'Returning to Father Socra, I don't forget he is from Osraige and so I thought he might know what was appropriate. Indeed, I sought his opinion as how the news of cancellation might be received in Osraige.'

'And what was his opinion?'

Colgú replied with a scowl. 'He felt that much would be made of it. Those supporting the prince of Osraige, Tuaim Snámha, would be claiming it was an insult. That it would demonstrate that we had no respect for Gelgéis and her bodyguard.'

'I still feel another champion of the Nasc Niadh should have been chosen, knowing the deep feelings Enda had for Cera.'

'Enda has duties to me,' snapped her brother.

'I am sure you don't mean that implication. Neither Finguine nor Gormán would agree with that. Your advice might have been different if Fíthel had arrived first.'

Colgú knew his sister had little admiration for Fíthel, the Chief Brehon. He admitted that she did have reason for her criticisms as he was a man who liked to intervene and score points, and had little toleration of anyone who criticised his interpretation of law. There would be no understanding of emotional stress with Fíthel; his interpretation would be based solely on whether the letter of the law was met.

'Anyway, Enda was the one who was supposed to be concerned about security. That task now is your concern while this matter remains a mystery.'

'That there is no clear explanation about the means of entrance to your sanctuary? It is a concern and I am apprehensive.'

'And you have no new ideas?'

'It is not ideas that are wanting, brother,' Fidelma sighed. 'It is practical evidence.'

'You don't mean that you have a suspect?'

'You misinterpret me,' Fidelma corrected. 'I don't have suspects, but that means there are now so many possibilities one cannot see who has had the most opportunity, both within the restrictions of the location and within the time of the attack.'

'You forget the guards could have ignored the rules,' Colgú murmured gloomily.

Fidelma knew exactly what was on her brother's mind.

'I forget nothing, brother. Only Luan had that advantage, being the guard by the stairway. I doubt that he would turn traitor and help an assassin. Otherwise, if you mean Enda, because he was in love with Cera and might have killed Cera, because love and hate are two aspects of the same emotion, I think you can dismiss it. You, and many here, have known Enda since his boyhood. Dar Luga was almost a mother to him. Eadulf and I have worked with him for many years.'

Her brother sniffed. 'You have often told me that the most unlikely person is not excluded from being a suspect until there is proof otherwise.'

Fidelma shrugged ruefully. 'You have a long memory, brother,' she admitted. 'I suppose one has to take notice of the impossible from time to time.'

Colgú spread his arms in a helpless gesture. 'If we cut out an unnamed intruder, we are back with our suspicion of Dar Luga.'

'She was certainly a suspect based on her having the opportunity, the finding of the bloodstained clothes and knife in her room, all put together with time restrictions and the security of your sanctuary. However, something is wrong somewhere.'

'I have heard that Eadulf argued with you when you were convinced that Dar Luga was the primary suspect. Is that not right, Eadulf?'

'Fidelma and I are in agreement,' Eadulf replied.

'Even if he disagreed with me it would not change matters,' Fidelma said sharply. 'I still would have had to make the decision myself. The law has not replaced my ability as a *dálaigh* yet, brother.'

'I was interested in his view,' Colgú replied, showing he could be as sharp as his sister. 'I admire Eadulf's ability even as much as you do, even if you do not often admit it. He has gained a reputation of high merit although you are hailed as a solver of these conundrums. I was interested to hear that you were both arguing over Dar Luga's guilt in the early stages.'

Fidelma's jaw jutted a little. 'Someone has long ears. I remember the saying of Brehon Morann: "Long ears distort sound."'

'Wasn't there another saying? If you don't wish to be overheard, then don't speak,' Colgú returned. 'A secret that three people hear is no secret.'

Eadulf decided to intervene.

'It has been a custom of your sister and me to discuss matters in the cases that we are investigating. Sometimes it pays for one of us to put forward a contentious opinion to provoke and test the strength of the opposing argument.'

'But now you both speak with one voice?'

'There was never a doubt we would do otherwise. We will only discuss points in this fashion when we have a need to be clear and not present an argument that is unresolved. Otherwise one is reduced to arguing just about the dimensions of the shadow of an ass. It is unanswerable.'

'I am pleased to hear this,' Colgú said quickly. 'I have found to my cost that even the commanders of our bodyguard have failed us on two occasions – there was Capa and then Caol, who served me for some time. They both had weaknesses. I was wondering whether we might invite Gormán to take temporary command of the household guards until this matter is over.'

'Gormán had the same weakness as Enda,' Eadulf pointed out, gloomily. 'Gormán fell in love with Aibell, married and resigned. Enda fell in love with Cera, but had no time before Cera was taken from him. Enda will recover. Gormán will always put Aibell first. That is nature.'

'I would venture that asking Gormán to replace Enda is not a good idea as it would penalise Enda,' said Fidelma. 'Enda has been in your service as a young man and served you and me very well. Do you recall that Enda accompanied me to Laigin when Eadulf was taken prisoner by the Abbess Fainder of Fearna? For that, and other times, I think we owe Enda some support now he is going through a crisis with the death of Cera. I found no fault in him relative with this mystery.'

'I am well aware of what Enda has done in the past. I am also aware of his role in all the conflicts that we have had with Fearna. Indeed, with the entire kingdom of Laigin.'

'I don't think Laigin will ever give up their ambition to control Osraige,' Eadulf pointed out.

'It has not lost my attention that I am married to Gelgéis, Princess of Durlus Éile, which is in the northern part of Osraige,' Colgú replied irritably.

'And why do you find that significant?' Fidelma demanded.

'It is significant only if it transpires that the motive for the attack was not on her attendant, Cera, but an attack on Gelgéis herself.'

'I think we are all just airing opinions,' Fidelma observed quietly. 'Let not our acts just be from our tongues.'

'A good maxim,' returned Colgú. 'But we must go through things systematically and not make leaps of suspicion.'

'At this time a closed mouth makes a wise head. Better to restrain our thoughts until we have more information.'

Colgú sniffed in disapproval. 'It is just so frustrating. I am barely married to Gelgéis, there are many matters of state that demand my attention, not least the demand from the High King on changes in the law, which I can't share with you until all the inner council are assembled, and always plots from within and without our family to consider, to protect my safety. This current matter must be settled quickly.'

'It can only be settled when it is settled, brother. No sooner, no later.'

Fidelma rose and turned to the door and, as she did so, there was a noise from above them, towards the back of the building. Colgú looked startled and turned to her.

'That is . . .?'

'Someone moving around up in your sanctuary,' Fidelma announced quietly.

Chapter Fourteen

'There should be no one up there now,' Colgú muttered nervously.

'Shouldn't there be a guard on the stairway to stop anyone going up?' Eadulf asked, opening the door of the reception room a fraction and peering out.

'Perhaps the guard has gone to search the sanctuary,' Colgú replied. 'But that would be unusual without informing me.'

Fidelma took the edge of the door from Eadulf and opened it wider, looking along the passage. It was deserted. Certainly, there was no one standing on the stairs to the sanctuary. She drew back.

'Perhaps the guards have not arrived to replace the former watch,' she suggested. 'Or maybe a guard has gone to check. That would be the right thing to do.'

'But I should be informed,' her brother insisted.

'We could wait, but it will be interesting to see who feels the necessity of being in the sanctuary without informing you,' Eadulf commented.

Colgú had moved to take one of the ceremonial swords from the wall it decorated.

'Then let us fulfil the interest,' he proposed quietly.

Stealthily they moved to the foot of the stairway. Colgú insisted on leading the way, sword in hand. Fidelma, with her practical mind, was relieved that the firm yew staircase had been so recently constructed so that there was no looseness in the workmanship. As they ascended their footsteps made no sound at all; not the faintest of creaks to alert any ears to their approach.

A step or so below floor level, so that his head rose high enough for him to see the corridor before him, Colgú halted. He drew in a sharp breath. At the end of the passage on the right side, outside the door to what had been Dar Luga's chamber, there was the shadow of a tall man. He held a lamp.

'Stay still or become a dead man!' Colgú yelled, scrambling up the remaining stairs with his sword pointed forward, ready to lunge.

The shadow turned and the light of his lamp illuminated his features.

'Enda! What are you still doing here?' Fidelma exclaimed at Colgú's shoulder.

Enda's features were immobile as he gazed at the trio crammed at the top of the stairwell.

'Forgive me, if I have alarmed you,' the young warrior said quietly.

'Easier to do so when it is known what one is forgiving,' Colgú snapped, lowering the sword.

'After we had discussed the problem and I had considered all the ways that the killer could possibly have entered here and attacked Cera, I came in an attempt to see how they could have entered and also left unobserved. Needless to say, I believe there is no way that Dar Luga was the assassin and was involved except as a victim. She could not have administered poison to herself. It was not in her nature.'

'So what have you discovered? Have you found anything more since we last talked?' Fidelma asked.

'Nothing significant,' admitted the warrior. 'But I am certain that someone else was in these rooms and carried out the killing.'

Enda's shoulders slumped a little. 'My search has shown nothing at all.'

Colgú stepped forward, lowering his sword, and laid a hand on the tall warrior's arm.

'Enda, you should go and leave this matter to Fidelma and Eadulf. I have urged you before. Fidelma has agreed with me. So, at least, go and take some rest. I understand your personal involvement but you do yourself no favours. I hear you have also attended the watching of the body. I would take some rest now. I presume you are due to command the guard tonight. Better to leave it to Luan or Aidan to take charge.'

Fidelma agreed with her brother.

'Didn't you purchase a small croft in the township below? Why not go there and get some rest before the funeral? Only come back when you have had some sleep. You are of no help to anyone when tired.'

Enda was reluctant. 'If I am not wanted to attend my duties as a guard then I would prefer to spend the time at the chapel. I don't trust this new chaplain . . . Father Socra.'

'Why not?' Colgú was puzzled.

'I have heard that he has been critical of Cera and insulting of Dar Luga.'

'Do not concern yourself on those matters,' Fidelma told him. 'We are aware of his extreme views. So far, he has not refused the proper rites. He has only hinted at them. Soon Abbot Cuán should be here and he will have a word with the chaplain.'

As Enda turned to leave, a thought occurred to Eadulf.

'We were told that you were able choose some of Cera's garments for the religieuse, Sister Sárait, to dress the body for the watching rites.'

'Sister Sárait did the choosing. She seemed to know the right things for a warrior's funeral dress, even to the weapons that should be placed with her. It was a task that I should have left to one of

Cera's comrades but I did not think anyone would object. Oh, that priest Socra had objections, but I am told Sister Sárait took charge.'

Fidelma felt sad as she gazed on the pain behind the young warrior's masklike features.

Eadulf asked: 'Was Sister Sárait satisfied with the choice?'

Enda frowned: 'She was. Why?'

'As you know, Cera was a champion of the Daughters of the Storm. It was her right to be dressed in her warrior's costume with her weapons alongside her.'

'That was fully understood by Sister Sárait. I did not have to point it out. She knew a warrior's ritual.'

'But Father Socra would have objected?'

'I am told there was a difference of opinion. But Cera's body is presented in the chapel as it should be. I believe there was some argument between Sister Sárait and Father Socra about the recognition of the honour rights of female warriors.'

'Interesting,' muttered Eadulf, thoughtfully.

Enda left them in the corridor and they heard him descend the stairway. The guards had arrived and he could be heard instructing them of the presence of the King, his sister and her companion in the sanctuary before leaving.

'I told you that he was taking Cera's death hard,' Fidelma told Colgú after a pause.

'I will have a further word with him to ensure he has made the right decision about taking part in the contest at the fair. He must do so only for the right reasons.'

'This has been a long and arduous day,' Fidelma sighed. 'Eadulf and I intend to visit the chapel for the watching, but it will be only a symbolic gesture tonight; just for a short time.'

'Gelgéis and I will also attend for a short period before midnight,' agreed her brother. 'There is much to do. I just wish Abbot Cuán were here. I would be much happier.'

They made their way down the stairway from the sanctuary and then Fidelma and Eadulf left Colgú going into his reception chamber, and made their way along the corridors, passing the newly arrived warrior guard to the main door.

Outside, low clouds were causing the day to darken. A figure was hurrying across the courtyard, head down, shoulders hunched. The head suddenly jerked up and a male voice shouted.

'Sister Fidelma!'

The figure had turned in midstride and was coming rapidly towards them.

'Did you want to talk with me, Father Socra?' Fidelma asked, recognising the new chaplain.

The slight, sandy-haired man halted with an inquisitorial posture.

'I wish to speak to you in your capacity as a *dálaigh*.'

'Then you may do so,' returned Fidelma.

'Since I have come to Cashel as the chaplain to King Colgú, I have been made aware, even though Gelgéis is a princess of Durlus Éile, in Osraige, that there is an ominous atmosphere that many from Osraige seem to encounter.'

'Why do you come to me about atmosphere?'

'Because you are a *dálaigh*, as I have said. I know there is the King's Chief Brehon, but he is absent and, in his absence, you are the arbiter of law in this place. You hold the second highest degree that the law bestows.'

'A degree only means that I have managed to gain some knowledge in a certain area, but it doesn't signify that one has more wisdom than most.'

'I felt you were the best person to bring your attention to this matter that concerns me,' the priest said.

Fidelma exchanged a quick glance with Eadulf.

'I presume that this matter is not concerned with the objections that you have raised concerning the obsequies of our *banmhaor*, the stewardess of the King's household, nor to your objections to allowing such rites to a female warrior?'

'They do not. Nor would I consult you on such matters, which are clearly in my capacity to assess and decide upon.'

'In that, we would debate,' Fidelma observed. 'Are you saying that you have already made decisions in the matters?'

'Unless arguments come to my attention that show clearly the woman Dar Luga did not take her own life, then I accept what the physician says: the matter is one of *fingal* – suicide. There can be no Christian ritual or burial. As for the girl, Cera, while I follow the statutes of the councils of Rome, I realise that these do not run in any of the five kingdoms . . . at least, not yet. So I will accept her burial and allowed her to lie in the clothes of a warrior. This was only through the intercession of Sister Sárait, who insisted on following such erroneous traditions.'

Fidelma's jaw tightened a little but it was Eadulf who replied.

'Hopefully Abbot Cuán, who is also Chief Bishop of the kingdom, and the Chief Brehon will be here by tomorrow,' he pointed out. 'If they cannot modify your views then perhaps there will be no need to explain to you the ominous atmosphere you say that you are encountering.'

'I need no advice from a foreigner; a *cú glas* . . .' Father Socra turned on Eadulf, his face contorted with anger.

Fidelma intervened quickly: 'Let us hope wiser heads will persuade you to the contrary on these matters. However, you say that you are concerned with something else? You speak of feeling a threatening atmosphere, for that is how I take the term "ominous".'

'And that is how I would measure it – menacing.'

'How does this atmosphere reveal itself?'

'I feel that I am being watched all the time. That people seem to be observing, inspecting me as if they are waiting for something.'

'Scrutinising you? Who is?'

'Your household guards, for example.' Father Socra's voice was filled with a fury she had not expected.

Fidelma countered with a pacifying smile. 'Would you not say that it is the role of the household guards to be watchful? They are here to protect the person and the family of the King. What is unusual and menacing by their fulfilling their duties?'

'I am the chaplain to the King. I should be above such scrutiny.'

'And is this scrutiny emanating from any other group?'

'Indeed it is. From that appalling band of women who believe they are the equal of men!'

'You mean Gelgéis's own bodyguard?' Fidelma's smile broadened even further. 'Well, don't they have a right to be as diligent in the protection of Princess Gelgéis as the Warriors of the Golden Collar are of the King?'

'Women trying brandishing weapons is an affront in the eyes of God.'

'Unless they brandished weapons in his name,' Eadulf muttered cynically.

Father Socra turned to him angrily and demanded his meaning.

'Only know what the sacred scriptures teach. Does not scripture tell us that Jezebel is the name for a woman as wicked, licentious and shameless?'

'There are a few women who ruled who were not nice – like Athaliah, who was queen of Israel and Judah for six years before the people rose up, dragged her from the Temple, where she had gone for sanctuary, and slew her by the stable gate,' Eadulf recounted mildly. 'Probably many more, like Miriam, a leader of the Israelites who challenged Moses when, approaching the land of Canaan, he decided to marry a Cushite woman. Oh, I grant you, if you pick nits in the ancient stories, you will find what you want. Perhaps in your case, condemning women who have roles equal to men, you should speak of Deborah, who was a ruler and judge of the Israelites. People flocked to her for her wisdom and judgements . . . as some people here seek out Fidelma.' He paused and grinned. 'It happened that Deborah was also a military leader and created the army that defended the Israelites against the Canaanites. The

Canaanite army was defeated on the Plain of Esdraelon. Wasn't it a woman name Yael who killed the Canaanite general, Sisera, when he was seeking sanctuary?'

Eadulf gazed vacantly at the sky for a moment leaving Father Socra staring at him in bewilderment, for it was clear his scholarship had not plunged into these stories from the scriptures.

'Yes, you are right to take note of the teachings of the Holy Scripture,' Eadulf sighed, 'but I don't think God condemned Deborah, who was in command of his army at that time. I think Sister Sárait has probably read her scriptures more closely.'

Fidelma hid her appreciative smile and turned to Father Socra.

'Doubtless you will have much to talk about regarding your views on women as rulers, judges and military leaders. But let us return to what you were asking. You say you are menaced by people here? So what are you seeking with me?'

For a few moments Father Socra stood as if unable to move, wondering whether he was expected to answer Eadulf. Then he sniffed.

'If I knew I would not be seeking your advice. It is known that you are close to your brother and, even more that, as a *dálaigh*, you have the knowledge of the current laws. You also know the guards in this fortress. It is their behaviour I find threatening.'

'What have they done? Can you give me any specific instance?'

'There is one warrior who distracts me and I feel his presence is also like an ill-omened wraith.'

'Harsh words, Father Socra.'

'Harsh, but apt.'

'So who is this wraith you speak of? Who haunts you?'

'The tall, young warrior. I was told his name is Enda and he commands the palace guards,' the man replied at once.

'Are you claiming that Enda is following you?'

'He has been in the chapel several times. He sits staring, saying nothing, and there seems to be no expression on his face.'

'Isn't that only natural?' Fidelma asked.

'Natural? I tell you, he has the features of a wraith staring out from the Otherworld as if contemplating evil.'

Fidelma shook her head sadly. 'Perhaps, if you had spoken to him, he might explained why he does so.'

Father Socra was clearly uncertain and so Fidelma continued.

'He was going to marry Cera, the young girl whose corpse is now being watched in the chapel. Of course, he is sorrowing. And, like many in this fortress, he looked upon Dar Luga as a surrogate mother. Hence, you should be careful about your opinions on her validity to be given a proper burial.'

There was a grimace of anger on the chaplain's features.

'Had Cera lived,' Eadulf added, 'they would have been married after the great fair.'

Father Socra shook his head with a frown. 'If they were scheduled to be married, it was certainly not in Cashel and he has made no mention of it to me.'

Fidelma glanced at Eadulf and shrugged.

'Well, if that is the only thing that worries you . . .?'

'No; there is also a short man wearing the accoutrement of a warrior but he has one arm.'

'And what has Dego been doing to distress you?' Fidelma sighed heavily.

'You know him?' frowned Brother Socra.

'We are a family in this fortress,' she returned dryly. 'Dego has been one of the household guards for many years. In fact, he was badly wounded in the arm during an ambush. It was Eadulf here who saved his life by amputating his infected arm. But he has not lost ability with his other arm. He is a trusty member of the household guard.'

'Then why does he seem to follow me about?' snapped Father Socra.

'Doing his duty, I presume,' Eadulf intervened with a smile of irony.

'I do not like the thought of being spied upon.' Father Socra was angry. 'Not just in the chapel but when I am practising at the back of the chapel.'

'Practising?' Fidelma asked mildly. 'Practising what?'

'I keep my hand in with archery. It is a skill that I do not wish to lose.'

'Really? That is surely enough to provoke anyone's interest, especially those who practise the art of arms. An odd choice of pastime for a member—'

'My interests are my own affair,' Father Socra retorted.

'You have to admit that it is an unusual interest for the chaplain of this fortress.'

'Is it forbidden?'

'Of course it is not forbidden. But as you tell me, you are free to carry out your interest just as the sentinels have a right to patrol the walls, in which, if you are practising your interest on the north side outside the chapel, where the sentinels patrol and even practise, someone is bound to take an interest.'

'And do those female harridans have a right to observe when I practise?'

'Again you make a reference to the Daughters of the Storm?'

'I do.'

'Are you saying they also watch you?'

'I am saying one of them certainly does.'

'That one being?'

'Crédh is her name.'

'I see.' Fidelma suddenly remembered a point Dego had made when he confessed to observing Father Socra at his archery. 'I would not worry too much. Possibly, if it has become known you practise archery, some of the warriors might want to observe to see how good you are.'

'Why?' Father Socra looked bewildered.

'You must know about the fair. Some may be wondering whether you will take part in the contests and therefore would like to observe your performance.'

'A reasonable thing,' Eadulf added. 'So there is no menace about your weapons practice at all?'

Father Socra was about to say something but, instead, showed his irritation by grimacing and turning away, then, without a word, walking across the courtyard to the chapel.

'I was sure that I was not going to have a good relationship with the new chaplain,' Eadulf mused as they watched the priest vanishing into the chapel. 'Now I know it.'

Fidelma was about to start towards the entrance to their apartment when her attention she caught by a light showing from the library.

'It seems young Brother Dáire is working late this evening. I want to speak with him. Let's go and have a word and that will save a task tomorrow.'

She turned along to the end of the courtyard, almost opposite the old apothecary of Brother Conchobhar, where the entrance stood to the archive and the library. The door was unlocked and Brother Dáire was seated at his desk with a single lamp, examining some papers. He looked up with a scowl as if about to rebuke the intruders coming to the library so late but, on recognising his visitors, he rose with a broad smile.

'You are the very people I was wishing to see,' the young librarian greeted them eagerly as they entered.

'You appear anxious,' Fidelma observed.

'In view of the recent events, I think most people are anxious,' Brother Dáire said dryly. 'It might be nothing, but to me it seems curious that it was only earlier today that we were discussing the plans of the sanctuary.'

'You said no one had asked to look at them.'

'That is right. We were talking about whether anyone had been able to secure sight of the plans of the sanctuary kept in the library.'

'And someone has?' Fidelma demanded quickly.

'Actually, no. The plans are still locked safely in the box and secured.'

'Then what are you . . .?'

'I was saying that even with the littlest enquiry or examination of archives, I could discover who had been looking for various subjects.'

'I remember,' Fidelma replied forbearingly. 'And so . . .?'

'You also remember Sister Ernmas was looking through the texts during her plotting to overthrow the King. Through the texts we were able to find out that she was in reality Aincride and the mother of Elódach, Prince of Áine, pursuing vengeance on those who killed her other son at Cnoc Áine. You were able to track down the conspiracy and those behind it.'

'And so?' she prompted, but this time with impatience.

'I discovered those same papers had been rifled through again. I could not believe it, for when you had finished with that case I remember gathering those documents and writing some notes of the way in which you used them to explain the case. I found the *forsundud*, the poem of the young brother's lineage, and one of the curious things was that the section on the descent of the princes of Glendamnach was missing. The *forsundud* is—'

'I know very well what a *forsundud* is, Brother Dáire,' Fidelma said tightly, speaking through almost clenched teeth. 'I am still waiting to hear what you are saying about the connection with the sanctuary.'

'I could see that someone was going through those documents—'

'Well, as you know, Ernmas – or Aincride – is dead. And I fail to see what that has to do with Colgú's sanctuary.'

Eadulf decided to intervene.

'I believe that what Brother Dáire is doing is using this as an example. You are saying that by the disorder of the documents you could tell that someone had been examining those documents without the knowledge of the library?'

'That, and my notes on how you used them to track down the perpetrator.'

'Do you know when these were used without permission?'

'All was in order when the King asked me to bring the sanctuary plans to you this morning. As you say, they were locked in a wooden box. I replaced them and, being in a hurry, I put them next to the file I kept with the genealogy of the Eóganacht Raithlind. That was where you traced the connection with Aincride, or Ernmas.'

'So the file was close by, but you believe someone had looked through it?'

'It was obvious from the disorder. Also, one page had been defaced. Whoever looked through this had scrawled after the name Aincride, the word "revenge!" That seemed odd.'

Fidelma thought for a moment. 'Perhaps not so odd because the name Aincride actually means "revenge". However, why are you connecting this with the sanctuary?'

'Because, I noticed that someone had tried to open the box where the plans were. Since this morning there were scratches around the keyhole as if someone had been digging around it with a sharp-bladed knife or dagger.'

'And had they succeeded in opening it?'

'No, of that I am certain. Perhaps they gave up when other people came close to where they were. The area was at the back of the archive, so they could have been unobserved for a while.'

'And when do you say this was done?'

'Today, lady. Having taken the box after you looked at the plans, I checked through it and ensured things were all in order. I had taken it to the back of the library and put it down, having become distracted by some queries. Instead of placing it in the cupboard in which it is usually locked, I left it on the table near the genealogical texts. So it was not until a short while ago, when I went to tidy and lock things away, that I saw it again.'

'But you can say that, in spite of the knife marks around the lock, no one had managed to open it?'

'You can rest assured about that. I know locks. Even if they did, what would they learn more than you? There is no other way into the sanctuary except by turning themselves into a kestrel.'

'You have not left the library?'

'I even shut the library during the main meal of the day.'

'Do you have a list of everyone who visited the library after you left the box in a vulnerable position?'

'There were very few people as, with the upcoming fair, people seemed to be taking time off from scholarly pursuits to witness the entertainers and traders and other people who are arriving. Few are currently searching for knowledge for the mind.'

'But you know who these were?'

'Oh, yes. Some of those visiting young women warriors from Durlus Éile. The commander of them. Crédh is her name. There was a companion with her whose name was Corbach. She has been frequently in our library. Then there was poor Enda. The new chaplain, Father Socra, has visited several times and he came this afternoon. Oh, yes, he even sent one of his people to check on something after he left because he had forgotten it. Then there was Sister Sárait, who has also visited here several times. And earlier today came the new physician, Síonna.'

'That is all?'

'I have a good memory, lady.'

'So what did they want to research – do you remember?'

'I have said that I have a good memory,' the young librarian said without apparent conceit. 'Síonna wanted to know what medical treatises we have and especially anything on poisons. That caught my attention after the news about Dar Luga, but then I found out she had done an examination of the body. We now have most of Brother Conchobhar's collection of texts, including foreign classics such as texts from Galen, Dioscorides, Avicenna, Serapion . . .'

'I know you have a good memory,' Eadulf intervened dryly. 'I, myself, have spent many long hours with those texts when Conchobar allowed me access to his apothecary. I envy you their keeping.'

'Go on, Brother Dáire,' urged Fidelma. 'Why did Enda come by?'

'An unusual request for him. Usually he comes by to play a game of *fidchel*, wooden wisdom. It is a game he excels at and often I lose to him.'

'So what did Enda want this time that was so unusual for him?'

'He wanted to know if there was anything about old pagan rituals in the archives. Particularly, death rituals.'

'When you say death rituals, what do you mean?' Eadulf asked.

'How the dead were treated and buried.'

Eadulf took a quick look at Fidelma. After what Enda had said about Cera, the reason for his search for such knowledge was obvious.

'Continue,' Fidelma instructed.

'I remember that I did have the file out relating to Aincride. I explained to Enda, and Sister Sárait, who was also there, that when Aincride fell from the tower, we had to bear in mind that she was of the Old Faith when we buried her. Father Fidach, who was then our chaplain, laughed and said a dead body wouldn't mind how they were buried. That had a strange reaction from Enda.'

'How did Enda react?' Fidelma asked.

'There was a strange look in his eyes and he took the file and read it. He said something curious.'

'What was that?'

'As far as I understood it was – there is hope from the mouth of man, but none from the mouth of the grave.'

'He is strangely emotional.'

'Well, Father Socra wanted to see the legal texts we have. Especially those relating to *fingal* . . .'

'Laws on suicides?' Eadulf queried. 'That also is obvious.'

'I heard that he was following the ideas put forward by Augustine of Hippo,' Brother Dáire agreed. 'I presume there will be some awkwardness because the new physician has told him that Dar Luga's death was self-administered and hence she was a *fingalach* in law – a suicide.'

'So that was what he came about?' Fidelma sighed. 'And his assistant?'

'She came because Father Socra had forgotten a reference.'

'And the two women – both of the Daughters of the Storm? What did they want?'

'They were concerned with the *Aenach Caiseal* – whether we had anything they could see to do with the fairs that had been held here before, and the martial arts contests. Anything general, that is. Oh, and Crédh was interested in what we had on the history and laws applying to the female warriors. The other one was wanting to know about records of combats and the most notable female champions. We have many stories.'

'And they were the only ones using the library at various times?'

'They were.'

'I can understand your concern at someone with a dagger or knife trying to open the lock on the box containing the plans of the sanctuary,' Fidelma mused. 'But why sort through that file on Aincride?'

'She was a strange one,' Eadulf agreed. 'Was she what you call a *taiscélaid* – an observer of omens? One of the old religion, too. Then she came here and adopted another name.'

Suddenly Brother Dáire frowned. 'I heard that you have found the weapon that killed the young girl and that it was a ceremonial dagger.'

'I suppose Enda told you?'

'He did. He said there was a symbol on it and such symbols usually identify the warrior bands they belong to, but this was not the symbol of the Daughters of the Storm.'

Fidelma took the dagger from her marsupium and handed it to Brother Dáire.

When the librarian looked at it, he shook his head. 'Enda is right, this dagger belongs to another warrior band.'

'So what does the lightning flash signify?'

The librarian thought for a moment and then he moved to a shelf, took down an ageing book and turned the pages.

'There was a group of Cruithne female warriors and this was their symbol. They were led by Prince Drustics, according to this record. I remember in the one of the lives of the Blessed Donnán it is said that he led some followers into the district and took possession of cattle from the local people.'

Fidelma smiled. 'Took possession?'

Brother Dáire shrugged. 'It sounds better than saying he stole the cattle and grain.'

'I presume he was from the Dál Riata settlements?'

'The Blessed Donnán and his men were encircled by a company of female warriors and slaughtered. There were at least fifty in Donnán's party. This was eighty years ago.

'Maybe this dagger was taken by one of the warriors who was in the battle against them. Here is the entry. The Defenders of An Sgurr. Their symbol was a silver leaf shape with two lightning rods and a great bear. The images are incised and picked out with red enamel.'

Fidelma breathed in. 'That is the symbol on the dagger,' she acknowledged. 'Defenders of An Sgurr? What is that?'

'An Sgurr is a high hill on an island in the new Dál Riata territory near Iona. There was a battle there in which the defenders were female warriors, who fought against the Dál Riata.'

Eardulf pursued his lips in a silent whistle. 'They were Cruithne or, as we call them, Picts? Now I know where I saw the symbol.'

'You said at Streoneshalh,' Fidelma pointed out.

'Remember when the Pict woman, Gwid, tried to stab Oswy?

The dagger she held bore that symbol.' He returned to the matter of documents. 'Did Enda talk about the death rituals as they were in the Old Faith? Was that one of the documents that he was shown?'

Brother Dáire frowned and then shook his head. 'I don't think so. But why would he be interested, just because Ernmas or Aincride were of the Old Faith?'

'If you remember,' Fidelma said, 'when Ernmas was cornered and fell to her death from the tower here, it was deemed she had committed suicide, yet she was buried in the burial grounds below.'

'But that would have made her death of more interest to Father Socra, if he was seeking information on suicides and how they were dealt with,' Eadulf observed.

'But Dar Luga was of the New Faith,' Brother Dáire pointed out.

'I believe Father Socra's interpretation of suicide originates from Rome, and in his eyes, that places her outside of the Faith.'

'At least he is not objecting to the watching rituals overnight.'

'It is when he has to perform the burial ritual that the problem will arise,' Fidelma pointed out gloomily. 'I think Enda might have some special ideas on that.'

'Then let us hope Abbot Cuán arrives soon, because if Father Socra refuses the Christian burial of Dar Luga, then there might be bloodshed.'

chapter fifteen

'I wish Colgú had cancelled this fair,' Eadulf announced, stretching himself before the fire and helping himself to a glass of *corma*. They had just returned from the chapel where they had joined the many that had gathered to take part in the first stage of the *aire*, the ceremonial watching of the bodies. It had been a late night because they had not only taken their turn in the chapel for the watching ritual but, of course, they spent time commiserating with Lassar, the sister of Dar Luga, who had come to the fortress from Ráth na Drinne where she and her husband, Ferloga, kept an inn.

Lassar and Dar Luga, who were twins, not only looked so much alike but had the same qualities of motherly sympathy. Ferloga had had to remain behind to attend to the inn, but Lassar had been welcomed into her friend Della's farmstead on the outskirts of the township. Della's son, Gormán, with his wife, Aibell, had taken charge of her. They had all come to take their turn at the watching. Even Rumann, the owner of the tavern in the main square, came with his son. Dar Luga was as well known in the township as she was in the fortress of the Eóganacht kings.

Certainly there had been many crowded into the chapel. Fidelma hoped that would send a message to Father Socra as to how popular Dar Luga had been, and perhaps alter his views. Certainly, members of the Nasc Niadh took it in turns to take their places, while the Daughters of the Storm also took part on behalf of Cera. Fidelma was surprised to see even the emissary from the High King seated for a while in the chapel. By chance they passed him on the way to take their seats and he came forward to greet Fidelma.

'You won't remember me, lady. But I was serving in the court at Tara when you resolved the mystery of the murder of the High King, Sechnussach.'

'And now you are emissary of Cenn Fáelad,' Fidelma smiled in return.

'Of that I cannot speak. Once your brother's council meets, you will doubtless know all.'

'Doubtless,' Fidelma replied solemnly. 'I should thank you for coming to pay respects tonight.'

The emissary sighed. 'I once served alongside a company of female warriors who went to Dál Riata to defend the settlement against the Cruithne, so I had great respect for the young girl, Cera. Other female warriors were there. Some groups disbanded. One went to study herbs, another to join the religious.'

Eadulf frowned as he knew in his tongue the Cruithne were called 'the painted people'. Now they had discovered the weapon that killed Cera was a Pictish dagger. He tried not to sound excited.

'Are you saying that the Daughters of the Storm served so far north? That they served the Dál Riata against the Picts?'

The young warrior shook his head with a smile. 'There are still other female bands across the five kingdoms. However, I thought I recognised a person among your people who had served against the Cruithne at the time that I spent with Domangat, King of the Dál Riata. I recall the warriors came from a group from the western province of this kingdom.'

'You recognised that person here, tonight?'

'I had only a glimpse. They were not dressed as a warrior so I might have been mistaken.'

'Are you sure they served against the Cruithne?'

'I would not say anything I am not sure of,' agreed the emissary.

'Then, if you see this person, let me know. It is of interest.'

Colgú and Gelgéis interrupted further conversation, coming to take their part with Finguine, the heir apparent, and other dignitaries. Fidelma and Eadulf had taken their son, Alchú, along with his nurse, Muirgen, and her husband, Nessan. Father Socra had kept any religious ceremonial to a minimum. The times when candles had to be reignited and bells rung to note the passing time were left to Sister Sárait and her helpers to observe. Thus the short while the King and his family had spent at the ceremony had passed without incident, although there had been much whispered conversation.

Now, as they stretched before the fire, Eadulf was reflective.

'There is a lot of unease about the fair,' he said.

'I think we have resolved the best course of action,' Fidelma said. 'People are uneasy, but if it were cancelled, they would start to whisper that my brother has given way to the fear of threats about his kingship. That would create more stories and dissension. You have to remember, Eadulf, unlike with your people, kingship is not passed on by primogeniture. The first born does not automatically inherit.'

Eadulf gave a mock groan.

'I know, I know. The most worthy inherit, although they must be of the bloodlines. I understand all about the *derbhfine*, the family council meeting, and their judging who is the one worthy to inherit.'

'Then remember that Colgú is only the second son of my father. Fogartach was the elder. And Finguine, while he is the approved *tanaiste*, or heir apparent, is the son of King Cathal, to whom Colgú was nominated heir apparent. So it does not necessarily mean Finguine will be confirmed as king if, God forbid, anything happens to my brother. Finguine has a younger brother called Ailill and he might equally be chosen by the *derbhfine* if they have a mind to.'

Eadulf raised his arms as if trying to ward off some unseen problem.

'I will never understand the intricacies of your system of inheritance,' he admitted. 'I think my people's tradition is simple and the best. The first-born inherits, plain and simple. It eliminates all the problems of casting votes.'

'Simple?' Fidelma gave a dry chuckle. 'It certainly doesn't stop the bloodshed that such a system encourages.'

'I don't understand.'

'In your system, if the people do not like the choice of the first-born, he is killed, or overthrown in other ways. I have seen the chronicles of your own people, the Angles. Eorpwald was murdered by his cousin, Ricbert, who was then murdered by his half-brother, Sigebert, who was forced into a monastery by another relative, Egric. Then, having been confined in the monastery for several years, Sigebert emerged and led an uprising, but both he and Egric were killed. Another cousin, Anna, became king and he was eventually killed by Penda and . . .'

Eadulf placed his hands over his ears with a mock groan.

'Enough, enough!' he cried. 'I concede. Both systems are dangerous fields to embark on. Personally, I am not sure I want to rule anything. My father was just an hereditary lawgiver, a *gerefa*. I was happy to follow in his footsteps until the Christian missionaries of your country came and taught the New Faith and I came and studied the healing arts here. Give me the texts on the healing herbs and I am well content.'

'Well, no time for reading tomorrow, for I fear it will be a busy day,' Fidelma said, rising from her chair. 'Now it is time to sleep until tomorrow's destiny guides our footsteps.'

It seemed hardly any time had passed before the ageing nurse appeared, bringing the morning light.

'The first meal is ready, lady. Your son is already agitating for his morning ride.'

'Excellent.' Fidelma turned and shook a protesting Eadulf by the shoulder. 'Eadulf will be taking him today,' she told the nurse. 'So we will need a good rider to accompany them. I have things to do.'

She rose from the bed and started to gather the necessities for her morning wash. Eadulf suppressed a groan but Fidelma heard him.

'You take little Alchú for his morning ride. We must not allow him to think that today is anything other than an ordinary one. I know Enda can't accompany you as he used to do, but there are a couple of stablemen who serve in the household guards who are available.'

Eadulf disliked Fidelma fussing so much. While he was no great horseman and would prefer any other mode of travel, he was determined to master his dislike and to do his share of the daily rides with his son.

'Today being anything but ordinary?' he queried, repeating her words.

'Unless there are changes, the funerals will take place tonight. If Abbot Cuán and Fíthel do not arrive we might have serious trouble with Father Socra. And, as you said, last night, it might even lead to bloodshed.'

'What are your plans then?'

'I want to take a ride by myself to get my thoughts together. I'll ride out towards Ara's Well. Don't worry, I should be back by noon.'

Eadulf had long accepted that Fidelma often liked to go on a solidary ride to clear her thoughts and to meditate on the problems she was faced with.

When Fidelma went to the stables to get her horse, Aonbharr, the Gaulish pony that had been a gift from her brother, she was hoping that a good canter in the morning air would drive away her feelings of exhaustion and irritability. She often liked to let Aonbharr have his head, galloping for a considerable period before halting for a drink in a cool mountain stream and having a short rest; Fidelma herself resting on the bank of the stream with a sweet apple to nibble while turning matters over in her mind.

That morning she decided to take the western track, thinking to pause at Ara's Well and exchange news with Aona, the innkeeper there, or Adag, his grandson. The summer's day was pleasantly warm as she cantered along the track bordered by tall, stately clumps of ash. Some of the ash trees showed where axes and saws had been at work, for it was a wood that was popular among farmers to build their carts or even items of furniture with. Several rowan had now established down the mountains to fight with the ash or an occasional elder, whose black berries were now providing food for enterprising birds.

The track twisted through these into stretches of grassland and bracken and gorse. The large number of whinchats did not seem disturbed by her passing, even though she knew their nests were hidden nearby in the thick ground cover that the bracken provided. She could see some of the males with white and orange breasts perched on higher growths of brambles where they found a commanding position to peer down with gimlet eyes at prospective prey.

Usually, for Fidelma, a ride was good for thinking through difficult problems. However, this ride brought her no closer to seeing reasons behind the attack on her brother's sanctuary. What did fill her mind she found depressing. She thought particularly about Eadulf's behaviour and especially his confession that he did not feel at home with her in Cashel. She realised how upset and anxious his confession had made her feel. She had taken for granted his acceptance in allowing her freedom to follow her career. She believed she was sincere in her determination that, as soon as this matter was resolved, they would go to Eadulf's home; to the land of the East Angles. But would that visit be enough to make him overcome his feelings of being a foreigner in her country? To her, it was as frustrating as it was worrying. She wondered how she would feel in his position.

Her brother had done all in his power to make Eadulf feel one of the family, even going through the legal form of adoption of him, as marriage usually made the wife part of her husband's clan and alien to her father's clan. So Eadulf, instead of being a foreigner without rights, was an Eóganacht kinsman; a 'kinsman by summoning', as the law had it. It had never occurred to her that Eadulf might one day feel uncomfortable and reject that position.

She had tried hard not to show her feelings when Eadulf had made his confession. Now, as she allowed her pony to slow to a walk, dark thoughts came to her mind. She knew that, while she could visit Eadulf's homeland for a short time, she could in no way do as Eadulf had done, which was to give up her native country, language and culture. The idea had never occurred to her before. Eadulf had travelled as much as she had and had never raised any matters about missing his home. He had spent time in the northern kingdom of the Uí Néill, had been to Rome, and he had travelled with her to many strange places. Never once had she considered that he could be unhappy in the kingdom of Muman, that he was discontented with life there with her and their son.

It was a shock now that she allowed her emotions to overcome the constraints of her analytical thought processes. It had been an easy answer to suggest a visit to his homeland. She now realised there should be more thought, more consideration, and that there were decisions to be made before rushing into the shadowy future. It was as if the summer's day had suddenly chilled and grown dark, with clouds rushing to cover the sunshine she had been previously enjoying.

She became aware of a carriage joining the track some way ahead. It was drawn by two mules; an ornate construction of red yew with a pole between the animals and four large wheels. There seemed a lot of polished brass fittings on the vehicle. There was some religious symbolism on it and the driver was clearly an ecclesiastic, by his attire. His companion, the coachman, was dressed similarly. As the coach drew close, Fidelma realised there were outriders behind the vehicle.

She waited, resting astride her pony, watching the coach as it reached her and halted. She had already recognised the symbols on it even before Abbot Cuán leant out with a smile.

'*Deus tecum*, Fidelma,' he greeted.

Fidelma edged her pony nearer.

'*Gratulor videre te*, Abbot Cuán,' she replied in solemn greeting.

He raised his eyebrows, hearing the relief in her voice.

'Why so thankful? Is there a problem? I know the fair is usually an anxious and troublesome period, but this fair should be one of celebration following your brother's wedding the other month.'

'Then you have not heard?'

'I have heard nothing, having been on the road from Imleach.'

Abbot Cuán had ordered the coach to halt until he was ready to give the signal to move on again. Fidelma swung off her pony and climbed up into the coach so that she could address him with lowered voice.

'There are two problems,' she told him. 'One is mine and the other can be averted by you.'

The abbot said nothing, waiting for an explanation.

'Two people were killed yesterday in the sanctuary my brother has built. One of them was Dar Luga, the stewardess, and the other was a young attendant to Princess Gelgéis, named Cera, who also served in the Daughters of the Storm. Resolving their murders is my problem. I believe the real targets of the attack were my brother and his bride.'

Abbot Cuán's eyes had widened, for he knew Dar Luga well.

'And the problem that I can avert?' he asked.

'Tonight Dar Luga and Cera are supposed to be interred, having been duly watched yesterday, last night and today.'

'And so?'

'The priest you recommended to act as my brother's chaplain, Father Socra of Sleibhte, is contemplating a refusal to conduct the interment of both of them.'

The abbot frowned. 'Why? I had recommended Father Socra because he is a moral man, but I also believed, having appointed someone from Osraige, it would help mend some of the tensions between Osraige and Muman after Osraige was made to pay tribute to Cashel for their involvement in that conspiracy plan of Fianamail of Laigin. I did not think Socra would exacerbate matters.'

'I understood that. But it seems that Father Socra is a believer in some of these new extreme ideas that are being agreed in the councils set up by Rome.'

'I did not think such decisions would affect burial rites. I thought he was fairly balanced about such matters.'

'Father Socra has implied that he thinks it wrong that Cera is buried with the usual rites because she is a female warrior, and such a calling is an affront to the New Faith. The female warriors will give demonstrations of the martial arts during the fair and that upsets him. The excuse not to bless the burial of Dar Luga is that the new physician believes Dar Luga's death, which was by poison, might have been self-inflicted and, according to Augustine of Hippo, by whom Father Socra sets much store, suicides cannot be buried by the New Faith.'

Abbot Cuán looked solemn. He had a quick mind.

'I presume this suicide was not your finding? You believe the administration of poison was done purposefully by someone else?'

'Dar Luga was murdered as much as Cera was. You know how much Dar Luga was beloved in Cashel, not just by her relatives and the local people but also by the warriors of my brother, who had come to regard her as a mother figure.'

'Have you and your brother spoken to Father Socra about this?'

'We have. He is a stubborn man. I think there will be much trouble if Father Socra refuses the rites of burial not only for Dar Luga but also for Cera.'

'Are you sure Father Socra understands all the implications? Does he understand the appropriate laws here, which are certainly not overruled by the laws of Rome?'

'Father Socra has been told. Whether he understands, I do not know. All I know is that he seems determined to enforce these new philosophies. He is a strange one. He spends most of the day prac-tising archery.'

Surprisingly, Abbot Cuán chuckled.

'I have heard about that. Before he joined the religious, he used to be a bodyguard employed by some *bo-aire*, a noble who lived along the banks of An Fheoir.'

'Not the Bhearú?' Fidelma queried sharply.

'One river bank is much the same as another. But he trained in the abbey of Sleibhte, which I thought was more sheltered from these new ideas of the Faith. I thought his voice would be moder-ate.' Abbot Cuán hesitated. 'How successful have you been in resolving the mystery of the attacks on your brother and his wife? Have you apprehended anyone or do you have a suspect?'

'There are suspects, but I have no conclusion that I can present to Chief Brehon Fíthel when he arrives,' Fidelma confessed.

'He is not at the fortress?'

'He is expected shortly. Like yourself, Fíthel has to play an official part in the official opening of the fair. The major problem is the joint funerals tonight.'

Abbot Cuán was reassuring. 'I will have a special word with Father Socra. You can be sure that I will remind him that he is answerable to the laws of this land and the religion that is still practised here, and not that in Rome. If he proves intransigent then I shall conduct matters myself.'

Fidelma smiled in relief.

'*Debitor tuus su, abba*,' she declared as she waved her obedient pony alongside the carriage and nimbly mounted it.

Abbot Cuán leaned forward with an answering smile. '*Omnia fortuna in via, Fidelma!*' He lifted his hand in a wave as she sent her pony into a canter.

The chapel bell was ringing to mark the beginning of the third *cadar* of the day. The sun was already at its zenith in a clear, blue sky in which a few white soft balls of cloud drifted. Eadulf arose from the light *etar-shod* or middle meal. Muirgen had brought him a traditional plate of *biror*, highly prized watercress, popular eaten raw as a salad with root plants called *mecon*, chopped carrot or parsnip and sometimes brooklime, accompanied by cheese and barley cake. He felt content as this had been accompanied by a mug of cider.

Having dedicated the early morning to his ride with his son and indulged in a few games with him before passing the boy over to the care of Muirgen, who would doubtless send him to one of Brother Dáire's assistants to be instructed on his letters and numerals, Eadulf considered his choices until the return of

Fidelma. He knew that she could lose track of time on her rides so it was of little concern that the day was passing swiftly. What he was concerned with was the fact that Abbot Cuán had not arrived. He knew that Fidelma was probably thinking the same thought. At least the abbot was not as fanatical as those who felt obligated to adopt the new ideas devised from the various councils that seemed to occur frequently under Rome's influence. The rituals and concepts of the New Faith were now changing. Someone of the abbot's stature was needed to stand up to the pedantic attitude of Father Socra.

Eadulf realised he should not waste time on such concerns. The main problem should be the resolution of the murders of Cera and Dar Luga. Unlike Fidelma, Eadulf did not consider going for a ride alone a good way to concentrate his thoughts. But he wanted to be alone and if he left the fortress and walked through the town he knew he would be distracted by those seeking information. The day after tomorrow the fair was to be officially opened by Colgú. The township would be swarming with people. There would be jesters, jugglers, gleemen and all manner of professionals who came to entertain. There would be contestants for the horse racing, ball games and other challenges. It was the martial arts competitions that brought his mind back to the murder of Cera.

He decided to climb to the outer wall of the fortress and take his stroll along the walkway. He knew the sentinels would respect his passing without distracting his thoughts by trying to engage him in gossip. However, it was not long before he found himself diverted. He was walking along the southern wall that led above the barracks of the household guards and the stables. At the end of this wall was the south-western corner watchtower. By the tower, stretched over the adjacent wall, was a figure. Eadulf saw the figure was dangerously balanced over the wall, as if peering downwards. He could not guess who it was. There was no sign of a sentinel in the watchtower who might have encouraged caution.

Eadulf started to hurry forward with a cry of warning. The figure immediately thrust backwards to a firmer position, stood and turned to face him. It was Sister Sárait. She had a puzzled and rather angry expression on her features. Eadulf came to a halt before her, slightly breathless.

'Are you all right?' he asked.

'Why should I not be?' she demanded.

'You were balanced precariously,' he replied, surprised at her tone of belligerence. 'I was worried you might lose your balance.'

Her expression softened. 'I was in no danger. I had a good hold.'

'Even so,' Eadulf pointed out, 'it is a long fall and there are rocks directly below.'

'I saw them then. Part of the rock on which this fortress is built. But I would not have fallen. I was just looking around for, since arriving here to assist Father Socra, I have not really seen this fortress. These great walls with this walkway seem the perfect place to view it from. I would not have fallen.'

'I have seen someone fall from this very spot,' Eadulf confided. 'I am not completely sanguine about the safety prospects.'

'You have seen someone fall?' The girl was suddenly interested. 'They fell from these very walls?'

'It was such a terrible sight,' Eadulf confirmed. He had memories of how he and Fidelma had cornered a fanatical killer at that very corner.

'Who was the person who fell?' the girl demanded.

'It was a woman calling herself Sister Ernmas, but that was not her real name.'

'Then who was she?'

'Her real name was Aincride, wife to a former prince of the

Eóganacht Áine, and mother of Prince Elódach. The mother was a crazy fanatic who wanted to destroy Colgú in vengeance for the defeat of her husband at the Battle of Cnoc Áine. She stole the sacred sword of the Eóganacht and killed an old friend, Brother Conchobhar.'

The girl frowned. 'Why so?'

'The battle at Cnoc Áine was fought several years ago. The victors were Colgú and the Eóganacht princes. Aincride wanted to replace Colgú with her son, Prince Elódach, as ruler in Cashel. When the plot was uncovered, she tried to escape and fell here.' Eadulf motioned to the battlement. 'It only happened back in the spring, in the month of the geese flying north.'

'So what happened to Prince Elódach?'

'He was killed during a last attempt to eliminate Colgú of Cashel.'

The girl turned and looked curiously back over the battlement.

'A sad, wasteful ending,' she commented.

'Not an ending that I wish to see repeated, which is why I cried a warning to you. So how are you finding serving in the chapel here? It is sad that you come at a time when there are more unnatural deaths to contend with.'

Sister Sárait grimaced, almost with humour.

'It sets me wondering how popular King Colgú can be among his people if there are often attempts to overthrow him.'

Eadulf frowned. 'I don't think popularity has much to do with it. The discontent arises from avariciousness or covetousness that some people nurture. Such feelings are often found among families. Here, of course, those feelings are much played on by rival factions from Laigin and even from your home territory of Osraige.'

'Osraige is not my home,' the girl replied automatically.

Eadulf was surprised. 'Oh, I thought that you had come from Sléibhte with Father Socra?'

For a second, he felt the girl looked embarrassed. 'I said I had joined Father Socra at the abbey of Sléibhte. I did not say I came from there.'

'I am sorry,' Eadulf smiled apologetically. 'Where is your home then?'

'I have been in several abbeys. I spent some years of study with Cumméne Find, when he was abbot on the Holy Island.'

'I-Shona – the island of peace? That is among the Dál Riata. I have heard of it as that is where several of the princes of the Angles have sought education and refuge. But you are not of the north; not of the Dál Riata?'

Sister Sárait shifted her weight. 'I went to study there.'

'But from where?' pressed Eadulf, feeling he was being distracted.

The girl looked annoyed but seemed to realise she must make an answer, for Eadulf could be like a terrier after a bone. She shrugged.

'My first abbey was on the island of Faithlinn.'

'That's in the west. It's in the territory of the Prince of Locha Léin.'

'You seem to know this kingdom well, Brother Saxon.'

'Brother Angle,' rebuked Eadulf with a smile. 'I know that your people do not have a word for an Angle but only a Saxon.'

Sister Sárait looked bewildered and then shrugged again. 'You will forgive me but I have several tasks to attend to. Tonight at the start of the first *cadar* the remains of the dead will be taken to the burial ground to be interred.'

'Does Father Socra agree to it?' Eadulf pressed.

'I have heard nothing otherwise,' replied Sister Sárait in a distant tone. 'The corpses are still being watched as the ritual prescribes. I have tried to advise Father Socra on the law here.'

She turned to the tower and was down the stairwell before Eadulf said anything further. A moment later a red-faced sentinel reappeared on to the walkway. He saw Eadulf and raised his hand in an embarrassed salute before turning and apparently resuming his duties. Eadulf knew the sentinel should have been at his post the whole time and not disappeared on whatever errand took him away from his duty. However, it was not his concern and he was about to resume his exercise when there was the sound of an arrival at the main gates. He retraced his step to look back towards the main entrance and felt relief as he saw the coach of Abbot Cuán entering the courtyard with Fidelma alongside.

chapter sixteen

It was early evening when Fidelma was told her presence was wanted in her brother's private reception chamber. She was told that Fíthel, the Chief Brehon, had arrived a short time before, and Colgú had summoned all the members of his inner council to attend him. As she entered the room, she was surprised to see that she was the last one to do so. Colgú was sitting with his heir apparent, Finguine, on his right. On the King's left was the Chief Brehon, Fíthel. Just behind him was Urard, his scribe. Next was Abbot Cuán, in his role as Chief Bishop of the kingdom. Fidelma took her seat as her brother's personal legal adviser. Brother Dáire, the librarian, now acting steward, also had a prominent seat.

Packed into the chamber, attending as advisers to the council, were Enda, the commander of the household guard, with Gormán, commanding the King's standing army, and Father Socra, the chaplain. Fidelma was pleased to see that Eadulf had been invited to attend as a *fine thacair*, one adopted under the law into the King's family. While not being members of the council, family members could advise if invited to do so.

At first, Fidelma thought the council had been gathered to discuss Father Socra's objections to the burials that were due to take place at midnight, but Colgú quickly disabused her of the idea. He opened the proceedings by taking out a parchment.

'Some of you will know that I have received an emissary from the High King, Cenn Fáelad,' he began without preamble. 'This emissary came yesterday and awaits a response. It is a matter that I need to consult with all of you before responding. Depending on our response, it may be that we will eventually have to convene a special council of all seven Eóganacht princes with their brehons to affirm whether they agree with us or not.'

Finguine, the heir apparent, appeared impatient at this preamble.

'Shall we be told what it is that the High King requires us to do?'

'I am obviously coming to the matter,' Colgú grimaced irritably at Finguine's sarcasm. 'The High King requires our views on holding a special council of the kings and brehons of all the five kingdoms of Éireann. The purpose of that council, which would be held under the authority of the High King and his Chief Brehon, would be to discuss and, if accepted, promulgate a new law that would replace our current laws relating to the subject.'

Fidelma now recalled that her brother had mentioned something of this when she had noticed the arrival of the emissary the previous day.

'The messenger has arrived and is waiting, so I thought this would be an appropriate time to test our views in this special council.'

'We should begin by announcing what the proposal is that the High King suggests and why,' Fíthel pointed out unenthusiastically.

Fidelma eyed the Chief Brehon with interest. If he knew the contents of the proposal, then he seemed disapproving of it already. From her knowledge and encounters with him, she knew that Fíthel was conservative when it came to the laws and their interpretation. He would disapprove of anything radical that was being suggested on principle.

'I should begin by saying that the proposal originates from a scholar of the Cenél Chonaill, who has recently joined the abbey of I-Shona.'

'A scholar from the abbey of I-Shona?' Brother Dáire immediately queried. 'That is in the land of the Dál Riata, across the sea in the north-west. I thought that proposals from scholars in abbeys to change laws would first have to meet with the approval of their abbot and his community? After that, it would be presented to the local king and his brehon. If he is proposing it from I-Shona, in the territory of the Dál Riata across the water, and not the Dál Riata in Ulaid, that would be Domangart, the second of his name, who has made that territory independent.'

'I think the original proposal is from a scholar named Eunan, a prince of the Cenél Conaill, who is now a scholar at I-Shona,' Colgú said.

Brehon Fíthel interrupted with a sniff. 'Permission from the abbey is irrelevant if this Eunan is of the Uí Néill and their family. No wonder this proposal has reached the hands of the High King so rapidly . . . they are all the whelps of Niall Noigallach, who have been in conflict with the Eóganacht since Eremon and Eber Fionn fought each other for which half of this land they were to inherit in the time before time.'

Abbot Cuán raised his hand almost as if bestowing a blessing. 'There should be no need for me to remind the learned brehon that we are all the descendants of someone.'

'And sometimes the historians have been known to use their imaginations to make connections to ancestors that never existed,' Fíthel replied in condemnation, 'especially when it comes to the Uí Néill. We can presume that this scholar has the approval of his abbey to make his proposal?'

Colgú referred to his parchment. 'It seems he had the authority of the new abbot of I-Shona, Failbe mac Pipain, the eighth abbot of that foundation. It mentions that he now takes a religious name: Adomnán the timorous.'

Brehon Fíthel groaned aloud. 'And supported by Abbot Failbe . . . who is also of the Cenél Conaill, whose family have provided that place with seven out of its eight abbots! Only the sixth abbot, Suibhne, was not of that family, and he did not last long as abbot. I am sure some members of the Cenél Conaill saw to that.'

Abbot Cuán looked uncomfortable. 'Do I also have to remind a brehon to guard his claims unless he is prepared to prove them?'

'If the learned Abbot of Imleach listened carefully, he would have heard I only made a statement of fact,' retorted the Chief Brehon in annoyance. 'It is so recorded in the chronicles.'

Colgú looked towards the librarian, who confirmed this with a nervous cough.

'For the sake of clarification, I have to say that the sixth abbot did serve only a short period before death cut him down. All the other abbots served far longer periods in office—'

'I do not think we need to be so pedantic about where the proposal emanates. It does come from the High King,' Colgú interrupted.

'But we should be precise about what we claim here,' Abbot Cuán protested.

'Then we should accept Brother Dáire's word in pointing out that my remark was accurate,' Fíthel added sourly.

'Getting back the point,' Fidelma decided to intervene, 'what do we know of this scholar? Whatever his family, is he a worthy scholar? If so, let us consider what he proposes.'

'Eunan is not the first of his family to reincarnate as a religious,' Brehon Fíthel said sarcastically. He was not to be distracted from his obvious dislike of the Cenél Conaill. 'I remember that the first Abbot of I-Shona was also the Cenél Conaill prince named Crimthann the Fox.'

'Crimthann joined the religious and became known as Colm Cille, "the dove of the church",' pointed out Abbot Cuán.

'A fine churchman,' Fíthel muttered. 'He was the one who was found guilty of stealing property from Finnán, the Abbot of Magh Bhíle and then refused to pay fines, having been pronounced guilty by the High King's Chief Brehon. This "dove of the church" then raised his own clan, resorting to his princely rank, and led them into battle against the warriors of High King Diarmait mac Cerbaill.'

'That is a controversial charge,' Father Socra shouted indignantly.

'Father Socra,' Colgú turned to him with a tone of disapproval, 'you are attending only to give advice when that advice is requested.'

'Even so,' Fíthel said angrily, 'if my word is questioned, what does our historian have to say?'

Brother Dáire stood up nervously. 'The battle at Cuil Dreimhne took place one hundred years ago. The High King was killed in that conflict,' he confirmed. 'The annals are clear on the reason for the conflict. Three thousand warriors perished. The Council of the Brehons was held at Tailteann, the famous place of meetings in the Middle Kingdom. They found Crimthann the Fox, whom we call Colm Cille, guilty and he was sentenced to exile. The sentence would have been worse, but he left with some followers to the lands across the sea claimed by the Dál Riata. It was there he established the abbey on I-Shona.'

Fíthel was smiling. 'Our young librarian is correct. Crimthann, or Colm Cille, set himself up on the island which he called the Island of Peace. His missionary work among the Dál Riata and their neighbours, the Cruithne, in Alba, brought him restitution and he was able to return on visits to the five kingdoms, attending the council called by the High King and appearing as the counsellor to the King of Dál Riata.'

'This is not helping me, Fíthel,' Colgú said impatiently. 'Let us forget families and get down to what the High King, Cenn Fáelad, wants. It matters not who this scholar is, but what he proposes and on which the High King thinks we should consider.'

Brehon Fíthel smiled grimly. 'Very well. So another religious of the Cenél Conaill is demanding that brehons make changes to our law system? I suppose we must hear the proposal. What is so important that it will not wait until our regular brehon council convenes for consideration of the laws that need to be updated or discarded?'

Colgú looked at the parchment. 'The proposal is that a council of the five kingdoms – not just the brehons, but the kings and their chief bishops – be held to amend the laws relating to the situation of women, regardless of rank and position. This first proposal is to bring our laws into line with the Christian councils who adhere to the words of the Blessed Paul of Tarsus . . .'

'Which are?' Finguine demanded. 'What words?'

Colgú handed the parchment to Abbot Cuán.

'This refers to Paul's letter to his disciple Timothy, in which it states that he forbids women to teach, or to usurp authority over men, but to remain silent in all matters.'

Fidelma flushed. 'That is totally contrary to our laws. We would never have accepted those words when we accepted the New Faith.'

Abbot Cuán gestured uncomfortably. 'Nevertheless, the words are from the translation into Latin of Paul's letters by Eusebius of Stridon.'

'But most people hold that the old texts of the early church did not have restrictions on women that are now being placed on them,' Brehon Fíthel said, surprising Fidelma by his support. 'Now it seems certain scholars find words in the translations to support their arguments that women should remain relegated to slave-like positions, as they once were in the Roman Empire.'

'Is this what this scholar Eunan is talking about?' demanded Finguine.

Abbot Cuán glanced at the parchment that he now held. 'Eunan ironically proposes the name of the law in Latin rather than in our own language. He names it *Lex Innocentium* . . .'

'Law of the Innocents?' Fidelma muttered. 'I don't understand. Innocent of what?'

'The proposed law abolishes the equality of women bearing arms and being able to defend themselves and others as the equal of men.'

'And that will lead to a complete loss of their status,' Fidelma assured them.

'Explain,' Abbot Cuán demanded.

'The scholar who proposed this as law seems to have lived much of his life outside of the five kingdoms or in isolation in abbeys where the laws of the brehons are unknown. What is claimed here is that women in our society should be mere slaves.'

Abbot Cuán peered at the parchment again. 'The right for women to bear arms – such as the Daughters of the Storm do – is, according to this scholar, merely an opportunity for the commanders of our armies to sacrifice them in conflicts rather than sacrificing male warriors.'

There was a murmur of surprise from those gathered.

'How is that?' Gormán was stung into demanding, although he attended only as an observer.

'The King showed me the manuscript sent to him,' Brother Dáire intervened. 'I have read the proposed text and claims of this scholar. It claims that we strip our women naked and force them into battle; even whipping our unwilling wives into the conflict, being indifferent to their wounds and suffering. Furthermore, it states these women are also forced into sexual relations before and after combat with males.'

There was an outburst of astonishment and anger from those gathered.

'That is as shocking as it is untrue,' Finguine ejaculated.

Colgú turned to his sister. 'Only you, among us, have travelled beyond the seas and have even been in Rome. Tell us your thoughts on how this fabrication could be made against us?'

Fidelma paused thoughtfully.

'My personal attitude is that the more fantastic the lie, the more oft repeated, the more people begin to believe it. During the last centuries, since it was first brought to us, the teachers of the Faith have changed much from the original ideas. In many places, the Greeks, the Copts and those in lands beyond the eastern kingdoms, have departed from Rome and its new ideas. Even the Nazarene sect, where the New Faith was born, has rejected the reform of Rome. We have debated with these new attitudes at Streoneshalh, and at Autun in Burgundia, and in other councils.'

'And lost,' Fíthel pointed out with a sigh.

'The pro-Roman faction is now seeking to replace our laws, and this is yet another attempt,' Fidelma declared. 'This Eunan, or Adomnán, whatever his name may be, is the latest attempt to change us.'

'I agree,' Brehon Fíthel said. 'This Eunan is attempting to recreate our laws in the image of Roman law. That is alien to our nature. The Faith that we first accepted in this kingdom was that taught to us by Ailbe of Imleach, by Déclán of Ard Mór, by Ciarán of Saighir in Osraige and by Ibar mac Lugna of Beag Érin. We were taught the Faith long before the Uí Néill in Ard Magh started to make claims about the teaching of the Briton, Maewyn Succat, who was arrogant enough to claim to be a patrician or aristocrat of Rome and even adopted the name Patricus.'

Brother Dáire was nodding in agreement. 'This Prince Eunan appears to be pushing forward dark propaganda, to support his claims for abandoning the right of women to carry weapons, which is the first step to removing their rights as co-equal with men. As an historian, I object to such lies as told by this Eunan. If one has no eyes to see, then read the law texts.'

'Can you be specific?' Abbot Cuán asked, obviously feeling uncomfortable at the criticism of a fellow churchman.

'The claims of how we treat women warriors are a fantasy by someone who has shut themselves away from reality,' the librarian replied. 'If he declares that women have to be whipped to make them fight in battles by male warriors then he does not live in the same world as we do.'

'Sadly, some of the abbots and bishops have started to adopt these radical ideas from the new teachings from Rome and set up what they call the rules of their communities,' Fidelma added. 'They call them "Penitentials", rules they apply not only to the religious within the abbeys and monasteries but anyone who dwells within the influence of them. The fact is that most of the abbots and bishops are also nobles of the area and believe they have some right to impose their will.'

'I know that you have tried to challenge the use of Penitentials, Fidelma,' Abbot Cuán sighed. 'Bringing in such rules is not something I approve of. I am content with the laws we have held since time immemorial.'

Fíthel agreed. 'I know many abbots in this kingdom have tended to accept the new edicts from Rome. These rules, which the council of Autun agreed a few years ago, tried to insist that all abbeys and Christian institutions should be ruled according to a set of regulations from a churchman called Benedict. Recently, it has become popular for some abbots to set up rules called *Aithrigech*, the Penitentials, which have no bearing on the philosophies and attitudes of our people.'

'So you are against any amendment to the law?' Colgú enquired. 'Are we agreed? For my part, there seems no harm in the declaration that a woman has a right to bear arms to protect her community and, furthermore, that it is a duty and a source of her pride to do so.'

'I am against amending any of our laws, especially changing laws by removing any rights from any group, whether women or men,' the Chief Brehon declared firmly.

'I think many of the rules and regulations that are now being forced through as law, inspired by the new ideas from Rome, are done so under the assumption that women are incapable of determining their own destiny; they have to be instructed and governed by men,' Fidelma declared. 'If the right to be a full member of the tribe, which is the right to bear arms and thereby to sit in military councils, were changed, where would the line be drawn? It would mean that after this loss of rights, women would be ultimately prevented from fulfilling their place in all occupations – even from being lawyers, such as myself, and judges. After that, they would have to be removed from all forms of scholastic life; prevented from being healers and physicians. The names of women who excel in medicine – and, indeed, in all the professions – are well known. What then? Ironically, those women who have achieved high places among the leadership of the New Faith would also be relegated to subservient roles. Their social rights and property and inheritance would be denied; the rights of women to instigate divorce from cruel husbands . . . what then? Where would it end?'

'You have made your views clear, Fidelma,' Colgú murmured.

Eadulf, who had been sitting in silence, had never seen Fidelma so fiery with outrage. As an hereditary *gerefa* of his people, he felt guilty because he had willingly followed the laws of the brehons in recent years, laws as explained by Fidelma. But he knew well that the laws of his own people, which followed closely the laws of the Salin Franks, who, over a hundred years before, had started to codify their *'leges barbarorum'*, had little place for the rights of women.

'So what do we do in response to this proposal?' Colgú enquired, gazing round at his council.

'As far as the High King and his Chief Brehon are concerned, we have simply been consulted as to whether we are in favour of the High King holding a special council to consider this proposal,' Brehon Fíthel said immediately. 'My recommendation is total rejection. This is a farrago of foreign ideas from those who have lost all sense of our cultural reality.'

'I support the Chief Brehon,' Fidelma agreed. In this, she surprised even herself for she disagreed with Fíthel far more than she agreed. 'I would also point out another council will have to consider this. In a few days' time, during the *Aenach Caiseal*, the great fair, there is traditionally held an *arecht* or women's council to consider any matters pertaining to women in this kingdom. You may be assured that they will hear of our decisions.'

Colgú glanced at Abbot Cuán.

'Abbot Cuán, as Bishop of Cashel, as senior religious leader of the kingdom, can we be assured that, in rejecting this, we are not rejecting a fundamental teaching of the Faith?'

'I think we have already answered the question within our law system,' Abbot Cuán smiled thinly. 'I am not saying that this Eunan, or Adomnán, as he is now known, lacks ability, but his scholarship is not in favour of his own people. He is partisan of a particular sect that expounds a different culture from ours.'

Colgú glanced around. 'And you all agree that this is what we should do?'

'I would add one point,' Fíthel interrupted. 'A worrying aspect is that this proposition would change the Cáin law, which must apply to all the five kingdoms. That may well devour the Urradhus Law, our customary law. It is not even a proposal to change the rules within the New Faith but a means of changing the law in all the kingdoms and that law must be obeyed.'

'I think it would make things clear if I add another matter of history,' Brother Dáire suggested. 'It may help everyone understand the current situation. From the time when most of this kingdom accepted the New Faith, it has never been the custom, as it has been in other lands, to dictate the Faith by law. Teachers of the New Faith were there only to influence the people. They did not bind them to obedience of the Faith by law.'

'I thought our laws were changed when the New Faith was accepted?' Colgú frowned.

'In the tenth year of the reign of the High King Laoghaire, with many accepting the New Faith, a council was set up which included the High King as well as our own Corc, King of Muman, and Dáire, King of Ulaidh. The Chief Brehon of High King Dubhtach, the Chief Brehons Ross of Muman, and Feargus of Ulaidh, attended. In addition, representing the New Faith were Patricus the Briton, and Benignus and Cairneach. And they and their scholars considered the laws of our people for three years.'

There was a little stirring of impatience from those gathered.

'So what are you saying, Brother Dáire?' Colgú demanded.

'I wanted to remind everyone what it says in the introduction to the laws that they revised and adopted. It says: "What did not clash with the word of God in the written Law and in the New Testament, and with the conscience of the believers, was confirmed in the laws of the brehons by the ecclesiastics and the princes of the five kingdoms of Éireann . . ." So the decision is already made.'

Fíthel was smiling in satisfaction at the young steward and librarian.

'What was good for the New Faith and its influence on the law of the brehons then, is also good enough for the New Faith in these kingdoms now. We can legally reject the idea of this so-called scholar who has exiled himself to the land of Dál Riata across the sea.'

'I protest!'

Everyone turned in astonishment as Father Socra leapt to his feet, seemingly shaking with rage.

'You have been advised that you are here only as an adviser when the advice is asked for,' Colgú warned him immediately.

When Father Socra seemed reluctant to re-seat himself, Fíthel tried to explain.

'You are here as the new chaplain to the King. You have no vote on this council. You attend only to give information when asked.'

'But you have heard only one side,' the priest shouted. 'There is the writing of the Blessed Mo Chua, who has condemned female warriors as an abomination. You ignore him at the peril of your souls.'

'Which Mo Chua do you refer to?' Abbot Cuán's brows came together as he searched his memory. 'There are several bearing that name.'

It was Brehon Fíthel who answered. 'He means Mo Chua of Balla in Máigh Eo, the Plain of the Yews. His real name was, of course, Crónán, son of Bécain. Mo Chua is just a pet form of his first name meaning "the swarthy one". He died the very year that you were born, Fidelma.'

'A northern ecclesiastic? Should we know about him?' Colgú asked.

'His work should be essential in considering this matter,' protested Father Socra. 'I base my condemnation of the Daughters of the Storm on it.'

'I doubt it is well known,' Brother Dáire reflected. 'There are at least fifty religieux of that name, as Abbot Cuán has observed. All of them use this pet form of Crónán. I don't think his religious scholarship is well known.'

Colgú turned curiously to his Chief Brehon. 'But as you knew the year of his death, Fíthel, you must know something about him.'

'I met an aged brehon from the north who told me a story, and one that might account for this Mo Chua being antagonistic to female warriors.'

'Share it with us,' Fidelma immediately insisted.

'It seemed that a local noble in Balla hired female warriors for his protection. But he did not pay them well or regularly. They protested and even went to Mo Chua, the local bishop, and asked him to arbitrate with this noble. Not only did he refuse, but he declared his support for the noble. Whereupon two of these female warriors left the noble's service and took to the highways, robbing the friends and relatives of this noble. One day Mo Chua and his companion passed through a ravine where the two female warriors were. They captured him and dangled him by a rope over a precipice until he agreed to pay them a ransom. He had little option. They let him go but he never forgot nor forgave what he considered the shame.'

There was laughter, to Father Socra's mortification.

'Did these female warriors have names?' Fidelma asked with a smile. 'It sounds as if they should be well known.'

'Oh, yes,' Fíthel nodded. 'One was called Bec, the small one, daughter of Cúchoreg, and the other was daughter of Attret, a girl called Líthbán the beautiful. It should be a salutary story.'

Even Abbot Cuán was trying to hide a smile.

'I think that we have spent enough time on this matter,' Colgú declared with an air of relief. 'Fíthel, I will ask you to draft a reply with your scribe, Urard, so that it may be given to the emissary to take to the High King. We can declare this council closed. There are now other matters for us, as individuals, to attend to.'

They all rose and began to move to the door. Fidelma was hesitant before she made to join Abbot Cuán, having observed that Father Socra, clearly fretting at having his views dismissed, was leaving.

Abbot Cuán waited as she came to him.

'I thought I had better check on whether you had spoken with Father Socra,' Fidelma opened.

The abbot inclined his head. 'Do not worry. Since we spoke on the road, I have had a discussion with him. I shall take over for the services tonight and he will make no attempt to interfere.'

'I am pleased to hear it.'

'I feel it is my place to do so. I knew Dar Luga, and I was sure Princess Gelgéis would not object. There will be no problems with following the right obsequies and I have already conferred with the grave diggers that the proper graves are measured in the place of interment below the rock.'

'But I suppose Father Socra was not happy?'

The abbot shrugged; a gesture of indifference. 'I think I may have made a wrong choice when I supported his chaplaincy to Colgú's household. But we shall see. He would be more comfortable at one of the other abbeys, even one that has started to adopt the Penitentials as their rules.'

Fidelma noticed a brief expression of humour on the abbot's features.

'Not that we would want to attract support for these rules that are contrary to our law,' she said dryly. 'But with regard to the rituals tonight, there are no problems?'

At that moment, Colgú joined them, smiling grimly. 'There will be no problems for the services tonight. But otherwise . . .' he shrugged. 'We have only one more full day before the fair and I was hoping that you and Eadulf would have been able to present some explanation of the murders. I fear that that is going to be the great concern, and not the prejudice and antics of Father Socra.'

Abbot Cuán raised a brow. 'We all have our prejudices,' he shrugged. 'I made a mistake with my recommendation. I shall correct it. But why would another day matter, provided Fidelma is able to find the right person?'

'The day after tomorrow is the official start of the fair.'

'This I know,' frowned the abbot. 'And so?'

'I and Princess Gelgéis have to officially open the fair.'

The abbot looked bewildered. 'I also know that. I have been told the procedures. We all have to stand on the platform to take part in the opening ceremony. There is nothing new about it.'

'I think what my brother is implying is that he would be far happier had the matter of the responsibility been explained by then.'

Abbot Cuán was still puzzled.

'If the intrusion into the sanctuary was an attempt on my life and that of Princess Gelgéis,' Colgú began, 'then another attempt could be made. It would be an ideal time.'

Comprehension dawned in the abbot's expression.

'And what better time and place for that attempt would be when we are exposed on a platform with a vast crowd of strangers mingling about?' finished Colgú.

chapter seventeen

'Not again!' was Fidelma's first thought when the rapping on their bedchamber door penetrated her mind and she came awake in the darkness. This time Eadulf was already awake and moving to the door. Once more it was Muirgen who stood on the threshold with a lamp, looking nervous.

'Colgú has sent a message bidding you both to come to the sanctuary immediately,' she announced.

'Another death?' Eadulf groaned.

'I don't know,' the old nurse admitted. 'I do not think so. The messenger did not say so. Only that you are both to go there immediately.'

It took a short time for Fidelma and Eadulf to splash water on their hands and faces, and get dressed, during which Eadulf said sourly, 'If this is another attempt, it is stupid for the assailant to return to the sanctuary.'

'It is said that lightning does not strike twice in the same place,' Fidelma replied.

'In my experience, there is always an exception,' Eadulf muttered cynically. 'If the killer was able to break in once, they could do so twice.' He suddenly regretted his comment as he remembered it was Fidelma's brother and Gelgéis who were in danger.

Fidelma did not respond. When they emerged into the courtyard it was still in that curious gloom of pre-dawn. They judged it was almost the second *cadar* of the day. There had been a recent shower of rain, causing sparks of light where their lamp reflected on the water. Inwardly Eadulf groaned and wished they could get through a night's sleep without being awoken with an alarm.

It had been a late night. Abbot Cuán's arrangement of the obsequies for Dar Luga and Cera had been protracted, due to the attendance of so many who had come to pay their respects. Dar Luga had been popular not only in the fortress but the township in its shadow, as well as the surrounding countryside. The funeral party had left the chapel to move in solemn procession to the graveyard below the towering rock, so that the bodies could be interred at the traditional time of midnight. They had returned in the early hours and now Eadulf was complaining of missing what he considered to be a good night's rest. He realised his thoughts were not helpful. But if there had been an attack that had harmed Colgú and his new wife, he was sure they would have been informed immediately.

As they emerged into the paved courtyard before the King's resident they saw several members of the household guard were active. To their left, there were lights in and around the warriors' barracks and the gatehouse, but the great wooden doors of the fortress were closed. The dim, flickering lights of the burning torches highlighted the sentinels.

'Unusual activity,' Eadulf muttered.

As they crossed towards the main doors of the King's residence, a familiar one-armed figure was on the steps awaiting their coming.

'What's going on, Dego?' Fidelma greeted the warrior.

'You have not heard?'

'Only that we have been sent for. Is anyone injured?'

They both had a feeling of relief when Dego replied in the negative.

'It is another intruder,' the man added grimly. 'Or probably the same one.'

'An intruder? Did they break into the sanctuary. Have they been caught?' Eadulf demanded.

'Colgú and his lady were asleep and were awoken because they heard someone moving on the roof. I best let the King tell you the details himself.' Dego opened the main doors. Aidan was awaiting them inside and spent no time in greeting them, but led the way to the stairs leading to the sanctuary.

'Your brother and Gelgéis are above with Luan.'

'I thought Enda was going to resume his duties. Is he here?'

'I think he has been sent for.'

'Do you know what happened?'

'I am told that someone was trying to break in through the skylight into the master bedroom.'

'So lightning does strike twice in the same place,' Eadulf muttered cynically.

Fidelma was already ascending but, pausing on the top step, she called out to announce their presence.

Colgú came out from the master bedroom and waved them forward. Gelgéis was sitting on the bed, comforting a nervous young girl whom Fidelma recognised as one of the attendants who must have taken Cera's place. Gelgéis was handing her a mug of something to drink. Under the skylight of the bedroom, Luan was standing, staring up at it. He glanced across as Fidelma and Eadulf as they entered behind Colgú.

'We were asleep,' Gelgéis told them. 'Lucky that the previous events caused our sleep not to be so deep. We both heard movement on the roof. Colgú immediately called to Luan, the guard.'

'I came at once and alerted Aidan and Dego,' Luan volunteered. 'I was hoping we would have found a ladder of sorts to get up to the roof or through the skylight.'

'It would be impossible to negotiate a ladder into this room to reach up to those skylights,' Eadulf pointed out.

'So you are all saying that there was someone on the roof?' Fidelma asked.

'Someone who had apparently been trying to gain entrance,' Colgú confirmed. 'Had my sleep not been shallow following that first experience, then the killer might have succeeded in achieving what they tried in the first attempt.'

'Has anyone gone up on the roof?' Fidelma demanded. 'That would be the first thing to do.'

Luan looked a little affronted at the implied rebuke. 'I sent to alert Enda who, I am told, has taken a guard to observe the roof from that of the main building. As you know, that would be the only route to the roof above this.'

'Tell me what sounds alerted you,' Fidelma asked her brother.

'As I said, I was awoken by someone moving on the roof,' Colgú confirmed. 'I heard sounds around the skylight and swung out of bed. Gelgéis was awake and alerted. I took my sword and was going to give a good account if the person succeeded in opening the skylight and attempted to drop into this room. I think the moonlight caused a reflection on my blade, for the movement stopped.'

Fidelma seemed sceptical.

'I doubt if your blade could cause a reflection from that angle. Anyway, you have only to see the measure of the skylight from the floor to know that if anyone had tried to drop into this room from that height it would have resulted in a serious injury for them. You would hardly have needed your sword to defend yourself.'

'Then . . .?'

'If there was a way to fix a rope, they might have planned to come down using that method.'

'I have seen it done,' Luan confirmed. 'Although the person would need to be very slender but strong to do that.'

A moment later Aidan returned to the room to answer Colgú's previous request for a ladder. He reported that it was impossible to negotiate into the sanctuary with a ladder long enough.

'What if the intruder is still hiding on the roof above?' Colgú demanded.

'Luan has just said that Enda and another warrior have gone up to see. We will have to wait until daylight before we can do a search above,' Fidelma replied. 'I am afraid your design has excluded any easy method of getting on to the roof in the darkness.'

'Except for the ability of this intruder,' Eadulf muttered.

'What do you mean?' Colgú did not understand.

'I think that you have to ask how this would-be intruder was so secure in their knowledge that they were able to get on to the roof in the first place, and know that they had the expectation of descending through the skylight, which we are unable to do.'

Fidelma was shaking her head. 'I do not intend to go scrabbling about the roof in darkness, even if I could get on it,' she said firmly. 'It is dark and cold. I suggest you and Gelgéis get some rest. If you are happy to remain here, you can double your guard. But I don't think the intruder will be back now, having failed in their task. When it is daylight we will come back and, hopefully, Enda might have seen something we can follow up.'

After Colgú and Gelgéis decided to remain, it took a little time for everyone to disperse. A guard was posted outside their door as well as one at the entrance to the stairway. Fidelma and Eadulf waited until the guards were there before they left to return to their own apartment.

'Well, I suppose this answers one question,' Eadulf said, as they left through the main doors.

'Which is what?'

'It seems that the intended victim of the assassin was either Colgú or Gelgéis or both of them.'

'I think it was obvious almost from the start,' Fidelma muttered absently.

A voice called Fidelma by name. They turned to see Enda hurrying up. His excited expression showed that he had something to tell them.

'I have someone you should speak to,' he announced. 'A witness.'

They regarded him for a moment in astonishment.

'A witness?' Fidelma repeated.

Enda turned and called for someone to come forward.

'This is Luchar-súil,' he explained, as a young man, in the warm clothes of a sentinel who has been on watch during the night, approached.

'And you are a witness . . . to what?' Fidelma stared at him.

'I saw the person on the roof of the sanctuary. They were attempting to break through the skylight,' the young man replied.

'You saw . . .? How so? From where? And why have you not spoken before?'

'I am a sentinel on the west wall. Having seen what I saw, I came round to the main doors as quickly as I could. I found Enda, who was about to go up to the main roof, which overlooks the roof of the sanctuary. So I told him what I had seen.'

'We went immediately to the roof,' Enda explained quickly. 'We saw no one there. We looked for a person but saw no one.'

Fidelma turned to the man, frowning slightly. 'Speak then. You saw the person attempting to enter the royal apartment through the skylight? How could this be? It is only just getting light enough to see.'

'I am a sentinel on the outer walls. My name is aptly given for—'

'I know, I know,' she interrupted impatiently, 'you are named because you have the eyes of a hawk. It was not yet dawn, so my question is – how could you see?'

'I could observe shadows, lady. My task is usually patrolling the west wall. I usually have the night watch, the first *cadar* of the day. Perhaps that is why you have never seen me before. Along the wall, during the hours of darkness, there are brand torches.'

'Are you telling me such torches would illuminate the roof of the sanctuary?'

'Of course not, but they create shadows.'

'Go on.' Fidelma gave a tired grimace.

'Very well. I was walking the western wall in mid-watch. But there was also a bright moon,' he smiled, perhaps a little triumphantly. 'I forgot to mention the moon.'

'So you did,' Fidelma replied sharply.

'Naturally, as a watcher on the wall my attention is fixed to the outer area beyond the walls. It is not concentrated on the inner buildings of the fortress.'

Fidelma tried to maintain her patience. 'That much is obvious.'

'So I was on the stretch of wall looking to the west. I had reached the little watchtower on the wall opposite, where the new royal apartment is. The one now called the sanctuary. In fact, I had gone into the turret for a moment or two.'

'For what reason?'

The man hesitated and looked embarrassed. 'There are times when one needs to descend the stairs and use the ground below the walls, lady,' he explained.

'Speak plainly then.' Fidelma was not amused and growing annoyed. 'And then?'

'Then I climbed back to the wall. As I was emerging from the turret I heard a noise from the sloping slate roof of the sanctuary. It was as if something was scraping at wood. It was like a scratching sound. The roof was in shadows, except now and then the bright moon reflected on one or other of the skylights. I am not sure whether it was the light reflecting or the sound that I heard that alerted me. Maybe they were simultaneous. Anyway, I saw a shadow, the shadow of a figure bending over the skylight and I believe they were trying to ease it open. I was thinking of running to the warning bell, which we have in each of the watchtowers, when there was a light showing through the skylight and I heard a shouting, which indicated that the intruder had been spotted. My warning bell would not have done anything more, for lights appeared in the royal residence.'

'And what did this person on the sloping roof do?'

'The moment the alarms were raised the figure drew away from the skylight. I swear they were not human for, on that sloping roof, they ran upwards over the tiles. No mortal could have gone so quickly. They ran!'

'Ran?' Eadulf sounded incredulous.

'I take oath, they moved swiftly and silently and nimbly, like a cat.'

'To the spot where the sloping roof of the sanctuary joins the main building is quite a height. Did you see a ladder placed against that wall by which they climbed on to the adjacent roof?' Fidelma asked.

The sentinel was shaking his head. 'No, lady. There was no ladder. That is what froze me in surprise. The figure ran up the sloping roof, reached the dividing wall and then . . .'

There was a silence.

'What then? If they had gone upwards all they could meet was the higher wall of the main buildings. A high wall of fifteen metres. So what did this shadowy figure do? Vanish?'

The sentinel looked offended.

'I swear it is true, lady. I saw this dark figure spring lightly up the tiled roof as nimbly as a cat. And when they reached the vertical dividing wall, they seemed to leap upwards. They scrambled up the wall, climbing like a spider. Up they went and vanished.'

Fidelma stood shaking her head at the sentinel's description. She could see that he believed the story that he was telling her.

There was little point in her pressing him on its accuracy. She turned to Enda.

'What part of the old residence adjoins the sloping roof of my brother's new addition? Remind me what part of the old residence lies behind it.'

'Most of the chambers are used when the visiting kings and princes come to Cashel. Finguine, Fíthel and Abbot Cuán, when he visits, have apartments there. Most of it is empty and used only when we host the council of the seven Eóganacht princes,' Enda explained.

'And the apartments are currently fairly empty?'

'That section is empty, lady.'

'But there is no other way of getting from the main residence to the roof of the sanctuary except by a long drop?'

'On to the sloping roof of the sanctuary?' Enda shook his head. 'No other way.'

Fidelma now turned back to the sentinel. She could not prevent her sarcasm.

'So you say your figure ran up a sloping roof to the towering wall, reached it and just vanished. So what has happened to the name you bear? Hawk-eyes? And where did the moon go? You said it was glinting on the skylights and was bright. Did that vanish as well?'

The man drew himself up as if defensive against her sarcasm.

'There were clouds in the sky, which often obscure its light. I will swear to what I saw. The figure ran towards the dividing wall and for a moment, as I said, I saw it leaping upwards on to that wall. It seemed like spider, with arms and legs outstretched as it scrambled upwards, and then it vanished.'

'So you say that this figure . . . a human figure? . . . ran like a giant spider?'

'I can only say what I saw.'

Enda interrupted with a cough. 'I should add that Luchar-súil is known to me as a trustworthy sentinel, lady. He came immediately and reported this to me and accompanied me up to the roof of the main residence. We searched the building but we found no one there.'

'You went to the roof together?' Fidelma mused.

'Yes, lady. Although it was still in semi-gloom, there was enough light to see there was no one there.'

'Clarification can often come with daylight. So let us all meet here during the middle of the second *cadar*, when we will go up to the roof and examine it.'

The sentinel was leaving when a second thought occurred to Fidelma and she called him back.

'You described the shadow. What type of shadow? A person; yes. But tall, short, broad in frame? What aspect did this shadow have?'

The sentinel thought for a moment, rubbing his chin. 'They were small, of that I have no doubt. Small, like a youth.' Then he paused. 'Small, like a boy or maybe a girl.'

Dawn had long broken over the eastern mountains when Fidelma gathered with Eadulf, Enda and Luan, with a couple of members of the household company. Among them was the sentinel called Luchar-súil.

She first insisted on leading them around the building to the area between the western wall and the watchtower opposite, where the sanctuary building rose. Fidelma examined the walls carefully. It was obvious that the sloping roof could clearly be seen from the sentinel's watchtower and wall in the daylight.

'There is no way any person can climb up to the roof of the sanctuary from this aspect,' she said. 'I just wanted everyone to be assured of that.'

'We have no ladders long enough to reach, lady,' Enda confirmed.

'Any comments, friend of the hawk-eye,' Fidelma smiled at the nervous sentinel, Luchar-súil.

'I swear there was someone on the roof, lady,' he stammered defensively. 'They must have leapt from the roof of the building. I would have seen any ladder placed against the building.'

'I do not doubt you. I just wanted everyone to be sure that there was no other way.'

'I said that there is no ladder long enough to reach the roof,' Enda repeated.

A thought occurred to Eadulf. 'So how was it when the building was being constructed? They must have used scaffolding then.'

They stared at him in bafflement and it took him a moment or two to realise he had used an Anglo-Saxon word. He thought hard, trying to dredge up a local word.

'I mean a *táibled*,' he guessed.

Fidelma smiled impulsively. 'That means a fighting galley or a tower used to storm a fortress wall. I think that you are looking for *colba*. We call those structures from which workers are able to work on the taller parts of a building the *colba*.'

'It was one of the things the lady Fidelma asked me,' Luan smiled, 'when she asked about the sanctuary's construction. A *colba* or scaffolding was certainly erected. But that does not exist now, nor are there any ladders available that can reach such extremities. If there are any repairs needed, then the builders would have to construct scaffolding all over again.'

'Besides which . . .' Luchar-súil began, then stopped abruptly, glancing at Fidelma as if realising the company he was in.

'Besides which,' Fidelma went on with a grim smile, 'the figure of this person was seen climbing from the sloping roof up towards the high wall of the adjoining building at the back. I suggest that we now climb up into the turret to observe the roof and wall as the sentinel did.'

It did not take long to the reach the position and make the observation.

'And that helps us not at all,' Eadulf commented dryly. 'From the *forlés*, or skylights, one could see that the slope of the roof was dangerous to climb on and with rain or mist, or with a frost, such an enterprise would certainly have ended in disaster.'

'However, the night was dry and so the endeavour was feasible,' Fidelma observed.

Luchar-súil was pointing. 'The shadowy figure moved to the ascending wall and—'

'Then vanished,' finished Fidelma.

'And, as we can see in the daylight, it is a blank wall. No door, no windows,' Luan said dryly. 'I'd say that it was at least five metres to the top.'

'Maybe six or seven,' corrected Enda.

'Still, an impossible climb from that sloping roof, even in semi-darkness.'

'And what is atop the wall?' Fidelma asked.

'A flat roof,' Enda said immediately. 'It covers the main building. From there, from that roof, the intruder would need acrobatic ability to descend to the sloping roof; to climb down and attempt to enter through the *forlés*.'

'I think it is time I did some exploring on the roof of the main building,' Fidelma said.

She turned and made her way down the turret to the ground. At the foot of the turret, she dismissed the sentinel, not seeing any need for his further involvement.

'Perhaps we need Brother Dáire and his plans from the master builder,' Eadulf suggested to her as they made their way round towards the main doors of the residence.

'They have become superfluous,' she replied. 'We now know how the intruder entered on both occasions.'

Eadulf concealed his surprise. Before he could question her, they met her brother, Colgú, at the main entrance. He appeared as if he had not slept at all. He seemed to be giving instructions to Urard, the scribe to Fíthel.

'Have you discovered anything of importance yet?' he demanded as they approached.

'We are still building up pieces,' she assured him. 'A little more patience is needed. Those pieces we can identify as in a game of *fidchel*, wooden wisdom. I can now see the game, but it needs a final piece or so. Be assured, it will come together very soon, brother.'

'Not soon enough for my liking,' her brother returned.

'None of us likes being faced with the riddle that holds the game.'

Colgú left with an uncomplimentary word, but whom it was aimed at was uncertain. Enda kept his eyes lowered. Eadulf muttered in disapproval: 'A little harsh.'

'My brother is not renowned for his patience.' Fidelma smiled tiredly. 'Now let us go and look at the roof. Lead the way, Enda.'

The tall warrior led the way up the main staircase, which ascended from the corridor in front of the great feasting hall. A guard on duty stood aside with a salute to the company. It was not long until, having negotiated several stairways, they emerged on top of a flat slate roof, with narrow walkways that covered the main building. There was a slight slope to it for the rainwater to drain off, so the angle of even this broad roof needed careful footwork to move across. They followed Enda to the parapet, which formed a border around the roof of the great building. There was no need for Enda to indicate which side was above the sloping roof of the sanctuary.

Fidelma, who had a better head for heights than Eadulf, looked down over the small parapet wall. Directly below was the sloping roof of the sanctuary. She gauged it was six or seven metres below. Directly opposite from where they stood, they could see the rising small tower on the western wall of the fortress where Luchar-súil had stood.

'Too high to scramble up from the roof below,' muttered Luan, peering down to the sloping roof. 'The brickwork is too smooth for any foot or hand holds. The sentinel's eyes must have been deceived. There is no way anyone could climb up.'

Fidelma did not reply. Instead she was making her way along the parapet very slowing, peering closely at it. She kept glancing across as if to measure her position to that of the turret opposite. She had not moved far before she gave a grunt of satisfaction, peering down at the parapet wall.

'You've seen something?' Eadulf immediately asked.

'You will observe that every few metres along the parapet wall, a stone is laid that is larger than the others so that it protrudes. I remember while we were talking to the builders at Imleach Iubhair last month that I was told this was done for a purpose; something to do with wall strengthening, or for securing possible supports for renovation work. So every so often you have a brick or stone standing proud from the wall.'

Eadulf was grinning as he began to understand. 'And thus something could be hooked on to it? A rope? Not very secure, but for someone with skill . . .'

'Someone with skill and a good rope,' Fidelma agreed.

'Whoever was on the roof of the sanctuary last night, and the time before, was indeed the acrobat we joked about. Last night they came to this main roof, secured a rope and lowered themselves to the sloping roof below.'

'Exactly. And the shadow that the sentinel saw was the intruder. Having realised they had been heard, they hurried back, making their way up the sloping roof to the wall, and were able to climb up. What he thought was the figure making a leap into the darkness at the wall was actually the person using a rope to scale it with ease, the shadow of the wall obscuring them.'

'With ease?' Luan sounded a little derisive. 'Lady, I have served a long time in the bodyguards of the Cashel kings. With all that length of time and training, that is not something I would do readily in daylight, let alone in the darkness of the night. The person who did this must have been a very skilful acrobat.'

Eadulf's eyes suddenly widened. 'You mean we have to look for a fanatical killer who is an acrobat?'

'Tomorrow the fair will open.' Luan was suddenly excited. 'The township will be overflowing with all manner of acrobats. There will be hundreds of them. Some of the best acrobatic talents of the five kingdoms will be attending to demonstrate their talents.'

Fidelma shook her head. 'The only thing wrong with that is the tense.'

'I am no scholar, lady.' Luan was puzzled. 'What do you mean?'

'We are not looking for an acrobat who is coming here in the future but one who was here the last few nights,' Eadulf explained. 'Moreover, that acrobat was here in the fortress and known to the point that they could pass among us without question. That acrobat also had to have a knowledge of preparing and administering a poison. You have forgotten the wolfsbane.'

'I had,' Luan admitted. 'But it must be someone with acrobatic knowledge.'

'Certainly. What was it our friend of the hawk-eyes said?' Fidelma asked as she stood still staring down at the sanctuary roof below.

'He gave the impression the shadow moved nimbly and like a cat,' Eadulf replied.

'More precisely, he said they could have been a young boy or . . .' She paused as if expecting him to finish the question.

'Or a girl!' exclaimed Eadulf.

Fidelma turned to him. 'And who might fit that description?'

'The Daughters of the Storm!' Enda spoke for the first time. His tone held barely concealed anger.

'That could be the reason why Cera was killed,' Luan said triumphantly. 'She could have recognised the intruder as one of her own company of female warriors. Of course, she had to be dealt with if she recognised the assassin. If we accept this then it would confirm that the intended victim was Princess Gelgéis.'

'And your reasoning for that solution?' Fidelma queried.

'The Daughters of the Storm were directly descended from the female bodyguard warriors of Osraige in the time before time. Being of Osraige, maybe their primary allegiance is to Tuaim Snámh and not to a princess of Osraige. As we know from the past, it seemed that the ruler of Osraige was happy enough to form an alliance with the King of Laigin. Gelgéis marrying Colgú was the final straw. By this means he could cease paying the tribute. What appears as a riddle is now solved. An easy solution.' Luan ended with a jubilant smile.

'A question or two.' Fidelma's voice was soft. 'Which of the Daughters of the Storm would you accuse? Or are you saying that all of them were in this as a conspiracy?'

'Why . . .?' Luan began, and then paused.

'You have to be specific. Was it Crédh, Corbach, Cumann or Bec-Odras? Or all of them? I presume that you are accusing the leaders of the troop and not the others?'

Luan stood scowling as he considered the choices.

'Apart from Crédh, I don't even know their names,' he admitted.

It was Eadulf who added quietly: 'I have to point out that Crédh did admit to a love for Cera, and that Cera rejected her. That could be a motive.'

'It could. Yet before such accusations you need to make more enquiries,' observed Fidelma. 'You present two possibilities, but on the first one, the question you should pay attention to is: if the assassin were a member of the Daughters of the Storm, and Cera recognised her and thus was killed to prevent her revealing the identity, why would this warrior-cum-assassin poison Dar Luga? Why do so in the manner that the poisoning was done? It was a poison that was not fast working, so it was not done for the same purpose as the motive for killing Cera.'

Luan, who had been listening to the exchange, was now looking troubled.

'I had forgotten. Now I realise my idea might be wrong. I should have thought of it before.'

'Thought of what, Luan?' Fidelma asked.

'I am not clever, lady. I am a warrior, as you know, and there are simple codes. If Cera was killed by a fellow warrior, why did they do so in a way no warrior would do? It breaks all codes and training.'

'Not to mention the poison, in the case of Dar Luga,' Fidelma added pointedly.

'Well, I will accept these arguments.' Luan was resigned. 'But I think the method of entry needed someone of the acrobatic ability and training similar to that undergone by the Daughters of Storm.'

Fidelma turned to ask Enda a question, but, to her surprise, the tall warrior had vanished. While they had been arguing with Luan, it seemed Enda had quietly left them. She was worried about his behaviour although it seemed that the others had not found anything unusual in his sudden disappearance.

'That's another point,' Eadulf was saying thoughtfully. 'There is another person in the fortress who doubtless would admit to that acrobatic ability, and they also have the knowledge to distil the poison. Síonna, the physician, who was once a member of a female warrior group.'

'But she had not arrived in the fortress until after midnight on the night Cera and Dar Luga were killed,' Fidelma pointed out.

'Well, that exonerates her, then,' Luan sighed.

'Síonna, the physician, is the perfect suspect,' Eadulf insisted. 'She has admitted to being a warrior before she qualified as a physician. And she *was* here on the night of the first attack at midnight. She entered the fortress at midnight and we did not know it until the next morning. And who greeted her and gave her a room until she could report officially the next day? Are we saying that she did not have an accomplice?'

Chapter eighteen

Eadulf was surprised when Fidelma declined to confront Síonna immediately.

'There is little point until we get more firm evidence,' she pointed out. 'Everything we have talked about so far is circumstantial. Think about it. It certainly fits our interpretation, but we need more. One of the things that is lacking is a clear motive.'

'But surely your laws have guidance on indirect evidence,' Eadulf protested.

'And on inadmissible evidence,' Fidelma pointed out. 'These matters are very specific. Even when eyewitnesses claim to have seen incriminating behaviour by the suspect, the law acknowledges that these grounds for suspicion must be carefully backed by evidence, or by proven lies by the suspect in response.'

'But there are surely grounds to interrogate the physician now?'

Fidelma shook her head. 'Such hearsay evidence, and indirect evidence, is not of itself conclusive. Also, the character of the suspect must be taken into account, and if the suspect has no known criminality recorded against them they can clear themselves just by taking an oath called the *fír tesa*.'

'So what do we do now?'

'Well, firstly it is my turn to take young Alchú for his morning ride. As for you, perhaps Brother Dáire might advise if there was any way of discovering the physician's family background. If Síonna was known as a warrior who engaged in exhibitions of the martial arts before she became a physician, she must have left some footprint behind that will lead us to her family.'

'Surely it would be easier simply to confront her?'

'It is not the way of our law, Eadulf. We must seek what information we can about Síonna by other means. The family connections might give us some clue to any motive.'

'But, in the meantime, Colgú and Gelgéis may still be open to attack.'

'Tonight, members of the household guard will also be on duty on the main roof to stop anyone performing acrobatics to get down to the sanctuary,' she assured him.

'What about Enda?'

Fidelma frowned. 'What, in particular, about Enda?'

'The way he disappeared when we were discussing things on the roof? I still find his behaviour suspicious.'

'I think you have forgotten that Enda agreed with Colgú to continue to represent the warriors of Cashel in the martial arts contest with the Daughters of the Storm. So he has been attending practice in the same manner that he did when Cera was to be their champion.'

'I still think it was a bad decision,' Eadulf sighed.

'But the decision has been made, even though I agree with you.'

'Well, I will see what I can find out from Brother Dáire. And you?'

'After I have taken our son for his ride I promised to go into the town and see Della and Lassar. There are things to be done for the fair tomorrow. So some of my time is best devoted to making the fair as successful as possible and as normal as possible. If the attempted attacks on my brother and Gelgéis are intentions to replace him as King, then the fair must be one that gives confidence to the people.'

*

For Eadulf, the day passed with increasing frustration. Even with the advice and assistance of Brother Dáire, he was able to find nothing of significance other than what Síonna had already told them, although her transition from warrior to physician was clearer. Eadulf had discovered she was the daughter of a *bó-aire*, a local minor noble. There seemed nothing suspicious at all other than she had grown up in the territory of the Uí Fidgente, whose princes had long been arguing with the Eóganacht of Cashel until a peace accord was made with Prince Donennach. As the Abbey of Mungairit was in that territory it was obvious she should have studied there. It was the most famous teaching school in the vicinity, founded by Mainchin, son of Setnai of the Dál Cais, who was named the Wise, renowned for his learning. Eadulf found out that Síonna also did exhibitions of martial arts to help fund her way through her medical studies.

Eadulf became side-tracked looking for disputes that could have led to blood feuds, but found nothing. There was nothing to distinguish Síonna as a fanatic, or even related to any branch of the Eóganacht family who would have any conflict with Colgú's family. Even as he thought this, Eadulf had to remind himself of the curious way that the kingship was passed on in Fidelma's country. Even with Brother Dáire's invaluable knowledge of such things, there was nothing in the library that showed the physician had any motive in attacking Colgú or Gelgéis.

By mid-afternoon Eadulf was so exhausted that he made his way back to his apartment and asked Muirgen to prepare him something to eat. He felt very tired, in fact, too tired to even play with little Alchú, whom Fidelma had delivered back after her morning ride so that she could go on to the township to advise on the arrangements for the fair. Eadulf felt guilty that, having eaten his late meal, he had fallen asleep and awoken finding that he had achieved no simple afternoon doze but must have slept for some time. The sky was darkening. When he entered the living chamber, he found Muirgen stoking the fire. Fidelma had not returned from the township.

'It is unusually dark,' he commented, as he asked Muirgen to bring him a glass of cider and some barley cakes.

'Thunder clouds coming from the west,' sighed the old woman. 'Taranis will be visiting us soon.'

Eadulf no longer smiled at the old women's preference for ascribing natural phenomena to the ancient pagan gods. Muirgen had been raised and had lived in the isolated mountains in the west before Fidelma and he had brought her – and her husband, Nessan – to Cashel as nurse to their infant son.

'Won't the bad weather destroy the fair tomorrow?'

'The storm will vanish after midnight,' Muirgen replied confidently.

Eadulf often wondered how she knew such things but he no longer questioned her. She could be relied on. She seemed to have knowledge of the skies, the movements of clouds and the positions of stars, and was accurate in her predictions.

'So tomorrow will be a good day?'

'Cloudy but without rain. Taranis and his escorts will have ridden across the skies by the morning. Do not worry.'

Eadulf smiled. 'And now will you prophesy when Fidelma will be returning home?'

Muirgen looked at him as if she doubted his sanity.

'She is a free spirit but a conscientious one. So she will make sure her friend Della has all the information necessary for the fair before she returns.'

After Muirgen had gone, Eadulf stacked another log on the fire. Although it had been a warm summer's day, as evening approached it was growing cold. He spent the time reading a few texts but did not stir much until Muirgen came to announce the main meal of the day. She explained that Fidelma had sent a message that she was not going to return until early morning as there were some complications with the organisation of the fair. That irritated Eadulf, and while he was wondering how to occupy himself, there was a knock on the door and Muirgen answered it.

'A boy with a message,' she announced. The child remained outside and whispered something to Muirgen. Muirgen thanked him, came back in and shut the door.

'Who was that?' asked Eadulf, sinking into a chair before the embers of the fire.

'A stable boy with a simple message,' she replied.

'For me?'

'From Enda. He asks you to meet him in the chapel just before the start of the first *cadar.*'

Eadulf was surprised. 'That's rather late, isn't it?'

'I did not choose the message,' Muirgen replied, but there was no humour in her voice for she did not understand irony.

'I just . . .' began Eadulf. He paused, not wishing to explain irony to the solemn-faced nurse. 'I'll have the main meal here and cider to drink.'

It was just before midnight and the start of the first *cadar* when Eadulf made his way down to the courtyard and walked along to the chapel entrance. The chapel was in almost complete darkness. Eadulf stopped. That was unusual. The chapel had been constructed without sufficient windows or lighting outlets, and those that did exist had been put at angles, which reduced the interior to an almost permanent state of darkness.

It was a different scene from the previous night when the candles were ablaze for the obsequies before the interment of Dar Luga and Cera.

There were usually two small lamps lit at the main doors and directly opposite the entrance to where steps ascended into the bell tower. Sometimes tall candles were lit on the altar, although this was usually during the time of a service, and there was one by a door on the far wall. That was an entrance into the religious quarters. If the lamp by the main door was not lit, which was very unusual, the other lights would emit a faint glow, which would spread the softest of lights through the building. At the moment there was nothing but the disturbing and encompassing blackness of the enclosed building.

Eadulf moved forward a step and halted cautiously.

'Enda? Are you in here?'

There was no response. His voice echoed a little in the high-roofed building. He closed his eyes for a few moments, knowing that when he opened them he had a better chance of focusing in the blackness. However, he could see little better. It took him a few moments to realise that he had been in the same position when he had been pursuing the killer of Brother Fidach in this very chapel. Even as he grew used to the shadows, there was nothing to be seen. It was clear that Enda was not inside the chapel. Eadulf knew that on the far side of the chapel there should be an open door, which led into a passageway off which were the doors to the quarters of the religious. Obviously the door must be tight shut because he knew this passage was almost permanently lit by lamps, and he could see no sign of light emanating around it.

He tried to line up with the door in his mind and began to move step by step slowly forward. He had not gone more than a few steps when his right foot hit something; something soft.

He halted and looked down.

Even in the gloom he could tell that this was a human body. Balancing himself, he lowered on to one knee and felt over the body. His searching fingers found the head and the warm flesh of the face. He could tell that the body, although not reacting to his touch, was still warm and alive. He could hear the faint gasping of breath.

Eadulf rose, knowing he could do nothing without light.

With a muttered curse, despite his location, he turned in the direction of where he thought the main doors were. Slowly, hands held out to protect him from any immediate disaster, he progressed until he could go no further. The first thing his exploring hands came into contact with was cold metal, and in a moment he had registered the outline of a hinge from which he quickly felt his way to the edge of the door and down to the handle. A moment later he was out into the night, which, after the chapel, seemed a place of brightness.

He stood for a few moments, taking in the cold night air and, as if timed on his exit, the rain started to pour down, heavy and vertically. Then, causing him to jump, came the first flash of lightning followed almost immediately by the crash of thunder. Muirgen had been right. Taranis, the thunder god, had arrived.

'Brother Eadulf?' called a young voice.

A second flash illuminated the figure of a young warrior.

'This is he. Is that Cano?' Eadulf screwed his eyes up in the direction of the youthful voice.

'You should not rely on lighting to see your way here. It is dark. You should be carrying a lantern,' the young man admonished.

'Do you have tinder and flint to light a lamp for me? I need a lamp at once.'

All warriors were known to carry flint, steel and kindle in what was called their girdle bag or pouch, and were trained to be able to light candles, lamps and so on without wasting time. Cano moved across and they re-entered the entrance hall of the chapel. It took more time than usual, but with Eadulf locating a lamp purely by touch, eventually it was lit. With the curious young warrior at his shoulder, Eadulf turned back across the chapel.

'Were you supposed to be on guard here this evening?' Eadulf asked.

Cano shook his head. 'There are no watches needed by the chapel. I was on my way to the barracks when the storm started and you appeared . . .'

A groan permeated the echoing space of the chapel.

Eadulf swung round, holding the lamp high. The sound came

from the direction where he had stumbled across the body in the darkness. He moved forward rapidly and found the body, which was stirring as though just coming to from a deep sleep, and not realising the circumstances of where and how they had fallen asleep. The figure groaned again and turned its head slightly towards the lamplight.

'Father Socra!' Eadulf gasped.

The chaplain made no reply but was trying to lever himself into a sitting position. He was clearly weak and confused.

Eadulf gave the lamp to Cano and turned to help the chaplain to an upright position, guiding him to the side of the chapel where there was a chair.

'My head hurts,' Father Socra groaned.

'That does not surprise me,' Eadulf replied. With Cano holding the lamp high, he could see some blood on the forehead of the chaplain. 'Do you know what happened?' he asked.

'I have a painful head, that is what has happened,' the chaplain almost snapped.

'How did the painful head come about?' Eadulf replied with a forced smile.

'If I knew that I would not have been unconscious on the floor,' Father Socra replied testily. It was clear the incident had not improved his temper.

'I understand that.' Eadulf tried to keep his irritation under control. 'So let me interpret matters. You were in here and someone hit you on the head, knocking you unconscious?'

'That is all I know,' the priest confirmed.

'All? I thought it was enough,' Eadulf smiled.

Father Socra was rubbing his forehead with his right hand. 'I would like to be taken to my room so that I can bathe my forehead.'

'Naturally. I shall see to it.'

Some memory stirred with Father Socra. 'I nearly forgot. You studied the healing arts. Well, so long as I am not charged a physician's fee, you may examine the wound.'

'It is not in my habit to charge, but if you demand to see the main physician because you think I am not sufficiently qualified, then you may know Síonna is not allowed to make a charge to any of the King's retinue. Shall I have her sent for?'

'May you not see the cuckoo or the corncrake,' Father Socra swore in response.

Eadulf smiled at the chaplain's resort to an ancient curse, although it was a bad curse, for it meant a wish that the cursed one may not live to see another spring. However, Eadulf decided to ignore it.

'Do you still wish to be taken to your chamber?' he asked in a mild tone.

'Do not play the fool with time, Brother Eadulf.'

'I was not aware that I was.'

'Take me to my chamber!' the chaplain almost shouted.

'You can light the way, Cano,' Eadulf said to the young warrior, who seemed awed at the interchange of the older men. 'When you have finished, I shall want this chapel thoroughly searched.'

'For what?' Father Socra's voice was almost a sneer. 'Do you think someone is still lurking around, ready to attack us again?'

'I would not take a wager on it, but one must observe precautions. Once I know what happened I can be better placed to give the right advice.'

Father Socra began to calm now and sound more reasonable.

'When I went into the chapel it was dark. Whoever attacked me was waiting in the darkness. I saw and heard nothing until I felt the impact on the side of my head. I do not think I even had time to cry out. I was plunged into a deep pool of darkness until I awoke and saw you above me.'

'So you could not identify your adversary?'

'I did not even see my attacker,' the chaplain admitted.

Directed by the chaplain, Cano held up the lantern and guided them through the side door and along the passage to his chamber. Father Socra collapsed into a chair in the corner of the room, by his bed. When a lamp in the chamber had been lit, Eadulf told Cano to find others to help check the chapel and search for signs of the attacker.

Eadulf then turned back to Father Socra to examine his head.

'An abrasion, a little bleeding and there will be a bruising on the side of the head, I would say the blow was struck by a heavy stick. A smooth quality wood that did not inflict a heavy blow. Now heavy oak would—'

'Can you just do something to help?' Father Socra almost wailed. 'My head hurts.'

'I will wash it and add a balm and, in exchange, you could tell me what you know.'

The chaplain stared at him in disgust. 'What would I know? I know nothing. I was knocked unconscious.'

'Let me put it this way,' Eadulf said with patience. 'A person is not attacked for no reason. So if you were attacked in your own chapel, you were attacked for something. So have you any idea why you were attacked, which might lead to discovering who attacked you, or have you led such a blameless life that there is really no reason why anyone should sneak up on you in the dark and hit you over the head? And, if I may say so, that blow could well have been fatal had it been slightly more to the side of the skull.'

The pronouncement caused Father Socra to stare questioningly for a moment. 'Are you serious?'

Eadulf saw the surprise in the man's eyes. 'I have seen enough deaths in my time to know that the human skull is just as delicate as the shell of an egg.'

'Then if the intention was to kill me, it does not make any sense.'

Eadulf frowned. 'Now you're confusing me. Can you elaborate?'

'You are suggesting that I was attacked in the darkness. That someone swung a stick at my head and that maybe they missed the place where they were aiming. That would have been an intended fatal blow.'

'That's about it.'

'It makes no sense as there were lights in the chapel when I was hit.'

'Lights?'

Father Socra made an affirmative gesture. 'I went into the chapel to extinguish the two candles that were burning on the altar. I had previously left them burning after saying the prayer starting the first *cadar* of the day. I say a general prayer then. A similar thing is now done in Rome, which they are calling the midnight Angelus. As usual, there were lanterns at the door and by the entrance to the bell tower. So the chapel was lit.'

Eadulf had good reason to remember the bell tower. He shivered, for it was in the tower he had found the body of the previous chaplain, Brother Fidach, hanging upside down and with his throat cut, the blood dripping down the stairwell in red droplets. Then a frightening thought came to him. He remembered how the throat was cut. It was in the same manner that Cera's throat had been cut.

He turned to Father Socra again. 'But if the place was well lit, surely no one could have come up behind you unseen?'

'I saw no one. I must have felt the blow but I was simply rendered unconscious. I can't remember much before that.'

'How was this? Explain where you were.'

'I was about to intone the final blessing before extinguishing the candles. So I was before the altar and kneeling in prayer. That was when I was hit.'

'So kneeling before the altar? Kneeling with head bent and concentrating on your prayer?'

'I suppose someone could have quickly emerged from some hiding place and stepped lightly up behind me and dealt the blow.'

'Now I see what you mean. If they had meant to kill you they would have brought the stick or cudgel down on your head where it would do most damage, and brought it down enough times to ensure it did. But this person knocked you unconscious and then went quickly round extinguishing the lights before disappearing. It makes no sense.'

'Will you get on with bathing my head and work it all out afterwards?'

Eadulf turned to the basin, found some cold water and began to bathe the wound.

'I am afraid I have left my *lés* in my room.' Even though he had never properly qualified from the famous medical school of Tuain Drecain, Eadulf had always made it a habit, on his journeys, to carry the medical bag by which most doctors could be recognised. Indeed, he had several times been essential to Fidelma's inquiries through his medical knowledge. 'So if you have a headache, perhaps Síonna will have something for you? Ah, I see you have some lavender over your bed. A sniff of that will help. If you need something else, ask Síonna to make you a poultice of foxglove leaves to place on your forehead. It is to lie externally on the forehead and not to be taken internally, otherwise . . .'

He shrugged before turning back and staring around the small room. It was then he noticed an unstrung longbow hanging on one wall.

'Now that is a powerful-looking weapon,' he observed.

'I told you I practise regularly. I was taught archery when I was a child. My father taught me how to bring small game to our table. Nobles could feast on deer and cattle but we had to be content with hares, badgers or an occasional otter.'

'It is a bow to be admired,' Eadulf said, peering closely. 'If you feel better, I presume you may well be entering some of the archery contests in the fair during the next few days?'

Father Socra grimaced uneasily. 'It was my intention to do so,' he admitted.

At that moment Sister Sárait entered the room, obviously in a state of anxiety.

'Forgive me, Father, but what is happening? I was in my cell preparing for sleep when there was noise in the passage and suddenly there were warriors searching and demanding to know where I was a short time ago.'

'It is your turn to forgive me, Sister Sárait,' Eadulf intervened. 'The warriors are searching at my orders. Father Socra was attacked in the chapel a short time ago and knocked unconscious.'

The girl gasped. 'Attacked by whom?'

'That is what we are trying to discover. However, he is now recovering with no more than a bruise and a bad headache.'

From his position on his bed, Father Socra scowled. 'It is nothing to be made light of. I still have a headache.'

Eadulf ignored the chaplain and turned to the anxious girl.

'Father Socra tells me that he was about to extinguish the candles when the attack happened. Where were you?'

'I should have gone to the bell tower to ring the bell to mark the first *cadar*. I usually do so, but Father Socra said he would do so this evening.'

Eadulf turned to the chaplain. 'So had you gone to the bell tower before you went to extinguish the altar candles? I can't recall the sounding of the bell.'

'I went to extinguish the altar candles first.'

'So you did not make it to the bell tower? How are the times for the bell to be rung measured?' Eadulf queried. 'Surely someone noticed the bell had not been rung?'

'There is a tall tallow candle in the tower with portions marked by a pin. The pins mark the passing of each quarter-day.'

Eadulf turned to the girl. 'And where was Father Socra at the time you, Sister Sárait, adjourned to bed?'

'I think he had gone to the main doors to ensure everyone had left the chapel. I was certainly on my way to bed.'

'So you also did not see anyone in the chapel before you went to your quarters. Is that so?'

'I was drowsy and fell asleep immediately. As I told you, the noise of the warriors searching disturbed me. I was passing here when, seeing the light from Father Socra's cell, I came in.'

It was then that Cano rejoined them.

'We have searched the chapel and the grounds close by and found no one who had cause not to be there,' he announced.

Eadulf frowned. 'Who did you know had cause to be here and who had not?'

The young warrior actually blushed in the lamplight. He seemed embarrassed by the question.

'I meant no one who had no reason to be within the vicinity of the religious quarters. There was Sister Sárait, of course.' He nodded to the girl. 'And the four religious assistants who look after the chapel and religious dormitories. Oh, nearby, there was Sister Síonna in her apothecary. Oh, and passing, there was one of those women warriors. Everyone could give a good account of themselves.'

Eadulf groaned inwardly. 'Perhaps it should have occurred to you, young Cano,' he said heavily, 'that if you had just attacked someone nearby and then been accosted and asked what you were doing there, you, too, would be able to give a good account of yourself. You would not lack an explanation so as to create suspicion about your presence.'

The young man swallowed. 'I had not thought of that,' he muttered. 'Do you want me to go round and question everyone again?'

Eadulf found himself smiling. 'I doubt whether that would do any good. They would either have to deal with any weaknesses, or have created a better story. No, I have made a note of whom you say you saw and, if need be, we will have to examine things again in the morning.'

Father Socra uttered a long impatient sigh. 'So long as I can get some balm, for my head begins to throb again after all this talk.'

Sister Sárait was immediately concerned. 'I can get you something for that, Father Socra,' she said solicitously. 'I am adept at mixing herbs. I recently made a potion for a condition where I sneeze among budding flowers and plants. It is something distilled from the bark of the willow that grows by running streams. We call it *salicin*. I found it also helps with a headache.'

Eadulf nodded in agreement.

'I have heard of the efficacy of willow bark. What with the odours of lavender there, above your bed, and a small drink of the distilled *salicin* you will be better in no time. How did you come by such herbal knowledge, Sister?'

Sister Sárait replied with a nervous grimace. 'My knowledge is minimal. I gathered a little in the abbey apothecary outside the chapel.'

When the girl had gone off to get the potion, Eadulf turned to Cano. 'You can dismiss your men, but leave one about the chapel, although I think whoever perpetrated this deed will not be back again.'

He frowned abruptly as he remembered why he had come to the chapel in the first place, and called back Cano.

'Has anyone seen Enda?'

The young warrior shook his head. 'He is not in the fortress tonight. I think he went to that place he has in the township. A lot of the men in the guards say he's seemed to avoid their company these last few days. So he is not spending time in the fortress.'

Eadulf turned to Father Socra. 'I presume, now Cera is buried, Enda no longer meditated in the chapel this evening? However, was he here at all?'

The chaplain appeared a little surprised as he considered the question, but he shook his head.

With Sister Sárait returning, Eadulf stood up and left through the chapel and out of the main door into the courtyard. There he exchanged a few more words with Cano about keeping a careful watch. It was while he was walking back to his chambers that his mind returned unwillingly to the bell tower and the time he had found Brother Fidach hanging upside down with his throat cut. There was something oddly familiar about it. Was it the angle of the insertion and the way the small-bladed dagger was drawn across the throat? But the killer of Fidach had been identified and was many months dead. She had perished as she had fallen from the battlements of the fortress. Yes, the vengeful Ernmas, as she had called herself, was dead; long dead and buried.

Why then did he keep thinking about the way Brother Fidach had been slain? Why did he keep thinking of the way the man's throat had been cut?

CHAPTER NINETEEN

The sounds arising from the township below announced that the fair had started even before the official ceremony by the King and his wife. The bright light of dawn was spreading across the distant black peaks of the eastern mountains. Fidelma had already returned to the fortress after spending time with her friend Della, planning last-minute aspects of the fair. Now she stood at the window of the apartment she shared with Eadulf, looking southward and watching the last greys of the retreating nocturnal light. From what she could see of the first streaks of the white light of dawn, without any threatening warning red in the sky, it was going to be a fine day. It was something she remembered her old mentor, Brother Conchobhar, teaching her: at certain periods, the rains usually ran from west to east, so sunrise often brought a reddish sky and that would mean rain. The old shepherds knew this well and would take shelter.

'I presume the events have started,' came Eadulf's voice from behind her. He had been awakened early by Fidelma's return.

'As you can hear,' she sighed. 'I was up before dawn at Della's, and so came back here immediately. I just wish we were able to come to some conclusions about the assassin before Colgú is called upon to open the fair. If only he did not have to stand so exposed to make his official opening.'

'*Idealis non semper habetur*,' Eadulf replied solemnly. 'The ideal is not always obtainable.'

'But we must always strive for it,' she countered grimly.

'Perhaps your brother should have delegated opening the proceedings to someone else?' Eadulf suggested.

'That would be playing into his enemies' hands. The ceremony will go ahead when the sun is at its zenith. Meantime, in these early hours of the day, events such as the chariot and horse racing can take place before it gets hot.'

Eadulf sniffed deprecatingly, but then realised he should update her as to the events of the previous night. She listened attentively without asking a question. At the end of his recital, a smile crossed her features.

'That's interesting,' she finally commented. 'Do you think Father Socra will be well enough to enter the longbow contest today? I see that he had put his name down for it.'

'He had a headache but not a physical disability,' Eadulf replied. 'At least it was not a self-inflicted wound as I suspected. But who did it and for what purpose?'

'You told me this morning you found the boy who brought the message but all he could say was that it was not Enda who sent it, but instead it came from a female figure in dark robes he could not identify.'

'I am wondering where Enda disappeared to and if he will go ahead with the contest against Crédh?'

'It has become a point of Eóganacht honour. It was Colgú who wanted this contest carried out because he has some jumbled notion that he had put his honour at stake by promising Gelgéis a contest between her warriors and his warriors. I do not think my brother understands the emotional storm that rages within Enda, which you witnessed. Let's hope we can find him and assess his feelings.'

'Can't your brother forget this honour business?'

Fidelma frowned in disapproval. 'You have been here long enough to know that our society's whole existence is based on the principle of honour. That is, when we present ourselves before arbitration in any matter, we are judged and fined by the status of our honour price. The worse thing that can happen to anyone is to lose their honour price. As King of Muman, my brother's honour price is valued at sixteen *cumals*, that is . . .'

'I know.' Eadulf was resigned. 'That is the worth of forty-eight milch cows.'

'Yes,' confirmed Fidelma. 'More than the worth of the chief bishop of the provincial kingdom, more than the level as an *airch-innech*, the administrator of the biggest abbey in the land. What does the law say? "The King's honour is more sacred than any other claim."'

'So nothing may challenge the King's honour?'

'Enda knows the imperative to defend the King's honour,' she said simply.

'And that takes place . . . when? I would like to be there to cheer him on.'

'At the third *cadar* of the day.'

'So what's first on the list?'

'I am attending the *airecht*, a woman's council to discuss matters pertaining to women. I mentioned it in the council the other day.'

'I'd like to attend that.'

'You've been here long enough to know that no man is allowed to be present,' Fidelma smiled. 'Anyway, we have a long day ahead. While I attend to the *airecht*, I am afraid the duty of taking Alchú for his exercise falls on you. I suggest we meet up at Rumann's tavern just before the official opening.'

The major fair green, the *faithche*, was to be in the centre of the township. A wooden platform had been erected outside Rumann's tavern, which faced the main square of the township. It was from here that Colgú and his entourage would announce the opening of the fair, the results of contests would be made known and the prizes given. All this was ultimately governed by the Chief Brehon, who ensured the rules regulating the fair, which had been set by time-honoured custom over centuries, were observed. The authority of the Chief Brehon was maintained through the fairground by minor officials.

Around the central square of the township, lines of smaller tents and pavilions had been erected. Together with a few open sites, these had already been awarded to those plying their various trades. In this area the numerous stalls were devoted to selling food: meat, fish and vegetables, corn and fruit. Rumann himself, as tavern owner, had the franchise on all drinks sold in the square, although some cheap ale stalls were discreetly set up in other places in the township. Across the square were stalls with a variety of clothing and footwear, and carpentry stalls with wooden board sets for *fidchel* and *brandubh* on sale. Next to them were some foreign merchants dealing with gold and silver artefacts and semi-precious stones. These merchants had brought with them their own guardians to watch over their goods, large angry-looking men who did not have the refinement of professional warriors.

It was almost impossible for Fidelma and Eadulf to meet up inside the tavern because of the surging crowds. Arriving first and taking a place nearby, Fidelma soon spotted Eadulf pushing his way across the square.

'We'll take a walk around,' she told him. 'There is plenty of time before the official opening.'

In the surrounding fields, livestock were being readied for what promised to be a lively trade in cattle, sheep, goats, horses, asses and hounds. In fact, the trade for animals had begun early, especially for those looking for watchdogs, beagles being the most highly prized. Sadly, to Fidelma's eyes, there were cages to one side with dogs whose destiny was not to be sold, but eventually to be entered into the many dog fights on which wagers were placed.

Among the livestock merchants were dealers in hares, otters, badgers and some deer. There were even two bears chained under a tree, which were drawing attention. Fidelma knew these were a disappearing species – they were now almost legendary in the five kingdoms. Stretches of land had been prepared for the foot racing, single-horse racing and chariot contests, as well as hare coursing. Other spaces were marked out for weapons contests, like archery and javelin throwing. Prizes were offered for athletic feats, races and team games like hurling. But generally the fair was a time when many fortunes were lost and some won on wagers.

Bands of jugglers and acrobats, jesters and gleemen moved through the crowds, usually led by an *obláire*, a chief buffoon or clown, hoping to attract attention for the act. These were to be watched carefully as they sometimes included light-fingered folk who would not hesitate to augment their riches by swiftly removing items from the unsuspecting.

Among the tents, pavilions and shelters of all types housing the acts, there was even one set aside for the Daughters of the Storm. This was their gathering point, for most of their announced events would be in the open: horse racing, chariot demonstrations, archery and spear throwing. The great event would be the contest between them and Colgú's Warriors of the Golden Collar, which would begin with a series of preliminary archery and spear-throwing contests, and end with a display of swordsmanship.

Eadulf was impressed at the size and scope of the fair, even though he had attended such events before.

'I am beginning to see why your brother couldn't cancel this,' he admitted. 'It brings great prestige to the kingdom.' He hesitated. 'I have not seen Enda. I am worried about him.'

'I was told that he has been seen. Importantly, Cano, who spoke briefly with him, said Enda had no knowledge of arranging to meet you in the chapel last night. That means that we have to find the stable boy who brought you that message. I thought it would be so when you related the incident to me this morning,' Fidelma said.

'So he will turn up for this exhibition of combat with Crédh?'

'If I had my way, Enda would have been allowed to spend days to himself to come to terms with his grief over Cera.'

'It is difficult to discern Enda's mood but there is something changed in him.'

It was hard to concentrate on these matters surrounded by the good-natured crowds who – even when arguing with one another over the price of this and that, or laying wagers on the forthcoming races and the prowess of the competitions, or arguing with those who supported an individual and against those who opposed him – seemed in happy mood. The din was almost deafening when a cheer rose for some event or for somebody who had won some competition or achieved a feat of excellence.

'It looks as though the fair will be successful after all,' Eadulf repeated, having to shout to make himself heard.

'I don't think the success was ever in doubt,' Fidelma returned. 'Fairs are never unsuccessful unless they are held in times of plague or famine, and we have had our fill of both in recent years.'

By coincidence, they were approaching a stall where a man stood clad in black robes, with a chain of polished silver around his neck, from which hung a crescent moon. His long black hair and straggling black beard were unkempt and seemed to have lives of their own, blowing this way and that in the little gusts of wind that cooled the day. He had a deep bass voice, announcing that within his tent were all kinds of medications and spells to rid every known malady and pestilence on the face of the earth. Each medicine was personally dispensed and guaranteed by Corruine, the greatest apothecary of all the ancient kingdoms.

Eadulf gazed at him with a derisive smile. 'I suppose you are the famed Corruine?' he asked sardonically. 'The greatest apothecary of the ancient kingdoms . . . the ancient kingdoms of where?'

The man regarded him good naturedly. 'Ah, a Saxon by your accent?'

'An Angle,' Eadulf returned sharply.

'Angles? I have heard of them. But Saxons or Angles, it's the same difference. They wouldn't understand herbal cures for illness. They only sacrifice and pray to their gods. A hare sacrificed and left to rot above the porch of a hut is no cure at all for those inside. However, I suppose it does provide a good meal for your priests.'

Eadulf glowered. 'Then you must be confused who the Angles are. I come from a civilised land.'

'At least you seem a little more educated than most of your countrymen that I have encountered,' the man replied, stroking his beard as if in thought.

'Let me tell you, I was trained at Tuaim Drecain in the healing arts. I know something of the law of this land . . .' Eadulf replied hotly. 'I know the law here recognises that it is easy to deceive a person who falls ill and is seeking a cure for his malady and so will grasp at anything that is claimed as a cure. The law says anyone who is not qualified and presents themselves to be so, especially in the field of the healing arts, will be punished. They stand without the law.'

It was difficult to see if the bearded man was smiling. Fidelma, who had been annoyed that Eadulf had chosen to start an unnecessary fight, now moved forward, thinking to end the argument.

'I am a *dálaigh*,' she announced. 'Eadulf here is correct when he states the law is clear that anyone not qualified cannot be allowed to make concoctions and claim them as cures. For this you may be reported to the convener of the fair and made to pay substantial fines.'

The man calling himself Corruine turned to her and seemed to examine her carefully. But he was smiling.

'I suppose that you are Fidelma, the sister of Colgú?' He made the enquiry as if passing the time of day.

'You do not seem concerned?' Eadulf snapped, showing his annoyance more at the man's lack of concern than his lack of deference.

'Why would I be?' the other replied offhandedly. 'Before we continue I should say that I studied the art of healing herbs for many years at Sliabh Fúair, where the school of Fingéin still stands. There I attained the level of *Clí*, if that is what worries you.'

Both Fidelma and Eadulf were surprised. A *Clí* was a sixth level of degree and only one below the degree Fidelma herself had obtained. It was regarded as 'the pillar of the house', taking no fewer than six years of study.

It was Fidelma who finally responded after a moment's embarrassment.

'So what is an apothecary of your rank doing, having come all the way from the northern territory of Ard Magh?'

Corruine, still with an amused tone, replied, 'Poets go on circuit, as do lawyers. So why not an apothecary of my reputation, even though that reputation seems to be confined to the Uí Néill kingdoms? I am here telling all the five kingdoms of my reputation and promoting my skills.'

'Then I ask for your pardon, venerable doctor.' Eadulf acknowledged the position of the apothecary and held out his hand. 'I am used to so many fakes and frauds who sell their concoctions at these fairs. I did not expect to meet anyone of your distinction doing so.'

'Nor did I expect to meet the famous Fidelma and Eadulf, whose services have been sought by High Kings as well as by others, wandering in a fairground even though it be under the shadow of the fortress of your brother, the King,' returned the bearded man in a solemn tone. 'Are you just enjoying the fair, or are you on some dark mission with a mystery to resolve? I am always ready to hear a good story about a new and bizarre form of murder.'

Fidelma dismissed the subject with a negative shake of her head. 'I am afraid new forms are not usually among the skills that assassins bring to their craft. Strangulation, for women, often suffices. Sometimes, if they are clever and know of herbs, then something poisonous. However, the time-honoured weapon for men and women tends to be the knife or something similar.'

They could tell that Corruine grimaced behind his beard.

'The wounds caused by a blade are often brought to the physician or apothecary for healing. Or for us to give evidence about when the wounds are beyond our skills. I suppose it is our fundamental work.'

'Well, we now and then get poisonings,' Eadulf admitted.

Corruine let out a soft chuckle. 'Poison, now? That is a method that challenges the mind. It is messy, because it is often slow and agonising. It is not what many men would prefer as a method of killing someone. The swift kill is often better, for the blade is quick once one knows how to insert it in the right place. No, poison is not quick.'

'I thought wolfsbane was fast working,' Eadulf said, turning to Fidelma. 'What is it called here – *ciarsú*? I thought that was a strong and quick poison.'

'So it is,' Corruine confirmed. 'I have read it is known in many countries under a variety of names. In spite of Pliny once claiming it came from some eastern city port from which it took the Latin name he gave it – *Aconitum* – it is a poison that grows everywhere. Well, I suppose if one was using it, it would be effective. I am told that the first touch of the root or leaves, properly prepared, placed on the tongue, creates a tingling and numbing sensation. But imbibing it tends to lead the victim to lethargy, mumbling and becoming as if they are sickening for something. There follow palpitations of the heart, which lead to a final spasm in which death occurs.'

Eadulf glanced quickly at Fidelma.

'So it is not used among physicians or apothecaries in any curative role?' she asked hurriedly.

'Not by me,' Corruine replied firmly. 'But there are some who will use it as a sedative or as a means of reducing fever. I will not prescribe it because of its intense poisonous nature. I do not believe anyone should attempt to mix and administer a correct dose, for there is no known antidote should a mistake occur.'

'So it certainly should not be used in any form?'

'I have heard of several who have experimented, but without success.'

Eadulf examined the man sharply. 'Without success? What does that mean?'

Corruine actually chuckled again, a dry ironic sound. 'It means their failure was a fatal one. I heard of a case at Mungairit which—'

'At Mungairit?' Fidelma asked quickly.

'A physician poisoned himself while trying to demonstrate his technique with the poison with his students. He killed himself and nearly killed a student. The student, being a physically strong young woman, was able to survive after suffering an illness.'

'And this was at Mungairit?' Fidelma pressed.

Corruine caught the note in her voice. 'They have a large number of students of the healing arts there,' he added. 'But you must know that. The place has a reputation among the teaching abbeys. Some of their scholars are well respected.'

Fidelma waited a few moments and then said: 'My brother's new physician was a *sui-liaig*, a professor of the healing arts, at Mungairit.'

'Who might that be? I travel a lot and am acquainted with many professors.'

'She is named Síonna.'

There was a look of surprise on the man's face that not even his generous black beard could disguise.

'Síonna? A woman who is now not much older than yourself, lady? Dark hair and, withal, very attractive?'

'I'll accept your male perceptions, but – yes. Do you know her then?'

'As the ancient says – *parva mundi* – it is a small world. Síonna was the student who survived the experiments of her professor on what he claimed was the efficacy of wolfsbane. There!' he exclaimed. 'You did not have to ask me about wolfsbane. You have an expert in the royal household if she is now physician to your brother, the King.' Then he paused thoughtfully. 'Has something happened that you bring up this subject at this time?' he asked slowly.

'You will doubtless hear about it. However, was this Síonna a martial arts expert doing exhibitions before she went to study at Mungairit?'

The apothecary considered this for a moment.

'I cannot confirm that from personal knowledge, but there were stories. She was the daughter of a minor noble killed at the battle of Cenn Braga in Connacht. The story was that she trained in the martial arts. While she was still young, she had a friend badly wounded in battle. It was said that Síonna tried to save her life and could not.'

'And that is why she gave up a career as a warrior and studied the healing arts?'

'That is what I have been told, lady.'

'It is a sad story,' Eadulf reflected.

'Sad as it is, you were mentioning wolfsbane. Has something happened to connect this Síonna and a case involving wolfsbane?'

Fidelma regarded the bearded apothecary, trying to weigh up what she should say.

'All I can say, at this time, is that there has been a death. Wolfsbane has been involved. And we are making an investigation.'

'Has Síonna been consulted?'

'As she arrived to take up her position as physician to my brother's household just at the time of the poisoning, she was naturally included in the investigation, but not as a suspect, as a physician.'

Corruine adopted a sceptical look. 'It seems almost too coincidental,' he said.

'The world is full of coincidence,' Fidelma replied shortly. 'And now, I will ask you to respect the confidence of this exchange, on your honour.'

The pause in which the apothecary considered her request made Fidelma examine him with a serious frown.

'This is a serious matter,' she emphasised. 'You do not need me to advise you that I am requesting your silence in my position as a *dálaigh*. You have informed me that you are of the rank of *Clí* and I am judging your honour price as worth two milch cows and a heifer. That would be your fine if you break this *géis*, this request for your oath to silence. Do you understand that?'

The bearded man looked hurt. 'You do not have to demand my oath to silence. You were speaking as one professional to another.'

'Your hesitation did you no credit, Corruine.'

'Nevertheless, I would not break faith. You have my word on it.'

'And your word is accepted.'

The penetrating noise of trumpets was signalling the moment when the great fair would be opened by Colgú. A throng of people flocked into the square of the township. Fidelma and Eadulf now assured Corruine that they would call by his stand later, and they began to push their way through towards Rumann's tavern.

Outside, the platform was being made ready with a few adjustments. From here, the fair would be opened by the King and blessed by Abbot Cuán in his role as Bishop of Cashel. Already the household officials – Chief Brehon Fíthel, Prince Finguine, the heir apparent, and others – stood waiting. Enda, as commander of the household guard, was there as well as Gormán, who stood slightly apart and made no attempt to join them. Instead, his eyes were clearly on the crowd. But now the trumpets were announcing the approach of Colgú with Princess Gelgéis. The crowds began to press in around the platform to obtain the best positions.

When Colgú and Gelgéis ascended to the platform, the other officials took up their allotted places. Colgú had turned to Gelgéis, squeezing her hand in an act of encouragement. Then he turned and stepped forward to address the people. When it was discussed afterwards, it seemed that Colgú had forgotten that his herald should have given a special salutation on his horn. Finguine, as heir apparent, had leant forward to remind him, stretching an arm to point the King towards his herald, now raising his trumpet.

That was when the arrow embedded itself in the flesh of Finguine's forearm. A fraction of a second before, it would have buried itself in Colgú's heart.

chapter twenty

The herald had started his trumpet fanfare at the precise moment of impact and Finguine dropped his arm with a curse, pulling at the arrow embedded in it. Fíthel, the Chief Brehon, moved to Finguine's side to assist. while Colgú stepped backwards to his chair, his face registering his shock. Several of the warriors from the household guard moved rapidly in front of the royal party, shields and swords ready, with Enda at their head.

The crowd erupted into pandemonium, with many turning to escape from whatever enemy they could imagine. But they did not know which way to move. In the brief moment that the arrow impacted, Fidelma had seen in her mind's eye the direction and the angle in which it struck Finguine's arm. She turned and looked across the heads of the crowd, searching for the spot from which the bowman must have stood to make his shot. In one corner of the square stood an old barn that she knew usually held cattle. Most of the wooden planking was now loose and some had decayed, so there were plenty of holes in what had been a hayloft, from which a good sight of the platform could have been made.

'Eadulf!' she called urgently, and began to push her way through the panicking crowds.

Behind her she could hear the sonorous tones of Abbot Cuán, who had made his way forward, leaning on his stick and calling for calm. Members of the household guard were still screening the King with shields.

'The King and his lady are not hurt,' the abbot shouted. 'It was some accident, so please be calm.'

Fidelma and Eadulf were thrusting their way towards the old barn. Even before they reached it, Fidelma realised that trying to find the bowman would be a futile exercise. The bowman had one clear shot at the King and had missed, thanks to the unexpected movement of Finguine. In the following furore, they would have fled immediately.

As Fidelma expected, the barn was full of cattle, which would probably be put forward in a sale later. The cattle were nervous so it certainly was not the safest place to be, should anyone have descended among them to make their escape. However, without exchanging a word, Fidelma and Eadulf moved quickly along the side of the old building, checking if there was any other way to a position of vantage within the barn. At the back there was a long wooden ladder lying against the wall, which told an obvious story: an easy way to climb to the loft.

'Don't ask me to go up that ladder,' Eadulf said at once.

'There will be nothing to find . . . now,' Fidelma sighed. 'The bowman would have left as soon as they realised their arrow had not met its intended target.'

'So Colgú was the target?'

'We can be assured of that now.'

'The person who loosed the arrow, the person who climbed up to the firing point, shows not only skill in archery but an acrobatic skill. It does seem to indicate that we are dealing with an Osraige intrigue.'

'Certainly we are dealing with someone who has acrobatic skills.'

Yet Fidelma's mind seemed elsewhere. Eadulf could read the signs.

'But you are not convinced?'

'Not convinced that there is a plot to kill my brother? Oh, I am convinced of that. But what else? Who and why? A simple scheme about Laigin wanting to use Osraige to destabilise the kingdom to gain some advantage is not reasonable. I don't think things are as simple as that.'

'In heaven's name, Fidelma,' Eadulf said, exasperated, 'what more do you want as proof? I think there is enough to present the case before Fíthel and to accuse the Daughters of the Storm . . . all of them, if need be. Personally, I believe it will turn out to be Crédh, who is leading them in this enterprise.'

Fidelma began a negative response but then hesitated and said: 'I think we'd better get back to my brother.'

As they returned into the township's square, they saw that Colgú and Gelgéis had been escorted away under a company of the household guard led by Enda. Fíthel and Abbot Cuán had gone with them. Finguine remained seated on the edge of the platform, where Síonna, the physician, was finishing bandaging his forearm. Two members of the household guard were keeping watchful eyes on the surrounding people.

'How is he?' Fidelma asked.

The physician shrugged. 'The arrow has been extracted. It had gone through the flesh of the forearm but did not penetrate deeply nor touch the bone. It might easily have passed completely through the small area of flesh had it been travelling with more velocity.'

'It is nothing, cousin.' Finguine forced a smile. 'A momentary pain where the arrow head cut into the flesh. It did not even strike the bone. I've had worse wounds in sword practice.'

The physician clicked her tongue in disapproval. 'Just so long as you allow time for the flesh to come together and don't let any dirt in to infect it. Keep it exceptionally clean.'

'But I can consult with you in the fortress later?' the heir apparent asked with a grin. 'I will need someone to ensure the bandage does not come adrift.'

Síonna did not bother to answer, but gave him a disapproving look, picked up her medical bag and moved off into the crowd.

Finguine turned back to Fidelma with a shrug of resignation.

Fidelma was equally disapproving of her cousin. 'Your reputation does you no credit,' she said.

Finguine opened his eyes wide and assumed what he considered was an innocent look.

'Why, cousin, you know I am well considered by many ladies of the kingdom.'

'At best as a lovable scoundrel,' she replied in censorious tone, 'but I will not tell you what worst is said.'

Still mocking himself, Finguine assumed a pained look. 'It is not something I would consider worthy of you. Anyway, you must excuse me . . . I must consult with Colgú and see if there is anything I should do in his absence from officially opening the fair. It is best if Colgú remains in the fortress until matters are resolved.'

'I will not argue with that,' Fidelma agreed. 'It is fortunate that you went to point to something at the moment you did, so that your arm took the impact of the arrow.'

Finguine picked up the discarded arrow on the platform and glanced at it. It was still intact. The arrowhead and the feathered flight were not damaged although they were smeared in the *tánaiste*'s blood.

'Your brother was about to speak when I had to remind him that he had to wait until the herald made to sound the attention.'

'Lucky for my brother that you did so, although it meant taking the impact of the arrow in your arm.'

Finguine grimaced. 'It was meant to be. *Fatum non disputandum*, as I presume you will quote from one of your favourite Latin philosophers. There's no arguing with destiny. Abbot Cuán's announcement claimed it was an accident in an effort to try to calm the people down, but I think we both know that this is now serious. Do you and Eadulf have any ideas?'

'Ideas aplenty. Suspicions by the score. But nothing by which I can put a name to the culprit.'

'I saw you were both heading through the crowd to that old barn. I gather that the bowman made the shot from there.'

'But had vanished by the time we reached it.'

'To shoot from there and at that angle means the bowman was no amateur.'

Eadulf held out his hand for the arrow, which Finguine was now holding. The heir apparent handed it to him. Eadulf turned it over, trying to avoid getting blood on his hands.

'This seems familiar,' he suddenly said.

'There are a lot of people with bows and arrows at the fair,' Finguine pointed out. 'Don't forget there are to be archery contests.'

'But it is unusual to see this type of arrowhead,' Eadulf frowned, holding it up.

'You are remarking that this has a bronze arrowhead, a cast bronze with a socket into which the wood is inserted? It has a good flight at the end. So you will say that it was no disgruntled farmer or cowherd that shot with it?' Finguine had a reputation for his sense of humour.

'I would doubt it.' Eadulf did not rise to his irony.

Fidelma took the arrow and stared at it.

'And you think you have seen arrows like this before, too?' Finguine asked, observing her interest.

'The bronze cast of the arrowhead seems familiar.'

'Well, keep the arrow,' the heir apparent said. 'When you find its sister, let me know. Meantime, we must maintain calm among the people attending the fair. I should make some announcement. I see the Chief Brehon returning and he can assist me.'

The Chief Brehon, Fíthel, made his way directly to Fidelma.

'Colgú and Princess Gelgéis have decided they should not leave

the fortress until we have identified the culprit. He has been persuaded to hold a *dáil* to find out what we know. You are requested
to present us with your findings so far.'

'Finding a resolution to the problem, as you know, is not a
matter of luck,' Fidelma replied distantly, feeling her old antagonism to the young Chief Brehon rising again. 'It is a matter of
concentration as one considers all the information. If one has
enough information then the crime can be solved. I am not ready
to present my claims before a *dáil*.'

Brehon Fíthel looked shocked. 'You refuse? Then I can take over
this matter as you have not succeeded in making developments.'

Fidelma's facial muscles tightened a little. 'There is no need at
all to do so. You have been misinformed that there are no developments. It is not a question of no developments, but putting the
kernel of each development together to build up a pattern of
the whole. I shall be able to continue my considerations and create the certainty of a resolution shortly.'

Fíthel stood undecided for a moment or two. It seemed to Eadulf
that one could almost hear his thoughts as he tried to put them into
some order. His mouth opened and closed a few times as if he were
about to speak. Then Finguine called to him. He turned, hesitated,
and then glanced back to Fidelma.

'I shall want to be appraised of these developments,' he said
shortly. 'But at the right time. Let us leave Fidelma to pursue her
final questions.' Fíthel hesitated. Then he shrugged. 'The King will
await you in his council chamber as soon as you return to the
fortress.'

'Well,' Eadulf muttered as he and Fidelma left the brehon and
Finguine and made their way through the crowd, 'our friend Fíthel
did not like that. He does not like the fact that you have an ability
to override his authority although he is Chief Brehon. I suppose he
wants to be the only person to have the final answers on matters
of law.'

'I am not responsible for his likes and dislikes,' Fidelma responded. 'But I acknowledge he is Chief Brehon. But I have to be certain of the evidence to present to him. So now let us put our heads together about where you have seen this type of arrow before.'

'I was going to suggest that we should be going over to the pavilion of the Daughters of the Storm.'

Fidelma glanced at him with narrow eyes and a questioning frown.

'Since we found that the person had to be athletic to get to the roof of the sanctuary, I am convinced that the assassin will be found among them,' he declared. 'A moment ago you were not sure where you saw a similar style of arrow. I think you recognised it then, as you do now. They use the bronze heads.'

'I realised the type of arrowhead is one that warriors or persons of wealth and noble rank would use. I know the Daughters of the Storm use them. It is not absolute evidence,' Fidelma pointed out. 'Anyone can pick up an arrowhead.'

'A *bronze* arrowhead?' Eadulf asked with cynical emphasis.

'Most people are proficient with the longbow. Easy to find discarded arrowheads.'

'But *bronze* arrowheads?' Eadulf repeated.

'All right. Mostly arrowheads are flint or hard wood. They are a favourite hunting weapon. A lot of people have a bow of between four and five feet in length, but used for competition shooting games. Take a look around, Eadulf, at the number of people carrying longbows as they are going to enter the games later. The longbows come from all parts.'

'And how many use *bronze* arrowheads?' he emphasised again.

They had reached the pavilion assigned to the members of the Daughters of the Storm. Two banners hung on either side of the entrance – one was the colours of Osraige, which Princess Gelgéis was entitled to bear. The other was what Fidelma and Eadulf had come to recognise in recent days as the banner of the Daughters of the Storm. A well-built girl was standing at the entrance and she straightened as she recognised them both. Fidelma was searching for a name.

'Greetings, Corbach.' The name came to her at the last moment.

'Lady,' the girl acknowledged with a brief glance at Eadulf. Fidelma recognised her as second in command of the company after Crédh. The name she bore was relatively rare, but was the female form of Corbb, who was a great warrior leader. He was Corbb, the Defiler of the Fomorians, in ancient stories.

'Someone told me there had been an attempt to kill the King, lady. I heard the cries and confusion of the people and someone running by told me that he had escaped and was safe.'

Eadulf decided to answer. 'Yes. Someone tried to shoot him, using a longbow.'

Corbach looked at him in amusement.

'None better to shoot the distance and with such accuracy,' Eadulf pointed out.

'Except the crossbow. That would be an accurate weapon of choice for an assassin.'

'You are knowledgeable?' he observed suspiciously.

'I am of the Daughters of the Storm,' replied the girl.

'But you use longbows?'

'Of course. We are warriors, not assassins,' she returned with humour.

'May I see?'

She stood aside. In the pavilion there were racks for weapons, shields and helmets and chain-mail coats. Next were racks of swords and stands for javelins. Then a stand from which quivers of arrows hung, alongside longbows.

'Quite an armoury,' observed Eadulf, looking round.

'We find people like to come and examine the weapons when we give our various martial art displays,' Corbach replied. 'As you see, we only use longbows during the archery contests.'

Eadulf went to examine them, but he was really interested in the quiver of arrows.

'Who constructs your arrows?' he demanded.

The girl lifted one shoulder and let it fall eloquently. 'We always use the same artisan back in Durlus Éile for our arrows. He has made our weapons since I can remember. We use no other for our metal working.'

'I see you use the cast-bronze tips.'

'They lend more accuracy.'

Eadulf turned to Fidelma. He had been hiding the arrow that struck Finguine under his cloak. Now he held it up.

'I have found not only a sister to this, but an entire family,' he smiled at Fidelma, referring to Finguine's comment.

While Corbach gazed at him in bewilderment, Fidelma, who had remained silent the whole time since greeting, took a pace to the quiver, took out an arrow and held it against the one Eadulf was holding. The similarity was obvious.

'The cast is the same?' she queried, looking at Corbach. 'The craftsman who made it is the same?'

'What are you saying?' Corbach was still puzzled.

'As you saw, Fidelma holds one of your arrows that is from that quiver. You identify that it is used in your martial arts demonstrations. In my hand is the arrow that struck Prince Finguine when he deflected it in the attempt to kill Colgú. Would you not agree they are cast by the same craftsman?'

The woman seemed mystified. 'What are you saying? Are you accusing us—'

'We are seeking an explanation,' Fidelma cut in sharply. 'A short time ago an attempt was made on my brother's life by someone shooting an arrow from a longbow . . . the arrow now held by Eadulf.'

319

'The arrow from your quiver is its replica,' Eadulf said. 'So an explanation is needed.'

'So you are accusing one of us in this attempted assassination?' Corbach was clearly angry.

'What's this?'

A sharp voice at the entrance to the pavilion caused them to turn round.

It was Crédh who had entered.

Corbach turned, almost thankfully. 'They are accusing us of being assassins.'

Fidelma held up her hand to stop Crédh's outburst.

'That is not exactly correct,' she said. Quickly she outlined the attempt on Colgú's life, the arrow and its comparison with those in the pavilion of the Daughters of the Storm.

Crédh moved forward and took the arrows, carefully comparing them.

'It is true that they are both made by the same craftsman,' she finally agreed. 'They are cast especially for us.'

'So there are two conclusions,' Fidelma said firmly.

'The one being, as Corbach has just said, that you are responsible for trying to assassinate Colgú,' Eadulf said.

'When you say "you", that is all or one of our troop?' Crédh asked with narrowed eyes.

'Probably just one of you, if the evidence is watered down to essentials,' Fidelma said.

'You mentioned two conclusions?'

'The other, I am sure that you will not be long in arguing,' Fidelma said with a thin smile.

'It is one that cannot be ignored,' Crédh replied. 'We try to maintain one person on watch at the entrance of this pavilion. Sometimes we cannot always be so vigilant. So it would be easy for an ill-intentioned person to sneak in, purloin one of our arrows and later use it for their nefarious purpose.'

Fidelma glanced to Corbach. 'What would you like to add?'

The girl hesitated and then sighed. 'It is true that I was not here the whole time. But I was not gone for long. I left to get a drink of cider and to see an exhibit I wanted to watch. There was no one here then. But I did not think anything was disturbed when I returned.'

'If it was just an arrow being taken from a quiver, nothing else would be disturbed unless the person who took it was extremely clumsy,' Eadulf muttered, seeing the logic. 'And how long would that take? Moments?'

'The person who took the arrow knew exactly what they were taking,' Fidelma agreed dryly. 'They knew what they had come to take and for what purpose.'

'But that person was not one of us.'

'Not necessarily,' Fidelma agreed reluctantly. 'But it does not exonerate any one of your troop.'

'If you are unsatisfied with the answer I give you, then you are welcome to examine the other members of my troop,' Crédh replied.

'I shall do so when a time is convenient. Meanwhile, is there a way that we can be sure only one arrow has been taken?'

Crédh was not happy, but she turned to Corbach with the silent question.

'The quivers are for nine archers. Each quiver has nine arrows. No more is needed because they are for certain demonstrations.'

'Then we can check by the number left in each quiver?'

Corbach went down the row, quickly counting the arrows in each quiver.

'There are only three arrows missing: one from each of the three quivers near the entrance.'

'Interesting,' Fidelma acknowledged. 'They took one from each of the first three quivers, perhaps in the hope that a single arrow would not be missed from a single quiver. It could also show that they were confident in being able to complete their task without the need for more. Only expert marksmen would do that.'

'It still does not add to our knowledge,' Eadulf pointed out.

'On the contrary,' Fidelma argued, 'no matter how small the information, it helps build the picture, until the picture is big enough to realise the whole. It means that two other arrows are missing.' She fell silent for a moment or two before turning to Crédh. 'I hear that you have completed most of the single combat contests with Enda?'

Crédh sniffed deprecatingly. 'We have done the archery, the javelin contests, the horseback riding, and now all that is left to us is the combat with sword and shield.'

'And that is to be held soon?' Fidelma demanded.

'It is marked for the middle of the third *cadar*. Any moment now, the trumpets will summon us. The combat will be held in the square outside Rumann's tavern.'

'What is the procedure?' Eadulf asked.

'There is to be the single mock combat using sword and shield. The judges then decide who has scored most points during the entire contest and declare the winner.'

'We have missed the early stages,' Eadulf confessed. 'So who are the judges?'

'Chief Brehon Fíthel arbitrates, with Gormán, as commander of the King's warriors. He has a co-judge, someone called Conrí, who commands the warriors of Donennach, Prince of the Uí Fidgente.'

Fidelma had not realised that their old friend Conrí was attending the fair, but it was logical he should, and she looked forward to seeing him. She thought for a while and realised there was nothing further they could usefully pursue with Crédh at this time. For the moment, the assassin had vanished again.

'I look forward to seeing your combat, Crédh. We will have to return to this matter again, but there is little further we can do for the moment.'

She left the pavilion, reluctantly followed by Eadulf. When they were some way away, Eadulf could not restrain his impatience.

'I think we are letting them get away with murder,' he declared.

'Letting who get away?' Fidelma asked.

'We should demand to question them all and make one of them confess.'

'Forcing a confession is not my method, Eadulf,' she rebuked. 'Unless a confession is freely given it is no confession at all. A confession may be accepted in the light of the evidence, but not forced. How would you extract a confession without evidence?'

'Some would not be reticent at using some force. When one considers the force a murderer must use, surely it is not to be condemned if one uses a degree of force, or threat of it, to extract an admittance of the crime?'

Fidelma shook her head. 'I suggest you look closely at the law texts on admitting and acknowledging a criminal act. If not given legally then the confression is immediately dismissed as a false judgment, and that is an end to any further consideration.'

'Then what are we to do?' Eadulf demanded.

'We will go somewhere quiet and have a talk. After the combat between Enda and Crédh this afternoon, I accede to Fíthel's demand to convene a *dáil*. Then I can put the facts before the court.'

Eadulf looked astonished.

'A court to hear what? You said you need more information.'

'I will put my findings to the court. After all,' she smiled, 'it is basically your inquiries that have pointed to the guilty one.'

Chapter Twenty-One

It had been decided, much against Colgú's wishes, that he and Gelgéis should remain in their quarters in the fortress with a company of the household guard never out of their sight. It was not until mid-afternoon that Colgú had finally prevailed upon Gormán to let him and the princess return, under a heavy guard, to the main square to witness the highlight of the first day's events: the mock single combat between Enda of the Nasc Niadh and Crédh of the Daughters of the Storm.

Under heavy guard, the King and his retinue – even the bandaged Finguine, Chief Brehon Fíthel, Abbot Cuán, Brother Dáire and others – came to take their places on the platform. The household guards were everywhere, so that any attempt to attack would be sheer suicide. Colgú was advised not to move forward to make any announcement, and the role fell to Gormán to announce the main event called the *Roé*, or single combat, between Enda and Crédh.

The centre spot of the township, outside Rumann's tavern, had been cleared and the townsfolk and other guests gathered around it under the watchful eye of Luan, who, as second in command, had placed the household guards in every overlooking prominence. Fidelma and Eadulf took positions nearby Luan.

Gormán, in his role as judge of this mock combat, had seen to the arranging of the ground. A pole had been placed along the middle of the combat zone, dividing the contestants. At the sound of a single trumpet note, the contestants, Enda and Crédh, came into the centre with only their swords and shields. They took up positions on either side of this pole.

There was another blast of the trumpet and the two contestants stood facing one another, feet wide apart and hands raised. In one hand was their sword, in the other their shield, thus showing they had no concealed weapons.

Gormán addressed the crowd.

'What you will see now is a demonstration of the skills of these warriors. This is a mock combat; a duel between Enda of the Nasc Niadh and Crédh of the Daughters of the Storm. They have already shown equal prowess in their skills on horseback, in the shooting of three arrows at a stationary target, as well as the casting of three javelins at the target. Now comes the final test . . . their ability in the *Roé*, the single combat.

'You will see the combatants stand each side of a pole laid along the ground. This is called "the wood of contention". Neither combatant is allowed to step across this pole, otherwise they are immediately faulted and the victory awarded to their opponent. This follows the rules of single combat when a challenge is given and accepted in any real conflict. However, we remind you that this is only a simulated combat. The combatant who is adjudged to have the most points will be presented with a ceremonial dagger by their patron – whether it is Colgú or Gelgéis.'

There was a pause.

'Are the combatants ready to engage?' Gormán demanded.

Both answered with the affirmative cry *'Airlam!'* and dropped into crouching positions, sword swinging in one hand and shield down in defence in the other. At another command, the two immediately touched sword blades as if testing their strength. Then the clash of blades striking one another began to resound. It did not last long. For a moment, no one could believe what had happened.

The shocked gasp that rose from a hundred throats was followed by deafening cries and screams. Two of the bodyguards pushed their way through to the arena with Fidelma between them. It seemed that neither Crédh nor Enda had moved. Crédh appeared frozen in her forward lunge position, her sword stretched out, connecting to Enda's chest. Crédh seemed to be staring unseeingly ahead, her features immobile in a mask of horror.

Even as Fidelma reached Enda, he was sinking to his knees, his shield dropping to one side and his sword falling from lifeless fingers on his other hand. Blood was spurting from his chest where the girl's sword point had entered. Even as Fidelma reached forward, Enda had fallen to the ground on his back.

Fidelma went down on her knees alongside the crumpled body of the young warrior. His face had gone white and there was a trickle of blood at the corner of his mouth. Curiously, she thought that he was smiling. His eyes were open and fixed upon her. The lips moved. He was trying to say something. She bent an ear to him. It was no more than a sighing breath. It sounded like 'I join with . . .' and then his head fell back.

She was aware of angry sounds rising around her. She glanced up. Crédh was now being held by two female warriors, one of whom had removed the sword from her hand. Gormán had pushed his way through the crowd with two other members of the Nasc Niadh. He gazed from the supine figure of Enda to Fidelma with a question in his eyes. She answered it with a negative shake of her head.

'Take Crédh up to the fortress,' he instructed. 'No harm must come to her.' The two female warriors closed in protectively on either side, while the members of the King's bodyguard moved forward as protection from the now hostile crowd. The group moved reluctantly to open a passage for them to pass.

Gormán was looking round and spotted Eadulf over the heads of the crowd, trying to move forward to reach Fidelma and the body of the young warrior. A quick word to his companion and they pushed people back to allow him to come forward to join Fidelma kneeling by the body. Eadulf made a quick examination and raised his eyes to her, the expression confirming what she already knew.

'Gormán, get your men to take Enda's body to the fortress. We will follow at once,' Fidelma instructed.

Gormán hesitated for a moment.

'Should I order the fair to disperse?' he asked quietly.

For once in her life Fidelma felt unable to make an immediate decision. The fair had been days in the organising and people had come from many parts of the kingdom. But an assassination attempt had been made on the King and now the death of his champion had occurred. Deaths had occurred at fairs before and had not led to their immediate closure.

'Gormán, find the Chief Brehon and check with him. If he agrees, find Brother Dáire and tell him to inform the musicians to start playing as loudly as they can. Don't they have a little platform here, outside Rumann's tavern? Start them performing and distracting the crowds.'

Fidelma and Eadulf stood back while Luan and another warrior came forward to lift Enda's body on to a litter, which had been brought. As they moved forward up towards the main gates, with Fidelma and Eadulf following, they were joined by Dego.

'Did you see what I saw, lady?' he asked in a shock tone, falling in step with them.

'It depends on what you saw,' Fidelma responded. She was trying to sort out her own muddled emotions. She had known Enda for many years, since he had been a youthful warrior, accompanying her, Dego and Aidan to rescue Eadulf from facing execution in Laigin.

'What I saw was that Enda invited death,' replied Dego.

'Explain yourself,' she said shortly.

Eadulf, who had been quiet, his mouth compressed into a thin line, replied before Dego.

'An invitation to death? I am afraid that is certainly a way of describing it.'

'How would *you* describe it?' Fidelma, demanded, trying to understand what she had seen and feeling only intense anger.

'The combat had been good and fair,' Dego commented. 'Enda and Crédh were well matched. Crédh was a good replacement for Cera to demonstrate the martial arts, although, of course, Enda had boasted about the prowess of Cera for some time. As you saw, of the challenges, there was little difference in the ability of either Enda or Crédh. True, Enda was able to demonstrate more ability with the horse. He was able to match her score with two casts of the javelin, out of the three, on the target. Crédh was able to put her three arrows on the centre of the target with Enda only narrowly missing one of his shots.'

'We have been told all this,' Fidelma replied irritably.

'Much remained on this final round – the single combat with sword and shield.'

'I know the procedure.' Fidelma's voice was distant. 'It was a combat Enda had proved himself adept in many times.'

'But it was a combat that no one was supposed to be hurt in,' Eadulf said bitterly.

'We all know the rules,' Fidelma snapped. 'Speak on, Dego.'

'It is why I say, watching it, Enda invited death,' Dego replied firmly.

'And you are submitting this as a witness?' Fidelma asked.

'That is what I have to do.'

'Tell me what you saw.'

'I saw two evenly matched warriors engaging in single combat for the purposes of an exhibition. The rules are well known. Sword and shield were to be used so that each should be able to inflict a blow without inserting the point of the blade or cutting into the flesh. The person with the advantage was to constrain their lunge when it was shown the blade could inflict damage.'

'I know this.' Fidelma exhaled in annoyance.

'All was fine. Even I could see that Crédh was working with blade and sword into a fairly traditional attack. I was sure that Enda would have seen the way she was developing the attack. He had negotiated himself into a position where he had a choice. Either to bring his shield across his chest to prevent the blow or to knock her blade aside with his sword. You saw what happened as clearly as I did.'

'Which was?'

'He stood in the position ready and Crédh rocked back a little and then, with right knee forward, she made the lunge. Her sword aimed straight and true, and she expected the shield to be brought across or her blade to be knocked aside. It was so sudden I did not believe it. Enda dropped both arms to his side. The shield on his left, the sword on his right. The blocking motion that Crédh was obviously expecting disappeared. Her momentum carried her weapon forward straight under the ribs and into the heart.'

There was a silence.

'As I said, lady, it was an invitation to death,' Dego finished.

Fidelma made no rely.

'That is how I saw it, too,' Eadulf admitted.

'I am afraid that I agree,' she said then.

'We must now inform Fíthel, the Chief Brehon, since you present yourself a witness to this accident,' Eadulf added.

'This was not just a mishap,' Dego muttered. 'It is a catastrophe. The truth has to be made clear. Especially as it was witnessed by hundreds and, by tomorrow, it will be spoken of in all parts of the kingdom.'

Fidelma's face was a grim mask. 'You speak sense, Dego, and

distorted truths will always travel faster and be more enduring than actual truths. Virgil tells us as much. I will speak to Brehon Fíthel as soon as we get to the fortress.'

It was only a short time later that the news was announced that Brehon Fíthel had convened a *dáil* by order of the King. The King and Gelgéis, Finguine and Abbot Cuán were in attendance with Brother Dáire and Urard, scribe to Brehon Fíthel. Crédh was escorted by two members of the Daughters of the Storm. Luan, Dego and Gormán were also there, and the new physician, Síonna, with Father Socra and Sister Sárait, and anyone else who held office in the fortress.

The facts were presented by Brehon Fíthel himself, and no one who had witnessed the event challenged them. It was seen that during the bout every rule had been scrupulously observed, until, at that last moment, it was clear that Crédh was about to lunge forward and Enda had dropped his defence instead of protecting himself.

Chief Brehon Fíthel continued, 'I have also discussed this matter before this *dáil* with Fidelma, who is qualified to speak on the law attaining to such affairs, because it is a law that is accepted in every jurisdiction of the five kingdoms. So to her is the judgment.'

Fidelma stood forward, slightly surprised that Fíthel had deferred to her, even though he had asked her advice beforehand.

'In this matter the resolution must be regulated by the laws relating to the rules applied to the *Róe.*'

No sooner had she started than Father Socra was immediately on his feet. '*Róe* – the laws relating to a duel? The Faith refuses to recognise such a thing,' he protested. 'Therefore no judgment can be given about it.'

'Father Socra, I think you may be confused,' the Chief Brehon intervened in a gentle tone, which disguised his rebuke. 'The advocates of the New Faith merely state that a duel, as a means of settling an argument, is wrong. It does not say any matter of single combat is wrong, especially that of a contest.'

'You are twisting words!' shouted Father Socra.

'The words of our laws are quite clear,' Fidelma replied quietly. 'I am afraid that this is not the first time that you have misinterpreted matters of Faith and Law.'

Father Socra was frowning as if trying to drag up a memory. Then his expression lightened.

'Wait, is it not said that single combat – the rules of *Róe*, or whatever you want to call it – is illegal unless it takes place with prior permission or agreement, and that can only be given by the authority of the King!'

There was an uncomfortable stirring and Crédh continued to stare in front of her, her features set.

Fidelma was shaking her head. 'Father Socra quotes the words of the *Din Techtugud* and I have to congratulate him for the accuracy of his knowledge of the laws.' She turned to where her brother and Princess Gelgéis were sitting. 'I have to ask two questions.'

Colgú gave a gesture of agreement with his hand.

'You knew that a display of martial arts was taking place and that this display was to end in a single combat, which, although it was a display, a mock combat, it had the appearance of a *Róe* or duel. Were you aware of this?'

'Of course.' Colgú was puzzled. 'It was agreed that the mock single combat would be between a warrior of the Nasc Niadh and one of the Daughters of the Storm.'

'So it was agreed by you?'

'I have said so.'

'And did you, Gelgéis of Durlus Éile, also agree to the Daughters of the Storm, your own bodyguard, taking part?'

'I did.' Gelgéis spoke uncertainly, not sure of the point Fidelma was making.

Fidelma then turned back to Father Socra with a grim smile. 'So permission was given. No law was broken because it is stated that a wound inflicted in a legal duel or single combat – at which point the combat should stop immediately, as it was – is not actionable. Therefore I have one expert witness in this matter. I ask Gormán to speak. Gormán remains Cashel's most trusted warrior and expert in martial arts. He serves as the marshal of the fair and oversees the martial exercises and games. He stood as referee of the entire combat.'

Gormán immediately rose.

'You saw this combat as referee,' went on Fidelma. 'You have heard the eyewitnesses. Have you reached a conclusion on the legality of the combat? Did you see any action from Crédh, during the course of the single combat, that delivered a blow against the rules; that a blow was delivered furtively, slyly and unfairly, with cunning and malice?'

'I can only tell the truth as I saw it and, as the other witnesses told you, there was no fault on Crédh. I say with sadness and with regret that it was Enda who chose the termination of his life. He lowered his defences when he must have known that Crédh was expecting him to use the obvious defensive tactic. She was given no time to pull back on her lunging stroke.'

'Therefore, it was entirely legal under the law of this land and no blame is attached to Crédh?' Fidelma said firmly. 'That is also the judgment that I submit.'

Brehon Fíthel was nodding and he turned to Fidelma.

'Unless you have any further comment, I have heard enough and confirm your judgment. Enda's death was a misfortune, which was apparently brought about by some error of judgement or some hesitation; an aberration of thought.'

Again, Father Socra was on his feet.

'But a crime has been committed and must be punished!'

For a moment Fíthel was astonished at the intervention. 'A crime? What crime?' he demanded.

'If Crédh did not kill Enda and Enda killed himself then his death must be tantamount to *fingal*. That is, suicide! This warrior, Enda, cannot be admitted to burial in sacred ground. If he invited the female Crédh to kill him, even though it was not of her own volition, this action is still of his doing. He is guilty of the crime of suicide and she might be considered to have aided that act and also punished.'

There was a loud muttering of dissent, but Brehon Fíthel held up his hand for silence before he turned a disapproving look on the chaplain.

'I am confirming judgment in this court, Father Socra. My ruling is that it was an error of judgement of Enda's part, which resulted in a misfortune, an accident, by which Crédh could not stop her forward momentum. And Fidelma has already made it clear that the law says that a wound inflicted in such a combat is not actionable.'

'We have heard clearly from the witnesses that he dropped his guard purposefully, knowing the sword of his opponent would kill him,' insisted Father Socra.

'I do not believe that you are listening, Father Socra. Unless you bring forward evidence showing that you are able to know what was in Enda's mind, I will not hear you.'

'I know he was having an affair with Cera, the girl who was killed. When she was killed, the Evil One was able to enter his mind and seduce him from the ways of God. He was always in the darkness of the chapel, alone with his thoughts, and it is obvious what dark thoughts they were.'

'Perhaps the chapel should not have been in darkness,' Fidelma said. 'Surely a chapel should be a place of light and understanding?'

Father Socra swung round to her. 'The chapel is a sacred place, not a place of light and celebration. It is a place of obedience to the laws of God!'

'Then, perhaps it should try to be a place of worship and of giving thanks for God's promise for eternal life? We have been allowed to bathe in the light of this world and not hide in the darkness of caverns,' she replied irritably. 'If Enda was in a place of darkness then darkness would have dominated his thoughts. If religion has anything to offer, it is the comfort of light and the prospect of peace and a better existence ahead.'

'*Sutor, ne ultra crepidam*!' the chaplain shouted angrily. There was a gasp as several recognised the abbreviation of Pliny's words that a cobbler should not judge above the sandal – in other words, should not talk about things they were not qualified to do so.

Brehon Fíthel seemed amazed as he gazed at the chaplain. 'Sister Fidelma is competent in most fields, if not all the fields that have been raised here. And I, as Chief Brehon of this kingdom, concur with all her statements. I have already given judgment on the matter.'

'It is clear Enda committed suicide and I will not preside over his funeral,' Father Socra argued.

'In that case,' Abbot Cuán rose and his tone was heavy, 'as senior bishop of the kingdom of Muman as well as Abbot of Imleach, I will preside over the interment of this unfortunate warrior who, as I know personally, served us all so well and devotedly.'

'Then you will have to face a higher authority!' Father Socra's tone was belligerent and threatening.

Colgú, who had been sitting quietly with Gelgéis since they had answered Fidelma's few questions, now rose after a whispered word had passed between them.

'I am sure Abbot Cuán will rebuke you for your misconduct here in his own good time. My wife, Princess Gelgéis, and I will be leading the mourners to the grave. Abbot Cuán will lead the services and we would like Enda's body to be borne to his resting place by members of both my household guard and of the Daughters of the Storm.'

'With my blessing,' Abbot Cuán agreed. 'Furthermore, I would take the opportunity, in this *dáil*, of declaring that Father Socra has shown himself unfit for the position of chaplain to the King. I have already overruled his applying ideas formed by councils of the Roman Church about *fingal*. The law of this country is clear. While he may have his own views on his faith, he cannot defy the laws of this kingdom and force the rules by which his faith is conducted as law in this kingdom. Such a conflict must obviously lead to disaster. I suggest that he be advised to remove himself from this fortress forthwith.'

There was an icy silence and no word was spoken in Father Socra's support. Colgú glanced towards the stunned priest.

'Be it so. You are dismissed, Father Socra. And now, with the permission of the Chief Brehon of the kingdom, I declare this *dáil* over.'

'Stop! This court has more business to consider before it is closed.' It was Fidelma's voice that rang out in the chamber.

Chief Brehon Fíthel was puzzled as he turned to her. 'What other matter is important to consider at this time?'

'The matter of the death of Cera and Dar Luga. I should add, it was Cera's murder, the murder of one who was devotedly loved by Enda, that drove him to such despair. He could not face the future and allowed his life to be taken. So a third death is due to this killer. Now is the time to reveal who the murderer is.'

The Chief Brehon sat back heavily. He exchanged a glance with Colgú before he turned to Fidelma.

'Are you ready to present a case against an accused?'

'I am ready to name the culprit and the motive.'

'Is the one you accuse in this chamber to defend themselves?'

'They are.'

'Then this *dáil* remains constituted for this hearing. I will invite Fidelma to proceed.'

Fidelma glanced confidently at Eadulf and shifted her weight to a more comfortable position.

'A few nights ago an assassin managed to infiltrate the sanctuary that my brother has recently built. The motive was the assassination of my brother as pure vengeance. The victim was to be specifically my brother, Colgú. However, in the course of the attempt it was Cera, Gelgéis's maid, who was stabbed and Dar Luga, our stewardess, who was poisoned. Both were victims of one assassin.

'The assassin knew who was in the rooms of the sanctuary and prepared their entrance, believing they only had to be careful of Dar Luga as she was a light sleeper and late to bed. Her room was also close to the royal bedroom. So it was planned that Dar Luga would be incapacitated by a mixture of wolfsbane. This was administered while the assassin was talking with Dar Luga in the kitchen before she went to bed in the sanctuary.

'This allowed the assassin, who was physically very fit, to be able to clamber on to the sloping roof of the sanctuary and enter Dar Luga's room through the skylight by means of a rope without disturbing her drugged sleep. Indeed, to pick up the steward's keys to all the rooms. But Cera was alerted by the assassin's movements once inside the sanctuary. As she went to investigate, she was killed. The dagger used was an unusual one. A Pictish trophy gained in battle. I'll come to that shortly.

'The assassin was able to exit by the same way that they came, leaving some incriminating items behind. Dar Luga was a strong woman, or perhaps the wolfsbane she was given was not strong enough. So when the alarm was raised, she was able to function to a certain degree. Stupidly, I did not realise she had been poisoned and was already dying. I let her go back to the kitchen where the assassin was waiting for her and persuaded her to take a more potent mixture of wolfsbane, from which she died.

'We know that the assassin made a second attempt, using the

same route into the sanctuary, which did not work. It was their belief that we would think, as some did, that lightning would not strike twice in the same place. That was a failure. So a third attempt was made when Colgú was opening the fair. Thanks to Finguine, the attempt was thwarted and the assassin escaped.'

Fidelma paused as if to gather her thoughts. It was a technique she had learnt when presenting a case, and she knew it kept her listeners focused.

'So who were we looking for? A young athletic woman. For we had a witness during that second attempt. It was a physically fit female who had obviously had the training of a warrior. Then we realised it was someone who was a fine archer. We were also looking for a young woman who had knowledge of plants, specifically how to mix wolfsbane. The dagger that killed Cera was left behind purposely and meant to lay a false trail when the attempt failed. The symbol it carried was of the female warriors of the Cruithne – the Defenders of An Sgurr. That is a high hill fought over by the Dál Riata and the Cruithne, not far from the abbey of I-Shona.

'It was a dagger with the symbol of a silver leaf and a bear, with two lightning flashes. Rather than a false lead, it turned out to be a clue. As there are no members of the tribes of Cruithne here, the question was, who would have access to such a weapon? It was someone who had served the Dál Riata and collected the dagger as a trophy during that conflict.'

She paused again.

'So who could fit this description?' Brehon Fíthel prompted, unwilling to allow Fidelma the same theatrics again. 'There were several in the fortress on these nights who might answer to such clues.'

'At the start we were not one-hundred-per-cent certain who the intended victims were, so we looked at the question of whether it might have been Cera herself. As you know, Enda and Cera had developed a relationship and it was their intention to be married.

Was that a motive? Jealousy? Lovers' quarrel? Even I briefly wondered about Enda's motivations. But his shock and agony over Cera's death were obvious to us all, so that now we can see the reason for Enda allowing his own death. Quite simply, he thought that he could not face the future alone.'

Crédh was sitting with facial muscles clenched in red-faced anger, almost visibly preventing herself from movement or voicing protest.

'Perhaps he felt it was not without symbolism to meet his death at the hands of Crédh? Crédh had become a suspect when she confessed that she was in love with Cera. Cera had rejected her attentions. Crédh told me that she had accepted Cera's rejection. But had she? She was my first principal suspect. This theory was dismissed when I realised the intended target was Colgú.'

'You were looking for a female warrior,' Fíthel reminded her.

'For someone with a warrior's training,' Fidelma corrected.

'Plenty of suspects here,' Fíthel shrugged. 'Are you going to say there were too many suspects for you to solve this matter?'

'I thought I started out by saying that I was prepared to present my case as to who the assassin was?' Fidelma asked sarcastically. 'If allowed, I shall do so, but in my own way.'

Brehon Fíthel flushed in annoyance.

'If that is your purpose, then proceed as quickly as you can,' he snapped.

'My next suspect was Síonna, the physician.'

The physician jerked round in her seat to stare at Fidelma in anger, but said nothing.

'Gormán and Enda both recognised her. Gormán had seen her performing martial arts exhibitions at the fortress of the prince of the Uí Fidgente. So she had the training as a former member of a female company of warriors. She also – and this was important – had the knowledge of the effects of wolfsbane and had access to old Brother Conchobhar's apothecary.'

'I deny this.' The physician suddenly rose from her seat.

Brehon Fíthel turned to her. 'You protest that the statement from the *dálaigh* is inaccurate? Did you train as a warrior?'

Síonna seemed to struggle with a degree of inarticulateness.

'If you do not deny the accuracy, we may continue,' the Chief Brehon intoned heavily.

'I would have pointed out that two factors tend to clear the physician,' Fidelma interceded. 'She did not arrive at this fortress until midnight, or just after; that is, after the start of the first *cadar*. She was greeted by Father Socra and, as the stewardess, Dar Luga, had retired to bed and had already been poisoned, she was given a bed in the religieuses' quarters. There was no time to arrive, find out how to enter the sanctuary, mix the poison and administer it to Dar Luga. That would have been impossible.'

There was a puzzled silence.

'There was another thing you should all have observed a short time ago. Síonna was also the first to reach and attend Finguine. No time to get from where the arrow was fired to the point of impact in Finguine's arm. She was not the assassin who fired at Colgú.'

Síonna sat down abruptly, scowling that she had even been named.

'And so? Where now?' Brehon Fíthel asked, almost clenching his teeth in exasperation. 'I declare that you have lost me.'

'Well, now we could come to Father Socra. He is young and slight enough to pass as a woman in the darkness. Dego had been the first to point out that Father Socra was an excellent bowman. Dego had witnessed his practising and, of course, Father Socra seemed to confirm this for we found he had put his name forward to some of the archery contests during the fair.'

'This shows my innocence!' Father Socra shouted. 'If I needed to hide my capabilities, I would have forborne such contests and thus not drawn attention to my abilities.'

'A good point,' Fidelma smiled. 'Yet you were not truthful when you were asked about your abilities and how you learnt them.'

'Not truthful?' Father Socra had an almost threatening ring to his voice as he challenged her.

'Abbot Cuán informed me that you were once bodyguard to a local noble whose territory was at the river inlet nearby where the Feoir joins the Bhearú, just south of Tigh Moling on the Laigin bank. Is this not true? You were once a bodyguard in service to a Laigin noble? Or do you say that Abbot Cuán is deceiving us?'

Father Socra's mouth was a thin grim line. 'That was another life; a younger life,' he protested.

'But still part of a life. That would place it in the local territory of the Benntraige, who rule on both sides of the river – in Osraige and Laigin. Are you of that tribe?'

'I am of no tribe but the tribe of Christ!' declared the angry religieux.

'Nevertheless you were of the war band of Benntraige and there your warrior skills were learnt. It is lucky that when Síonna arrived at the abbey, when the assassin made the first attempt on Colgú, you were at the gate to meet her. I suspect that you had met during your martial arts days. But it does provide a mutual alibi for you. Anyway, Father Sorca, you were seen at an archery contest at the time the arrow was fired at the fair. So you were eliminated, not to mention the fact that in no way could you have fitted through the skylight in the sanctuary.'

'But there was a silly attempt to draw him into the conspiracy by creating more confusion,' Eadulf said sharply.

'Which was?' asked Abbot Cuán.

'When Socra was knocked unconscious in the chapel last night and I was lured there by a fake message, purporting to come from Enda. Was it set to divert suspicion from Socra to give him more freedom?'

'That is nonsense!' shouted Socra.

'It was certainly done for the purpose of decoying but from whom?' Fidelma queried. 'Eadulf was able to find the messenger boy who confirmed it was not Enda who sent him the message. It was given to him by a dark-robed figure in the shadows – a woman.'

'But surely this clears Father Socra from suspicion,' Abbot Cuán pointed out.

'The idea was to imply that the wound was self-inflicted but the attacker, being a warrior, was a little too enthusiastic.'

'Are you back to women warriors?' Fingiune interrupted.

Chief Brehon Fíthel uttered a loud exasperated sigh. 'This is going nowhere, Fidelma. You are playing games. You name people and then exonerate them. Are you going to name anyone else as the possible killer?'

'Maybe you are overlooking the remaining possibility?' enquired Fidelma. 'Thankfully, Eadulf here had been gathering information, which last night made me realise who the assassin was.'

Several people were looking at one another in bewilderment.

It was her own brother, Colgú, who understood the direction of her mind.

'You said earlier that I was the target of the assassin. Why? Is it that motive that points to the killer?'

'The assassin is the daughter of a previous assassin,' conceded Fidelma. 'That first assassin also came here disguised as a religieuse to destroy my brother and steal the sacred sword of Frecraid, The Answerer, to discredit him. That is the sword that hangs above the King's throne. Legend has it that it was handed to our progenitor Eógan Mór by Nuada of the Silver Arm. So there came to us one who called herself Sister Ernmas, whose real name was Aincride, mother of the late and unlamented Elódach, a prince of the Eóganacht Áine. Aincride's husband and eldest son were defeated and killed by Colgú at the Battle of Cnoc Áine eight years ago. Her motive was vengeance. Her punishment was that she fell to her death from these fortress walls while trying to escape justice. The assassin is her daughter.'

She paused dramatically.

Several of those gathered were shouting, demanding a name, before they realised Fidelma was looking at the woman who called herself Sister Sárait. The girl rose, then hesitated, which was her undoing, because before she had braced herself to try to make for the door, strong hands had grasped and pushed her back down in her seat, despite her twisting and turning.

'Elódach of Áine?' Colgú was musing softly. 'His father and brother had given support to the Uí Fidgente in an attempt to seize the throne of Cashel which culminated in the battle at Cnoc Áine. His mother never forgave our victory at that battle in which her husband and eldest son died. Elódach, who survived the battle, surrendered and made peace, but he was a weak ruler. You say that this woman, Sárait, is the sister of Elódach and her mother was Aincride?'

'I do not deny it! They murdered her!' the girl suddenly shouted. 'My mother was murdered by being thrown from your battlements. You bathe in the blood of my family and I seek retribution. We declare the *dígal*, a blood feud, until our deaths are revenged. I cry blood feud on all your kind.'

Fíthel was whispering something to his scribe, Urard, who was recording the proceedings. He then turned to Fidelma.

'A confession is admitted so usually there is little else that needs to follow it. However, for the interest of the court you may tell us how you reached this conclusion.'

'It was thanks to Brother Eadulf, who was able to ascertain that Sister Sárait was not from Osraige as originally thought. She spent time among the Eóganacht of Loch Léin at Faithlinn's island after her family and their allies were defeated. Eadulf began to suspect Sárait when she made the slip after Socra was attacked. She said she was asleep which was a deliberate contradiction.'

'As to specifics, when I spoke to Dar Luga, not aware that she was dying, she said she had been up late talking with someone. That person, we later realised, had administered the poison. There had, she said, been much talk about the new chaplain. In retrospect, I would say that it was Sárait, in her guise as a religieuse newly arrived with Father Socra, for who else would have such details? That should have struck me earlier.

'Enda was surprised when he told us that Sárait knew what warrior's clothing to use for Cera's grave clothes and what weapons to lay with her in spite of the protests by Father Socra. It became clear that Sárait had a female warrior's training. When the emissary from the High King arrived here he recognised someone as having served with the Dál Riata against the Picts, where he himself had served. He did not name her. However, she admitted to Eadulf she had gone to I-Shona, in the land of the overseas Dál Riata. Eadulf had seen her martial art abilities for she practised with Father Socra, and Dego and others admitted witnessing her practices. She did not serve in the abbey but as a warrior. I-Shona is not far from An Sgurr. From the Pictish defenders of An Sgurr she was able to get, as a trophy, the dagger that was left to mislead us.

'By the way, Eadulf had been worrying about the similarity of the dagger technique used on poor Cera to that he had seen when Aincride had used the technique on others like Brother Fidach. It was not conclusive, but I believe it was a stroke taught by mother to daughter.

'Another point that should have alerted us was when Eadulf found her interested in the spot from where her mother fell from our battlements in her attempt to escape justice. We had to look beyond the evidence. Sárait said she studied at Inis Faithlinn as many of those of the Áine clan do. Brother Dáire, our librarian, found that after Sárait had visited our library, part of the genealogies of the Eóganacht Áine had been cut out of the texts to eliminate her origins.'

'But did she know how to mix the poison?' Fíthel explained. 'That is essential.'

'I should have thought more about that. She admitted to Eadulf she knew about mixing herbs last night when Father Socra was attacked, so she was able to mix the wolfsbane.'

'You mentioned the family of Áine.' It was Finguine who asked; as the Prince of Glendamnach, the territories of Áine had been assigned to him.

'I am sorry that we are speaking of our cousins, Finguine, who were removed from their position by the *derbhfine* of your family. It is no reflection on you and your branch that created the peace between us again. When she visited the library, Sárait removed the evidence that Elódach, Prince of Áine, not only had a brother but also a sister. You all remember the vengeance his mother, Aincride, tried to inflict. She actually took the name "Vengeance". Sister Sárait was more than interested in the fate of her mother, who fell to her death from our walls.'

Colgú was looking coldly at the girl as his warriors escorted her away, still struggling hysterically, screaming for all to rise in a blood feud against the destroyers of the Eóganacht Áine. 'Vengeance,' he sighed. 'Blood feuds. What a waste of life.'

Fidelma grimaced. 'It is impossible to believe that a wrong has been done without the belief that someone should pay for it. It is a fact that in every complaint we make against someone, every claim of wrongdoer to us by others, there is the seed of vengeance in it. It is probably a human condition.'

Fidelma allowed her pony, Aonbharr, a free rein to climb the small hill where the *bó-aire*, the noble Cumascach, had his fortress home. But his fortress and two small unconnected dwellings were small compared to some. Fidelma liked pausing to talk with Cumascach, for he had been an old warrior in her father's service whose military preparation earned him his nickname, which meant 'the confuser'. She paused at the top of the hill and looked back to the north-west, where the high limestone thrust of rock on which her brother's fortress was built dominated its surroundings.

If she was honest, she felt the need to ride to old Cumascach's homestead as a means of distraction; of escape after the tensions of the investigation and the court hearing of the day before.

She admitted to herself that she feared for the future. For her, the emotions of love and relationships were ever complex. Eadulf had upset her thoughts, although her years of training in law had taught her never to wear her emotions on her face. She wondered if she had made the right decision. The thought of agreeing to journey with Eadulf to the village of his birth in the land of the South Folk, in the kingdom of the East Angles, worried her. It was a decision she wondered whether she would regret. Fidelma saw the future with great foreboding and almost fear.

ḣistorical afterword

R eaders will be interested to know that the story recited by
Brehon Fíthel concerning the two female warriors who held
St Mo Chua and his attendant to ransom by dangling them over a
cliff on a rope, is recorded in some of the early stories about the
saint. It is also given in *Annála Ríoghachta Éireann*, otherwise
'Annals of the Four Masters.' Bec (the 'little one'), daughter of
Cúchorag, and Líthbán (the 'beautiful'), daughter of Attref, are
described as *ban-gaisgedach* or female highway robbers. The story
is, more or less, as Fíthel describes it. Mo Chua's proper name was
Crónán mac Becáin, of the Uí Néill family, who settled and became
Abbot of Balla in Mayo.

The attempts made by the Cenél Conail prince, Eunan (AD 624–
704), who later became known as religious scholar Adomnán, the
eighth Abbot of Iona, to ban female warriors, did not succeed until
twenty-five years after the setting of this story. The *Cáin Adomnán*,
or Adomnán's Law, was accepted at the Council of Biorra in AD 697.
Biorra, now Birr in County Offaly, was on the border of the Muman
(Munster) kingdom, in the territory of Éile. The council was attended
by the High King, Loingsech mac Óengusso (d. AD 704). Loingsech
was Adomnán's cousin. Attending, for the Eóganacht kingdom, was
Ailill mac Cathail (d. c. AD 698/701), the brother of Finguine, who
appears in these stories as the heir apparent to Colgú.

The Abbot of Imleach, Conamail mac Carthaig (d. AD 708) and the Abbot/Bishop of Armagh, Flann Feblae mac Scandláin (d. AD 715), attended with Coeddi, Bishop of Iona (d. AD 712). Representing Laigin was Aedh, Abbot of Sléibhte (d. c. AD 700), who had acknowledged Armagh as having the primacy over the Laigin abbeys. A famous historian from Laigin, Muirchú moccu Machtheni, was in attendance. He was author of *Vita Sancti Patricii*, which was the first text to claim Patrick had converted all Ireland and was clearly a propaganda text to attempt to unite the churches of the north and south of Ireland. Dedicated to Bishop Aedh of Sléibhte, Muirchú's work had a distinct literary quality to it, although it tells us more about the late seventh century than of Patrick's time. Also, among other churchmen listed at the Council, was a Pictish bishop named Coretáin.

With his relative, the High King, supporting Adomnán, it was obvious that the Council of Biorra would give approval to the *Cáin Adomnán*, also then called the *Lex Innocentium* (Law of the Innocents). This was claimed to be the first recorded and successful attempt by ecclesiastics to graft Christian ideas and Roman legal ideas upon the indigenous native law system.

Whereas women had always enjoyed a high status in all Celtic societies, including the right to bear arms as a duty and source of pride in defending their society on equal terms with men, this right was now taken away. Women now found they had to pay for their exemption, being subject to a new special tax. Of interest was the fact that the law stated that each *derbhfine*, or family branch, had to provide an *aitire*, or surety official to observe and confirm the compliance of the law and the taxes dues. Adomnán's law assumed that women were incapable of determining their own destiny. This became the thin end of the wedge, as between AD 697 and AD 887, ecclesiastics also managed to have nine more laws passed amending and changing Brehon Law.

The position of women was gradually eradicated, and they lost the right of qualifying in all professions as lawyers, judges, physicians, professors and scholars. It is reported that Tairrdelbach ua Bríain (1009–1086), King of Munster and then High King, accepted the influence of Pope Gregory VII (1020–1085) and amended even the Brehon marriage laws. The decline of women's rights in Irish law was not all done immediately and many rulers and lawyers refused to meekly accept the 'alien ideas' of Roman cultural concepts being brought into Ireland by Christian ecclesiastics.

We can say that it was the Council of Biorra that was the start of the diminution of women's rights in the indigenous law system. This falls just outside the period in which our stories are engaged and Fidelma would have been sixty years old when that historic council took place where Adomnán's law was endorsed. One wonders, looking at the loss of rights and position of women that followed, what Fidelma's interpretation would have been on Adomnán's name as coming from the Irish word *adomnae* meaning 'great fear'. Dr James Cameron, in his book *Celtic Law* (1937) wrote of 'the passing of the law, the necessity for, and the effect of which, are grossly exaggerated'.